CLASSIC

CAMPFIRE STORIES

CLASSIC
CAMPFIRE STORIES
FORTY SPOOKY TALES

WILLIAM W. FORGEY
ILLUSTRATED BY PAUL G. HOFFMAN

GUILFORD, CONNECTICUT

FALCONGUIDES®

An imprint of Globe Pequot
Falcon and FalconGuides are registered trademarks and Make Adventure Your Story is a
trademark of Rowman & Littlefield.

Distributed by NATIONAL BOOK NETWORK

Text copyright © 2017 by William W. Forgey, M.D.
Illustrations copyright © 2017 by Paul G. Hoffman

British Library Cataloguing-in-Publication Information available

Library of Congress Cataloging-in-Publication Data available

ISBN 978-1-4930-2909-9 (paperback)
ISBN 978-1-4930-2910-5 (e-book)

∞™ The paper used in this publication meets the minimum requirements of American
National Standard for Information Sciences—Permanence of Paper for Printed Library
Materials, ANSI/NISO Z39.48-1992.

Printed in the United States of America

To the memory of Thomas Andrew Todd (1963–2016) who, as the Publisher of ICS Books, started many of us on our writing careers. To his many friends he was also a cherished canoe, rafting, and adventure travel companion.

We will all miss him greatly—I more than most.

William W. Forgey, M.D.
Crown Point, Indiana
August 5, 2016

From Ghoulies and ghosties and long-leggety Beasties
and things that go bump in the night,
Good Lord, deliver us.

—Cornish Prayer

CONTENTS

ACKNOWLEDGMENTS

I wish to thank my editor at Falcon/Rowman & Littlefield, David Legere, for making this project possible and Paul Hoffman for creating the illustrations. I created many of these stories around campfires during hundreds of trips with my boy scout troops in North Carolina and Indiana—the youngsters deserve the credit for providing the inspiration for those stories. And then there are the great writers of macabre whose works are included here—they also were a great source of inspiration.

But of particular note in this volume are the additions made by David R. Scott and Scott E. Power. In 1991 I sponsored these two (at that time) young men for a one year expedition into far Northern Canada where they lived in a remote wilderness cabin. Their story can be found in more detail at www.forgeyexpedition .com and in the book *Paradise Creek* by David Scott. I gratefully acknowledge the courage these two men had and appreciate being able to include the product of the labor which they produced during that year while sitting around the wood-burning stove and arctic campfires of their youth.

—**William W. Forgey, M.D.**
Crown Point, Indiana

HOW TO TELL A GHOST STORY

by Mark Twain

A perfect example of storytelling technique was recorded by Mark Twain in "How to Tell a Story." I have extracted a portion of that essay which quite well stresses the seemingly impossible task of perfect timing during delivery. But don't let this section worry you. By watching the faces around you it is actually quite easy to sense just when it's time to make a loud shout, or as in this case, to get the pause before the shout just right.

The pause is an exceedingly important feature in any kind of story, and a frequently recurring feature, too. It is a dainty thing, and delicate, and also uncertain and treacherous; for it must be exactly the right length – no more and no less – or it fails of its purpose and makes trouble. If the pause is too long the impressive point is passed, and the audience have time to divine that a surprise is intended – and then you can't surprise them, of course.

On the platform I used to tell a ghost story that had a pause in front of the snapper at the end, and that pause was the most important thing in the whole story. If I got it the right length precisely, I could spring the finishing shout with effect enough to make some impressionable youngster deliver a yelp and jump out of his seat – and that was what I was after. This story was called "The Golden Arm," and was told in this fashion. You can practice with it yourself – and mind you look out for the pause and get it right.

The Golden Arm

Once 'pon a time dey wuz a monsus mean man, en he live 'way out in de prairie all 'lone by hisself, 'cep'n he had a wife. En bimeby she died, en he tuck en toted her way out dah in de prairie en buried her. Well, she had a golden arm – all solid gold, fun de shoulder down. He wuz pow'ful mean – pow'ful; end at night he couldn't sleep, caze he want dat golden arm so bad.

When it come midnight he couldn't stan' itnomo'; so he git up, he did, entuck his lantern en shoved out thoo do storm en dug her up en got de golden arm; en he bent his head down 'gin de win', en plowed en plowed en plowed thoo de snow. Den all on a sudden he stop (make a considerable pause here, and look startled, and take a listening attitude) en say: "My lan', what's dat?"

En he listen-en listen-en de win' say (set your teeth together and imitate the wailing and wheezing singsong of the wind), "Bzzz-z-zzz" – en den, way back yonder whah de grave is, he hear a voice! – he hear a voice all mix' up in de win' – can't hardly tell 'em 'part – Bzzz-zz-W-h-o--g-o-t--m-y--g-o-l-d-e-n – arm?" (You must begin to shiver violently now.)

En he begin to shiver en shake, en say, "Oh, my! Oh, my lan'!" en de win' blow de lantern out, en de snow en sleet blow his face en mos' choke him, en he start aplowin' knee-deep towards home mos' dead, he so sk'yerd – en pooty soon he hear do voice agin, en (pause) it 'us comin' after him! "Bzzz-zz-W-h-o--g-o-t--m-y--g-o-l-d-e-n – arm?"

When he git to de pasture he hear it agin – closternow, en a- comin'! – a comin' back dah in de dark en de storm (repeat the wind and the voice). When he git to de house he rush up-stairs en jump in de bed en kiver up, head and years, en lay dah shiverin' en shakin' – en den way out dah he hear it agin! – en a – comin'! En bimeby he hear (pause – awed, listening attitude) – pat – pat

– pat – hit's a-comin' up-stairs! Den he hear de latch, en he know it's in de room!

Den pooty soon he know it's a stannin' by de bed! (Pause.) Den – he know it a-bendin' down over him – en he cain't skasely git his breath! Den – den – he seem to feel someth'n'n c-o-l-d right down 'most agin his head! (Pause.)

Den de voice say, right at his year – "W-h-o – g-o-t – m-y – g-o-l-d-e-n – a-r-m?" (You must wail it out very plaintively and accusingly; then you stare steadily and impressively into the face of the farthest gone auditor – a young scout, preferably—and let that awe-inspiring pause begin to build itself in the deep hush. When it has reached exactly the right length, jump suddenly at that youngster and yell, "You've got it!"

If you've got the pause right, he'll fetch a yelp and spring right out of his shoes. But you must get the pause right; and you will find it the most troublesome and aggravating and uncertain thing you ever undertook.

Mark Twain

2

THE VALLEY OF THE BLUE MIST

by Doc Forgey

About a hundred years ago there were three boys who decided that they would go to the gold fields in California and try to strike it rich. In those days, youngsters very often left home at an early age. The discovery of gold in California could mean wealth, perhaps more important, a chance for adventure and to leave hard and drab work in the East.

These three youngsters decided to band together—after all, they had known each other all the way through grade school. They liked and trusted each other, and had helped one another often before. It was a dangerous long journey. They took the money that they had and were able to buy passage on an ocean going ship that would sail around Cape Horn off South America. They arrived in San Francisco and from there they headed to the gold fields.

Well, they were late in arriving. When the news of gold spreads, it spreads fast. Adventurers from all over the United States, from the Orient, from around the world had made the trek to California.

As they traveled to areas where the latest rumors told of great finds, they did so as part of a large, milling mob of eager gold seekers. Life was expensive. This was the frontier and everything had to be brought in from small communities that were not large enough to support such demands on their farms and craftsmen.

Local farmers and workers had frequently deserted their work and had joined the gold seekers.

But a living COULD be scratched out, and who could tell, but anyone might strike it rich by finding a mother lode. So they joined the crowds and kept working the placer deposits, finding a little color (as gold was called when found mixed with the stream gravel). Placer deposits are hard work. Gold which has been washed down from the hills by the rivers is mixed with the stream gravel. By scooping up pans full of this mixture and washing the lighter stones away from the heavier gold, the prospectors could separate the valuable gold dust and nuggets.

But the goal was to find a Mother Lode—the source of the placer gold. Prospectors always tried to follow the grains of gold up the river beds, hoping they would be led to the vein of gold from whence these nuggets were cut and carried by the water. Then, instead of washing and washing for mere specks of gold, they would have a solid vein of pure gold to cut away from the surrounding rock! They would have wealth beyond their wildest dreams!

One day the three boys came upon a river that only had a few miners working the placer deposits near a fairly large, but abandoned tent camp. They thought that there wouldn't be much gold there, otherwise there would be more miners. But when they started to pan, they found some of the best gold that they had come across! They were excited! By working this stream they could make a fortune if the gold help up!

Soon dark approached. They joined the few other prospectors at the tent camp to cook supper and were invited to stay in an abandoned tent. They were amazed at how rich this stream was, and yet how few miners were working there.

An old man told them, "You need not be surprised boys. You may not be here long either. There are things more important than gold! But whatever you do as long as you stay in this valley, get into the tents by night-fall. Don't get caught in the valley in the blue mist. People die who get caught by it. It carries some sickness, but we have survived it. Do as we do, get into your tent before the blue mist comes down the valley!"

And that night, the blue mist again came. At first fingers of a thick blue fog rolled down the valley and curled around the tents. It was dark, about 10:00 p.m., and the lantern cast an eerie glow with the fog lapping higher and higher on the tents, until finally all was obscured.

The three friends were safe in a tent, hardly believing what the old timers had told them, but not wishing to dare their luck either. Day after day they worked the riches of this stream; night after night they sought refuge in the tents as the blue mist slid down the river from higher in the valley, obscuring everything and bringing all activity outside the camp to a stop.

And as they would work any other river, by day they panned further and further upstream, looking for richer color, looking for a concentration of gold that might mean that they were nearing the Mother Lode. But they always made sure to heed the old men's' advice to be back in the tent camp by night-fall, long before the fingers of blue mist curled down the valley.

One day they spotted an abandoned cabin, high in the valley. Its door was unlocked and upon checking it out they found it fully furnished, apparently abandoned by the owner. That night they asked the old timers about this cabin, so conveniently located high in the valley closer to the richer source of placer deposits which they had worked their way to.

"Stay in the cabin by day, if you must. But whatever you do, get back to this camp by night fall. Don't let your greed cause you to get caught out there over night. That cabin wasn't abandoned—the owner was Bill Murphy, who some say was the first prospector in this valley. He died in that cabin, and by the way they found him it was a horrible death. The same horrible death that kills anyone caught by the blue mist."

More than that the old timers couldn't tell them. But they were obviously afraid for their lives. The valley and its blue mist was holding some terrible secret and these old men would be of no help in solving the mystery . . . .

Mike, one of the three boys, finally had enough of the long trek back down to the tent camp, especially when there was a fully equipped cabin so close to their diggings. He announced one day that he was spending the night in the cabin. That morning he took his bedding, several days of his rations, and packed them along to the diggings. Tom and Roy tried to talk him out of it.

"Why take the chance?" Tom asked. "We have it OK at the tent camp. We are making good money. And it's obvious something terrible has happened in this valley. Those old miners aren't afraid of anything, except the blue mist. Let's just stay together and forget that cabin!"

Mike wouldn't hear of it. He worked with them during the day, but that night Tom and Roy had to return to the tent camp without him. And as the night wore on, they anxiously awaited the coming of the mist.

About 10:00 p.m., as usual, the fingers of thick, blue mist curled through the tent camp—soon obscuring all view of the twinkling light from the cabin up the valley. Finally, about 1:00 a.m., they heard something—they thought—way up the valley, possibly from the cabin. Tom couldn't believe that they had let Mike stay up there alone.

"We promised each other that we would stick together, no matter what," he reminded Roy. The old prospectors were furious that they had let Mike stay up there, for they had learned to like these three boys from the East. They didn't want anything to happen to them, and here they had gone and challenged the deadly blue mist.

The night was terribly long. Tom and Roy couldn't sleep that night as they waited for dawn so they could scramble up the valley to the cabin. The old prospectors also spent the night awake, worrying about their new friend.

But morning finally did come and they left as soon as the sun shined into the valley over the mountains, burning off the blue mist and sending light into the dark valley.

When they got to the cabin, they couldn't believe their eyes! Mike was dead. And worse, the cabin door was open and he lay half out of the door with a look of terror frozen on his face. A fear that struck the others right to the heart. The old men said that they had enough, they were leaving this valley for help. It wasn't safe to stay any longer, no matter how much gold was there.

Roy and Tom were stunned! And sick at their loss. And mad that they had not helped their friend as they had promised when they set out from home together.

In a daze they returned to the now abandoned tent camp after burying their friend near the cabin. They had to decide what to do. Should they return home to tell Mike's parents? They had enough money to return home, but not enough to buy a farm or to start a business if they returned now to the East. But more than that, they mourned their friend. This mourning turned to anger and frustration. Tom finally told Roy that they could not leave until they had done something to solve the mystery of their friend's death. They could not go home without being able to tell Mike's parents what had actually happened. Some beast or some person must be responsible for this, and whoever—or whatever—it must be punished.

Tom could think of only one way to do this. They must return to the cabin, armed, and spend the night. That way they could solve the mystery of the Valley of the Blue Mist!

Roy was horrified! No way was he going to spend the night in that cabin! He thought the idea was crazy and he told Tom so in no uncertain terms. Tom was rigid in his plan. He felt that it was their duty as they had abandoned their friend—they owed this to him.

Roy could not talk him out of it. But there was no way that HE would go up that valley and spend the night in the blue mist. As evening approached, the boys each had their mind made up. Tom packed his gear, including their only rifle, and headed up the valley to the cabin. It was already late when he left, and he had to hurry to beat the blue mist.

When he got there he made sure that the door was latched and windows shut. He moved the heavy table in front of the door, and to help support it, also slid the heavy chest of drawers against it.

Down in the valley Roy was alone in the tent camp. The old timers had left in a hurry, not even taking their equipment. An old clock ticked on as night fell. He realized what a terrible error he had made. His friend was trapped at the cabin, he was alone in this dreadful valley. Just two nights ago he had been with the two best friends he ever had—without a care in the world. Now he was exhausted, alone without a rifle, and his remaining friend was at the head of a valley that was full of death and mystery.

The minutes on the old wind-up clock ticked by. A proud possession of one of the miners, it had been left behind in the hasty abandonment of the camp. Soon it was 10:00 p.m.; the fingers of mist again curled through the silent tent camp. Terror struck—he waited and listened. He could hear nothing. The swirling mist climbed higher and soon obscured all view of the stars and the other tents. He was utterly alone. Oh, how he wished he had stuck with Tom in the cabin—or wherever he wanted to go. After all, Tom was his best friend and might even now need his help. And how about him—alone and without a gun in abandoned tents—alone in a thick, swirling mist.

The night lasted and lasted, as nights full of terror always do. Soon the glow of the sun penetrated the thick fog, and the mist started lifting from the valley.

Roy scrambled up the valley to the cabin. From the river's edge he shouted for Tom—but there was no answer from the cabin! He climbed up the path . . .

AAAUUUGGGHHH!

THERE AT THE FRONT OF THE CABIN—THE DOOR OPENED, WAS HIS FRIEND'S BODY! Twisted in an agony of death, the table and dresser knocked over, the rifle off to one side. The rifle had not even been fired! What could possibly have caught brave Tom so suddenly that he couldn't even get a shot off?

Roy now knew what he had to do. He could not return home now, he had to find out what mystery the Blue Mist held. He had to avenge his friends' deaths! Oh, how he wished he had stayed with Tom. How could he have been so stupid to have let him stay in this cabin alone, but now he had to make all of that up to both of his friends.

He immediately returned to the tent camp. There he got nails and a hammer. He brought extra kerosene for the lantern and two extra lanterns. He brought rope and some old, empty cans. He would return to that cabin and avenge the death of his friends, come what may!

Weighted down with his supplies, he took a last look at the now abandoned tent camp. He trudged up the now familiar stream bed that he and his friends had worked together for so long.

At the cabin he noted that the old clock which his friends had started was still ticking, and the time seemed correct. He took nails and went to work on the windows, boarding them up—nailing them soundly shut. Nothing could possible get in. He strung the empty cans on the rope around the cabin, so he could hear anyone, or anything, approach. He raked the dirt so that he could see any foot prints the next day. Finally, everything outside seemed ready. He shut the door of the cabin for the last time, and firmly nailed it shut.

He moved the dresser in front of the door. Thinking to further barricade it, he tried to move the large trunk located along one wall of the cabin. The trunk was incredibly heavy, too heavy to move. Opening it he found only a layer of old clothes, a belt, and a few odd items. The trunk had been nailed to the floor. Leaving it there, he filled the kerosene lanterns. He made sure the rifle was loaded, and then started the long wait for night.

Night comes suddenly in the mountains. When the sun finally lowers towards the horizon, it will suddenly dip behind a mountain top and be quickly lost from view. Shadows appear immediately and soon thereafter it is night.

With night in this valley comes more than darkness. The dreaded blue mist starts forming in the chasms and rivulets that form the valley on the mountain side. As Roy waited, he watched the clock. Soon it was 10:00 p.m., and the mist started swirling beyond the cabin door, filling the basin of the river and sliding its way down to the abandoned tent camp. Fingers of mist slid between now empty tents.

At the cabin Roy continued to wait. His heart pounding, he thought of his friends and he thought of his own danger. The night deepened and outside the mist covered the cabin. He listened intently for any sound amongst the tin cans outside, any evidence of movement from the nearby forest.

And finally he DID hear something. At first it was a quiet whisper. Then, more of a hiss. It sounded close, very close to the cabin. Could it be a snake? Or a whole coil of snakes? Surely there would have been some sign earlier when the others had been killed.

The hiss was close, near the window, SUDDENLY HE FELT A TIGHT CONSTRICTION GRABBING AT HIS THROAT. He thought he was losing his sight, the cabin was becoming darker! No! It was the kerosene lights, they were flickering out!

AAAUUUGGGHHH!

VIOLENT SPASMS TWITCHED HIS BODY, HE GASPED FOR AIR, HE STRUGGLED TO ESCAPE! He couldn't breathe! The light from the lamps went out, the hissing, more of a sighing was louder now. Its location was easy to identify—IT WAS COMING FROM THE EMPTY TRUNK!

He grabbed the dresser and threw it aside. The planks! He ripped at the planks, the spasm racking his body!

Early the next day a column of men proceeded up the valley. It was the group of old miners, leading a posse from the nearest town. Upon finding the cabin sealed shut, they took their pikes to the door and smashed their way through. Inside they found the contorted body of the last of the three friends.

These men decided that they would take matters into their own hands. Furiously they would destroy this cabin where so many had died. They started tearing it apart, board by board. When they reached the flooring, they too noted the old trunk nailed to the floor. Breaking it apart they made an incredible discovery. The trunk apparently had a secret, false bottom. It covered a shaft leading into a hidden mine. And that mine proved to be the Mother Lode! Rather than claiming this rich vein of ore for what it was, the miner had simply staked a claim and built his cabin over the spot. Then he concealed the shaft opening with the trunk, a much better concealment than a trap door under a rug in the cabin. But unknown to the old miner, he eventually reached a pocket of deadly gas within his mine. When night fell in the valley, the barometric pressure dropped. On the outside this caused the blue mist to rise up from the ground. But inside the cabin, it allowed the mine shaft to start blowing air out its opening, just as a cave entrance will do when the pressure is right. But this mine air was laced with deadly cyanide gas, which, when it caught its victim, racked them with spasm and a very quick death.

This mine eventually became known as the Empress Mine, one of the richest finds of the gold fields. But a mine with a tragic beginning, one that killed three good friends in the midst of their life of adventure together.

Story Outline

I. Three young friends left their homes in the East, about a hundred years ago, to try their luck in the western gold rush.

II. They were panning for gold, like most prospectors—but always hoping they could follow the gold specks to the

Mother Lode, the vein of pure gold from whence the rivers washed the nuggets.

III. They found a beautiful valley with only a few prospectors. Much to their surprise the panning was rich in gold yield. An old miner told them of the legend of the valley— he warned them to be inside camp before the dreaded blue mist formed in the valley at night. Some people died when caught out in the blue mist.

IV. The boys worked further and further upstream, panning a higher and higher yield of gold. The distance to camp was becoming longer each night. Finally they found a cabin which had been abandoned way up the valley.

V. Mike, one of the boys, decided to spend his nights there, rather than make the long trek back to camp. The others couldn't talk him out of it.

VI. Tom and Roy couldn't sleep that night worrying about their friend. Finally daylight came and the mist burned off. When they and the other prospectors reached the cabin they found Mike dead, half lying out of the cabin, with a look of terror frozen on his face.

VII. The miners left for help, but Tom and Roy stayed behind. Tom told Roy that they had to find out what had killed their friend. He insisted on spending the night in the cabin with the rifle. Roy could not talk him out of it, but there was no way that he would spend the night out in the valley of the blue mist.

VIII. That night Tom barricaded himself into the cabin, moving the heavy furniture that was there and spent the night, his rifle ready for any trouble.

IX. Roy was alone in the tent camp, afraid for himself and his friend. The next morning he scrambled up the valley to the cabin and there AAAUUUGGGHHH! (loud scream) was his friend's body, twisted in an agony of death, the door open, the rifle off to one side, unused.

X. Roy was now determined to avenge his two friends' deaths. He gathered supplies at the cabin, returned to it and nailed the door shut, covered the windows and sat waiting for the mystery of the valley of the blue mist.

XI. Finally, in the night he heard a hiss that grew louder and louder. He realized that the hiss was coming from the trunk that was nailed to the floor of the cabin. Suddenly he started choking, gasping for air.

XII. The prospectors returned the next day with a posse from the nearest town. They found Roy's body and decided to tear the cabin down. When doing this they found that the trunk was covering a mine shaft entrance. It was the entrance to the Mother Lode.

XIII. But the mine had encountered deadly poisonous cyanide gas—and when the night came and the barometric pressure dropped, when the blue mist formed outside, at that time the mine entrance would start blowing air out, rather than sucking it in. And the poison gas would claim another victim.

XIV. The mine became famous as the Empress Mine, one of the richest ever discovered. But a mine that killed its discoverer and three good friends in the midst of their life of adventure together.

3

THE HUMAN HAND

by Doc Forgey

Stories to be good have to be credible. An example is the ridiculous situation of a severed human hand crawling along the ground trying to strangle its victims. The following is a story utilizing a human hand, but told in a manner that lends it credibility. I have been told that this is actually a true story. It is a story that has circulated about my old alma mater, Indiana University, and it is supposed to have happened back in the 1930s.

The girls in a particular sorority at Indiana University, back in the 1930's, had a terrible thing happen to them.[1] A group of six of them were being dated by a particular group of boys. This group had become very close. They shared all of their free time together and generally enjoyed talking about all of the things which they did during the day. Whenever you are in school, working, or doing anything during the day—what do you talk about when you get together at night? Well, generally it's about what happened during the day. You talk about the professors you have, the tests they gave, your other classmates—even though you are trying to get away from it and want to relax at night. You know yourselves, you frequently talk about what you did during the day. And the same was true of this group.

---

1 If telling this story to a group of young scouts, you may have to tell them what a sorority is.

There was a law student, two business students, a chemistry major, and also two pre-medical students. And therein laid the problem. Because one of the girls was extremely squeamish. She couldn't stand hearing them tell stories about the laboratories, about cutting up cadavers (human bodies), about doing any of their work. So these two poor kids could never say anything about what they were doing during the day. At first this was OK, but as time went on it became a real nuisance to everyone concerned—all of the others felt kind of sorry that this situation was going on. But she was just absolutely rigid about it—she would not let them discuss the things that they did in class.

One day they all got together talking, when she wasn't with them, and they thought: "You know, we ought to teach her a lesson. We ought to do something to just kind of get rid of this nonsense." And they came up with an idea . . .

Now in Indiana during the winter it gets dark rather early, around 4:30 P.M. They decided they would tell her that they wanted to go out for a movie after supper. It would be very dark.

In this sorority all of the girls had their rooms upstairs, but they ate their meals and entertained their guests in their living rooms and dining room on the first floor. In their individual rooms upstairs the girls had electric lights, but because it was so many years ago, the fixtures were very simple. Every light was simply turned on by pulling a string that hung down from the ceiling.

The plan was that they would go to the cadaver laboratory where they kept the dead bodies. There they would cut off a human hand. And they would take that human hand and they would tie it to the electric light switch string hanging from her ceiling. They would make an excuse so that she would have to go up to that room alone. And when she went up to that room, she would reach up to turn on the light, and she would GRAB THAT HUMAN HAND!

So, sure enough, the boys arranged it. They managed to sneak a hand out of the cadaver laboratory. That night they all sat around and had supper together over at the sorority before going to a movie. It soon got dark out. Finally they were sitting around discussing their evening, when one of the boys said "Isn't it about time that we left for the movies? And the girls all said "Oh, yes. Let's get our coats." And they all stood up as if they were about to rush on upstairs, but then the five of them knowing this trick that they were about to play—and which had already been arranged by one of the boys during supper—hung back seemingly to make last minute minor conversations with their boy friends, while she went up stairs . . . to turn on that light!

And as she disappeared around the corner of the stairs, they all fell silent. They were waiting for the scream.

A scream that never came.

Finally, they could not stand the suspense any longer. They all as a group traveled up the stairs, not caring that boys were not allowed upstairs, and they looked down the hall of the dorm.

Nobody . . . nothing was in sight.

The door was standing open to her room . . . and the light was on!

They rushed down the hall and they OPENED THE DOOR TO THAT ROOM—nobody was there.

One of the girls went down to the end of the hall to the bathroom, opened the door, went in . . . nothing. She wasn't there.

ALL OF A SUDDEN ONE OF THE BOYS RAISED THE SKIRT AROUND THE BOTTOM OF THE BED . . . nothing was under the bed.

They couldn't believe it. The light was on, the hand was gone, the room was empty. Where was she?

Then one of them went over to the closet door . . . OPENED UP THE CLOSET DOOR—AND THERE SHE WAS! DOWN AT THE BOTTOM OF THAT CLOSET! HER HAIR TURNED SOLID WHITE . . . AND SHE WAS GNAWING ON THAT HUMAN HAND.

She had gone entirely insane. She had grabbed that hand off the string and just started gnawing on it. She was totally mad. They had to take her away from school and she had to be locked up the rest of her life in an insane asylum. The boys were afraid that they might be kicked out of school, so they took that gnawed human hand from there and drove it outside of town and buried it. They buried it in a place that to this very day can be found on the maps—a little town just east of Bloomington called "Gnaw Bone, Indiana!"

Story Outline

I. A group of 6 boys were dating girls from a sorority at Indiana University back in the 1930s.

II. While they all liked to talk about their actions during the day, one of the girls was so squeamish that she would not let the two boys who were medical students talk about any of their activities.

III. The group finally decided to pull a trick on her to cure her squeamish ways. The medical students stole a hand from a dead body and hung it from the light string in her room.

IV. After supper, during a dark winter evening, the girl went upstairs to get her coat before going to a movie.

V. They waited to hear her scream, but no scream ever came.

VI. They scooted upstairs, but could find no sign of her in the room, down the hall, or under the bed.

VII. Finally, they looked in the closet and there they found her . . . totally insane, gnawing, eating on that human hand!

4

LA CUCARACHA MINE

as told by Doc Forgey

As a new lieutenant in the Army, one night in 1966 I was called upon to lead a group of Boy Scouts on a camp out – and they called upon me to tell them a story. Thinking on the spot, I managed to tell three. This is one of them. The others are in this book also: The Graveyard Rats and The Human Hand.

Not so many years ago there was a group of young men, a little older than you boys, who were in college. They developed a hobby, and that hobby was to try and find buried treasure. They felt that the best way of doing that was to learn Spanish. Not regular Spanish, but the old Spanish, the Spanish spoken by the *conquistadores*. These ancient soldiers had captured the Indians of Central America—the Inca, the Mayan, the Aztec. Stealing their gold and other treasures, they would bring it back to Spain in their galleons. They kept meticulous records because this gold was the property of the king. The instant they laid their hands on it, it was considered the king's property. So they kept very good track of it—their lives were forfeit were they to lose their accounting of these treasures.

In Spain at the Alhambra, the old royal castle where these records were sent, there are piles of ancient documents which are old records of the gold shipments. The boys felt that within those archives there could be some secret that might let them find a lost treasure. Indeed they studied these records carefully. They went over there during the summer and spent weeks and weeks poring over all sorts of these ancient journals. They had explained to the officials that they were there for academic purposes and therefore they were allowed access to the archives to help their studies.

One summer they found it. There was a record of a mine, a very rich mine, located in a province that today is in southern Mexico. The Spaniards were running it with Indian slave labor and getting tremendous quantities of gold. Year after year the gold was being shipped back to Spain, when suddenly . . . it stopped!

Something mysterious had happened. There was no more gold from this area.

Several things could have happened. The Indians could have mutinied and actually killed off the guards. But if that were to have happened, the Spaniards would have sent more guards and an army detail to restore order, for this was a very wealthy mine. So that could not have been it. A disease could have struck killing off everyone in that area. But again, with that much value to this mine, surely the mine would have been reopened regardless of the cost.

Something mysterious had happened to have caused this whole operation to have just closed down. The name given to the mine was: "*La Cucaracha.*"

The three young friends took all of the money that they had and formed an expedition to go down deep into the jungles of lower Mexico. They had an approximate location from the old Spanish name of the district, and so they went to find *La Cucaracha.*

They went to small towns in the highlands on the jungle edge to see if they could get any clue about where some mysterious things may have occurred. In one town there was a bar with an old man there—he did not know anything about *La*

Cucaracha, but he said: "You know, there is an Indian legend about a mine called: *La Antigua*, in the back country. It means "The Old One.""

That was the closest of anything they had come upon, the only thing that they had to go with, it certainly sounded mysterious. Maybe the Indians had a different name for the mine than the Spanish Conquistadores. They asked the old man to take them to *La Antigua* and they headed off into the jungles on their quest.

They cut their way through the thick underbrush, SLASHING their way through the foliage, and finally after they had gotten way out in the jungles they found a mysterious shaft. This shaft HAD to be man made. It was cut out of solid rock, a shaft that just disappeared into the depths of the bedrock of the earth.

They had to find out what was at the bottom of this pit. They dropped a rock down it . . . they could hear nothing. So they rigged up a wench, and one of the guys climbed into a parachute harness. The Indians working with his two friends would lower him into the shaft.

He had a head light on. Soon he was below the surface of the ground and the darkness of the musty pit closed in around him. As he was being lowered further and further into the shaft, the rope started to slowly spin around. he slowly twirled around and around as he went down deeper and deeper. Pretty soon he could see no light from the top of the shaft at all. There was just a tiny light way up above as he was being lowered into that shaft.

As he was being lowered deeper and deeper, he noticed that the walls were turning a rusty brown color. As he went further down he though that maybe he could see the bottom of this mine shaft. But he was spinning faster and faster, too fast to clearly make out what was below.

He needed to slow down, so he reached his leg way out to touch the wall of the mine shaft to stop the rapid spinning. As he did this, while spinning around, his foot literally gouged into the wall of the shaft—suddenly he realized what that rust color was. Thousands, millions of cockroaches had climbed up the side of the shaft—indeed as he looked further down he could see that the bottom of the shaft—the place to which he was being lowered—was a teeming mass of cockroaches. He was being lowered to his death, he was about to be buried alive by cockroaches!

AAAUUUGGGHHH! He shouted as loud as he could, hoping his friends would hear him and stop lowering him into that ocean of writhing insects.

His foot had dislodged the cockroaches on the walls and millions came cascading down, some falling, thousands flying. A suffocating mass of whirling wings. Trying to get his breath for a second scream he choked on a mouth full of the vile insects. They were in his ears, in his nose, his throat gagged with wriggling, struggling insects. He was suffocating, he was gagging—trying to scream and vomit at the same time.

He had learned the dread secret of *La Cucaracha* Mine.

And closer to the bottom of this pit—closer to being buried alive in a mountain of cockroaches. All light from his helmet obscured by the massive number of insects, he knew he was closer and closer to the bottom of the shaft. THOUSANDS, AND THOUSANDS OF THE ROACHES POUNDED HIM ON ALL SIDES. HE COULDN'T GET HIS BREATH, BUT HE HAD TO BREATHE! Desperately he struggled for air.

They were down his shirt, swarming around his head, thousands, and thousands of them.

HELP!!!! His screams were muffled by the millions of whirling cockroaches. He shouted again, and he shouted again—desperate

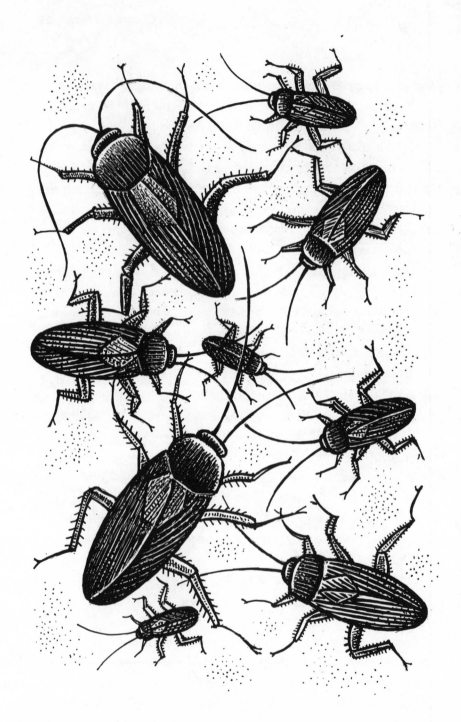

for help amongst their nightmare of cockroaches. Cascading cockroaches were burying him alive!

Suddenly . . . he jerked to a stop!

He felt himself being raised, raised as rapidly as he knew his friends could. Once on the surface, he lay gagging and choking—trying to breathe. His friends on the surface realized something was wrong. Thousands of cockroaches suddenly began swarming out of the entrance to the shaft, and when they saw that they stopped lowering him and immediately tried to get their friend out of there. They now all knew the secret of *La Cucaracha*!

Subsequently the village people made certain that the shaft was boarded up so that never again would somebody be lowered into the sprawling mass of insects that had taken over *La Cucaracha* mine.

Story Outline

I. A group of students study old Spanish documents to study the movement of the gold taken from the New World by the conquistadores.

II. They learn of a mine called *La Cucaracha* whose rich supply of gold suddenly and mysteriously stopped.

III. Forming an expedition to the section of Mexico where the mine should be located, they find a deep shaft in the jungle.

IV. One of the young men is lowered into the pit. As the rope starts spinning faster and faster, he notices that the walls of the shaft are turning a rusty brown color.

V. He thinks that he might be able to see the bottom of the shaft. Putting out his foot, he touches the wall to stop his spin. Suddenly, he dislodges a mass of cockroaches.

VI. He tries to shout to his friends to stop lowering him into the pit of cockroaches, but the flying insects practically suffocate him, preventing his friends from hearing him.

VII. Just as he is about to be lowered to his death, his friends stop lowering him. They have been alerted to his trouble by the flying hoards of cockroaches that start coming out of the shaft entrance.

VIII. They have learned the secret of *La Cucaracha*—the Cockroach Mine.

5

THE ICE WALKER

by Grey Owl

Grey Owl was one of the unusual breed of Englishmen who became so infatuated with the natural life in the wilds of Canada that they immigrated and became woodsmen. Grey Owl went so far as to assume the identity of an Indian. He was adopted into an Indian tribe and given the name Wa-sha-quon-asin. *He had the talent of writing about his many experiences and his epic stories of the vast North Land, of the men— both Indians and white—of the animals that live there, and of the trees and rivers which are its sentinels and highways, make the Canadian wilderness come alive for us. Living in a primitive and isolated area, Grey Owl once encountered this story of adventure in the Northland. When telling this story use plenty of tap, tap, tap and tock, tock, tocks to describe the incessant noise of the ice walker Grey Owl is encountering. Using the descriptive phrases that Grey Owl includes of his journey through the icy wilderness makes this a great, scary campfire story.*

For some time past I had heard the man coming. The tock, tock of his pole as he tapped the ice had been audible from a distance of perhaps a mile, the sound magnified and carried far and wide, as is the way with a blow struck on glare ice.

This testing ice by sound is often necessary during the early part of Winter, the pole being swung naturally and easily in the stride, the end being allowed to drop with its full weight at every fourth step, much as a drum major wields his staff.

The timing of the strokes in this case was such that the traveler seemed to strike the ice at every other step the steps of one who is unhurried, walking slowly, but steadily. And as he walked came the *tap tap*, of the pole, regular as the "tuck" of the drum of marching infantry. It was late Fall, and I knew the ice to be bad, especially at this place, a large shallow lake bottomed with a treacherous, gaseous slime, which spelt death for him who should break through and be sucked into the hungry maw of the shifting ooze. The lake itself was walled in by the towering black palisades of a gloomy spruce forest, into which no ray of sunlight ever penetrated, and was backed by miles of almost impassable swamps.

A desolate region, and one that I avoided as much as possible in my goings and comings on the trap lines.

Suddenly remembering my duties as probable host to a tired man, I stirred up the smoldering fire, put the cold tea on afresh and endeavored to make some semblance of a meal out of the remains of the lunch I had just eaten. As I so busied myself, I wondered a little what even could bring a stranger into my hunting ground, at a time when the Fall hunt was in full swing.

My temporary camping place was not visible from the lake but the smoke was plain to be seen, and I knew that the voyageur would not fail to turn in and stop awhile, as is the custom with those who travel in the Wilderness. So I sat by my fire and smoked, and anxiously awaited the newcomer's arrival, for something in the manner of his coming indicated (for a lifetime on the trail trains the faculties to a degree of perception in such matters), that he who had penetrated so far within my boundaries was no ordinary trapper. There seemed, for one thing, to be some peculiar quality in this man's method of feeling out the ice; in the first place there was his unusual action of striking at every third step as though marking time on a line of march, and then the additional resonance he produced by the unusually heavy blows he struck, as though he carried a weightier staff than was commonly used. And over and above that was the changeless, unbroken rhythm of the strokes, which were as measured and uniform as the ticking of some gigantic clock.

And his slow, unfaltering strides seemed to suggest a dogged persistence, as of a man with a mission to fulfill, and a man, moreover, not easily swerved from his purpose. Onward he marched, his every step timed by the steady, persistent tap of the pole, *tock, tock, tock*, until the regularity and monotony of the sounds exercised an almost hypnotic influence on my mind as I sat and waited. He seemed long in coming, walking slowly as he did, yet so persistently that he should have long ago arrived. And then quite suddenly I realized that the sound was now beyond the stopping place and that the wayfarer, whoever he might be, had ignored the presence of my camp, in spite of the smoke and the light sleigh in full view on the shore, and had passed on. An unusual, nay, an unheard of proceeding amongst bushmen, and unaccountable unless the man be blind, or an enemy.

There does not live the man of any character who has not made at least one enemy in his lifetime, and this last thought stuck in my mind.

I went out onto the ice, but the passerby was already out of sight beyond a point, for the lake was one of irregular shores and many deep bays and inlets, in which concealment for purposes of ambush would have been an easy matter. And I could still hear plainly the measured stroke of the pole, a sound which, from being merely eerie, had now become ominous, seeming to tap forth a challenge, or a threat.

I hastened out to the center of the lake for a fuller view, and still saw no one, so I returned to my camp, extinguished my fire, and quickly arming myself, started in pursuit. I traveled at a dog-trot the usual gait on glare ice, taking, as I did so, full advantage of the excellent cover that the broken character of the shore line afforded, having as a guide to the line of march of my quarry, the steady, never ceasing rapping on the ice.

For an hour or more I followed the intruder. There being now no necessity for testing the ice where one had passed ahead of me, I lost no time, yet great as was my speed, and slow as his appeared to be, found that I could in no wise catch up to him.

In spite of his apparently leisurely progress he seemed to be able to keep his distance. The sound swung off to my right, and following it, I saw that the chase had taken me into a deep and apparently endless bay, of which, up to that time, I had had no knowledge. Down this I pursued the elusive, baffling tattoo for miles, always trotting, and the invisible stranger always walking with his measured steps.

Almost it was as though the man carried a huge metronome, or that the creature itself were not a human being but a robot. Grimly determined to get to the bottom of this mystery, I followed mile after mile, regardless of where this will-o'-the-wisp of sound was leading me; over wide expanses of lake, through narrow gorges, along winding forest-bordered streams, but always on ice, and ever to the accompaniment of that unvarying and monotonous rapping.

Eventually I found myself in a part of my hunting ground that I had never before set eyes on, a barren desolation of blow-down, burnt lands, and black impenetrable swamp. How this section had escaped my observation after some years of constant traveling in the district, I could in no way account for, and I was somewhat piqued to think that a stranger knew more of my own territory than I did myself. More than that, the nature of the whole proposition began to border on the uncanny; even the wild and inhospitable appearance of the landscape, with its grotesque and twisted piles of shattered trees, and dark reaches of brooding swamp, seemed to reflect that atmosphere of weird unreality of this adventure.

The chase was long and I began to tire, and no longer able to run, I now walked; and strangely, I was still able to keep that haunting sound within earshot, and at about the same distance as before. It appeared as if the stranger was cognizant of my fatigue, and was, by some means unknown to me, able to gauge accurately my speed, and thus keep his progress timed to mine, never allowing me to catch up, yet never drawing away from me. And there occurred to me with startling suddenness, the possibility that he did not want to outdistance me, that I had blindly followed where he had led me, and that I had been decoyed with devilish ingenuity many miles into a country of which I knew nothing; for what purpose I could only guess.

The sun had set, and there was no moon; night was coming on and I was alone in a trackless wilderness with an unknown and evidently competent enemy. I became conscious of a feeling of uneasiness, and halting in my tracks, formed and rejected a dozen swift plans of action. Co-incident with my stopping, the sound slewed off to the East beyond a fringe of timber, and I noticed with a feeling of distinct relief that it seemed to be going further away. This, and the fact that I had no provision, decided me to turn back, resolving to return with some supplies and solve this vexing problem on the morrow. Snow threatened, and in that event, the man of mystery must at least leave some tracks.

I squatted on the ice and mapped out as well as I could the tortuous itinerary over which this man-hunt had taken me, in order to devise a short-cut back to my main trail, but found the project hopeless. I was now faced with the necessity of covering the entire route, most of it in the dark.

So I started on the long journey back to my launching place. Off to one side I could still hear that infernal *tock-tock*, and as I proceeded I seemed to be unable to get away from the now hateful sound; in fact it seemed to be coming closer. I stopped and listened. It was approaching without a doubt, outflanking me from behind the thin fringe of timber just mentioned, which now proved to be an island behind which it had passed; and a sudden turn in the route brought the sound dead ahead of me, blocking my trail, and coning my way! I could no longer disguise from myself the certainty that this thing, whatever it was, was intentionally heading me off, and mixed with my feeling of affront at the overt act, was more than a hint of fear.

Nearer it came, nearer and yet nearer, and still no one was visible; a slow measured advance, as immutable as the onward march of Time itself; *tock, tock, tock*; now no longer reminiscent of the strokes of the homely metronome, but more suggestive of the ticking of an infernal machine, stalking me, marking off the seconds till it should close with me and destroy me. In something of a panic I sheered off, and it followed like a nightmare; I doubled, and the Thing crept on behind me.

I ran and the sound kept its given distance; I slowed up with a like result. I twisted, turned, and back-tracked; I tried every shift and subterfuge learnt in a calling where stratagem and expedient become second nature, but without avail. I could not shake off my fiendish familiar. And I now knew in cold reality the awful fear of one pursued by some hellish monster in a nightmare.

I was no longer the pursuer but the pursued, and I was being hunted by some person or thing that could see without being seen, and could accurately forestall my every move. Escape into the bush was impossible, as the whole country was covered by a fallen forest that had been blown down by some recent hurricane, and in places newly burnt. And always behind and to one side or the other, that sinister tapping herded me relentlessly and inexorably on my way, as a steer is herded by a skillful cowboy. For I dreaded now to meet the one I had so assiduously sought, and kept as much distance between him and myself as the shape of the waterways allowed, for I felt that even armed as I was, weapons would be of little use against a being who could apparently so flaunt the laws of nature. I burst into a clammy sweat.

The terrible hitherto unbelieved tales of the man-eating windego and the Loup Garou, the were-wolf of bush mythology, flashed across my mind, tales of trappers found dead in ghastly and unexplainable mutilation.

The horror of what I now knew to be the supernatural drained the last vestige of resolution from my being, and I abandoned all attempts at a considered or calculated retreat; I no longer hoped to outdistance this Thing, seeking only in my desperation to delay as long as possible the awful moment when it should catch up to me and work its will upon me.

I lost track of my direction, except to see that I was being driven deeper and deeper into a savage Wilderness, the like of which I had never before seen; yet the terror of that unknown presence behind me goaded me on and on, whither, I no longer cared, so that I kept beyond the reach of this invisible peril. I was fatigued beyond measure, and knew that I could not much longer continue my flight. I became obsessed by the idea that if I could only leave the ice I could outdistance my pursuer, but I seemed held from making the attempt by some diabolical power beyond my control.

I then made the alarming discovery that the body of water on which I traveled was coming to an end. Towering, impregnable cliffs walled it in on either hand, closing in on me as the waterway narrowed, and at its termination, no great distance ahead of me, was a bristling rampart of torn and broken tree-trunks, through which no man could make any headway. I now saw that the matter had been brought to an issue, and that be it man, beast, or devil that was hunting me down, I must at last stand and fight it.

My aim was now to reach the foot of the narrow sheet of ice, where I would have protection of a kind on three sides of me, the walls of rock to my flanks and the masses of fallen timber in my rear. The phantom sound was almost upon me, and not daring to look back lest I lose this terrible race, I stumbled forward with feet that seemed suddenly turned to lead. With a last despairing burst of speed I gained my objective, when hope suddenly sprang to life within me as I descried, by the failing light, a narrow trail that had but lately been hewed through the tangled slash before which I had intended to make my stand. This, I thought, must undoubtedly lead to some human habitation, or failing that, would at least enable me to leave the ice, and so perhaps outdistance my pursuer, whose element it appeared to be, and I made for it with all possible speed. My relief at finding my feet on solid ground, where my pursuer would be no longer able to tap out his accursed measure, was indescribable. And then, too late I discovered that a frozen creek ran parallel to the trail, hidden from it by the wall of prostrate tree-trunks, so as to be only intermittently

visible. My faulty strategy had now given him the advantage that he needed.

And as, almost at the point of exhaustion, my face streaming with perspiration, and gasping for breath at every step, I staggered along the narrow pathway, the ceaseless *tock, tock, tock, tock,* beat its threat of a nameless horror into my reeling senses, as it marched alongside me on the ice of the stream, an invisible, but ever present escort. I could now no longer turn to right or left, and ever the Thing was beside me; I felt as one who walks with Death.

And then, to my unutterable relief, I saw a clearance ahead of me, and a cluster of log cabins. The stream was now plainly visible, and on its bank a group of men were gathered around some object on the ground, and them I approached with the feelings of one who has escaped from the very edge of the pit. The sound from which I fled was now close at hand, and I lost no time in acquainting those present with my predicament. To my surprise they looked coldly on me, and my remarks passed unheeded. No one spoke, and a strained silence, such as greets the appearance of an unwelcome visitor at any gathering, fell upon the assembly, until one man said, pointing at me:

"There he is now, that is the man; show him his work."

At that the group opened up, and I saw stretched out before me the dead body of a young man, terribly mutilated, evidently murdered with the utmost brutality.

"Who has done this?" I asked, even as there was borne upon me the frightful realization that these people, for some reason, accounted me the guilty party. My question remained unanswered, but all eyes were turned on me with cold, staring hostility. These men were all rough prospectors and trappers, strangers to me, every one of them, members of a community that I had not known even existed, and their deadly calm and purposeful demeanour showed me that the situation was fraught with terrible possibilities.

I made some attempt to clear myself, telling them who I was, and where I had been this two months past, stumbling over my words and faltering in my speech, as an innocent man will, when confronted by the evidence of his supposed guilt.

My disjointed and incoherent protestations met with no response; the men ignored the fact that I was speaking, staring at me in stony silence, on their faces the set expression of an unalterable purpose. Finally the man who had accused me spoke again. "This thing must be finished before dark. Here comes the boy's father; let him decide what is to be done." And at that instant the persistent, unearthly rapping that had driven me to the scene of what was liable to be my doom, at length caught up to me and, almost at my elbow, abruptly ceased. Turning, I now for the first time saw my pursuer, an old, old man dressed in faded buckskin, and armed with a heavy, steel-shod hardwood pole. His frame was so attenuated, being almost fleshless, and his demeanor so strange and wild, that he had all the semblance of one risen from the grave, or of a being from another world. His hair was white and hung in snaky locks below his shoulders, and a full beard covered most of his face; and out of this his burning eyes glared into mine with an unwavering stare of such malevolence and hatred, that it chilled me to the bone; for I plainly saw what he would desire to be done.

Without speaking he advanced on me slowly, raising above his head as he did so the heavy staff that, having driven me to my place of execution, was now to be the instrument of his just but misdirected vengeance.

The first blow struck by the parent as his unalienable right, I would then, without a shadow of doubt, be literally shot to pieces. Stiff with horror, held by some awful fascination in the old man's insane stare, I was struck dumb, until at last:

"Wait, men, wait." I screeched rather than shouted "I am not the man," fumbling meanwhile in my pockets with fingers that refused their office, for some identification. Two men leaped forward quickly, and held me full in the path of the descending shaft. In my dire extremity and with the strength of despair, I tore myself loose with a mighty effort. A great light flashed before my eyes, and I awoke to find the landlord of the little frontier hotel, where I was passing the night, shaking me violently with one hand, while he held a lamp before my face with the other.

And at the same moment there came to my ears the steady and resonant ticking of the large kitchen clock that was suspended on the wall over my bed.

Story Outline

I. Grey Owl is in his cabin and hears the steady *tock, tock, tock,* of a man coming closer, testing the ice on the lake as he comes.

II. In the tradition of the north country, he prepares a warmer fire and fixes tea and something to eat for his arriving visitor.

III. He is shocked to realize that the man has passed by the cabin. This is an insult in the north country—he rushes out to chase the man down and find out who he is.

IV. For over an hour he follows the man, thinking to easily overcome his slow pace. The sound swings to the right down a deep bay, unfamiliar to Grey Owl.

V. For hours he continues, following the steady *tap, tap, tap*—through gorges, over wide expanses of lakes, along forest bordered streams, but always on ice listening to the *tap, tap, tap*.

VI. It soon begins to get dark, and Grey Owl is becoming fatigued. He notices that the tapping has slowed, as if the man knows he is tiring. He decides that he is almost lost in unknown territory at night, with an unknown enemy ahead of him. His best plan would be to return. The tapping man has gone into the forest and the sound is fading.

VII. As Grey Owl starts his trip back, he finds that the tapping man has simply gone around an island and is now heading straight for him!

VIII. Grey Owl shears off to one side. The *tock, tock, tock* of the tapping is louder and following him, like a monstrous machine closing in to destroy him. If he ran, slowed, changed course, it followed.

IX. He realizes that the lake he is on came to a dead end with cliffs blocking his retreat. He decides to make a stand in a protected bay, but upon reaching it is delighted to find a new trail recently cut into the wilderness.

X. Hoping to find humans, he takes the trail. The tapping follows him as there is a stream running along side of the trail. On this narrow trail, he can turn neither right nor left to escape from the tapping monster that is right beside him.

XI. To his relief a clearing is ahead with several men standing beside the now visible river. The tapping is right behind him. He approaches the men, only to see a crumpled figure lying at their feet.

XII. One of the men points to him, saying: "There he is now, that is the man; show him his work." At their feet lays the terribly mutilated body of a young man, apparently murdered.

XIII. The men pay no attention to Grey Owl's telling them he was innocent. They state that here comes the boy's father now, let him decide what should be done.

XIV. Grey Owl is horrified to hear the tapping resounding behind him ever louder; turning it is the boy's father, a wild looking man, who looms closer and closer with a fierce stare of hatred. The old man approaches Grey Owl and raises the heavy, metal tipped staff he has been using to strike the ice, raises it to smash it down on Grey Owl's head.

XV. Grey Owl pleads with the men, who are holding him for the old man to strike. Grey Owl struggles and struggles—suddenly he finds himself being shaken awake by the landlord of the little frontier hotel where he has fallen asleep, with their large kitchen clock ticking loudly on the wall suspended over his bed.

6

THE MESSAGE

by Doc Forgey

At Fort Bragg, North Carolina, the father of one of my scouts got himself into trouble. This is an area that has a lot of nice sandy soil, beautiful pine trees—it is also an area of swamps. And, in those swamps, one has to be careful and remain alert as to what he is doing. You should not become too mesmerized by walking and day dreaming, by enjoying a walk in the woods without maintaining at least a certain amount of vigilance.

This particular hunter was very smart because when he left for a pheasant hunt he told people where he was going and when he would be returning. He went alone, which always increases the risk one might run when traveling in the swamps, but at least he notified others of his planned whereabouts.

A long day hiking in the hot, North Carolina sun tends to exhaust a person. Enjoying the beautiful countryside at the same time also lulls one into a comfortable, mechanical stride that minimizes the effort. He was walking along, paying no attention to where he was going. As he was moving, he failed to notice that he was entering a depression, a shallow valley-like area. Suddenly, something moved catching his eye and jarring him to reality!

What moved? To his astonishment it was a snake at his feet, but not just a snake slithering away from him, but a sudden excitement and rippling movement of dozens of snakes, all Eastern diamondback rattlesnakes, lying virtually on top of each other, spread all throughout the depression area and surrounding him on all sides!

Reacting with instinct, he gave a leap upon a stump that was moldering in the ground next to him. He stared in horror at the writhing mass of snakes, all deadly poisonous and now all awake and active—crawling over each other, hissing, and even striking at each other. The heat in this depressed area was oppressive. But fear more than the heat made the sweat stream down his face. He had his .410 shotgun with him, but he knew that he did not have enough shells to clear his way through this mass of snakes.

As he stood there staring in fascination looking all about him, the movement of the snakes gradually quieted down. They again became dormant—fewer and fewer of them seemed to have noticed the intrusion upon their resting place. He could not believe what had happened. His heart was still pounding at the thought of his narrow escape and with apprehension about his present situation. He could not understand how he walked into the middle of this mess without being bitten! But now here he was—stuck in the middle of a swampy depression, surrounded by poisonous snakes, any one of which could possibly kill him, or at least cause terrible injury.

At least they were not attempting to climb up the stump to get him. But if noise and excitement seemed to have left this valley, the heat had not. Standing there on the stump, the heat seemed more and more oppressive. Afraid to move a muscle for fear of arousing the snakes, the hunter wisely stood as motionless as possible. He hoped that the snakes would leave this area when the day cooled down towards evening. Perhaps then he could find a pathway out of this mess.

The minutes passed like hours, slowly—almost imperceptibly. The heat and sweating added to the thirst of his earlier

activity. His mouth was parched, his legs fatigued. His only hope was that these snakes would leave the valley after it cooled. Perhaps they would become fearful of owls or other creatures of the night—if only he could just remain perched where he was until night fall.

Perching on a stump is never easy. In this case, it was sheer torture. It seemed as if the sun would never lower, that the day would never cool.

SUDDENLY, a clatter and hissing snapped him awake! His shotgun had fallen from his sweaty grasp! While this commotion continued for a few minutes, the heat of the afternoon soon caused it to slow down. Soon the only sound was the occasional buzz of a fly, the occasional slither or hiss of a restless snake.

But finally, the imperceptible movement of the sun, lower and lower towards the horizon, did make a difference. It became cooler and more tolerable, but this dimming of the sun's rays caused a stir throughout the depression. The snakes were becoming more active, they were moving in anticipation of feeding— more at ease in the cooler evening temperatures!

The hunter stared in horror as the snakes raised their heads, hissing at each other. His skin crawled whenever some of the nearby snakes seemed to notice the stump, when their actions seemed to indicate an interest in his position. His escape at night now seemed in doubt.

Darkness finally came. He had stood on that stump as long as he possibly could. He was dehydrated. He was exhausted. The snakes were still twined all around the stump and escape had become impossible. There was no moon. The stars seemed distant and unfriendly. If he stared at one too long, it seemed to move— almost as if it wanted to pull him off that stump!

And that stump. His feet were now made sore by every lump and irregularity on it. The pain did not stop at his feet. It traveled up his legs making every muscle in his body ache.

AAAUUUGGGHHH!

A shout, a scream broke the silence of the night! The noise started him awake—almost startled him off the log. (*If the above is handled properly, when you scream, everyone at the campfire will think that he has fallen off the log, hence the scream!*) Bright lights shined in his face, making it impossible to see in the surrounding darkness!

With a startle he realized that his wait was over—a whole group of rescuers had found him, had shouted to him and turned their lights upon him. Calling encouragement to him, they carefully started shooting the snakes that were crawling near their position or along the pathway they had chosen to reach the stump. He was saved—saved because he had left a message where he could be found!

Story Outline

I. A hunter decided to leave for a walk in the woods of North Carolina looking for pheasant. He went alone, but he left a message telling his family where he would be going and when he would be returning.

II. The hunter became entranced with the beauty of the walk, paying no attention to where he was going. Suddenly a movement caught his eye—it was a snake, in fact he had wandered into a depression full of snakes!

III. He jumped upon a nearby stump, watching in horror as the snakes crawled, hissing around him.

IV. The day slowly passed, the hot sun, the aching of his legs, the drone of an occasional fly—suddenly a clatter and hissing snapped him awake. His shotgun had fallen from his sweaty grasp.

V. The snakes quieted down until the setting sun allowed the valley to cool. This seemed to cause the snakes to become more active. Escape seemed impossible.

VI. Darkness came. He was exhausted. The ache in his body traveled up his legs into every muscle in his body.

VII. AAAUUUGGGHHH! A loud scream broke the silence of the night. The noise startled him awake. He realized that the lights and noise were the rescuers, that his wait was over.

VIII. He was saved—saved because he had left a message where he could be found!

7

THE CURSE OF THE AUSTRALIAN GOLD

by Doc Forgey

It is hard to discount or ignore tales told by well-established important men in their community who insist that they have been cursed; that ghosts have contacted them. These men cannot be dismissed lightly. Such a tale was told by George Woodfall. He was a wealthy man from Sydney, Australia. This is a strange, supposedly true, story of a curse and ghosts that haunted him in the middle of the last century in this story adapted by Doc Forgey.

George Woodfall was originally from England. He was from a well-respected family, but he lost all of his money in business dealings causing him to immigrate to Australia to seek his fortune. And what better way to seek one's fortune in the outback than prospecting for gold?

He found two partners, Harper and Freeth, and together they searched the back country of Australia for gold. Woodfall was hoping to find enough that he could rebuild his fortune. Harper and Freeth were typical prospectors—two rough characters looking for an easy strike so that they could live it up awhile in town before heading out again to look for more gold.

They were lucky, little by little they found gold. The nuggets and specks kept adding up until they were happy with their find—at least Harper and Freeth were. They were slowly working their way back to Sidney, Australia, to spend their fortunes when they noticed a remarkable waterfall leaping out of the side of a cliff. Such a remarkable sight was made even more appealing for the mountain slope contained considerable quartz, which is frequently a gold bearing rock. Even from the ground they could see a cave entrance near the waterfall. Certainly they should look into such a find!

They crawled up the rubble slope to the cave entrance. Once there they found that the cave entrance was a vertical shaft straight down. Chopping up some sturdy small trees, they fashioned pegs which they could drive in cracks in the rock, thus making a ladder that they could climb down. In this manner they were able to make it to the bottom of this cave. It was very impressive, with a vast cathedral like ceiling which reverberated to the thunderous roar of the nearby waterfall. Large stalactites and stalagmites[1] glittered in their torch light. Beautiful quartz crystals in the walls reflected their light. Excited by the possibility of a rich find, they set to work, digging into the quartz veins in the walls, heedless of the extreme beauty that surrounded them.

But beauty was all that they would find, for the quartz had very little evidence of gold in it. At one point they smashed a large quartz formation, finding a small den of a cave behind it. Exhausted by their work, they decided to rest in the small den before climbing out and proceeding on their way to Sidney. They were able to gather firewood from the shattered trees that had fallen down the shaft. In the warmer confines of the den, they lit their fire and settled down for the night.

Their talk that night, as usual, was of their gold, calculating its worth and describing the meals they would eat and the fun

---

1 Stalactites are the rock formations that hang down from the ceilings, while stalagmites grow from the ground up.

they would have when they reached Sidney. But Woodfall fell into a silent brooding since he was an impatient man. Each had a respectable amount of gold, but these men he was with had little ambition. The gold they had would soon be squandered. If he could only have the entire amount, then he would be wealthy enough to really make a come-back!

There would be no chance of simply robbing his two companions and running to Sidney or anywhere else with the gold. They would follow him to the ends of the earth. As he pondered the situation, he eventually came to a bone chilling plan. He would murder his companions. But they were both strong men, both clever desert travelers. He would have to be swift and sure of himself.

The fire was dying down—he would need light, but just enough light to accomplish his task. Not so much light that they might notice his movements. How would he kill both of these men almost at once? Would they never stop talking, laughing, carrying on? He took some of the breakfast fire wood and added a little to the fire. Neither man seemed to pay attention to him. And soon, fortunately, they seemed to fall asleep. He waited until he could hear the even, deep breathing one expects in sleeping men.

His plans well laid, he waited until the fire died—he could barely see Freeth, his closest victim. He would have to dispatch him and instantly roll to Harper's position and hit him anywhere he could. Sweat was standing on his brow, even in the cool damp cave. His muscles tense, he knew the time was right—it was now or never.

Quick as a flash, he struck Freeth a death blow right to the heart! There was scarcely a gurgle, simply a convulsion as the man received this lethal blow. Then he flung himself towards

Harper. Woodfall had failed to count on the almost sixth sense that a woodsman develops to danger—that sixth sense had caused Harper to spring awake. Harper had turned to grab for his pistol as Woodfall lunged at him. Woodfall tackled him—both the knife and gun clattered away onto the darkness of the cave floor. Woodfall had the advantage as he grabbed Harper around the throat and squeezed like a mad man. Harper had been unable to get a breath of air and thus soon thrashed, tangled in his bed roll as he convulsed from the lack of oxygen. Woodfall let the unconscious man loose, but searched for his knife. Locating it by its glitter in the dim light, he instantly turned back towards the strangled Harper. Harper was sitting, unable to speak as he was still gasping for breath, but his pitiful face could be seen, his face flushed, his eyes protruding. He looked up at Woodfall desperately, putting his hands together, praying for mercy. But Woodfall had gone too far to stop now. He plunged the knife straight into Harper's chest.

AAAUUUGGGHHH!

Harper died with a terrible scream that echoed and reverberated through the great room of the nearby large cave.

Even though it was the middle of the night, Woodfall decided to leave that place at once. He combined the gold which they had all mined into his pack. The twisted bodies of his companions were too much for his conscience, and he decided to bury them. Perhaps he could hide any evidence of his crime forever in the bottom of the small grotto.

But digging in that cave bottom was harder work than he thought. The floor was clay, packed hard as concrete, with many small rocks. He chiseled away at it, but tiring he decided just to lay them in the shallow grave he had constructed and lay what debris he had picked from the floor over them. There would be little chance anyone would find this remote location, and if they did, there was nothing that could connect him with their deaths anyway.

Thus he left them, partially covered with loose rubble. He attached a rope to his now heavy saddle bags, then carefully climbed up the treacherous wooden stakes they had placed in the entrance shaft. He left this horror behind him for Sidney, where his fortune awaited him. The date was September 20th—a day that would soon mean a lot to George Woodfall.

Once there he established himself as a wealthy man from England, who was interested in investing his money in various Australian enterprises. Woodfall was obviously a man who took chances. When the opportunity arose, he invested nearly everything in a new mining property called the Benambra Mine, soon to become one of the wealthiest mines in Australia. The shares skyrocketed and he found himself a very rich man.

He purchased an estate in an exclusive area of Sidney called Pott's Point. There he lived in a grand style. He entertained lavishly and soon had many friends in the highest levels of society. But soon September came around. After one party he sat alone by an open window in his sitting room, staring across the dark waters of Port Jackson to the harbor lights at the Heads. More and more of his conscience ate at him—he would have given back all of his wealth, if only the terrible deed which he had done could be reversed. In this frame of mind, he had a strong inclination to go to the police and confess his crime. Soon this mood passed. He sank back into his chair thinking that at least dead men could tell no tales, and those men were hardly fit to have owned that wealth which they would have merely lost within a month.

Suddenly, he heard a voice in the room say, "It is time. Let us begin."

Sure that he had overheard burglars, he slipped to his desk and obtained a revolver. He searched the house, but was unable to find any evidence of intruders. He returned the revolver to his desk. Deciding to go to bed, he put out the lights in the room and started for the door. He had hardly taken a step, when he said that he heard a heavy thump, like a body falling at his feet. As he staggered back in alarm, he began to hear sounds—the sound of a waterfall reverberating in the room, then worst of all came an ear piercing scream, just like the last terrible cry made by Harper when Woodfall plunged the knife into his chest. There were other terrible, unknown noises which shook and rebounded through the room.

He collapsed into a corner, covering his ears against the terrible bedlam, but he was unable to drown this living nightmare out. It was as if he was back in the cave, reliving that night of terror—the night he sent two of his companions to the next world.

He expected his servants to hear this racket and come flying down from their quarters. But no one came and he soon guessed that only he could hear this nightmare of sounds—the devil's concert as he later called it.

At the height of this noise it suddenly ceased. Then, next to him a voice spoke, plain as day. It was the voice of the slain Harper.

"You are growing forgetful, George. In a week's time it will be September the twentieth. We are here to remind you."

George Woodfall remembered the voice—without doubt it was Harper's, whose nightmarish scream had haunted him so long. But he also felt, rather than heard, another presence. That of Freeth whom he had killed so suddenly.

"Your time has not come yet, George, but before it does we will teach you to remember. We will expect you in the cave on the twentieth. Don't forget to come. That is the only way you will escape us."

"Yes, I will come," Woodfall answered, and then he fell into a dream.

Was it a visit from beyond, or merely the tortured mind of a man who had committed cold blooded murder?

Nevertheless, Woodfall returned to the cave, fearful of disobeying the dreaded specter who had contacted him beyond the grave. The trip back had to be made alone and in secret. Once there he had to again thrust in the wooden pegs to support his weight as he climbed down into that chamber of horrors. Woodfall later said of his experience that there he spent "a night of such agonizing horror that I wondered afterwards how I came to retain either life or reason."

What actually took place in the cave that night? We can only guess, but it would be doubtful that Woodfall could have touched the decaying bodies of his victims, covered with the thin layer of rocks.

Each year after this he repeated his ghastly journey, spending a whole night in this hellish pit—listening to the roar of the waterfall. Each year the bodies rotted more and more, becoming more skeletal, more decayed. It was only by going back there that he felt he could have peace between times. But each year his dread of September twentieth mounted.

During the fourth year he decided that he would not go. But there was to be no escape, for again Harper and Freeth visited him at Pott's Point, turning his home into a raging hell. From that time on, he never tried, never hoped to avoid the yearly pilgrimage to this cave of death.

This grim yearly ritual had one major effect upon George Woodfall. It changed his whole attitude towards life. No more did he hold frivolous parties. He tried to make up for his deed by giving to charity. He went to church regularly. He became one of Sidney's most respected citizens. His importance to the community is the reason that we are so aware of what eventually happened to him.

No one could possibly have guessed that he was a murderer. He had kept his gruesome secret well. Even his yearly trips had been carefully planned so that no one followed him, or even missed him. But the urge to confess his deed was constantly beneath the surface. Perhaps Harper and Freeth would leave him in peace if he confessed to the authorities? Anything would be better than the visit to the dreaded cave.

Finally, after twenty wretched years, and after nineteen terrifying visits to the cave of horror, Woodfall decided that he would make a complete confession. He felt compelled to make one more pilgrimage. But before he left, he sat down and wrote out his confession, noting the details of the murders, his many trips to the cave in penance, but particularly the visits of the ghosts of Harper and Freeth to his home at Pott's Point. He then left his home, never to return. His disappearance was a sensation in Sidney. All of his property and business dealings were found to be in perfect order. A statue was erected to the memory of this great civic leader. But, his disappearance was also a mystery that would not be solved for five years.

The mystery was solved by William Rowley, the architect of many canals in New South Wales, and the Reverend Charles Power, of St. Chrysostom Church, Redfern, Sydney. They went on an expedition into the wilds of the Blue Mountains, gathering specimens for Rev. Power's large collection of butterflies. Both of them had known George Woodfall personally.

It was the twentieth of September when they came upon the spectacular waterfall which had first attracted Woodfall, Freeth, and Harper nearly 25 years before. They camped near the base of the waterfall, delighted with the beauty of the area. Just after supper, while relaxing around the campfire, a thunderstorm rolled around them. A deep red glare shone through the clouds which seemed to turn the pouring torrent of water to a crimson, blood color. This caused them to stare closely at the waterfall and in so doing they noticed the figure of a man—rather the image of a man along the edge of the waterfall. The image seemed to be beckoning them up the slope.

Although it was dark and treacherous, they scrambled up the hill. It took them an hour and a half to reach the place where they saw the man. They were following a dim trail along a steep precipice, with the mountain towering above them steeply in the night. In another hour they had reached the summit where the waterfall leaped off into the valley below. There they noted an ironbark tree which had been blazed with an arrow pointing directly downwards.

In the nearby brush they found the entrance of the cave shaft. They held their lantern over the black pit and noted the wooden pegs which had been driven in the shaft wall. The stakes seemed secure, so the two men daringly descended. After a struggle with the treacherous entrance shaft, they found themselves at the bottom of the main cave, standing in awe at its size, listening to the roar of the cascading falls nearby. They examined the magnificent chunks of broken quartz, the beautiful cave formations, and the large boulders that littered the cavern floor.

Finally Rowley found the entrance of the smaller cave and entered it! His cry of horror brought Reverend Power hurrying in after him. As Power joined him, Rowley said, "Come, let's go back. This is no place for us!"

"For heaven's sake, what is it?" Power demanded.

Rowley then turned the full effect of his lantern upon the scene in the grotto. There in front of them was the shallow open grave, the tools used to dig it still scattered about, but sitting on the edge of the grave was a skeleton, bush clothes rotted to tatters, sitting as if he was peering, grinning down into the grave.

Two more bodies lay in the grave, one on top of the other. The one on top was similarly an almost complete decomposed skeleton. The one underneath was not as decayed as the other two!

Rowley reached down with a sapling and brushed aside the top corpse to view the one beneath. He was in the last stages of decay, but the dried flesh on the face made him seem vaguely familiar. There was something obviously strange about the positioning of the bodies. Why was one less decomposed than the others on the bottom? The other two had obviously been dead a much longer time. How was it possible for the man who had died last to be found underneath a man who had died many years before?

They noted some camping gear and searched through it. In an old coat, fallen apart from age and the dampness of the cave, they found a flat metal box containing the inscription: "George Woodfall, Pott's Point, Sidney." Within that box they had the answer of the mystery which they were staring at, or at least a part of the mystery. Inside was the confession of George Woodfall, how he had killed Harper and Freeth for their gold, and how they had made him return to this place every year.

In his confession he wrote that he was making this, his twentieth trip, his last trip. He planned to return to the authorities and turn his confession over to them. He would never again return to this horrid cave.

But he did not return from his twentieth trip. He did not leave the power of Harper and Freeth ever again. How was he killed?

He had originally laid the bodies of his two victims in the grave which he had dug. And there they had laid during the twenty years of his visits, slowly decomposing. Because of his fear and loathing of this horrid place, it is hard to imagine him in anyway disturbing or touching their bodies.

But he said that this would be his last visit to this place—from this point on he would attempt to free himself from the power of the dead. And to help him do it he would give himself up to the authorities, to be locked in prison so that he could NOT return, even if he wanted to try. Perhaps the ghosts of Freeth and Harper which had such great power over him prevented his ever leaving again. Perhaps he arrived to find them sitting on the edge of the grave awaiting his return? Or perhaps he went hopelessly insane during this, his last visit to the cave.

The Reverend Charles Power felt that there was something very devilish about the whole thing—that the place smelt like the very pit of hell.

The two men buried the three bodies, the Reverend Power saying a prayer over them. A cairn was constructed outside the entrance of the grotto marking their grave site—a cairn made of beautiful gold-bearing crystalline quartz from the cavern floor.

Story Outline

I. George Woodfall murders two companions in a cave located near a waterfall, high on a cliff, to steal their gold. Freeth he kills instantly, Harper struggles but is finally half strangled and then stabbed to death.

II. Woodfall invests his money well and becomes a very wealthy and respected man in Sidney, Australia. But he is haunted on the anniversary of the murder—voices in his house and the sound of the waterfall convince him to return to the scene of his crime.

III. He returns yearly, spending the night in the cave with the bodies of his victims, during the next 19 years.

IV. Finally, he decides he will return only one last time and afterwards make a confession to the police. He never returns from this secret trip to the cave.

V. Five years later two men stumble across the waterfall. They notice the appearance image of a man who seems to beckon them up the hill, where they find the cave.

VI. Inside they find the bodies of three men. Two have been dead a long time. Two men are in the shallow grave dug by Woodfall—and he is one of them! One of the older corpses is located on top of him; the other is sitting on the side of the grave. They find Woodfall's confession, thus learning the whole incredible story, which was recorded in the Sidney newspapers.

8

THE LOST HUNTER

Doc Forgey

The Adirondacks has many beautiful places to camp. It is an old, and in many places a wild area. There have been many stories that have come from the Adirondack Mountains. This particular story, told in the Pennsylvania region, is a story of a lost hunter.

One weekend a group of guys went hunting, back into the remote hills of the Adirondacks. In that country there are plenty of deer and they all hoped one of them would be lucky enough to get one for their families. It was a very cold day, one threatening to snow. They had permission to use a cabin from its owner, so they felt they would be safe in case of a storm.

At about the time that they arrived at the cabin, a very light snow had, indeed, already begun to fall. The one essential thing was to be able to keep warm in that cabin. They opened the door and found that everything was intact, no damage had been done. The cabin had a nice Franklin stove to one side of the room which looked sturdy and which should maintain a good, warm glow throughout the night.

There was one problem which they now discovered. There was no firewood where the wood pile should have been located. The previous occupant of the building had failed to cut firewood and replace what he had burned. There was not a stick to be found. Obviously they were going to have to get out in the few remaining moments of day light and gather some wood real fast. Darkness was coming as well as the possibility of an approaching storm. With snow clouds formed overhead, darkness would indeed come early.

They scattered out around the cabin, each man trying to find some wood. If a cabin has been built for any length of time, generally it means that all of the readily available wood suitable for burning in that area has been used. All of the easily gathered wood has been picked up or pulled off the trees already. One has to then go further and further away to get a firewood supply. And that was just the case for these men. There was no wood that they could use right near the cabin and they had to spread out further and further to find the wood that they so desperately needed.

There was one man, John Butler, who did wander and wander. He strayed down into a little valley ravine where he hoped to find downed squaw wood to burn. The tricky part about wandering in an area which is cut up into ravines, ridges, and valleys is that you may feel you know where you are, but by climbing over a ridge into a wrong ravine you can easily be led into a maze of wrong ridges and your directions can easily become very twisted and confusing. You can end up not heading in the direction that you thought you were going. This, indeed, proved to be the fate of John Butler. For on this cold, stormy evening he disappeared into the night.

The snow was cascading down worse and worse. The darkness settled in, which combined with the swirling snow, made visibility virtually zero. His friends returned back to the cabin fairly soon for they realized how dangerous it was to be out at night in a snow storm, especially in territory that they really weren't familiar with. But John Butler had been caught, extending himself out too far, and was trapped in a swirling snow storm in the Adirondacks in Pennsylvania.

His friends were really quite concerned about him. They waited impatiently for him to appear. When he didn't return after about 2 hours, they felt they would have to get out there and look for him. It would take too long to get into town, the road may not be passable, and his tracks would certainly disappear if they waited much longer. The temperature was dropping and John could be getting into trouble, maybe he was even injured!

They took the lanterns that they had brought and placed kerosene lights in the cabin's two windows. They tried to follow what they thought might be his trail, each person trying to determine who had made the marks that they were following, trying to determine if they were following the trail of the lost hunter.

It became quite apparent after struggling in a fiercer and fiercer blizzard that it would be absolutely impossible to find him that night. The trails were becoming rapidly obscured. The weather was so bad, that the best they could do was to return to the cabin and try to survive the storm themselves. They had only found a few scraps of wood, so they didn't have a very pleasant night of it. But huddled there together, listening to the gale winds tearing at the cabin and the trees groaning outside, they feared for their friend's life.

When morning came, the snow continued. Two of the men took their 4-wheel drive vehicle and drove into town to get the sheriff who alerted the local Search and Rescue team. The rescue team soon congregated at the cabin site deep in the woods. They had brought their tracking dogs, food, clothing, and heaters to establish a base camp for the search operation.

They struck out looking for him. The dogs proved useless sin the confusion of tracks and the blowing snow drifts. The search drug on for days. Ridges were combed, valleys and ravines were checked. They gave up all hope of finding him alive. Indeed, when a person is lost in a driving snow storm, frequently their body will be covered so well that it might not be found until after the Spring thaw.

But the story of John Butler does not end there. While this area is very remote, it is still active with camping and hiking. A scout camp was located only thirty miles away and the Appalachian Trail passes through a neighboring section of land. The next fall a group of scouts reported an unusual occurrence.

Members of Troop 91 from Colfield had left the scout camp 3 days before on a fifty mile hike. The evening of their third day, three members of the troop were sleeping somewhat apart from the others, but near the cooking fire embers left over from supper. Harold Johnson, a Patrol Leader, was asleep in the area that had been the wood pile. Had been, I said, because all of the fire wood had been consumed cooking supper and for general warmth and campfire fun afterward. After hiking all day one tends to be tired, very tired. Yet, in the middle of the night John sensed something wrong and he just popped awake . . .

And he wished that he hadn't!

Standing next to him he saw a man, and the man was holding an axe! In fact, it appeared to be his troop's axe. John broke out in a cold sweat, his eyes barely open, peeking at what the man was going to do next.

Suddenly the man moved, *WHAM!* QUICK AS A FLASH THE AXE SLAMMED INTO THE TREE NEAR HIS HEAD!

John opened his eyes wide in terror . . . but the man was gone!

He bolted up out of his sleeping bag, paying no attention to the night's chill. He virtually landed on his two friends nearby, shaking them awake, telling them what he had seen. They fumbled for their flashlights and shined them around looking for any trace of the man John had just seen.

They did not see the man, but what they did see was a stack of firewood, left where they had laid their axe that night! Needless to say, the entire troop was awake within about 3 minutes with the guys looking for clues of this missing man. He vanished without a trace, no foot prints, nothing. Nothing but the stack of firewood and their axe stuck in the tree.

As the years went on, the stories of encounters with the Lost Hunter kept spreading out. The sightings started happening further and further away from the lonely cabin. People in nearby states started telling a story of a mysterious man visiting their campsite, of their finding firewood where none had been the night before.

It seemed that the ghost of this lost hunter was prowling around, just waiting, looking to find somebody who was impolite enough not to chop firewood to leave for people who might come afterwards, or perhaps lazy enough not to chop enough to have some there for emergencies—or for people who had burned all of theirs up and did not have any left in case the weather became bad or some problem developed. It became real important to everyone in that area to remember one of the basic courtesies and rules of camping—to plan ahead, to make sure that there was firewood available and to make sure that the campsite was left in better shape than when they first found it.

If you are out camping and the weather is bad, particularly as a snow storm swirls in, be sure that you have plenty of firewood, both for yourself or for others that might follow you. Campers who do not obtain enough firewood are apt to have a visit in the middle of the night from the Lost Hunter!

Story Outline

I. A group of hunters travel deep into the Adirondack Mountains to a cabin they have borrowed for a weekend of deer hunting.

II. When they get there a snow storm begins, there is no firewood for the cabin and they all struggle to find some as night approaches.

III. John Butler, however, becomes lost in the deepening night and swirling snowstorm. The Search and Rescue Team is activated the next day, but even with their dogs they are unable to find a trace of him.

IV. The next fall a group of scouts from Colfield Troop 91 have a visit from a mysterious man. He replaces their consumed firewood during the night, after scaring a patrol leader who saw him in the night.

V. Mysterious sightings are soon made in states further and further away, always by people who have used their firewood. A lesson is to be learned by this story—never consume all of your firewood or leave your campsite without replacing what you have used, especially if you do not want a visit from "the Lost Hunter."

9

THE BOG

by Doc Forgey

This original story went through a metamorphosis from its first telling, which had the four friends canoeing into a hidden valley that was reached through a cave entrance. Originally called "The Hidden Valley," it did not explain how such a neat valley could remain unfound on the maps. So I invented the bog.

Four members of Bensenville Troop 752 had been friends all their lives. Scouting had allowed them to cement that friendship even further on many canoeing and camping trips near their home town and on several high-adventure trips in Minnesota and New Mexico. But what lay ahead of them was far more sinister than any adventure they could have dreamed of . . . and it was going to happen practically in their own backyard.

Just outside of Bensenville there was a fairly large swamp, known locally simply as "The Bog." It was large enough to be deep and dense, but not large enough to attract attention of developers, park service personnel, or even conservationists. The bog had always been there. No roads went near it, no communities were positioned nearby—the bog sat by itself, tucked in a little-used portion of the state where time had passed it by.

The stagnant water in the bog seemed lifeless. It attracted no fishermen. There was an unusual scarcity of bird life, so no birdwatcher ventured into the hordes of mosquitoes to visit its remote water. Yet the bog seemed so dense that it was hard to imagine that there was not some living thing, even a whole slough of living things, within its borders.

Do not let me give the impression that this swamp was actually lifeless. Everyone who had ventured into the waters near its edge could vouch for the fact that indeed there was life in the swamp. The mosquitoes had neighbors—biting gnats, blackflies, swarms of bees, and although the waters seemed to produce few fish, leeches abounded.

Oh, the waters of the bog had been tested to determine if there were pollutants, radioactivity, or unusual chemicals dissolved in them. The tests had always shown nothing of interest. And so the bog continued to be abandoned.

It was abandoned for another reason beyond lack of interest: There just seemed to be something mysterious about its uncharted waters, perhaps something that might even be considered sinister. People tended to shy away from encountering the place—after all there was never a really good reason to go there anyway. Even the Indians who used to roam that area had apparently avoided the bog's confines.

But for Ralph, Bobby, David, and Chris, the bog held a special attraction. At first they paid little attention to it. They were having plenty of fun with Troop 752 just starting their camping adventures. Then those high-adventure trips consumed their interest. But with these trips behind them, their thoughts turned to "The Bog." They knew how to handle the bugs they thought. They certainly knew how to camp and canoe. The swampy ground might make pitching a tent difficult—and perhaps there would be snakes and other creatures slithering along the ground—so they decided to pack along army surplus jungle hammocks with netting, besides their two tents.

As Ralph and Bobby were slightly older than the other two, they would each take the stern of a canoe, with David and Chris manning the bow. Water filtration pumps, fire starter, hand ax and saw, as well as sleeping bags and other gear were divided equally between the two canoes—in case something happened to one of them. Each boy carried a compass. There was a topographical map of the area, but it was featureless in the vicinity of the bog, except for map symbols representing a swamp.

The boys decided that they would leave the week school was out for summer vacation. All was ready when the time came, and early one morning the four excited friends shoved off from the local highway bridge that spanned a watery section of the bog.

The wilderness opened up on all sides of them, with the air feeling heavy and smelling from the lush vegetation. They had expected mosquitoes, so they were ready with the bug dope to keep them off. What they did not expect was the maze of islands, which they were finding difficult to navigate around. Frequently the channels were choked with weeds or simply played out, ending on a marshy shore.

Bubbles of marsh gas occasionally caused a sudden splash in the water near them, which seemed to accent the eerie feeling that they were all experiencing. The boys stopped on a marshy piece of land for lunch the first day, carefully purifying their water, which they acquired by shoving down on mats of floating seaweed and thus allowing water to percolate into the depression that formed. The canoes were sluggish in their forward motion because of the drag of seaweed, which also increased difficulty in paddling.

The weather favored them the first night so that by sunset they had selected a suitable campsite, unloaded the canoes, pitched the tents, and collected and sawed a store of firewood. It was easier to prepare drinking water this time, as there was a deeper channel by the island that they had chosen for the night. They were all prepared for bad weather. The boys cooked a good supper and, as the mosquitoes were not all that bad, they sat around the camp-fire—happy to be in the great outdoors and on an adventure in an uncharted wilderness at that!

The strangest thing about that night was the almost total lack of wildlife. It was as if they were canoeing back into time, into some primitive swamp of the past. The deep stillness made many of the sounds around them seem amplified, and the boys' feeling a little keyed up also added to the startle each of them felt when they heard PLOP in the water right next to their camp. No further swishing sounds were heard, so the boys decided it was a lump of earth from the bank caving into the water.

In the night as they lay in their tents, once again they heard the swish of water.

It was barely five o'clock when daylight glowed along the eastern horizon of the bog. The two tents were capped and wreathed with smoky trails of fast-melting mist. In the open spaces the ground was drenched with dew. Ralph lit the fire so that an hour later, when the others got up, hot water would be ready and a bed of coals formed to make cooking breakfast less of a chore. He set forth on an exploration of his island but had gone barely ten yards when alongside the bank a giant WHOOSH occurred. Ralph caught his breath at the sound, but then he soon saw what was happening. A large bubble of methane gas had escaped from the swampy floor of the bog, and it suddenly surfaced, bringing large chunks of rotten vegetation with it. A whole mat of this material floated and bobbed in the wake of the sudden gas escape.

Ralph cut his exploration of the island short and returned to the campsite. He had to wait patiently for about half an hour

before the other boys got up, so he busied himself by fixing breakfast over the hot bed of coals that he had made, even though it was David's turn to be chef that day. After breakfast he told them of his discovery, about the source of the SWOOSH they had heard the night before.

"Well that explains these clumps of floating debris that I've been having to push out of the way of the canoe," Chris remarked.

"Yeah, and some of those clumps are so big that they seem to be pushing right back," David, the other bowman, added.

"I've heard of something like this before," Bobby mentioned. "In one of the large swamps down south, maybe it was the Everglades or the Okeefenokee, bubbles of methane gas bubble up large amounts of debris from the swamp floor. Those mats float around and act as a platform for larger plants to live on. They become floating islands. When roots from the plants became long enough, they anchor the floating islands, which become permanently fixed in one place."

Finished with breakfast, the boys were anxious to shove off before the day became too warm. The reflection of the sun on the water and the stifling thickness of the air made the work of paddling their canoes all the more difficult.

"Ralph, what will we do if these islands we are charting float around and change their positions?" Bobby called over from his canoe. "We could get stuck back in this swamp forever!"

Ralph shouted back, "I've been thinking along those lines myself."

A fairly large stretch of open water promised to be a pleasant interlude from dragging their boats through weeds and trying to pole through the muck at the bottom. As they approached the open water, they noticed that the bottom deepened, deepened beyond the reach of their paddles.

But it was not to be an easy crossing. As the boys paddled, they suddenly realized that they were not making much progress toward the opposite shore. It seemed as if they were glued to the water's surface. The light breeze was not hurting or helping them. It caused a small chop of waves, which was insignificant. It just seemed as if they struggled without progress. The breeze calmed down the insect problem, and it gave the boys a chance to yank off their shirts and the insect head nets. Ralph soon realized that they were all sweating hard with everyone paddling furiously, almost savagely along, but they were getting nowhere. "Rats," he shouted. "Hey, let's all cool it for a while. We're not going anywhere. Let's stop for a while and see what happens."

He got no argument from the others. They stopped and rested their paddles across the canoe gunnels, stretched their aching muscles, and wiped the sweat off their faces. They grinned at each other at first, feeling good about the workout they'd just had. Feeling weary, yet so strangely excited . . . It was in the middle of that lake in the bewildering chatter and confusion of explanations, that, very silently, the ghost of something horrible slipped in and stood among them. It made all their explanations seem childish and untrue. They exchanged quick, anxious glances—glances that were questioning and expressive of the dismay that they were beginning to acknowledge. There was a sense of wonder, of poignant distress, of trepidation. Alarm stood waiting at their elbows. This ghost was a realization that something they did not understand was having its way with them.

They now rested quietly after their initial joyful excitement, feeling the little quivers that the light, choppy waves made against their canoes. But as they bobbed, their quietness was a manifestation of the fear that each of them was beginning to know. And none of them seemed to want to hear the others acknowledge this same fear. But something really did seem to have them in its grasp! It soon was becoming evident that their canoes were drifting toward the north side of the lake, almost at right angles to their original line of travel.

"Hey, if this lake wants us to go to that northern shore—well, let's just help it out a little. Let's start paddling!" With that almost cheerful statement from Ralph, everyone bent to the task of paddling out of this lake, which they were beginning to fear. Even then it seemed as if their progress was just not what it should be, that the lake held them with some invisible glue.

Even with this slow progress, the marshy shore of the north end soon came close enough to view easily from the canoes.

"Check it out," Chris remarked.

The shore seemed to be penetrated at regular intervals by streams that were flowing away from the lake. The land between these streams was marshy, so swampy that no obvious stopping place was evident.

"Our next campsite will be knee-deep in water if something better doesn't appear," Chris continued.

Small, swampy islands located along the north shore were similarly unsuitable for camping.

"We've got to find someplace not only dry enough, but where we can find firewood, or we'll be stuck with just our gas stove. I'd rather be able to build a fire around this spooky place," commented Bob.

There was ready agreement on that, so that even though the boys were capable of pitching hammocks above the swampy ground and cooking with their Peak 1 stoves, they anxiously sought a piece of real estate where they could construct a more secure campsite.

After several hours of probing the streams, searching among the islands, and drifting along the shore, the boys found what appeared to be an almost ideal site.

"Jeez, this place looks like it was constructed for a campsite. This may not turn out so bad after all," one of them blurted out enthusiastically as they unloaded the canoes and started squaring away their gear.

There was a restless feeling in camp that evening, and none of the boys wanted to leave the protection of the campfire. It was as if something was alive out there, something moving—slowly, almost unperceived—but yet most assuredly moving about them. The very land seemed alive. The boys felt as if there were other people out there with them.

That night they were sure of it.

The swirling and sucking sound of the water washing along the shore, as well as the feeling of dread that they all seemed to have, caused the boys to gather as much firewood as possible and maintain their fire late into the night. The eerie night noises prompted them to peer out now and again into the black void of the night. Suddenly Chris saw something! It was a campfire flickering on an island about a mile away. Someone must be there! They all looked and watched as the small campfire burned down too low for them to see any more. After it disappeared, they all watched carefully for some sign of life, but they neither saw nor heard anything the rest of the night.

The mystery of that night deepened the next day when they decided to leave their camp set up but canoe over to the island where they thought they had seen the fire. There was a long, oval-shaped island, with large bushes in the center and several clearings, but no evidence of a fire. They spent the day searching other likely spots, but they could not find any evidence of the people whose fire they saw the night before.

The next night they again kept vigil by the fire. Sure enough, at about the witching hour of midnight, they again saw the fire flicker into life. As they watched, they thought they could see people moving around the fire. It was just too far away to tell for sure. Although there was surely more of the bog to explore, this seemed to be the crux of the mystery—to find out if a lost race of people were living back there.

The next day they again canoed over to the island where they had seen the campfire. They still could see no evidence of the campsite or indication of where the fire might have been built. Chris designed a plan to solve the mystery. He decided that it would be a good idea for them to move to the island and camp out there instead of staying where they were. But their present spot was so ideal that the others would not agree. They would have to cut firewood and canoe it over to the new site, the island seemed too damp, the clearings were small, and the bushes probably had too many mosquitoes. They all had reasons why they would not camp there, all that is except Chris. When he could not get the others to agree to spend the night there, Chris announced he would do it by himself.

"You've got to be crazy, Chris," Bobby, his canoeing partner, told him. But Chris was determined to solve the mystery.

"And besides you guys, the camp is only about a mile away. We can shout back and forth if we need to. I'll keep my fire burning all night if I'm scared, and one of you do the same. It won't be that bad."

But the others were buying none of it. They did not want anything to do with the swampy, mysterious island. They spent the rest of the day breaking out Chris's camping gear from the rest of theirs and gathering the firewood, food, and purified water that he would need. By nightfall they had him in his camp, and they were back at theirs. As darkness fell, the fires burned brightly in both camps.

Occasionally the boys shouted across the water to each other, Chris's voice sounding so alone and far away. At just about midnight, Bobby was poking the fire with a stick, watching the sparks leap skyward. He looked up just in time to see Chris's campfire suddenly disappear! He thought, "Boy, is he a brave one. I'd probably keep my fire going all night."

Thinking to reassure Chris a little, he called over, "Hey, Chris! Did the boogeyman get you?"

But there was no reply. Bobby shouted several more times, with the other guys also joining in. But they were to receive no answer from Chris's camp that night.

At first light the next day, the three anxious boys hopped into the canoe and paddled over to Chris's campsite. His canoe was floating free, not nestled up against the shoreline where Chris's camp should have been. When I say "should have been," I mean precisely that. The boys felt a sense of panic and sickness in the pits of their stomachs when they could find no trace of Chris's camp whatsoever.

"It's just like the fires we have been seeing the previous two nights," David remarked. "There is not a sign anyone has ever been here since the beginning of time."

The boys widened their search, checking nearby islands and the shoreline, but they could find no trace of Chris. Because they had his canoe, they knew that he did not canoe away. Their great adventure had suddenly turned into a horrible nightmare.

Late in the afternoon, after checking all the surrounding areas several times, even desperately calling his name during moments of panic and anger, the boys returned with the two canoes to their campsite.

They sat around their camp in a state of shock and disbelief, discussing what they should do. They felt the overwhelming urge to travel back to town and request help. But they did not want to leave Chris by himself, wherever he was. There was a remote chance that they could still solve the mystery of the island.

Before dark Bobby came to a decision. He announced to the other guys that he was going to spend the night at Chris's island to see if he could solve the mystery. Ralph and David objected, but Bobby would not give in.

"I owe it to Chris to see if I can find out what happened to him."

Bobby packed up his gear, taking his sleeping bag, his clothes, and materials for starting a fire. He took his canoe and paddled over to the island as the others watched. Both camps started a fire just before dark. That night a thin layer of fog caused the fire from Bobby's camp to glow peculiarly in the distance. Neither Ralph nor David were about to try to sleep. They watched Bobby's camp intently as the night wore on. They called back and forth, but the distance was too great to clearly hear what was being said. Then about midnight, the very thing that Ralph and David were dreading happened again. The light from the other camp suddenly went out! They were almost in a panic, but they could do nothing about it. They knew that canoeing in the pitch-black would be hazardous. And they were too scared to consider leaving their camp. They could feel the blackness of the night crawl closer around them. The water gurgled and swished at the shoreline. The chill of the night and the surrounding dampness made the night unbearable.

The first crack of dawn found them madly paddling their canoe over to Bobby's island. But his campsite was not to be found! There was no evidence of fire, and there was no sign of

Bobby's clothing, sleeping bag, or footprints. Nothing showing human habitation was left on the island.

The boys stood on the swampy island in a state of shock. They hardly knew what to do. Ralph wanted to go home, but David knew that he had to find the answer to this mystery and was not about to leave his friends behind. He would not listen to Ralph's pleas that they get out of there as fast as they could paddle. David sighted a gleam in the water that turned out to be Chris and Bobby's canoe floating full of water. Both life jackets and one paddle were missing.

Back at their campsite Ralph and David talked it over. "How can we possibly go back now? We may never find this place exactly again. You know how these islands seem to be floating around. We may never come to this exact point on the lakeshore or find the island that Chris and Bobby were camping on. And how about the mysterious campfires that we saw before they disappeared? If someone is out here, we must make contact with them. We can't tell their parents that we left them behind." And with that David completed their discussion. Except for one more thing. "Ralph, I know of only one way to solve this problem. We have to camp out on the island ourselves."Ralph would hear none of it. He was not about to stay on that island. "Well Ralph," David said. "I'm going to take that canoe and go over there myself, tonight. I'm going to find out for myself what's going on."

Ralph could not believe his ears. He was not about to spend the night on that island. The campsite they had was spooky enough. And now he would have to be there alone. But he was not going to the island!

They spent that day in brooding silence. Ralph was too mad at David to really talk to him much. That night David departed and set up his camp at the island. The night seemed to fall all too quickly for Ralph, and he was glad he had a good fire to hold back the edge of darkness that surrounded his camp. There in the distance was the flicker of David's campfire.

Then, almost precisely at midnight, the very thing that Ralph was dreading the most happened. The small flickering fire on the island disappeared. Ralph's heart was in his throat it seemed. He felt a sense of panic, for he knew that he was in this swamp all alone. But more than that, he felt an incredible lonesomeness. The best friends he had in the world were no longer with him. And there was not a thing he could do about it.

With daybreak Ralph canoed the lonely stretch to the island. Again he found nothing. He looked carefully to see if he was on the right island. Somehow it did not look quite right. He had tramped over the marshy area so much that he had begun to know it—or so he thought. Its oblong shape seemed smaller to him. But there was no other island close enough that he could be mistaken about the location. It had been in sight from the camp-site, and he had followed the same azimuth to reach it—a straight shot from the camp.

Ralph knew he really could do nothing for his friends, but he was also worried about how to get himself out of this mess. It should not be all that hard to do, he thought. But this time he would have to do it alone. Still he could not tear down his camp and leave just yet. He would spend one more night at their camp-site, still hoping that he might be able to make some sense of his friends' disappearance.

That night he watched over the dark lake, with both fear and sadness as competing emotions. As he sat contemplating the events of the last several days, Ralph was suddenly jarred into action by what he saw in the distance. A flicker of light appeared from the island campsite! He yelled out as loud as he could, but each time he listened afterward, he heard only the swish of water in return. Soon the light again disappeared, but Ralph felt a sense of hope.

In the daylight his position did not seem so bleak. And as he gained his courage, he also resolved to do the very thing he knew all along deep down inside of himself he had to do. He would have to move his camp to that dreaded island. He would have to find out for himself what the mystery of that place was. He would not leave his friends behind, no matter what their fate—or no matter what his might become.

He broke camp early that afternoon and returned to the island. The ground in the middle of the island was spongy, but he was able to clear an area for a safe fire. He erected his tent. Standing around here is like standing on a waterbed, he thought to himself, as he squared his campsite away. It was sure a let down from the comfortable camp where he had spent most of the previous week.

The wetness of the place made the camp miserable. Ralph decided to place his bedding and most of his gear in the canoe and tie the canoe to the shore, allowing it to float free. As darkness fell, he made sure he had plenty of firewood on hand, some of which he had brought over from the other campsite. In fact he had about three times as much firewood as he thought he would need, certainly more than the others had brought.

With nightfall the dampness became even more noticeable. Hour followed hour as Ralph stood around the eerie camp. Suddenly he heard a familiar sound: the SWOOSH of water as gas from the swamp's floor bubbled up to the surface. And although this attracted his attention, not too far away near the shore, he saw a flare of light upon the water's surface. He stared at it flickering, then climbed into his canoe for a better view, allowing the canoe to drift a little way from the island's edge. Suddenly there was a massive shift of the island, the entire center where his camp was located folding in on itself, his campfire disappearing in the rush of water and hiss of steam. A wave rocked his canoe as Ralph stared in disbelief. But now he knew the secret of the island.

The campfires they had been seeing were actually will-o'-the-wisp, the phosphorescent light sometimes seen in the air over marshy places. And the island was a floating island, just as they had all known. But what they did not realize was that this floating island was not able to support their weight for a long period of time. The center of the island would suddenly sink under the weight of the campers standing on it, just folding together and dragging the struggling victims underwater. With each collapse the island had grown smaller. And Ralph realized that his companions would be buried forever beneath the muck, quicksand, and water of the lake.

Story Outline

I. Four members of Bensenville Troop 752 have been friends all their lives and are looking forward to further high adventures in the mysterious bog that lay outside of town.

II. Ralph, Bobby, David, and Chris leave the week school is out to explore the bog by canoe.

III. They find the marsh a strange place, with bubbles of marsh grass and mats of floating vegetation. The water and weeds seem to slow their progress.

IV. As they camp the first night, they hear strange plopping and swirling sounds in the water. Ralph later sees a large bubble of marsh gas come to the surface, thus explaining the sounds of the night.

V. They enter a large stretch of open water, but still find the paddling difficult. Drifting, they find they are drawn to the north shore of the lake, where they find a good dry campsite after much searching.

VI. That night they build a large fire to ward off their fears. During the night Chris sees another campfire in the distance.

VII. The boys search for the fire the next day, but they do not find it. The next night they again spot the fire. Chris decides to spend the night on an island where they think the fire may be coming from to investigate the mystery.

VIII. The boys watch Chris's campfire that night, when suddenly it goes out. They shout over to him, but they receive no reply.

IX. The next day at daybreak they canoe to his island, but they can find no trace of his camp. They find his canoe floating nearby. They search everywhere for Chris but cannot find him.

X. Against the other boys' advice, Bobby decides he will also camp out on the island. They watch his campfire that night through a thin layer of fog, until it also suddenly goes out at about midnight.

XI. The next day at daybreak Ralph and David canoe over, but again there is no trace of the campsite on the island.

XII. David realizes that they cannot go back without solving the mystery. He ignores Ralph's pleas to leave and prepares to spend the night on the island.

XIII. Ralph watches intently that night, when almost precisely at midnight David's flickering fire disappears.

XIV. Ralph finds no trace of David or his canoe the next day. He spends the day searching and decides to spend one more night at the camp, hoping to learn something about his friends' disappearances.

XV. That night as he watches over the dark lake, he sees a flicker of light from an island campfire appear again. No one answers his shouts.

XVI. He breaks camp the next day determined to solve the mystery of the island by himself.

XVII. He moves extra firewood to the boggy island and makes his camp. He leaves his canoe floating but tied to the shore.

XVIII. During the night he suddenly sees a fire nearby. He gets into his canoe to view it better and realizes that they have been looking at a methane swamp gas flare, a will-o'-the-wisp.

XIX. As Ralph watches the flare, the island collapses, folding in the middle from the weight of the firewood. He realizes that his friends, standing in the camp in the middle of the floating island, made it collapse, causing them to be sucked into the muck, quicksand, and water below.

10

THE WALKING STICK

by Doc Forgey

Have you ever had one of those days, especially when you are hiking or climbing, when you just do not have the zip and vigor that everyone else has? On one such an occasion, I decided that perhaps I was just contending with an evil spell, for I certainly could not be that much older or in that much worse shape than the rest of my party. That got me started thinking about a possible source of an evil spell for a nephew who just could not leave his uncle's things alone.

Mike had a walking stick that used to be his uncle's. He always wanted to take it camping. Hiking with it now, with the rest of the kids envious of his stick, was something he was enjoying, sort of. Sort of? Well, Mike couldn't really enjoy this moment as much as he wished. You see, the stick didn't belong to him . . . yet. It was still his uncle's, and he had been warned to leave it alone. But there it was in his grandpa's house, down in a closet filled with things—all still owned by his uncle.

But that stick. It was special and stood out from the rest of the items—even his uncle's military uniform, the one with the medals. You see his uncle had always made it clear to Mike to stay away from that stick. He wasn't to touch it, play with it, even take it out of the closet—and here he was taking it on a camping trip with the other boys in the Scout troop, just as if it were his.

He never understood why he wasn't to play with it. His uncle had never told him. In fact he had always scolded Mike for coming near it or for even asking questions about it. His uncle had been in Vietnam for many years, and there were many things that he said that Mike knew he would never understand fully. This stick was obviously part of the stuff he had brought home from that war. Mike felt that there was something sinister about it, something evil. It didn't look like much—just a stiff, light, and straight pole. But the color was black. It came to a sharp point and broadened as it went up to the top, where it formed a smooth, flat head.

The stick would have been just right for his uncle to use as a walking stick, but it was a little tall for Mike. Still, it fit well enough in his hand as they scrambled over the rough ground. Mike was always having to hurry a little to keep up with the bigger guys. The sun was becoming a little hot; the ground was uneven at times, with logs and stones covering the trail here and there; and now insects were becoming bothersome—especially in this heat. It seemed that the insects were bothering him more than the other guys. Maybe he was sweating more. As he looked at the boy ahead of him, he could tell that Jim looked comfortable. His friend was walking along the trail in an almost carefree manner. Jim had not soaked through his shirt, but Mike had. The heat was clouding his vision, hurting his brain, even bothering his hearing.

The trip became even harder as the trail led up the hill to a fire tower. A natural spring had been tapped with a faucet, providing water for the little campground about three hundred feet beneath the hilltop. As they reached the campsite, the other kids wanted to run on ahead to scramble up the tower. Mike was too exhausted to even consider climbing that last three hundred feet of hill. He flopped to his back at the last remaining tent site, breathing heavily in the stifling hot air of that summer afternoon.

The sounds of the kids in his troop faded away, up the hill. The drone of the insects seemed louder and muffled the happy sounds coming from his friends. He swatted at them aimlessly, too tired to open his eyes. The hot sun made the vegetation smell musty and strong. The babble of voices seemed to continue in the background. As he lay exhausted against his pack, Mike hoped he would never have to move again. Clutching the walking stick, which he laid along his side, he became more aware of the strong smells of the forest. Now he was even less aware of the incoherent chatter in the background, coming from the hill above him.

He paid no attention, that is, until suddenly it dawned on him that there was something different about those voices. He could not understand even an occasional word. The voices were making choppy, peculiar sounds. The insects were competing with their swarming and buzzing. Strange that his friends did not seem to notice this horrible weather, these horrible bugs. What were they doing anyway? He no longer heard the occasional sound of his scoutmaster's voice.

Mike lazily opened his eyes. What he saw shocked him wide awake. The trees had changed! The weeds, the bushes, the forest—they all had changed! Just the heat was there . . . and those mosquitoes. And the voices from above him on the hill.

But the voices were different. Mike wasn't sure what he noticed first: the fact that he could see no other camping gear around him, that he was in a thick jungle of vegetation, or that the voices he heard were not those of his friends!

His first impulse was to call out, to yell his head off for help! But there was something scary about those voices. They were excited, shouting to each other, crashing through the thick brush

above him. He could tell that the people making the noises were thrashing the brush as they walked along through it, as if they were in a straight line beating the bushes, trying to flush something, or someone, out!

He thought that the voices were sinister, gruff. He realized that he should take no chances with these people. He must hide. He hated leaving his spot, because he was afraid that he would only get helplessly lost. Yet he feared for his life.

Still clutching the walking stick, Mike slid down the hill under the cover of a layer of large-leafed plants. The dirt from the forest floor stuck to his sweaty legs and clothing, the stick was slick in his sweaty hands. His movement must have attracted attention on the hill above him, for there was a commotion—the people all seemed to be coming, crashing down the hill directly toward him!

The jungle floor was steep, steep like the jungle-covered hills in Vietnam must have been where his uncle had served during the war. Mike was able to slide faster and faster, and he desperately tried to get away from the people streaming down the hill above him. As he looked up he could see them coming closer and closer. He could make out the peculiar helmets, the red star on their helmets, their rifles.

The bushes whipped him as he slid down the hill toward a stream that he could hear below. The willow-like wands of brush were cutting at his face, arms, and legs. It didn't matter. Just as long as he could get away! A bush with bright orange flowers and long spike-like thorns struck him, leaving a large thorn stuck in his right arm.

Suddenly, as he slid toward a large tree—CRACK! The walking stick slammed against the tree and was torn from his grasp! He suddenly plunged off a small gully—SPLASH—into a stream of cold water!

With a shock he looked around. The forest was hardwood, he was not in the jungle anymore. The voices from above him were those of his friends, who were excitedly climbing down the hill after him, looking for him! Mike realized that the walking stick was not in his hands any longer. The weather was pleasant and cool. The bugs were gone.

Mike could never explain to his scoutmaster or his friends what had happened to him. And he could not find the walking stick, no matter how hard he looked.

His mom took him to the doctor when he got home to have a large, strange thorn taken out of his arm. But what was really strange was that his uncle was never seen or heard from again. All traces of him vanished—and Mike wondered if his uncle could have taken his place, deep in some mysterious jungle in Vietnam! He would never know.

Story Outline

I. Mike takes his uncle's walking stick, a souvenir of the Vietnam War, with him on a hike with his Scout troop—even though he has been warned to leave it alone.

II. The troop is hiking in a forest up a hill to a fire tower.

III. While everyone else is enjoying the hike, Mike feels hotter and hotter—and is bothered by the bugs.

IV. When the troop reaches the campsite, Mike is too tired to scramble farther to the tower with the other kids. As he rests, he is surrounded by bugs and the heat.

V. Mike becomes aware that the voices of his friends have changed; the vegetation has changed—he appears to be lost in a jungle.

VI. He tries to get away from the people, probably Viet Cong, who are chasing him. As he crashes downhill toward a stream, he hits a tree and has the stick knocked away from him.

VII. After this crash, he realizes that he is back with his friends in normal woods.

VIII. The stick is lost. His mother takes him to the doctor to have a strange thorn removed from his arm. And his uncle disappears, never to be seen again.

11

DAVE'S PAUGAN

Pronounced "pooh gone"

by Scott E. Power

When I sent Dave Scott and Scott Power into the northern Canadian wilderness to live in a cabin for a year (www.forgey-cabin.com), they had several assignments to keep them occupied – basically to keep them from killing each other. Exploring, building another cabin, and writing campfire stories. This is one of my favorite campfire stories of all times —Doc

I had never believed in Indian legends until I met Dave, a Catholic priest and missionary from a remote trading post in the wilds of northern Manitoba, Canada, a land where Cree Indian legends prevail.

Dave and I met while I was on a canoe trip into the north. He needed transportation from Nueltin Lake back to his post two hundred miles north.

Although I was a safe canoeist, I wondered about my new partner, Dave. But within minutes of our shoving off, he proved to be an accomplished paddler. During conversation he explained that he had lived in the north for five years. He was supposed to leave after one year, but he loved it so much that he insisted on staying. He said that the Indians had taught him a lot, but he still had a lot to learn.

He explained that the Indians had taught him that every human being has a guardian angel called a *paugan*. The paugan is a protector or spiritual guardian. A paugan will only interfere with reality in extreme life-threatening danger. Typically, a paugan is a likeness of an animal. Each person's paugan is different. One person's paugan might be a cougar, for some an eagle or a wolf, but it is always an animal of significance, of great importance. But there is only one way for a person to discover what type of animal his paugan might be. He must fast and dream for a fortnight, for two full weeks of dedicated misery and deprivation. Only then will the Great Spirit show a person through dreams what his paugan is.

Dave said at first he didn't believe in it. But one day, while he was canoeing with Indian friends north into the barrens to hunt caribou, they found themselves in a wide turbulent river. The water was freezing cold. Even though it was late August, the air temperature was below freezing. Dave and his partner managed to get ashore once then realized how dangerous the stretch of river had become, but the other canoe was blown into the main channel and was being swept into the dangerous standing waves. An upset at this point could mean death for the two Indians, but there was a swirl under the canoe and to Dave's disbelief an immense moose rose up out of the water and the canoe was lifted upon its back. The moose plunged towards shore and then suddenly sank beneath the waves, but the canoe had been freed from the main current and the Indians, were able to desperately paddle their way to the shore.

Dave was dazzled with disbelief about what had happened. An Indian called Julyja, a good friend of the minister, explained that the moose was his own paugan and it had saved him once before as a boy. The canoe had been saved by Julyja's paugan.

Well, that was all Dave needed to see. He immediately believed in the reality of the paugan and he wanted to discover his own. He asked Julyja for instruction. Julyja told him to fast for a fortnight, swim naked with the fish, and dream each day. Whatever animal he dreamed about would be his paugan.

The following summer, Dave did all of this faithfully. At the end of his ordeal it was revealed to him that his paugan was a wolverine, one of the most independent and fierce animals of the north country. He had never been saved by his paugan, and it had been years since he had witnessed it in dream, but he knew that it existed and that it would watch over him.

I simply could not believe in any of this. Dave told me that my disbelief was wrong. The Cree Indian legend of the paugan was indeed true and if I didn't show respect my safety was questionable.

Several years later, I was making a solo canoe trip on a remote stretch of river in the forest country of northern Saskatchewan. It had been a pleasant trip and I was in no hurry as I was enjoying that beautiful countryside and its occasional sand beaches. The weather had been the best that I had ever had on a northern trip. Perhaps all of this lulled me into a feeling of over-confidence, because a fateful decision caused me to take a chance with a rapids that proved to be a mistake. A rock ripped my canoe open from stem to stern, causing the entire craft to disintegrate in the swirling rapids. My gear had been secured into the boat; perhaps the turbulence of the water tugging on my Duluth packs aided in destroying the canoe. By the time I had swum clear of the rapids, there was nothing to be seen of my canoe or any of my equipment. My initial relief of being alive soon turned to fear. I was hundreds of miles from any help with no food, tent, or extra clothing!

In some ways the first few days were the most difficult. I still had my mosquito netting and some insect repellent, so at least I wasn't eaten alive by the mosquitoes. There was plenty of fresh water to drink. But food—I had none at all. I became more and more miserable during the first several days. I didn't know a person could become so miserable, so hungry. I built myself a shelter and planned to stay in one place, hoping another party might come down the river that summer, or that an Indian trapper or fisherman would come through.

It was just as well that I stayed, for soon the lack of food made me weak. Travel would have been impossible. My repellent ran out and the mosquitoes started adding to my misery by biting through my clothing. My only relief came when I went swimming naked with the fish in the cold stream. Fish that I could never hope to catch.

As the days passed I became strangely tranquil. And while each day become a blur in my memory, there can be no doubt that I was accidentally fulfilling the quest for a paugan. After almost two weeks, a fortnight as Julyja had told Dave, I lapsed into a trance. While in the trance I started at the clouds above me and I slowly realized that the clouds were forming into a shape. I was lifted out of my daze by the realization that I was going to see my paugan, that it was going to reveal itself to me, that I might be able to appeal to it for safety and deliverance from a certain death in this wilderness.

But the clouds were forming a shape that I was unfamiliar with. It was, naturally, a white blob. The white image seemed to boil and slowly evolved into a strange image that I struggled to recognize. Then it suddenly dawned on me what I was seeing, what my paugan really was. It was not a giant creature after all. Oh, the cloud was large, but my paugan was not. I was staring at a cloud image of a grub.

An insect that lived in rotten trees, that formed a main food source for the mighty bears of the forest, who were so fond of ripping apart dead trees to devour those tasty morsels.

Yes, my salvation lay all around me in the forest. I came out of my trance and grabbed a large rock and easily found a rotten log. I pounded the log apart and revealed a swarm of the maggot-like grubs, scurrying for cover from the daylight. I scooped up entire handfuls of the white bugs and shoved them in my mouth. The bugs squirmed as I crunched them. The taste was surprisingly wonderful. There was, of course, the crunchy sensation as they were squashed between my molars and there was the delightful juice that squirted into my cheeks with every bite. I was delighted at the first taste of food that I had experienced in two weeks.

My life had been saved by my paugan. I could live for weeks, travel for miles, all because I had been saved by my paugan—the white maggot-like grubs hidden all around me in the rotten logs.

Story Outline

I. The story narrator tells of meeting Dave, a missionary, who joined him for a canoe trip back to his post in northern Canada.

II. Dave relates the Cree Indian legend of the paugan, a protective spirit in the form of an animal that everyone has, but the identity of which will only be revealed in a trance that occurs after fasting for two weeks.

III. Dave sees two Indians rescued from a turbulent river by a moose that suddenly rises from river, saving their canoe, before disappearing again beneath the waves.

IV. Dave is told by an Indian to fast for two weeks, swim naked with the fish, and dream each day if he wished to learn of his paugan.

V. The narrator does not believe in this legend, but several years later, while on a solo trip in northern Saskatchewan, his boat and all of his possessions are lost in a rapids.

VI. As he starves he can obtain relief from the mosquitoes only by swimming naked with the fish in the cold water, accidentally fulfilling two of the requirements of the Great Spirit to have the identify of his paugan revealed.

VII. After two weeks he lapses into a trance, thus fulfilling the last requirement.

VIII. The paugan is usually a powerful beast, able to protect the owner from dangers of the wilderness. But the narrator's paugan is not a powerful animal, but a grub.

IX. The lowly grub, a nutritious source of food for many forest creatures, was the only thing that could have saved him from starvation. The narrator had found his paugan and it saved him!

12

THE LOST PIECE AT BAD CACHE RAPIDS

(pronounced "Bad Cash")

by David R. Scott

I was waitin' fer one-eyed Mike to come strollin' into my store with his buckskin pouch a' gold dust. He'd always come in 'bout this time ta barter with me fer his winter trappin' supplies. Yet fer some strange reason he was nearly two weeks late. Now a woodsman simply don't worry 'bout a fellow woodsman, but the truth to the matter was that ol' Mike was late and that the river'd soon be froze. To add to the problem I was the only friend Mike ever had; everyone else thought he was a bit off his rocker—after all he did live beyond Bad Cache Rapids. Yet ol' Mike always told me, "If'n ya want the best apple ya gatta risk climbin' out on a limb at the top of the tree." Perhaps it was his risk that prevented him from paddling into town and provoked me into paddling up his way.

The water of the Black Hat River is fairly calm, except fer Bad Cache Rapids. I reckoned it'd take me 12 days to reach the rapids, if'n the weather was in my favor, and an extra four to reach Mike's place. I got Betty the barmaid to watch the store while I was gone. As I paddled on up through the windin' shores I remembered my Granddad tellin' me why the Cree never camped near the rapids.

"Bad medicine, couldn't hear an approachin' enemy if'n ya had the ears of a bull moose!" he used to say. Not to mention the other yarn 'bout the rapids spun by the folks in town, but I put them stories out of my mind.

Finally, in the mid-afternoon on the thirteenth day I could hear that faint drone of the rapids. Now I didn't believe the tall tale told by the town folk, yet fer some reason my fear grew with the building growl of the boilin' water. I paddled my boat a while longer 'till I couldn't paddle no more. I eased the bow of the canoe up onto a sandy bay on the south shore. Snatchin' up my pack baskets I headed upstream to portage, for there was no way I was campin' at or near them rapids. I was halfway up the portage trail when I seen it and I reckon deep down inside a my gut I was expectin' somthin' like this, just didn't want to believe it. Pulled up on the bank was ol' Mike's birch bark canoe an' there wasn't a track around it.

Now everyone knew 'bout the old cabin at Bad Cache, but no one knew whose it was and no one knew of no one who stayed a single night there 'bouts. I made a quick turn and started up the trail towards the old cabin. By now the sun was droppin' in the western sky and some rain clouds was movin' in overhead. Still, despite the conditions, I trudged on up the overgrown trail.

After a while I could see the ol' one-room shack through a green lace of pine needles. The door was hangin' up with one leather hinge (the other one was torn off) so it hung crooked in the door frame. I cautiously peered through the crack expectin' the unexpected.

"Mike . . . you in there?" It was a pretty small cabin so there weren't no use in askin' twice. I stepped on in.

The cabin was, as cabins go, typical for the north country. Scattered cast-iron cookware on the wall, a hand-made table and chair (which was overturned when I got there), one large oil barrel stove, one bunk hangin' from the west wall, and a few rusted traps hung by the door. On the table sat a small oil lamp which I lit, and then I commenced to workin' on the fire. Soon I had the place warm and my belly full a' bannock and moose tongue stew.

After dinner I undid my bed roll and sat on the bunk exhausted from the long day of upstream paddlin'. It was from there that I noticed Mike's pipe in the southwest corner of the cabin. It was a fancy pipe that ol' Mike got from his Granddad and he never went nowhere without it. I stepped across the room and picked it up. The stem of the old pipe had been bitten clean through and it was half full a' half-burnt tobacco. As I put the remainder of the pipe in my pocket, the rain started to come down a bit harder and the rush a' them rapids sounded a bit louder.

Before I believed ol' Mike to be off in the woods huntin' fer some grub . . . now I had my doubts. The small oil lamp cast a few dull and broken shadows on the round long walls and the fire could barely be heard over the rain and the river. I must admit that at this time I was feelin' my knees a-knockin' and my hands a-shakin'. Nonetheless, because a' that I dropped my pipe whilst I was loadin' it. The pipe gave a jump and then rolled under the low hanging bunk. I leaned my head over the wooden edge to the point where my hair was sweepin' the floor. Against the wall I could make out the bowl of my pipe but I also saw a small box that went unnoticed b'fore. I reached under, nearly fallin' off the bunk, and grabbed the both of 'em. I stared at the ol' box cautiously and finished packin' my pipe. The hinges was rusted and the wood was rottin'. I struck a match and set my tobacco aglow never once takin' my eyes off a' the box. What was inside this dern thing? Gold, WHAT? Fer all I knew it was a human skull, at least that's what the towns folk would tell ya. Maybe it was ol' Mike's skull! I sat there starin' at the box an' draggin' on my pipe for a long while till finally I flung open the lid.

Fortunately there was no human skull, unfortunately there was no gold nor anythin' of the sort. What was in the box made me double up with laughter. It was a child's jigsaw puzzle. Well I knew, bein' as scared as I was, that sleep was out of the question, so I thought I'd try my luck on the puzzle. I was too amused to wonder 'bout its origin so I spread the pieces out on the table and commenced to fixin' it right. On and on I puffed my pipe and worked on placin' the pieces in their correct spots. The roar of the rapids seemed to increase as the rainy night poured on, drownin' out the sound of everything in and outside a' the cabin. After a while of work I had the frame of the puzzle complete and for some strange reason the puzzle, what I could make out of it, looked familiar. Still I kept on workin' and placin' when suddenly I realized that the puzzle I was workin' on was a picture of the cabin in which I was holin' up in fer the night. Well, I did find that rather strange, but in lookin' at the good side a' things (at least to ease my fear) it did make the puzzle much easier to fix. One by one I placed the pieces of the puzzle in their correct spots and with each new piece the river grew louder and the lamplight dimmer. Every now and then I would check my backside 'cause if someone (or something) were sneakin' up on me I wouldn't a' heard it (even with the ears of a bull moose). Also, with each new piece, the puzzle became more and more like a picture of the cabin I was in.

I was workin' on the lower right-hand part of the puzzle when I noticed somethin' far too peculiar. That particuliar part of the puzzle happened to be in the northwest corner of the cabin where I had stored my pack baskets and shoot a monkey if my pack baskets weren't in the very puzzle itself! I started to drag on my pipe even though there weren't nothin' in it, still somthin' possessed me to work on the puzzle. Soon I discovered my bedroll, my hat, my leftover stew and then finally myself in this backcountry jig saw. It was almost complete, except fer a few pieces that were missing, which made up the one window at my back. Everything else that was in the puzzle matched the cabin's interior log fer log.

I relit my pipe and studied the puzzle. I checked the box, the floor and the table but the missing pieces weren't nowhere to be found. Leanin' back in my chair I pondered over my situation. The sound of them rapids was now over-powerin' and the lamplight just gave a flicker. Yet in the flickerin' light I found the missing pieces I was a-searchin' fer. Not on the floor and not in the box, but I saw the missing pieces in the puzzle itself. There they were, layin' on the bunk. I was almost too afraid to set my eyes on the old bunk but I had no choice but to do so. I lifted my head up and gazed over the flame of the tiny lamp. Sure enough, there the pieces were on top of my dusty ol' Hudson Bay blanket just wait'n to be dropped into place.

I walked around that corner of the old wooden table and grabbed the pieces in my sweaty hands. Again I sat down at the table and packed my pipe before placin' the pieces into the missing holes. These would bake up the windows of the cabin and complete the puzzle. I held my match up to the flame of the lamplight and watched it flood the room with a fiery flash. The smoke from my pipe hung about me like a heavy fog and the river roared on towards town. Finally I picked up the pieces and carefully snapped them into place. At first I didn't believe what I saw, but in the window stood Death itself. It was a figure almost human . . . but not quite. Its eyes were sunk deep into its skull, its face was wrinkled gaunt and grey, and its hair was long, stringy, and smoky white.

It didn't make a sound, jus stood there . . . starin' with a hungry, evil sort a' grin on its face, and if this puzzle was right (as it had already proved to be) this creature was standin' directly behind me. A bead a' sweat dripped down my forehead causin' my eyes to blink, and then rolled off a' my cheek and splashed onto the puzzle. I couldn't stand the fear no more. I grit my teeth, clenched my fists, an' whirled around in my chair ready and willin' to face anything for the sake a' my life.

Yet the creature was gone! Swallowin' hard, with my eyes wider than a river in the springtime, I let my breath out with a stutter. I looked back to the puzzle, a bit puzzled m'self. There weren't no creature in the puzzle neither, the window in the picture was blank! Had the puzzle lied, was this all just my fear playin' tricks on me?

A cool breeze blew its way through some holes in the wall causing my lamplight to flicker and my spine to tingle. Without a moment to dwell on my questions, the door of the cabin blew off a' its one leather hinge. There before me stood the beast in the window, the thing in the puzzle . . . there before me stood Death itself.

When it opened the door, it seemed as though the entire river poured into the cabin, the noise from the rapids drowned out my screams of terror. An' there it stood, almost human, but not quite. Its face seemed hollow, its eyes seemed evil and its teeth seemed anxious. It's hair was long grey and stringy and came to rest on its shoulders lying over a buckskin shirt that I recognized as one-eyed Mike's. As a matter a' fact the more deeply I looked at this . . . this . . . thing, the more it took to lookin' like ol' Mike. And when it smiled its hollow-toothed smile, I knew it was indeed ol' one-eyed Mike himself.

Instantly I grabbed the corner of the table and threw the entire thing on the creature that I had somehow constructed. At nearly the same time, I blasted out a' the door like an eight-legged

dog, and ran straight fer the rapids. I couldn't hear it' but I knew that the beast was right behind me. I made it back into town in two days, and four days later ol' Mike made it into town. Not by canoe, and not by horse . . . but floatin'. His face was mangled, his body scarred and his one good eye and buckskin shirt weren't nowhere to be found. In his mouth was the stem of the pipe his Granddad had given to him.

The townsfolk have since accused me of bein' a killer, after they found the other half of Mike's pipe in my pocket, and have sentenced me to be the guest of honor at a necktie party. I haven't told them my story for I'd rather face the steps and string than live knowing that creature still lurks in the black spruce forest near Bad Cache Rapids. But the next time one of them towns folk are up that way pannin' or trappin' they'll learn right quick, and you can bet a sack a' gold dust that it'll be my face in the missing window.

Story Outline

I. One-eyed Mike is two weeks late returning to town from the mysterious wilderness area called Bad Cache Rapids.

II. The story teller is about the only friend Mike has, so he takes it upon himself to travel upstream for 12 days to check on Mike.

III. When he arrives at the Bad Cache Rapids, he finds Mike's canoe, but is unable to locate him at an abandoned cabin.

IV. He is horrified to find old Mike's pipe as he knew that it was Mike's most prized possession and that he was never without it. He places that broken pipe in his pocket for safekeeping.

V. When spending the night at the cabin, he finds a small box with a puzzle on it that turns out to be a picture of the cabin's interior, even to include his own pack baskets sitting in a corner.

VI. Several of the pieces are missing, but upon studying the picture in the puzzle, he notes that they appear on the bed. Sure enough, upon checking the bed there they are.

VII. When he places the pieces into the puzzle, it shows the window behind him with the figure of Death, appearing as a half-rotten image of his friend Mike, looking at him.

VIII. He turns around, but the window is empty. Before he can get over this shock, the door blows off the cabin and there stands the creature of death.

IX. He throws the table at the creature and escapes back to town.

X. Mike's body soon floats into town, all mangled, but with the pipe stem still clenched in Mike's teeth.

XI. The town's people arrest, and are going to hang, the story teller as they have found Mike's pipe in his pocket.

XII. The story teller knows that they will not believe his story, but that someday one of them will also go up to that cabin and put the puzzle together, only to see his face in the missing window!

13

THE NIGHTMARE TRAIL

by Scott E. Power

I considered myself a rational and sensible person until that night. I don't blame anyone for disbelieving me. I often times don't believe it myself, but as soon as I close my eyes to sleep, there it is as vivid as that night. And as horrible.

I'm surprised at myself for trying to explain it all here again. I've told the story so many times. Each time people laugh in disbelief. I, too, would laugh if I heard such a story, if it had not happened to me. But it did. I can't deny it. If I hadn't been alone, maybe it wouldn't have happened at all. But I was, it did, and as a result, I will forever shun solitude.

Although I was anxious to arrive back at my cabin, which was only a mile down the river, I couldn't help but stop periodically to look around. All I could see through the falling snow was the river bank and jagged tree line, the black spruce stabbing the dark sky with their twisted tree tops. The whole panorama was illuminated by the soft light of the full moon, which was shining behind the thick cover of snow clouds. There was no sound. Only winter's silence literally humming in my ears. I have never understood how, when it is so silent in the north country, there seems to be a distant noise, not unlike the whine of a saw mill.

After a few moments of gazing at what appeared to be an enchanted fantasy land of a child's nightmare, which was really the frozen muskeg of northern Manitoba, I pressed on. The winter's silence was drowned out by the "crunch . . . crunch . . . crunch" of the snow beneath my snowshoes.

I was contemplating the epicurean delight of a hot cup of tea back at my cabin when I saw the tracks. They were large tracks, but not the tracks that moose leave behind as they move through the snow. They resembled tracks made by a human. But who?

No one lived within fifty miles of my cabin. I didn't remember making the trail. It ran perpendicular to my trap line and to my normal travels. I could not think of a reason why I would have gone that way, unless to satisfy an urge to explore. But the trail was fresh, made within the last few hours. I hadn't seen it earlier while hiking past. Someone, or something, had just traveled through here. If so, they must have seen my trail. What was it? A human? If so, who was it? What were his intentions? Why was he traveling on such a stormy night?

As I pondered these questions, I felt the rhythm of my heartbeat raise to a staccato pounding. The only way to know the answer to this mystery was to follow the trail and find out. If worse came to worse, I had my rifle. But surely this was the trail of a fellow trapper whom I did not know. I turned off my trail and onto the other, following it into the dark gloom of the trees.

I had followed the trail into the woods a hundred yards or so when I began to see dark splotches on the snow. It was a substance I didn't recognize. The splotches were sporadic and of diverse sizes. I took off my gloves to touch them, attempting to identify them by their textures. But of course, the cold temperatures had already frozen the substance into grains of ice.

The thought crossed my mind that possibly blood had dripped from dead game that this unknown person had hunted. I felt comfortable with this thought and ceased to puzzle over it any longer.

I stopped to look over the surroundings. I could no longer see the river behind me. All about me were sinister shadows of gnarled black spruce. Occasionally, I would brush up against a tamarack tree. The cloud cover had begun to thin out and the snow was changing into light flurries. The moonlight was swelling as the clouds dispersed.

The moon itself was full and ominous. The air seemed to be growing colder. I began to feel the frigid air stabbing me like pricking needles through my layers of wool and down. In the distance, I heard the hunger cry of an Arctic wolf.

The trail I followed was longer than I had anticipated and I began to feel as if it went nowhere specific. Just someone, or something, passing through. But that just seemed too outrageous, it had to be somewhere. Much to my surprise, as I continued trekking, I began to recognize various landmarks. I guess you could say I was experiencing a sense of déjà vu. I began to feel that I had been there before, but didn't consciously remember it. It was like a dream, or a nightmare.

Finally, just over the sounds of the snow crunching beneath my snowshoes, I heard what seemed to be the song of a Canadian Jay. But as I stopped to listen and discern, I realized it was the whistle of a human. As last I was nearing the mysterious person.

As I closed the distance between the whistler and myself, I began recognizing more and more of the surroundings. It was more eerie than bizarre. The hair on my neck stood up and the gloom of the forest was serenaded by someone whistling in the darkness. It seemed to me that I was walking myself into a realm of paradox and surrealism. The atmosphere reeked with the warmth of evil and frigidity of death. I tried to convince myself to turn around and go home. But not knowing what was ahead, whistling in such a dreadful context, would forever vex me. Besides, I had come this far, and I did have my rifle.

The stains in the snow had become more frequent. I lit a match to examine them more closely. As the match flame illuminated the snow, I saw a dark crimson color. It was definitely blood.

Exactly at that moment, the tune being whistled in the distance changed. At first it had been merry and delightful, however I did not recognize the melody. But now the air was filled with the robust melancholy of Bach's Toccata and Fugue. The sound was amplified throughout the forest and resembled a pipe organ more than a whistle. But that was impossible and I knew it. It was all in my head, made worse by my fatigue and terrible imagination.

I looked up from the ground and saw candlelight shining through a cabin window. A cabin! I couldn't believe it. I didn't think there was a cabin within fifty miles of my own. As I approached the cabin stealthily and with great curiosity, I began noticing that the cabin resembled mine. But it was difficult to concentrate and be sure, because the whistle was getting louder. It seemed to weaken me.

I was positive that the cabin looked like my own. The roof was an A-frame, the main cabin was about the same size and there were windows on the east and west walls. And even more peculiar was the fact the outhouse and woodshed were designed identically to mine.

Suddenly, the person inside stopped whistling. My ears were ringing in its absence. My heart was pounding like a sledgehammer. Although the temperature was below zero, I was sweating. The trail of what I knew to be blood went around the corner of the cabin to the far side, where I assumed the entrance was. Just like mine.

I gazed through the window from where I sat, some twenty yards away, hoping to see who was inside this cabin. Unfortunately,

I saw nobody, just a shadow dancing about in graceful glides. I un-lashed my snowshoes, took hold of my gun, and prepared my nerve to go look through the window at the person inside.

As I sat there, I looked down at my hands, which grasped the rifle with a white-knuckled grip, and realized how ridiculous I was behaving. If someone was to have seen me, they would have thought I was a child. I was ashamed. It was mere coincidence that this cabin resembled mine. It couldn't be mine. Besides, what did I think was in there? The windigo? The windigo is part of a Cree Indian legend that embodies all the fear, all the horror, and the wildness, starvation, misery and terrible cold of the North. The windigo is supposedly a man and cannibal. But it is an Indian legend, not reality. It simply doesn't exist!

I laughed at myself and my imagination. It crossed my mind that I had lived in that God-forsaken-land too long and I was becoming "bushed," as they say in the North. I decided to leave my gun behind and simply go look inside the window to check things out. Then I would knock on the door and introduce myself. Maybe that person would be kind enough to offer me a cup of java. I certainly needed a warm drink. With a huge boost of confidence, I got up from where I sat and walked, as quietly as possible, to the window.

However, as I got closer, my determination began to melt away. I began noticing debris and other objects that I recognized. The spool of rope against the wall. The kerosene barrel. And just a few feet away, I could see a sled that looked like mine. This was my cabin! But how? Who was inside? And why the blood?

Immediately, I grew weak with fright. Everything was too freakish for it to be normal. I felt I had fallen into a trap and there was no way out. I remembered my rifle, but it was too late, I was at the window. I could delay no longer. I had to look in.

I peered in. Everything was as I had left it, but there was a fire burning in the stove, obviously started by this foreigner. And some kind of meat was being fried on the stove. Maybe that was what the blood came from.

I could see the person inside, but not the face. It was a man. He was tall and husky with long white hair. There was something hanging in the corner, but I couldn't tell what it was. The man moved the kerosene lantern onto a table by the stove and I could make out a few more details. It was definitely meat of some sort cooking on the stove. But exactly what kind I couldn't tell. The carcass was still dripping blood and under it was a bucket to catch the fluids. The carcass was hanging from its hind quarters, and the forelegs, minus the severed one, were almost touching the floor. It was a large animal, probably seven feet from tip to tip. The head had been severed.

The man, whose face I still could not see, removed the meat from the stove and, with his back to me, began to eat it. My eyes went back to the carcass. I tried to identify it. I was truly puzzled. Finally, as I let my eyes sweep over the room that was mine, I noticed something next to the lantern. The shadows on it cast from the light were sharp and full of contrast. It was difficult to discern what it was.

I stared and stared until the realization of its identity burned my consciousness with an evil that could only be from hell. My whole body quivered. My heart was overcome with fear. That thing in the shadows of my cabin was a human head! And the carcass was a human body!

I thought I was mad . . . insane . . . hallucinating. But there it was. Swinging in the shadows of my cabin. A bloody fresh carcass of a slaughtered human being.

The fear and horror of the evil overcame me. I wanted to run away, but I couldn't move. My whole body was paralyzed and sick.

The cannibalistic man inside stood up from the table where he was eating human flesh, and walked toward the door. He was going outside! I must run! I turned to escape. As I did, I looked up and there he was in front of me! The windigo!

"You're next!" he sneered.

Darkness overcame me. I lost consciousness.

When I awoke, I was inside my cabin. Tucked inside my warm sleeping bag. It was daylight. All was serene.

I looked around. No one was there. He, or it, was gone. Or had he even been there? There was no carcass, no head.

It was all a dream, a nightmare! My terrible ordeal was only a dream.

How good it was to be alive! Really alive! No fear, no horror. All was well.

After breakfast, I had to check my trap line. As I left the cabin, I walked with a bounce, a joy of peace. But as I turned the river bend and approached the spot where my nightmare had started, I slowed with uncertainty. Had it truly been a dream, or not?

Yes! Of course it was a dream. I was still alive wasn't I?

But as I continued trekking, the scar of a freshly made trail perpendicular to mine became visible.

Story Outline

I. The narrator finds a mysterious trail leading into the woods, only about a mile from his cabin located in isolated wilderness.

II. As he follows it he notices drops on the trail that he eventually finds to be blood.

III. He comes upon an inhabited cabin that he did not know existed.

IV. Initially scared, his fear increases when he notes that the cabin and its belongings appear to be identical with his.

V. To his horror, he sees that the body hung in the cabin, and being eaten by its inhabitant, is that of a human being.

VI. He knows that he has come upon the windigo, the embodiment of all the fear, all the horror, all the wildness, starvation, misery and terrible cold of the North.

VII. He turns to run from the cabin, but the windigo is behind him suddenly and shouts (and be sure to shout this when telling the story), "You're next!"

VIII. The narrator wakes up, safe in his cabin. It has only been a dream.

IX. After breakfast he leaves to check his trap line and the story finishes with his noting a freshly made trail, perpendicular to his, just as in the dream.

⊶——14——⊷
A TRAPPER'S GREED

by Scott E. Power

Once upon a time, there were two boys who were very good friends. They had many common interests, especially camping. They loved to hike in the woods, set up camp, and spend the night under the stars. The sounds of the night were very alluring and mystifying to them; they really had a great appreciation for the wild in the wilderness. Growing up, they had participated in the Boy Scouts and learned much history and technique about camping, canoeing, survival and wilderness first aid. John's grandfather was even a trapper, third generation, and helped teach the boys about the woods and wildlife. He showed them how to live off the land and how to trap for pelts. He taught them everything he knew and they grew up always dreaming of a day when they could go to Grandfather's cabin in northern Canada and live for a winter and trap and learn what it was really like to live off the land and with the land.

Finally, it was high school graduation, and the first real chance the boys had to pursue their dream approached. Upon graduation, Grandfather promised that he would send them to the cabin for a winter to fulfill their dreams if they wanted. They immediately said, "Yes!"

The pre-trip planning went smoothly, time passed quickly, and before the boys knew it the departure date was imminent. These best of friends couldn't wait for the great adventure. It was their dream.

Most of their gear was food, clothing and books. Grandfather had the rest of the essentials already stored at the cabin. Traps, fur stretchers, knives, tools, fishing gear, tents, extra sleeping bags, some nonperishable food, all sorts of things. The friends were all set.

The night before the bush plane was going to fly them into the bush, one of the boys, Ricky, was talking with a local trapper and they discussed many aspects of the job, just like people with things in common do. When the subject of money came up the old trapper told Ricky that last season one marten pelt had sold for fifty to seventy dollars—and that the price was expected to stay high for the upcoming season. This news excited both John and Ricky. They didn't realize they could make so much money. It was exciting to think about and they determined to work together and do the best they could to make a lot of money to help offset the cost of their trip. If they could just get fifty pelts each, which was very likely, they would get seven thousand dollars. What a great thing! The friends were elated.

Once the boys got to the cabin in August, everything went well. It was very hard work to get the camp up and running, chopping firewood and planning trap lines and everything else that goes into preparing for a long, dark, northern winter.

Finally, the snows of November came and the boys could begin to set up their trap line. Before the trip they agreed to share the line and its maintenance since it was such a tough job, but as they started the line something weird began to happen. John began to act distant from Ricky, almost as if he wished he wasn't there. One night the truth emerged. John told his friend that he wasn't going to share the trap line anymore, that he didn't want to split the money either. He would move downstream and set up his own camp and trap line away from Ricky and his line.

Ricky couldn't believe his ears. This didn't sound like the best friend that he had come to know. John was acting greedy and Ricky was confused about why. He thought they were a team, a partnership, but suddenly John didn't want anything to do with his so-called friend. Ricky was hurt and did his best to convince John to reconsider, but John wouldn't hear it. He was to move downstream a few miles and live through the long, dark cold, winter nights without another person within a hundred miles, aside from Ricky.

At first Ricky hoped that John would get over it. "This is just a phase," he thought. But as the days turned into weeks and weeks turned into months, John never recanted or even came to visit. Ricky tried again to reconcile things but John was adamant. He wanted to be left alone. So Ricky finally gave up and left John alone. Meanwhile, Ricky continued with his life and trap lines.

Finally, as spring approached, the trapping ended and each boy had accomplished his goals. Ricky had trapped in the wilderness, living off the land, just as he had always dreamed. His trapping was good, but not as good as John's. Ricky had gathered twenty-five pelts, but John caught sixty. John worked much harder than Ricky; he really wanted money and at seventy dollars each, sixty pelts would bring in more than four-thousand dollars. In his mind he was gonna be rich, because to him four thousand dollars seemed like a fortune. He was already counting the money and still didn't want to be friends with Ricky. Ricky was hurt, but had come to terms with John's rejection, and accepted it. They had both done the best they could, according to their own goals.

Grandfather arrived at the cabin excited to see how the boys were doing and how successful they had been at living off the land. Upon his arrival he noticed something was wrong. The boys seemed happy to see Grandfather but didn't really seem very

cordial to each other. Grandfather figured something had happened, maybe an argument. Finally, when it was appropriate, Grandfather asked his grandson John confidentially if there was anything wrong between them. John said, "No."

Not satisfied with the answer, Grandfather later asked Ricky if there was anything wrong. Ricky told Grandfather about what had happened. Ricky explained that John hadn't wanted to share the trap lines or the profits, and that they had lived apart for the last six months. He explained that he had tried to reconcile things but John wouldn't agree. Ricky told Grandfather how hurtful it was for him to lose his best friend over the greed for four-thousand dollars. Grandfather was very hurt that his own grandson had missed the point of teamwork, had become greedy, and had ruined a once-cherished friendship.

In John's mind, though, it was worth it. After all, he was going to get at least seventy bucks per pelt and wouldn't have to share it. Yes, he wouldn't have to share his profits. But what John didn't know was that the price had dropped harshly because there had been a big drop in demand. Grandfather explained the price had been readjusted while they were gone to about five bucks a pelt. John was crushed. He wasn't rich after all. He was a loser. He had let greed and three-hundred dollars destroy what had been a life-long friendship.

Story Outline

I. A life-long dream comes true for two boys when John's grandfather sends them to his cabin in the far north to trap and live off the land.

II. Fur prices are quite high, and John becomes greedy, telling his friend Ricky that he has decided to live and trap alone and not share his catch.

III. Ricky learns to enjoy the North as best he can, without the friendship of John.

IV. When John's grandfather comes in to bring the boys home, he notices that something is wrong and finally learns of John's greed.

V. He then tells John that the fur prices have dropped. John has lived alone all winter and lost his best friend over a mere three-hundred dollars.

A KNOCK AT THE DOOR

by David R. Scott

Editor's note: In this story, Dave almost seems to be getting even with me for sending him to a remote cabin for a year-long expedition. You can learn more about the background of the adventure at the website: www .forgey-cabin.com. At least, he puts a character with my general description into a horrible predicament. —Doc

Long ago, I built a small log cabin in the northeastern corner of Manitoba, Canada. Every so often, I find two youngsters willing to capture the experience of a lifetime by living there for an extended period of time. I help them finance the expedition and they in turn pay me back by living out an adventure that I could not experience myself. The cabin is located 200 miles from the nearest town and at some points on the compass a thousand miles away from the nearest human. It is only accessible by bush plane. Once a crew is in the bush, I usually fly in once every four months to resupply them and to make sure they are in good health. (It is also a good excuse to escape to the cabin I love.)

I had sent two young men up for a one-year expedition and I had checked on them twice. It was now nearing Christmas time and I was on my way to take them out of the bush and back into the "civilized world." It was a trip that I had looked forward to with great anticipation, however it resulted in my worst nightmare.

The sound of the single-engine Beaver rang in my ears as I watched the Land of the Little Sticks pass beneath its skis. The temperature had plummeted to forty below that day and the thought of a hot cup of coffee and a toasty log cabin warmed my soul. I had so much to tell those guys about the world they had left behind. My heart began to pound in my throat when I saw the mighty Churchill River, I knew I was getting closer. It had always been such an exciting moment to fly low over the cabin and see two weathered woodsmen come running out with their faces full of smiles and their arms waving. Exciting, indeed, and relieving, for I knew at that moment they were alive and well. The thought of no one coming out of the cabin scared me more than anything, but it was the chance one took. And I had great faith in the crews I had sent up in the past.

Soon we were flying over the Smith River, and in the distance I could see the bend on which the cabin was located. I pointed it out to the pilot and he aimed the nose of the plane straight for the cabin, but something was wrong. No smoke was visible from the cabin's stove pipe. As we drew nearer my nightmare became a reality. Not a single sign of life was present. No tracks to the river, no smoke from the pipe, no firewood cuttings . . . nothing. I had the pilot buzz the cabin as low as he could. No one came out! The pounding of my heart increased with every beat. We flew up to the drop-off point one mile upstream and the pilot gently brought the plane down.

"I can't wait for ya or the engines'll freeze up. Do you wanna stay'r go?"

"Pick us up in one week," I replied. I used "us" simply because I refused to believe anything had gone wrong. I pulled my gear onto the bank and watched the airplane disappear into the empty Arctic sky.

Quickly, I strapped on my snowshoes and headed downstream toward the cabin, stumbling from time to time, intoxicated with fear. Finally, through the dense black spruce I could make out the roof the the cabin. To my ears my footsteps were silent, and the wind, though blowing briskly, made no sound. All I could hear was the beating of my heart.

The was no sign of life whatsoever . . . none! The front door of the cabin was wide open. I stepped in, and struck a wooden match upon the surface of the cast-iron stove top. The room flooded with a fiery flash and when my sight returned from a state of temporary blindness, I lit a small kerosene lamp.

Through the dim lamplight I could see both chairs were overturned, pots and pans were strewn about the floor, the stove pipe was disconnected and the ladder to the sleeping loft was broken. I picked up the one chair and placed it by the small table. After starting a fire I sat by the stove in a state of shock, I assumed I had lost two very good friends. It was from this point that I noticed Scott's closed journal on the floor along with some other fallen books. In haste and desperation I grabbed the journal and began to read, hoping to find some clues. It read:

Oct. 15, 1991
"I awakened in the middle of the night last night for reasons unknown. I was having a difficult time falling back asleep when I first heard it. There was a knock at the door. Three times in a slow steady progression. I knew that it couldn't possibly be a human for there is no one within 200 miles of here. I awakened Dave to see if he had heard anything, yet he had heard nothing. Perhaps it was a figment of my rather creative imagination, but I could have sworn that I did indeed hear a knock at the door.

He continued on with the day's events and weather documentation, but said nothing more about the knock until two days later.

Oct. 17, 1991
"Well, Dave and I are in the loft right now. Dave is almost asleep and I am catching up on my journal entries. The day has been great. Got a lot of firewood cut and started building a new table beneath the east window. Also went hunting and got a few ptarmigan so dinner was exceptionally good tonight. Dave and I are going to head up to . . . I just heard that knock again. Dave didn't believe me when I told him I heard it two nights ago, but now he hears it too."

I flipped the next pages but there was nothing more to be read—that was Scott's last journal entry. Jumping up from my chair I began searching for Dave's journal, tearing the cabin apart as I looked. After a great deal of difficulty, I found it up in the loft. The journal was wrinkled and appeared as though it had been through a battle. I found it face down, opened to the date Oct. 19, 1991. I read even though the writing was shaky and nearly illegible.

Oct. 19, 1991
"Scott has not returned since the night before last. He offered to check out the knock since I was nearly asleep. He went downstairs with the gun, opened the door, but never came back. There was no sound, no scream, no nothing; it was almost as if he was swallowed by the night in the black spruce forest. I spent all of yesterday and part of today searching for him, but have not found so much as a clue. I am in the loft right now. It is in the middle of the afternoon and I did not sleep last night because I,

too, heard the knock. Three knocks in a slow steady progression, just as Scott and I had heard the night before last. I am afraid and alone. My partner is gone and I have no choice but to stay here for two and a half more months, to stay here with whatever has been haunting us. I am going outside to try to find whatever it was that did this. I just pray that I am back to document the events tomorrow. If there is no more writing in this journal from this point, then my advice to you (whomever you may be) is to get the hell out of here as fast as you can. Chances are you'd be better off if you were. . ."

That was it, the rest of the journal was blank, Dave had never finished what he was attempting to write. I leaned my head against the wall, and in the dim lamplight I saw eight scratches running down the floorboards. I also saw a loaded rifle with the hammer back in the far corner of the loft. Whatever had been knocking on the door didn't wait for Dave to finish his journal entry, nor did it wait for him to come outside. Instead, it came and got him, dragging him and causing him to claw the very floorboards in an attempt to escape and save his own life!

My fear intensified. The thought of those guys having been killed was devastating, and the thought of what killed them was even more terrifying. Yet, I was also on the menu . . . I could feel it. By then the sun had set. I couldn't eat anything for I was nauseous. Instead I loaded my rifle and sat in the loft, too terrified to move. The night dragged on. Eventually my fire burned out, yet I didn't risk going downstairs to feed it. I simply sat shivering in my sleeping bag waiting for the dark night to fade into day.

Morning came with the singing of whiskey jacks and the fighting of martens. The sky was clear and the temperature cold. Soon, I had the fire going and coffee boiling on the buckled top of the old wood-burning stove. I was still in somewhat of a state

of shock, so I didn't even notice the coffee boiling over. Quickly I grabbed the pot off the stove, and with shaking hands poured myself a cup.

The day progressed as slowly as the night and my fear grew with each passing moment I was there. I spent the day cutting firewood and reopening an ice hole, always looking for clues and always looking over my shoulder. Soon darkness fell upon the Arctic land and once again I sat in the loft of my cabin awake with a fearful anticipation of the night. My eyes were wide, my knuckles were white, and my finger remained poised on the trigger.

Suddenly, without warning, something jumped in the far corner of the loft, and before I knew it, the rifle was jumping in my hands, emitting spears of sparks and splintering the roof logs with each and every shot. When the smoke cleared, I saw the culprit, although I hardly believed it possible for such a creature to kill two grown men. What I'd believed to be a horrid beast was nothing more than a small squirrel seeking the warmth and comfort of my cabin. Instead, he received six rounds form a lever-action .30-.30. He now was a permanent part of the cabin's floor.

"Let that be a lesson to ya," I shouted beyond the walls of the cabin and into the empty black forest. "Anything that moves within my sight will die within my sight as well. So help me God!" Outside the wind took a deep breath, causing the tree limbs to release their grip on the snow the which they so desperately clung. The wind lazily exhaled in a way that made me realize that my fear was of no importance to her. Whether I lived or died was far from her concern. After all, this was big country, and up here there are no corners in which to back into. A man can run . . . but he cannot hide.

The next four days followed the same pattern, and each day my fear grew to the point where I was too terrified to accomplish anything. Each new sound that echoed from the black spruce forest provoked a fear in me that I can not explain. Each new night became a gamble, a game of Russian Roulette. I never knew on which night I would hear the knock at my door. I never knew if I would live to see the light of tomorrow.

Finally, it was my last night in the cabin. Tomorrow the bush plane would come to take me out of my nightmare. I climbed into the loft of the cabin and zipped myself into my sleeping bag, laying the gun over my lap. I remembered giving the boys a quote by the famous woodsman Calvin Rutstrum, who said, "An absolute wilderness is a place where you can yell your head off for help and no one will hear you!" I knew I was in such a place. I was defenseless, helpless and completely on my own. Never before have I felt a fear such as that.

Outside the winds rose and fell as if the night were breathing once again. My eyelids became heavy and I could no longer fight the sleep that I had been avoiding for the past week. For the first time since my arrival, I was in a deep sleep. Thoughts of the bush plane filled me with hope.

Morning came bright and cold, I started the fire and set the coffee to boil. I was overwhelmed knowing that the bush plane would be arriving today to take me out of the bush, and out of this living hell. I was preparing to fry some back bacon when suddenly there came a knock at my door . . . three times in a slow steady progression . . . knock . . . knock . . . knock!

I bolted upright in my sleeping bag, clutching my rifle and sweating profusely. Morning had been a dream. It took me several minutes to catch my breath and to release the white-knuckled grip I had on my gun. I must have been asleep quite some time, for I noticed that the moon was nearly set in the western horizon. I laid down again and closed my eyes, listening as my own heart pounded the rhythm of absolute fear. I was between the stage of being asleep and awake when I heard it . . . three times in a slow steady progression, just as the journals had said, yet this time it was no dream. Knock . . . knock . . . knock!

My throat went dry, and my knuckles went white around the stock and grip of my gun. The noise didn't recur for several minutes and then it repeated. Knock . . . knock . . . knock!

I sat in silence for an eternity. My back was wedged up against the wall and my gunbarrel was aimed at the top of the ladder leading up to the loft. Even in the freezing temperatures my face was beaded with sweat. I didn't move from that spot for the rest of the night. Nothing else happened.

I watched the sun come up through the tops of the spruce trees. Its beams of light came through the frosted windows, illuminating the cabin with a cold light. Quickly, I packed my bags along with the boys' journals and headed for the drop-off point. I recalled the pilot telling me that he'd be there in the early afternoon, and that I should be ready and waiting. I was ready to say the least.

I arrived at the drop-off point at 1 PM. My ears strained for the sound of a bush plane. The wind was calm and the land stood still. Anxiously I panned the sky for my ride home. Was it getting late or was I paranoid, where was my flight?

Finally in the cool, clean air I could hear the drone of the engines getting closer and closer. The sound, however, demonstrated the Doppler effect, roaring overhead and then onward toward Churchill. Two more hours I waited, yet my plane never showed.

It had happened before in the past, but this was a time of desperation and due to the fact that my pilot was a freelance flyer no one else would know where I was. I hiked back to the cabin for another night of indescribable fear. I arrived at the cabin past dusk. The sky was on fire with vibrant reds and oranges. I relit the stove and set some coffee to boil on the stove top. I also lit all of the lanterns and began to read, trying to fool myself into believing that I was no longer afraid. Eventually I climbed into the loft with my gun and extra shells. I could hear the wind licking the treetops and my heart pounding with fearful anticipation. Once again I wedged myself into the corner of the loft, poised with the gun ready to kill anything that moved. My fearful anticipation was short-lived. Two hours after I had climbed into the loft I heard the knock, three times in a slow steady fashion. Knock . . . knock . . . knock. I held the rifle to my chest and closed my eyes, hoping that this thing would go away as it had done before . . . but it didn't. Instead I heard the hinges of the cabin's front door slowly squeak as it opened, and then, for a brief moment, they paused, and then they squeaked once more until the door met the wall. The front door was now wide open, and the creature was in my cabin. I jumped up screaming in utter terror for my life and began firing through the floorboards at whatever was beneath me. Finally, I heard the old wooden door creak upon its rusty hinges until it was shut. The creature escaped, and from the sound of its patient exit, it escaped unharmed. My fear increased in its intensity. I was too afraid to go below so I hid in my sleeping bag overcome by exhaustion.

I awoke the following morning still immersed in fear. For three hours I sat deaf to all sounds, blind to all sights and numb to all feeling. It was almost as if someone had shut down all of my senses.

The only thing I do remember was finally snapping out of my state of unconsciousness. I turned my fear into rage. I was angry because this "thing" hadn't put me out of my misery the night before. It was almost as if it fed off my fear, as if it could taste it, as if it enjoyed it. I reloaded my gun and climbed down the ladder. The moment my feet hit the un-level wooden floorboards, there came a knock at the front door three times in a slow steady progression. Knock . . . knock . . . knock.

A rush of adrenaline overpowered me and without second thought, I opened fire on the front door. Six shots I fired from the hip, screaming wildly as I pulled the trigger. When the smoke cleared, I heard the thing drop heavily to the ground.

Quickly, I reloaded my gun and stepped up to the door. I took one deep breath, pulled the hammer back on the rifle, and kicked open the door. There, in the crimson snow lay the bush pilot with blood pouring profusely from six large holes in his chest. His face displayed with the struggle of his final breath and his eyes were opened wide with shock. It was at that moment I realized that I had just condemned myself to a life sentence in a living nightmare. Off in the distance I heard a laugh echo throughout the black spruce forest, and soon after, the sun fell into the gaping jaws of the horizon.

Story Outline

I. The narrator visits a cabin in the far North where he had arranged for two young men to spend the winter.

II. When flying over the cabin, he sees no sign of human life, and discovers when he lands that the boys have been missing for some time.

III. In the cabin, he uncovers one of the boy's journals and finds out through reading its last entry that someone or something was knocking at the cabin door.

IV. He discovers through reading the second boy's journal that the other boy had vanished. The second boy never made another journal entry either.

V. All that week, he lives in absolute fear, for he does not know if or when the knock will sound at the door. Finally, the night before the plane is to arrive, there comes a knock at the door, but the thing goes away.

VI. The next morning, he leaves to meet the plane. But the plane never comes. Scared beyond belief, he is forced to spend another night in the cabin.

VII. Very late that night, he hears the knock but this time the creature comes inside the cabin. In blind terror he begins shooting down through the floorboards of the loft at the creature, and when he finishes firing, he hears the door slowly close.

VIII. The next morning, he is at first paralyzed with fear, then angry. When there are three knocks at the door, he fires all six rounds from the shotgun into the door, and hears the creature drop dead outside in the snow.

IX. He kicks open the door only to find the bush pilot with six holes in his chest, dead in the white snow. He has just signed and sealed his reservation into a living nightmare.

16

SCARED TO DEATH

by Scott E. Power

In a faraway land, but not too far, there was an old farmer. Through years of hard work and long days, he had become very strong and wise. In fact, he was regarded as the wisest person in the entire town. He was very proud of this fact. And he was vain enough that he never let anyone forget just how smart he was.

One day, while he was performing one of his many farming chores, ploughing the fields, he came upon a snake. It laid there in the dirt, motionless. The man wondered if it was dead. He questioned what kind of snake it was. It just laid there coiled up, appearing to be dead. The farmer couldn't stand his curiosity very long. He had to know if it was really dead or if it was just sleeping. Actually, the farmer had never seen a snake like it before. There were weird shapes on its back, kind of like the shapes in a spider's web. It seemed that it was an extraordinary snake.

The farmer bent over, stretching forth a stick to prod the snake, to see if it was alive. But after it was too late, he realized the foolhardiness of his behavior. For just as the tip of the stick was threatening to touch the snake, it sprang out of its coil as quick as lightning, bit the farmer, sinking its fangs deep into his flesh.

After releasing itself from the man's leg, the snake quickly slid away and coiled itself in the dirt. The shock and the horror of the bite was overwhelming for the farmer. He had seen snakes many times before, but had never ever been bitten. As he stood there in shock, wondering what to do, he realized that the nearest doctor

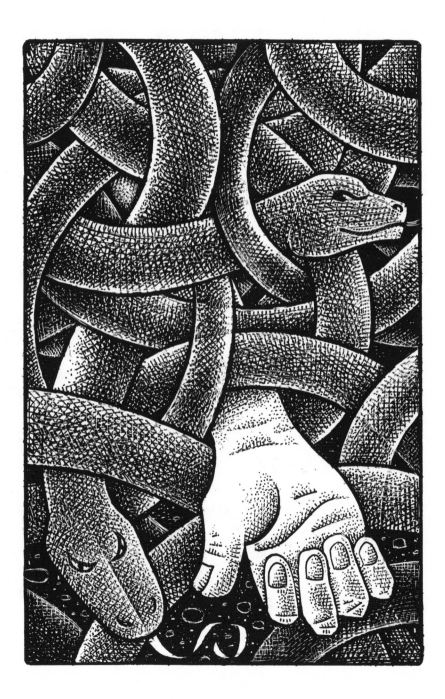

was more than one day's journey away. Immediately, the man fell dead.

Many hours passed before anyone found the man. His wife was the first to happen upon him. When he didn't come to the house for lunch, she got worried and went searching.

Upon finding the dead man, she also saw the snake and killed it with the backside of a shovel. She couldn't help but kill the snake, knowing intuitively what it had done. She took vengeance, stabbing the snake with the shovel, cutting it into many pieces. She wanted to find out what kind of snake it was, since it was obviously poisonous. Picking up the bloody remnants of the dead snake, the wife had wished she hadn't made such a mess. But she too had never seen such a deadly looking snake.

After having the snake identified, the farmers' wife was shocked to find the reptile was not a rare, lethal snake at all. It was just a common garden snake with unusual markings. The man did not die from poisonous venom. He had been struck dead by fear of a harmless strike of a common garden snake.

The moral of the story is to always be smart, but not too smart; scared, but not too scared.

Story Outline

I. An old farmer is in the field doing chores.

II. As he is working, he is bitten by a fierce looking snake.

III. Realizing the nearest doctor is one day's journey away, he falls dead.

IV. His wife finds his dead body. Seeing the snake nearby she understands what happened and she kills the snake with a shovel.

V. Later, she finds out the snake was not poisonous and that her husband died of fright.

VI. The moral of the story is to always be smart, but not too smart; scared, but not too scared.

17

TATANKA SAPA AND HIS MEDICINE BOW

by David R. Scott

Daniel Hawthorne lived with his father Joseph and his mother Annette in a tiny one-room log cabin. It was a time when the West was still "wild" and when each step had to be taken with caution. Rumors of "savage" Indian tribes were known by all the squatters in the area, and the people said that if the Indians didn't get you, then the land certainly would. Because of high upbringing, Daniel believed those rumors thoroughly, even though his folks were generally good people who didn't spread falsehoods.

One day, while hunting, Daniel came upon an old Indian man laying helplessly in the forest. His first thought was to flee, until he saw how sick the old man really was. His fear quickly passed and he felt he had no choice other than to help him.

Daniel helped the old man to his feet, and although no words were spoken—at least none that were comprehended by either of the two—a great bonding had taken place. Slowly the Indian, with the help of his new friend, made his way through the forest carrying with him the last of all he possessed. The Indian kept on speaking in a language foreign to Daniel, and Daniel kept telling the old man how much trouble he was going to get into when he got home. On and on the two walked until they could both see the tiny log home. Upon seeing the cabin, the Indian seemed hesitant—almost afraid. Perhaps he had heard equally frightening stories of the "savage" settlers.

Daniel's parents were furious with him for bringing home an Indian. In fact, his father wanted to shoot the old man. Daniel ended the dispute by stepping between the two and reminding his father of the lessons which he'd learned.

"If someone is in trouble, no matter who they may be, you help them. Remember what you told me?" Daniel told his father. At that point, the reluctant parents had no choice other than to help the old Indian.

Over the course of the next four weeks, Daniel and the Indian become very close friends. He discovered that the old man's name was Tatanka Sapa, Black Bull. From his bed, Black Bull showed Daniel how to knap arrowheads, set traps and play traditional Native American games. The two even learned words and sign language from each others language, but words did not need to be spoken for theirs was a friendship of the heart. As their friendship grew, however, the Indian continued to sicken.

Before the night of his death, Black Bull signaled for Daniel to come to his side. He reached beneath the bunk and pulled out a large bag made of animal skins, and motioned for Daniel to open it. Inside was the most beautiful bow, accompanied by ten meticulously made arrows. He gave the bow and arrows to Daniel and made the sign for brother, after which he passed away.

Several weeks went by, and one day Daniel fell asleep after finishing his chores. His mother and father were a half mile away gathering berries in the meadow. What they didn't know was that a grizzly bear was doing the same, keeping a careful eye on the couple at all times. The gnarled old bruin, eventually became bored with the two, and headed toward the cabin. Annette sensed that something was wrong. No birds were singing, no animals were chatting, even the wind was still. At that moment she saw the large bear enter the partially opened door of the cabin.

She and her husband rushed with great speed to save their son, yet they knew they were too far away to get there in time. When they finally reached the front door, they were astounded. There, sprawled out on the floor before them, was the great grizzly bear. On the bunk beside the bear lay their son fast asleep.

No one could figure out how the bear had died, for there was no obvious wound. But when Daniel's father was butchering the great beast, he found a beautiful handcrafted arrowhead embedded deep in its heart.

Quickly he dashed into the cabin where Daniel kept the bow and arrows given to him by the old Indian. The arrowhead retrieved from the bear's heart was a perfect match with the arrows given to Daniel, and when he counted the arrows in the quiver there were only nine, as for the tenth, it was gone.

Story Outline

I. Daniel Hawthorne lived on the frontier at a time when Indians were considered dangerous enemies.

II. He finds an ill, elderly Indian and brings him home to nurse back to health, much to Daniel's parents' objections.

III. The Indian returns Daniel's kindness with his friendship and a gift of a medicine bow. Then he dies.

IV. Daniel is asleep in the cabin one day, when his parents see a grizzly bear break into the cabin.

V. The frantic parents reach the cabin from their field, only to find the bear dead.

VI. Upon butchering the bear, Daniel's father finds an arrow has killed the bear and one of the arrows has mysteriously disappeared from the old Indian's quiver while Daniel slept.

18

PIQUA

by Scott E. Power

One hundred years ago, there was a man named Jonathan who worked for the railroad. His job was to bargain with landowners, primarily Indians, about the acquisition of the land needed to expand the railroad further west. His job was difficult and probably not worth the money. It was dangerous since people didn't like to give up land they loved. In reality, the landowners had little choice. The rich railroad owners, with their friends in government, would simply take the land if the rightful owners wouldn't give it up. It was unfair and unjust, but that's how it was done.

Word had spread amongst the natives that this sort of evil was happening. Other tribes had been "relocated" or simply killed off by mercenaries hired by the rich railroad owners. It was a no-win situation for the Indians.

Well, a certain tribe of Indians in what is now called Piqua, Ohio, decided they would fight for their land, even die if necessary, but would not give up their land to the railroad.

Word had reached the tribe that Jonathan would be coming to their camp to "bargain" with them for the land. The Indians knew the white man named Jonathan would make any promise necessary to get the land. And after that land was given over, the white man's promises would be broken like every time before. So the Indians would not give in. They would die first.

The Indians regarded the white man as evil. The white man called Jonathan was their enemy and like any other enemy must

be destroyed. So the Indians devised a plan to capture Jonathan and destroy him. They understood that truly evil people would only die if their spirit was burnt from their body on a stake. So the Indians arranged a traditional, ritualistic ceremony to burn Jonathan, their enemy, on a ten-foot stake placed on the sacred mound altar to the gods. When an enemy was killed at the stake like this, the ceremony ended after the spirit fled from the burning body to the abyss of the cosmos, never to return.

It was very easy for the Indians to capture Jonathan. He was traveling alone and wasn't expecting any trouble. He didn't know how despised he was amongst the natives. He didn't know they knew the truth. He didn't realize his very presence was a threat to their lives and culture. He didn't know he was so vulnerable. He didn't know it was a trap. He didn't realize he must be destroyed.

The Indians tied Jonathan's feet together and pulled him behind a horse, dragging him across the ground, through sticker bushes, against rocks and tree trunks. By the time they reached the ceremonial altar, Jonathan was covered with cuts and blood and bruises. His right arm was broken and he was screaming in pain and terror to stop. STOP!

It was no use. The Indians would not stop. Jonathan was an enemy, a white man, a paleface, a liar, a threat to the survival and culture of all Indians. He was to die an enemy's death. A death of terror, torture, pain, misery, and brutality.

By the time they had tied Jonathan to the stake he had lost consciousness. Once the fiery flames began to burn his flesh, Jonathan awoke to feel the pain. He screamed. AHHHHH!

Over the crackling of the flames, he could hear the drums pounding and the cries of the Indians as they danced and cheered the death of their enemy.

Jonathan could feel life leaving him, he no longer felt the pain. Things were turning black.

The Indians could see Jonathan dying. Burning black on the stake. They could see his spirit pulling from the body. They cheered louder and yelled louder. The drums were pounding at a frenzied pace. The death of their enemy was at hand!

Suddenly, there was a thunder and then all was silent. In the darkness, the Indians watched their enemy die as its spirit fled the cooked corpse. As the spirit left the body, the Indians heard it cry, "Otah-He-Wagh-PE-Qua" (Translated: He is risen from the ashes.) Even since then, the place where Jonathan died has been called Piqua.

He who works for evil eventually pays the price.

Story Outline

I. A tribe of Indians in Ohio hear that the railroad will send an agent to try talk them out of their land.

II. The Indians realize that these deals are always broken and are only a method of stealing their land.

III. The railroad land grabber is captured by Indians and burned at the stake.

IV. Upon his death his spirit cries "Otah-he-wagh-pe-qua"— "He is risen from the ashes."

V. Ever since then this place has been called Piqua.

19

THE LEGEND OF STIFFY GREEN

by the Reverend Mark M. Wilkins

Dogs, so the old proverb says, are man's best friend. While some might take issue with such conventional wisdom, for many others, dogs become more than mere pets—they become intimate friends and lifelong companions. And, if the tales told in the vicinity of Highland Lawn Cemetery in Terre Haute are to believed, at least one man has taken his relationship with his dog beyond life and into the realm of Indiana ghost lore.

According to legend, John Heinl was a well-known and well-beloved figure around Terre Haute in the early years of this century. An elderly gentleman without immediate family, Heinl spent much of his time taking long strolls through the town, his favorite pipe in hand, greeting and visiting his many friends throughout the growing area. Everyone, it seems, knew John Heinl, and the little dog that was the constant companion on his wanderings. Indeed, it seemed that the elderly gentleman was never seen in public without the company of his bulldog, Stiffy Green, walking protectively by his side.

Tradition suggests that the dog's unusual name came from the awkward gait of the animal, coupled with the fact that unlike most members of his breed, Stiffy was possessed of piercing green eyes. Indeed, new members of the community were sometimes startled when, stopping to speak to the affable Mr. Heinl, they found themselves under the close scrutiny of his small companion with the arresting green eyes. Stiffy Green was known to be fiercely protective of his master, never allowing strangers too close. It was even said that as John Heinl slept, Stiffy Green slumbered at the foot of his bed, guarding him in his sleep just as he did during the daylight hours.

In any case, the pair seemed inseparable, one never out of sight of the other. John lavished love and affection on his little dog, and Stiffy returned his affection by providing his master with company, comfort, and the companionship needed to ease the loneliness of his elderly years.

It was death that eventually parted the two boon companions. In 1920, the aged Mr. Heinl died in his sleep. While his passing caused much sadness among his many friends in the community, it was his dog Stiffy that was his chief mourner. The dog was inconsolable, refusing to leave his master's side even during his funeral and entombment in the family crypt at Highland Lawn Cemetery.

As the funeral service ended, several of Heinl's friends and distant relatives tried to leash the dog in order to lead it away to safety. At first, the dog kept his would-be rescuers away by snarling and showing his teeth. Even in death, it seems Stiffy refused to abandon his beloved master. Eventually, the dog was captured and taken to the home of one of John Heinl's distant relatives in Terre Haute. However, even in his new home Stiffy refused to be consoled.

Within a week the dog was reported missing. He was found shortly thereafter sitting mournfully by the door to the Heinl family mausoleum, patiently guarding the eternal sleep of his master. Again the dog was captured and returned to his new home, only to disappear once again. Over the next several months, this became routine. No matter how securely Stiffy Green was guarded or chained, eventually the little dog would escape the confines of

his new home, only to be found several miles away, at the door to the Heinl family crypt.

In time, Stiffy Green's new masters gave up trying to keep the dog at home, and allowed him to take up residence in the cemetery grounds. At first, workers there tried to bring food and water to the solemn little animal, but these were refused with a snarl and a grimace from those flashing green eyes. For weeks, Stiffy Green sat nearly motionless at the entrance of the Heinl tomb, seeming to challenge anyone who sought to enter. Through rain and cold and darkness Stiffy Green stood resolutely at his post outside the grave, as loyal as ever to the master within.

And it was here that his body was eventually found. Time, weather and lack of nutrition had eventually taken their toll. A word of the dog's death spread, a number of John Heinl's old friends gathered to discuss what should be done with the animal's body. While some recommended that it should simply be discarded, others suggested that it would only be appropriate to allow the animal to be entombed next to his master and friend. A fund was established, and the body of the dog was transported to a local taxidermist, who stuffed the remains and transformed his corpse into the unnerving semblance of life. The dog was stuffed in the sitting position he had maintained for months outside the Heinl tomb. The eyes were left open, with brilliant green glass orbs put in place of the real ones.

When the grisly job was completed, the body of Stiffy Green was placed inside the Heinl tomb, next to the crypt of the master he had served so long and so well. It seemed that his service to John Heinl was at last completed. But perhaps not quite completed. Several months after Stiffy Green took his place in the Heinl family mausoleum, a maintenance worker was leaving the cemetery grounds early one warm fall evening. Just as he was packing his car for the ride home, he heard the excited bark of a small dog coming from the direction of the Heinl family crypt. Since the presence of wild dogs was, of course, discouraged by the cemetery work force, he quickly decided to investigate.

As he neared the precincts of the Heinl mausoleum, the sound became clearer, and the frightened workman stopped in his tracks. Much to his horror, he realized that the sound he was hearing was a familiar one. He had heard it frequently, months before, in this very spot. It was the barking of Stiffy Green. Then, as suddenly as it had begun, the barking had stopped.

Summoning all of his courage, the workman crept closer to the grave site and stared at the mausoleum through the line of trees that surrounded it. He heaved a relieved sigh. There was nothing unusual around the crypt. Deciding that this had been nothing more than the barking of a stray dog, or perhaps the product of his imagination, the workman turned and began to walk back toward his car.

Then something else caught his attention. Out of the corner of his eye he caught the movement of a figure, or a pair of figures, in the distance. He turned once again and stared with horrified fascination at what he saw. Through the dusk of early evening, he saw, walking quietly along the fence that separated Highland Lawn from the surrounding community, the figure of an elderly man smoking a pipe. By his side, there padded silently the figure of a small dog. All of this, of course, was enough to unnerve the unfortunate workman. But there was one further aspect to the scene that caused his blood to chill; even from a distance, he could clearly see that the dog's eyes sparkled bright green.

Since that fateful day in October of 1921, legend has it that many people in the vicinity of Highland Lawn Cemetery have reported hearing the barking of a dog coming from within the confines of the cemetery grounds at odd hours of the day and night. A few have even reported seeing the figure of an elderly man, walking on cool autumn evenings, strolling amidst the windswept leaves. While their descriptions of the figure do vary slightly, they all agree on one point; walking serenely by his side is the figure of a small bulldog with green eyes – eyes now peaceful and content, since dog and master have been reunited beyond death itself.

Story Outline

I. The elderly John Heinl had a faithful bulldog. The dog was named Stiffy Green, due to its awkward gait and its piercing eyes.

II. The two were inseparable, until John Heinl died.

III. The dog, Stiffy Green, refused to leave the crypt mausoleum no matter how people tried to remove him from the area.

IV. The dog died of starvation and was stuffed and placed beside his master in the family crypt.

V. A worker one night heard a dog barking and upon investigating, saw an old man and a dog, resembling John Heinl and Stiffy Green, going on an evening walk – an event that continues occasionally even to this day.

20

ONE CRUEL JOKE

by Scott E. Power

On a particular Friday night—no one is exactly sure when but many believe it was Friday the thirteenth—three boys were walking down a dusty road, amidst the fields and farms of northwestern Iowa. The road was very well known to the boys. Each had travelled it many times before. But on that night it was said that the moon hid behind the clouds like a veil, and the darkness was so thick that the road didn't look quite right.

As the boys walked, each one tried to scare the others with frightful stories. Each laughed with disbelief, except Joe. The other two boys could sense that Joe was somewhat scared by the stories and the dark road, so they decided to play a trick.

Soon the boys walked by the gate of the local cemetery. Anyone who had died since 1901, when the cemetery had been established, was put to rot there. Many tall tales had been told about the graveyard, some saying that on certain nights a person could hear the voices of the dead crying out for life.

As the boys stood in front of the fog-covered cemetery and glared into the entrance, the mist seemed to swallow the tombstones and crosses into itself. Joe began to tremble with fright. When the other boys saw how scared he was, they knew it was time to play the trick.

"Inside the cemetery is a grave that is so filled with evil that anyone who stands on the grave and stabs a knife in the ground will die," said Chris.

The third boy, Frank, continued the story. "Yeah, they say that if anyone stands on the grave, sticks a knife in the grave they will turn white as snow and die. I would try it, but I don't think I have enough courage. Are you brave enough, Chris?" asked Frank.

"No way!" exclaimed Chris. "I'm a coward. But I know someone who isn't a coward. Someone brave enough to even stick the knife in the grave. Someone who is too smart to believe such nonsense."

"Who?" asked Joe.

"You, silly! You're the bravest and smartest guy I know. Even Chris says that. Only you can do it. Chris and I are cowards," explained Frank.

In the distance the boys heard an owl hoot in the night.

"Well, what?" asked Joe.

"Are you brave enough to stand on the grave or are we wrong about you? Surely you're not a coward. Are you going to test the evil grave or aren't you? You can even use my knife to stick in the ground and prove that you were there," said Chris. "It has my name on it. It will show that you really had the courage to stand on that grave."

"O.K.," Joe answered.

Frank and Chris led Joe through the fog and up to the cemetery gate. Of course, there wasn't actually a grave. But they knew of a grave with a really old, scary-looking tombstone. Joe was told to go to the old McDowell grave and stand on it—and to stick the knife into the grave to prove he had done it.

Approaching the cemetery with fictitious apprehension, the two boys stopped at the cemetery gate, "Here it is," whispered Frank.

"Boy, does it look bizarre. I would never be strong enough to do what you're going to do, Joe. For being just a kid, you're quite a man," Chris exclaimed.

"Well, are you going to stand there or go in? Or were we wrong about you?" threatened Frank.

Up until this point, Joe had been hoping that they wouldn't really want him to go through with it. His heart was beating fast. He didn't believe he would actually die, but how could he tell otherwise? Would there be such a legend if someone hadn't died while standing on the grave before? People wouldn't just make up something so horrible as a lie about an evil grave, would they?

Joe couldn't believe his friends thought of him as brave and strong. It made him feel good. But if he had known they were lying and playing a mean trick on him, he would have hated them. Joe hated being the sucker. They played jokes on him a lot, knowing he could be fooled easily. But they were his friends and the grave was a different thing. If they thought he would actually die, they wouldn't want him to do it anyway.

Joe said "O.K., I'll do it. If you think I'm so brave, I guess I am. You guys know me pretty well. Besides, I don't believe the legend anyway."

As Joe walked through the gate Frank and Chris looked at each other and grinned. They knew what to do once Joe was standing on the grave.

Finally, Joe was standing on the edge of the grave, looking at the tombstone. Through the darkness and the fog, he could barely read the letters on the tombstone. It said, "Russell McDowell, 1854-1901, The first man buried in this cemetery, Rest in Peace."

Joe stood in fear all alone in the cemetery surrounded by the swirling mist of fog. As Joe lifted his right foot to step onto the grave, his heart was nearly pounding a hole through his chest. His palms were sweating and his stomach began to hurt. "I shouldn't be doing this," Joe thought to himself, "I'm not brave."

But it was too late. His honor was at stake. Aside from that, his right foot was on the grave now, and his left was following. Within seconds Joe was standing on the grave. His heart was still pounding like a hammer. He was proud of himself for taking the step. Now all he had to do was stab the knife into the ground.

At that moment, Joe raised the knife high above his head and with all his strength stabbed the knife blade into the ground. But because of his intense nervousness, he wasn't watching where he was sticking the blade and consequently stabbed the knife through the canvas on the running shoe of his left foot. Joe's only thought was to get off that grave and out of there as quickly as possible.

He tried to turn and run, but it seemed something in the grave had grabbed him by the foot and wouldn't let him go.

Chris and Frank waited a long time at the cemetery gate, hearing nothing. Finally they decided that Joe had played a trick on them and had gone out the back way, leaving them standing around like idiots in the cold night fog.

It was only the next day when they realized how their trick had backfired. The police came to arrest Chris, for they found his knife stuck through their dead friend's shoe on an old grave at the cemetery.

Story Outline

I. Three boys are walking down a dirt road late one Friday night when they pass an old graveyard.

II. Two of the boys know that Joe is quite gullible and decide to play a joke on him.

III. They tell him that inside the graveyard there is a grave so filled with evil that if a person stands on the grave he will die.

IV. The boys tell Joe that they don't really believe it but are too cowardly to try it. They tell Joe that they think he is brave and strong enough to test the legend and suggest that he should.

V. One of the boys even gives Joe his knife to use to prove that he stood on the grave.

VI. Joe takes the knife and walks to the grave, where he finally gets enough courage to stand on the grave and plunge the knife into the ground.

VII. Joe tries to run but he feels as though something from the grave has grabbed hold of his leg.

VIII. The other boys get tired of waiting for Joe, thinking that he left them there in the night fog by themselves as a joke on them.

IX. The next day the police arrest Chris, for his knife was stuck in his dead friend's shoe in the cemetery.

21

BENEATH THE LONE POST

by David R. Scott

As a young boy, Brenton Fielding had always been fascinated with the lifestyles of Native Americans. Each day he would tromp through the fields near his home, combing the turned soil for arrowheads and artifacts. His room was cluttered with antique books, authentic clothing and other relics that he found in the woods.

In his later years he became less and less interested in Indians and began his career in agriculture. He enjoyed his life on the farm and enjoyed spending time in his fields tending crops. One day however, he found something that rekindled his love for Native Americans . . . a flint ax head. The ax still held its polished edge and became the farmer's most prized possession. He carved a beautiful handle for the blade and always carried it with him on his tractor when he worked.

One day, while reaping his autumn harvest, he accidentally lost the treasured ax head. Brenton did not continue working, but instead began looking for the missing artifact. Much to his dismay, he could not find it anywhere, and he sadly returned to his home.

That night, Brenton dreamt that he was again a small boy coming home from school through the woods. Suddenly, an Indian appeared and began chasing him down the path in the direction of his home. The Indian's face was painted black, and his hair was tied in long braids down either side of his chest.

Young Brenton ran faster than ever before, and with each step he could hear the Indian brave asking for his sacred ax to be returned. Brenton blasted through the front door, grabbed the ax and, out of fear, turned and killed the Indian with a blow to the head.

In his dream he dragged the Indian far out into the field so that no one would find his remains. He buried the body as deeply into the ground as he possibly could near a lone fence post.

A singe crash of thunder awakened him from his nightmare. Brenton walked over to the window and gazed though the curtain of rain sprinkling over his crops. Due to the darkness he could see hardly anything at all, yet suddenly, a great flash of lightning ignited the sky, and in that one instant the only thing he saw was the lone fence post of his nightmare.

Days went by, and then weeks. The urge to dig beneath the post was overwhelming, yet the fear of what he might find there was even greater. Winter soon set in and along with the cold months came constant torment. All Brenton could do was peer out his window at the post swirled with a beard of frosty white snow. Everyday he hoped he would come across the ax head, to prove that the dream was a figment of his imagination, but it never appeared.

The breakup of winter and the blooming of spring was fast upon him. Brenton had nearly forgotten about the ax simply because he was preparing for the planting season. But while carrying a sack of seed to the barn, Brenton noticed the long fence pole, and once more this torment returned. Running to the barn, he grabbed a spade and headed for the fence post.

Quickly he began digging into the soft muddy earth. His shovel was heavy and sweat poured from his brow, yet his pace was rhythmically steady. The spring mud slowly began piling up around his feet, and although tired he could not bring himself to slow down. Finally he heard a click.

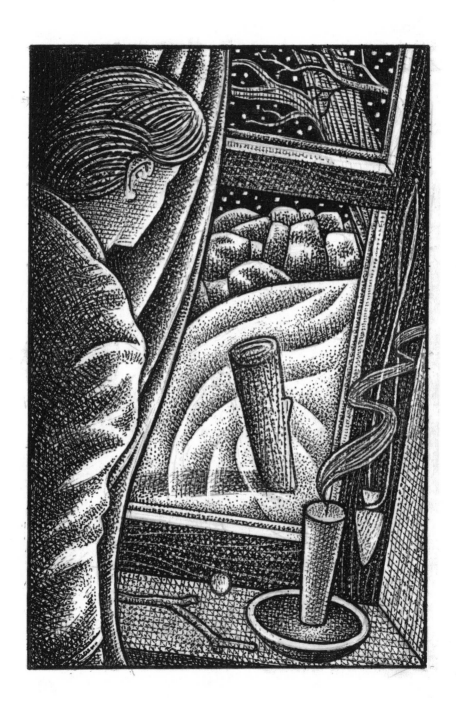

He cleaned the remaining mud away with his hands only to discover the missing ax head embedded deeply into a human skull. Next to the skull lay a rotting wooden handle . . . it was the handle that he had carved.

Leaving the items where he found them, Brenton filled the hole and placed his best arrowhead on top of the grave. The next day the arrowhead was gone, and from that day forth Brenton never revealed the story of the lone post to anyone.

Story Outline

I. A farmer finds an ax head, which he cherishes until the day he loses it in his field while working.

II. He dreams that an Indian brave is chasing him, asking for the ax back. In the dream he kills the brave with the ax and buries them both in the field near a lone fence post.

III. Thunder awakens him from his dream and in a lightning flash he sees a lone fence post on the property.

IV. He resists the urge to dig beneath the fence post until the following spring.

V. As he digs beside the fence post he finds the missing ax head, deeply embedded into a human skull, with the handle that he had carved for the ax rotting next to it.

VI. He reburies the ax and skull and leaves his best arrowhead as an offering on top of the grave.

22

THE NIGHT VISITOR AT LOCKWOOD INN

by David R. Scott

There are several versions of a similar folklore tale, but of those I prefer this adoption by David Scott for campfire story telling.

Tucked away in the corner of a New England village sat the Lockwood Inn, an old stone mansion owned by the Blanchfords. The Blanchfords had inherited a vast expanse of wealth from their deceased relatives, and because the mid-1700s were a dark time overrun by pillaging thieves, the Blanchfords were extremely careful about whom they allowed to stay at their Inn.

One night, William Blanchford and his son Craig were playing an arduous game of chess, while Martha Blanchford busied herself with her knitting needles. Every now and then she would chuckle at her husband, who cursed as Craig continued to destroy him in their game.

Outside the wind whipped the tops of the trees, and could be heard howling down the cobblestone chimney and blowing the coals to a deep glowing red within the hearth. The rains pounded the roof top, and an occasional flash of lightning would illuminate the dimly lit den. Beatrice Whitfield, the inn's maid, who had served the Blanchfords for over 35 years, stirred the coals beneath the cast-iron tea kettle.

"A bit more tea, Mrs. Blanchford?" the maid pleasantly asked.

"Why yes, thank you, Beatrice," Martha Blanchford responded with a radiant smile. "It most certainly is a dreadful night, don't you think so?"

"Aye, that it is, ma'am. Pleases the soul to be within the confines of a warm and cheery den," the maid said as she filled Mrs. Blanchford's tea cup.

Just then a heavy knock came forth from the inn's massive oak doors.

All faces stared down the corridor. "Now, who do you suppose that could be out in this dreary weather?" Beatrice said, walking down the lamplit corridor.

"Best let me answer it, Beatrice. Something may be wrong." William Blanchford stated impatiently, angered that someone would interrupt his game of chess.

William held the oil lamp in one hand, and opened the door just a crack to see a black-cloaked figure with a hood drawn loosely over the visitor's head. The drops of rain framed the hood with liquid beads, and the visitor's split leather boots were well-worn from travel. In one hand he clung to a knotted walking cane, and in the other was a small burlap sack.

"Please . . . please . . . I beg of you sir. Share with me the warmth of your fire and tea. Have mercy on a pitiful old man who has nothing." The old man's voice stuttered and cracked as it came forth from his lips.

William stood silently without expression while the chilling winds filled the warm room. He had sympathy for the old man, yet he was still rather apprehensive about letting strangers into his home.

"Oh William, can't you see the old man is freezing? Let him in," Martha said over her husband's shoulder.

William opened the door. "I'm sorry, old boy, but one can never be too sure anymore around here." William explained. "You do understand, don't you?"

"Aye, them bandits prowl on a night like tonight, yet all I ask for is a warm place by the fire, and a hot cup a' tea, then I shall be on my way," the old man said as he limped his way through the door. All eyes stared at the man's rather strange walk.

"Aye, 'tis proof that them scum roam the village on nights like this. One slit the back of me leg three months ago, and stole all I had," the old man solemnly said.

"Oh, you poor dear, sit down by the fire, and Beatrice will get you some tea," Martha said while helping the old man into a chair. Beatrice poured the old man a spot of tea, still not trusting his "good nature."

Soon the old man stopped shivering, and politely asked for another cup. Craig and William went off to their quarters, and Martha continued to pamper the visitor.

"Well, Beatrice, I am off to bed. Sir, if there is anything you need, Beatrice will help you," Martha finally said.

"Thank you ma'am, you are too kind," the old man said with a sinister smile.

In a few short moments, Martha's echoing footsteps were swallowed by the drone of the storm, and the only audible sound remaining was that of the dry wood popping as it burned in the hearth.

"Well my dear, where is it that you sleep? Do you not have your own quarters in such a lofty abode?" the visitor asked inquisitively.

"Yes of course, but I shall sleep here on the settee in case you need my assistance . . . good night sir."

"Good night," the old man said with a disappointed tone.

Beatrice laid on the settee pretending to be asleep. She breathed in a deep rhythmic pattern, and let her eyes open only as slits. She did not trust the old man in the black cloak; something about him drew her suspicion. Perhaps she was being foolish. Maybe he was simply an old man with no place to go. Maybe he was telling the truth, and maybe he did simply need the comfort and care of loving people such as the Blanchfords.

However, after an hour, her instincts proved not to be fiction. The old man slowly turned and stared with cold eyes for a long time into the eyes of the maid. She managed not to break her rhythmic breathing, and kept her face expressionless. She watched as the old man stood from his resting place and moved across the room, never limping once. In the flickering firelight, he grabbed his small burlap sack and untied the twine that sealed its opening. Beatrice watched as the night visitor reached within the sack, and then she froze in terror.

The old man had pulled from the sack a severed human hand, and placed it on the wooden table near the stone hearth. Beatrice bit deep into her lower lip to prevent herself from screaming. She wanted to run and fetch Mr. Blanchford and his son, but she figured her best bet was to stay put. The old man retrieved a candle from the fireplace's mantel, and poured the hot wax into the palm of the hand on the table. He then placed the candle in the wax to prevent it from tipping. Again he looked deep into the face of the old maid, but she appeared to be fast asleep.

And then, he chanted in a whispering tone:

"Ancient hand from forest deep;
Bring all within a soundless sleep.
Grant them sleep throughout this night;
To not awake till morning light.

Allow your fingers to unfold;
And point me to the Lockwood gold.
In silence now I watch and stand;
Now point, now point your hallow hand."

Suddenly the fire flared, and a flash of blue lightning filled the tiny room, followed moments later by a deep crash of thunder. The candle's flame grew brighter within the open hand, and soon its fingers moved. The index finger pointed straight while the others slowly closed, and then the hand began to spin on the small oak table. It spun around the room twice, slowed, and pointed not toward the gold's hiding place, but directly at the maid. Beatrice bit again into her lip, till it was bleeding within her mouth, yet still continued to breath rhythmically.

The old man seemed puzzled and repeated his chant. Beatrice could now clearly see the accents of his gaunt facial features in the flickering candlelight. His beady eyes were wide and wild with greed, and his teeth seemed to grind as he repeated the chant. His body was hunched over the candle and silhouetted by the fire, and his bony hands stretched skyward over the flames of the candle.

Again the somewhat withered hand spun around the table, only to slow and stop with its long wrinkled finger pointing in the direction of Beatrice. The night visitor slowly looked away from the candle at the maid, squinting from the blindness of staring intensely into the steady flame. She did not break her rhythm, even though her head was begging for oxygen.

The old man carefully picked up the hand, which was still pointed at Beatrice, and slowly crossed the room toward where she lay. Using the candle within the palm of the hand as an added source of light, the night visitor crept toward the maid. Then,

suddenly, he stopped when he heard a noise in the next room that startled him.

Quickly, he turned to see what had caused the noise, only to discover that it was the Blanchford's cat. Yet, when he turned the pointing hand away from Beatrice, he made another discovery -- the outstretched index finger had folded and closed.

Slowly, he turned and again faced the sleeping maid, and upon doing so, the index finger pointed at her once more. Her heart pounded and her mouth went dry. The old man slowly turned the hand away again, making an effort to watch both the hand and the maid as he did so. Sure enough the finger closed, yet when he aimed the hand at the maid, it opened once more, pointing directly as the needle on a compass.

Certainly, if the old man realized that she was awake he would kill her, yet she remained motionless and watched as the old man drew nearer. A wry smile painted its way across his lips, and his steel black eyes twinkled in the flickering candlelight.

Soon he stood hunched over the old woman, staring at her with the intensity of a hungry falcon. The candlelight seemed to lick her face, and the only thing visible through her partially open eyes, was the long bony finger protruding from the hand on which the candle was perched. It was, of course, aiming directly between her eyes.

The old man continued to study her face. Certainly he knew that she was not asleep . . . was he merely playing a game with her, or was he genuinely deceived. The old woman did not know. He seemed to stare for an eternity, and then finally retreated to the table near the stone hearth. Slowly, he placed the hand upon the old table and again said his chant, but the finger continued to point toward Beatrice Whitfield. She knew that she would eventually have no other alternative but to flee. Her mind raced and her heart beat wildly within the prison of her rib cage. The old man's eyes shortly fell once again upon the maid, waiting for her to move, when at last she did.

She exploded from the settee and ran up the massive staircase quickly as her legs would carry her. Behind she heard the night visitor coming after her, yet he wasn't running, he was merely walking, almost as though he knew he would capture her. Beatrice blasted the Blanchford's bedroom door nearly off its hinges, and shook both of them violently, but neither stirred. She screamed into their ears, but no avail. She could hear the heavy footsteps echo throughout the long hollow corridor, yet still they were not running, simply walking.

She ran to another hallway that led back down some winding stairs. She was about to run out of the front door when she glanced into the sitting room and noticed the hand pointing its gnarled finger and following her every step. Quickly, she lunged out and cast the hand within the flames of the hearth, and then headed for the door. The hand suddenly burst into flames with a violent explosion and the old man screamed in apparent pain. She heard a commotion upstairs as the Blanchfords suddenly awakened from their spell.

The old man fumbled with the front door and staggered through it into the blustery night outside, never to be seen again.

Beatrice was honored for her intuition and her bravery. It pays not only to have common sense, but the courage to back it up.

Story Outline

I. An old man is let into an inn owned by a family called the Blanchfords on a stormy night long ago in New England.

II. The housemaid, Beatrice, does not trust the old man and tells him that she will sleep in the main room with him "in case he needs anything."

III. Beatrice fools the old man into thinking that she is asleep. He pulls a severed hand from a bag, placing a spell on the family to make them all sleep. Then he asks the hand to point out the inn's treasure. The hand points at Beatrice.

IV. Beatrice sees her chance and runs for the owners' bedroom, but they are in a deep sleep.

V. She grabs the severed hand and throws it into the fire, causing the old man much pain, allowing the Blanchfords to awaken, and thus saving herself and their fortune.

The moral of the story is: use common sense and have the courage to back it up.

23

THE TELL-TALE HEART

by Edgar Allan Poe

True! – nervous – very, very dreadfully nervous I had been and am; but why will you say that I am mad? The disease had sharpened my senses – not destroyed – not dulled them. Above all was the sense of hearing acute. I heard all things in the heaven and in the earth. I heard many things in hell. How, then, am I mad? Hearken! and observe how healthily – how calmly I can tell you the whole story.

It is impossible to say how first the idea entered my brain; but once conceived, it haunted me day and night. Object there was none. Passion there was none. I loved the old man. He had never wronged me. He had never given me insult. For his gold I had no desire. I think it was his eye! Yes, it was this! One of his eyes resembled that of a vulture – a pale blue eye, with a film over it. Whenever it fell upon me, my blood ran cold; and so by degrees – very gradually – I made up my mind to take the life of the old man, and thus rid myself of the eye forever.

Now this is the point. You fancy me mad. Madmen know nothing. But you should have seen me. You should have seen how wisely I proceeded – with what caution – with what foresight – with what dissimulation I went to work! I was never kinder to the old man than during the whole week before I killed him. And every night, about midnight, I turned the latch of his door and opened it – oh, so gently! And then, when I had made an opening sufficient for my head, I put in a dark lantern, all closed, closed, so that no light shone out, and then I thrust in my head. Oh, you would have laughed to see how cunningly I thrust it in! I moved it slowly – very, very slowly, so that I might not disturb the old man's sleep. It took me an hour to place my whole head within the opening so far that I could see him as he lay upon his bed. Ha! – would a madman have been so wise as this? And then, when my head was well in the room, I undid the lantern cautiously – oh, so cautiously – cautiously (for the hinges creaked) – I undid it just so much that a single thin ray fell upon the vulture eye. And this I did for seven long nights – every night just at midnight – but I found the eye always closed; and so it was impossible to do the work; for it was not the old man who vexed me, but his Evil Eye. And every morning, when the day broke, I went boldly into the chamber, and spoke courageously to him, calling him by name in a hearty tone, and inquiring how he had passed the night. So you see he would have been a very profound old man, indeed, to suspect that every night, just at twelve, I looked in upon him while he slept.

Upon the eighth night I was more than usually cautious in opening the door. A watch's minute hand moves more quickly than did mine. Never before that night had I felt the extent of my own powers – of my sagacity. I could scarcely contain my feelings of triumph. To think that there I was, opening the door, little by little, and he not even to dream of my secret deeds or thoughts. I fairly chuckled at the idea; and perhaps he heard me; for he moved on the bed suddenly, as if startled. Now you may think that I drew back – but no. His room was as black as pitch with the thick of darkness (for the shutters were close fastened, through fear of robbers), and so I knew that he could not see the opening of the door, and I kept pushing it on steadily, steadily.

I had my head in, and was about to open the lantern, when my thumb slipped upon the tin fastening, and the old man sprang up in the bed, crying out – "Who's there?"

I kept quite still and said nothing. For a whole hour I did not move a muscle, and in the meantime I did not hear him lie down. He was still sitting up in the bed listening – just as I have done, night after night, hearkening to the death watches in the wall.

Presently I heard a slight groan, and I knew it was the groan of mortal terror. It was not a groan of pain or of grief – oh, no! – it was the low stifled sound that arises from the bottom of the soul when overcharged with awe. I knew the sound well. Many a night, just at midnight, when all the world slept, it has welled up from my own bosom, deepening, with its dreadful echo, the terrors that distracted me. I say I knew it well. I knew what the old man felt, and pitied him, although I chuckled at heart. I knew that he had been lying awake ever since the first slight noise, when he had turned in the bed. His fears had been ever since growing upon him. He had been trying to fancy them causeless, but could not. He had been saying to himself – "It is nothing but the wind in the chimney – it is only a mouse crossing the floor," or "It is merely a cricket which has made a single chirp." Yes, he has been trying to comfort himself with these suppositions; but he had found all in vain. All in vain; because Death, in approaching him, had stalked with his black shadow before him, and enveloped the victim. And it was the mournful influence of the unperceived shadow that caused him to feel – although he neither saw nor heard – to feel the presence of my head within the room.

When I had waited a long time, very patiently, without hearing him lie down, I resolved to open a little – a very, very little crevice in the lantern. So I opened it – you cannot imagine how stealthily, stealthily – until, at length, a single dim ray, like the thread of a spider, shot from out the crevice and full upon the vulture eye.

It was open – wide, wide open – and I grew furious as I gazed upon it. I saw it with perfect distinctness – all a dull blue, with a hideous veil over it that chilled the very marrow in my bones; but I could see nothing else of the old man's face or person, for I had directed the ray as if by instinct, precisely upon the damned spot.

And now have I not told you that what you mistake for madness is but over-acuteness of the senses? – now, I say, there came to my ear a low, dull quick sound, such as a watch makes when enveloped in cotton. I knew that sound well too. It was the beating of the old man's heart. It increased my fury, as the beating of a drum stimulates the soldier into courage.

But even yet I refrained and kept still. I scarcely breathed. I held the lantern motionless. How steadily I could maintain the ray upon the eye. Meantime the hellish tattoo of the heart increased. It grew quicker and quicker, and louder and louder every instant. The old man's terror must have been extreme! It grew louder, I say, louder every moment! – do you mark me well? I have told you that I am nervous: so I am. And now at the dead hour of the night, amid the dreadful silence of that old house, so strange a noise as this excited me to uncontrollable terror. Yet, for some minutes longer I refrained and stood still. But the beating grew louder, louder! I thought the heart must burst. And now a new anxiety seized me – the sound would be heard by a neighbor! The old man's hour had come! With a loud yell, I threw open the lantern and leaped into the room. He shrieked once – once only. In an instant I dragged him to the floor, and pulled the heavy bed over him. I then smiled gaily, to find the deed so far done. But, for many minutes, the heart beat on with a muffled sound. This, however, did not vex me; it would not be heard through the wall. At length it ceased. The old man was dead. I removed the bed and examined the corpse. Yes, he was stone, stone dead. I placed my hand upon the heart and held it there many minutes. There was no pulsation. He was stone dead. His eye would trouble me no more.

If still you think me mad, you will think so no longer when I describe the wise precautions I took for the concealment of the body. The night waned, and I worked hastily, but in silence. First of all I dismembered the corpse. I cut off the head and the arms and the legs.

I then took up three planks from the flooring of the chamber, and deposited all between the scantlings. I then replaced the boards so cleverly, so cunningly, that no human eye – not even his – could have detected anything wrong. There was nothing to wash out – no stain of any kind – no blood-spot whatever. I had been too wary for that. A tub had caught all – ha! ha!

When I had made an end of these labors, it was four o'clock – still dark as midnight. As the bell sounded the hour, there came a knocking at the street door. I went down to open it with a light heart – for what had I now to fear? There entered three men, who introduced themselves, with perfect suavity, as officers of the police. A shriek had been heard by a neighbor during the night; suspicion of foul play had been aroused; information had been lodged at the police office, and they (the officers) had been deputed to search the old gentleman.

I smiled – for what had I to fear? I bade the gentlemen welcome. The shriek, I said, was my own in a dream. The old man, I mentioned, was absent in the country. I took my visitors all over the house. I bade them search – search well. I led them, at length,

to his chamber. I showed them his treasures, secure, undisturbed. In the enthusiasm of my confidence, I brought chairs into the room, and desired them here to rest from their fatigues, while I myself, in the wild audacity of my perfect triumph, placed my own seat upon the very spot beneath which reposed the corpse of the victim.

The officers were satisfied. My manner had convinced them. I was singularly at ease. They sat, and while I answered cheerily, they chatted familiar things. But, ere long, I felt myself getting pale and wished them gone. My head ached, and I fancied a ringing in my ears: but still they sat and still chatted. The ringing became more distinct – it continued and became more distinct: I talked more freely to get rid of the feeling: but it continued and gained definitiveness – until, at length, I found that the noise was not within my ears.

No doubt I now grew very pale – but I talked more fluently, and with a heightened voice. Yet the sound increased – and what could I do? It was a low, dull, quick sound – much such a sound as a watch makes when enveloped in cotton. I gasped for breath – and yet the officers heard it not. I talked more quickly – more vehemently; but the noise steadily increased. I arose and argued about trifles, in a high key and with violent gesticulations, but the noise steadily increased. Why would they not be gone? I paced the floor to and fro with heavy strides, as if excited to fury by the observation of the men – but the noise steadily increased. Oh God! what could I do? I foamed – I raved – I swore! I swung the chair upon which I had been sitting, and grated it upon the boards, but the noise arose over all and continually increased. It grew louder – louder – louder! And still the men chatted pleasantly, and smiled. Was it possible they heard not? Almighty God! – no, no! They heard! – They suspected! – They knew! – They were making a mockery of my horror! – this I thought and this I think. But any thing was better that this agony! Any thing was more tolerable than this derision! I could bear those hypocritical smiles no longer! I felt that I must scream or die! – and now – again! – listen! louder! louder! louder! louder! –"Villains!" I shrieked, "dissemble no more! I admit the deed! – tear up the planks! – here, here! – it is the beating of his hideous heart!"

Story Outline

I. A kind, old man has a blind eye, which becomes the object of obsession for his housekeeper.

II. The housekeeper makes careful plans to kill the old man. He creeps into the gentleman's room each night to spy upon the old man and his "evil eye."

III. One night, as the eye watches him, the housekeeper kills the old man. After he is dead, the housekeeper dismembers him and hides the body parts under the floor in the old man's bedroom.

IV. The police arrive after he has cleaned up, saying that a neighbor heard a scream.

V. He says he screamed during a nightmare, that the old man is away, and shows them through the house.

VI. He sits with them in the old man's bedroom and places his chair over the floor where the dismembered body is buried.

VII. While talking with the police, he hears a noise which he is convinced is the beating heart of the old man.

VIII. He talks as loud as he can, rants and raves, even eventually throws his chair – but the beating continues while the police smile at him.

IX. He finally gives up and shows them where the old man is buried.

24

THE CURSE OF THE SILVER SEAL

by David R. Scott

The old wooden boat sliced its way through the sea, plotting a course due south toward the lost ship *Anna Marie*. Jonathan Moore had been a treasure hunter for years and with some degree of success; in fact he had supported himself solely on his findings.

His hardy crew of five gazed without expression at the vast expanse of water that heaved before them. Their faces were wind-swept and their hands were callused, yet their souls remained undaunted, and their lust for loot drove them forth regardless of Jonathan Moore's stories.

You see, this was not Mr. Moore's first dive on the *Anna Marie*; he had been on this quest once before with his lifelong partner Thomas Hues. They too had that gleam in their eyes, eyes which hunger for gold, that passion that makes man a slave of mammon. They too had ignored the legend and lore that surrounded the sunken ship in hopes of discovering a well-spring of riches. They had found the wreck and exposed a silver seal that stated that any man who dare venture near the ruins of the *Anna Marie* would either die or be forever cursed. When they dove a second time, only one came to the surface . . . and that was Jonathan. His partner's oxygen tank had somehow failed, leaving him prey to the merciless sea.

To that day Jonathan believed the drama to be an accident. His desire to strike it rich extended far beyond the curse of the silver seal. So, with his tiny crew, he looked out over the tossing mass of dark water, and dreamt of the *Anna Marie*. His movements matched that of the vessel as it crossed the hills and valleys produced by the churning sea. The sun hung low in the western sky, dipping every now and then beneath a rolling wall of water, then returning to provide the final light of day. Tomorrow was to be the greatest day in the lives of the crew, the greatest . . . or perhaps the last.

The wind beyond the cabin's wall pulsed throughout the night and the crew lay fast asleep. Jonathan remained awake however, poring over maps, double-checking compass headings, and pacing the deck due to his excitement—or was it due to fear? Surely not. Jonathan reassured himself that what happened on his last trip was nothing more than a terrible accident. Finally, he decided that it was time to turn in, for the day ahead was to be a long and hopefully a bountiful one.

Jonathan was on his way back toward the ship's main cabin when something caught his eye. It was a figure standing near the oxygen tanks, yet Jonathan could not quite tell who it was. The wind picked up and licked his face, and he squinted from the salt spray that washed into his eyes. The figure was hunched over with its back to Jonathan and it appeared to be checking the pressure in the oxygen tanks. Jonathan waddled with the rocking boat toward the figure, attempting to pierce the darkness with his tear-swollen eyes.

"Bishop . . . Bishop, is that . . . you?" he asked curiously, thinking it might be his first mate.

He moved closer still and repeated his question, the only response being the growl of the sea. Finally he stood above the person and played his hand on the man's shoulder. "Bishop, why didn't you . . ." At that moment, the figure rapidly turned around and Jonathan staggered back. He was too afraid to speak, too terrified to move. The figure before him was a man who had long since been dead. It was a man that Jonathan knew well . . . the figure was none other than Thomas Hues himself.

His face was pale, preserved, yet washed white from lying beneath the sea for so many years, and his long wiry hair came to rest upon his bony chest dripping wet with salt water. His eyes were as empty as the sea itself and his gaunt and bony body was hunched over. Thomas Hues' voice crackled as it came forth from his broken lips;

"A sunken ship 'neath stormy sea; a silver seal harken to thee.

Taunting treasure fathoms down; with gold from lands of Spanish crown.

Ignore the lust within your soul; or pay an old friend a heavy toll.

Turn back! Turn back and loot no more; stand safe upon the ocean shore.

If not, old friend, then you must dwell; without a soul in ocean's hell.

A hollow body fathoms deep; a nightmare that is absent sleep.

Harken to the silver seal, or dine well on your final meal.

'Tis best to have an empty purse, because, old friend, the curse is worse . . ."

The wasted man raised a gnarled knotted finger with a cast-iron evil stare pointed to Jonathan. "Because, old friend, the curse is worse . . . ." He repeated. And with that he leapt over the side of the boat and allowed himself to be swallowed by the sea.

Jonathan stood holding his breath. He had heard stories of men hallucinating after spending too many days at sea, yet this seemed far too real. At last he managed to let out his breath, which stuttered as he did so. Slowly he walked over to the railing on the starboard bow and peered over its edge. Below the black water swirled over the hull of the boat, but as for Thomas Hues there remained no trace.

Jonathan slowly walked back to his quarters. Hallucination or not? What did Hues mean by what he said—"best to have an empty purse . . ." Jonathan thought aloud. What could that have possibly meant.

In his hammock, Jonathan gently swayed to the rhythm of the sea. Sleep, after that episode, was beyond impossible, and he constantly reassured himself that the entire ordeal was a mere figment of his rather unfaded imagination. Still, Jonathan lay in his hammock patiently awaiting the break of morning light. He stared aimlessly toward the ceiling of the cabin, pondering the past and praying for the future.

The thought of the *Anna Marie* nearly drove away all his fear. However, in the closet of his mind lurked the memories of the silver seal, not to mention the death and rather blurry resurrection of his "late" friend Thomas Hues. Jonathan, regardless of his fears, finally managed to fall into a spell of deep sleep.

The light from the morning sun stabbed its way through the tiny portholes of the boat. Jonathan, as he had always done in the past, got up, poured himself a steaming cup of coffee and stood on the upper deck. The wind cut through his hair and his boat cut through the icy water below.

Jonathan knew that he and his crew were nearing their mark . . . he could feel it. Closing in on a sunken ship caused the blood to boil in his veins, and the thought of the gold that lay below in the murky depth, caused his eyes to grow wild with greed. Yes, they were indeed closing in, and his crew was hungry.

At long last, the moment had arrived. The anchor was lowered and the engines were cut; below a fortune awaited. Final checks were made on the equipment, and each man suited up for the greatest of all hunts.

One by one the crew held their mask and rolled backwards into the churning salt water. Their excitement had mounted to the point of hysteria, yet underwater, all was silent and serene.

Down the crew descended toward the ocean floor, spreading out in a rake formation as they dropped. Each man had a particular quadrant of sand to scrape, and each man felt certain that he would be the one to unveil the grandest prize. It was decided that the findings would be divided equally among the crew.

Jonathan drifted weightlessly away from the group. He had been there before and he never once forgot the hot spots of a site —he had a nose, a sixth sense for gold.

His feet tingled when they touched the sandy bottom. Deep inside his instincts told him exactly where to go, yet also deep inside he remembered the curse of the silver seal. His mouth went dry and his heart thumped. Perhaps he should have taken the seal's warning a bit more seriously, maybe a curse did in fact exist.

Above the rippling sea scattered beams of sunlight desperately attempted to reach the murky depths. Jonathan carried his fear like an uncomfortable pack, yet when he saw a gleaming object protruding from the sand, all fears melted away. Weightlessly, he bounded toward the object, with his greed and lust for gold stamping out all other emotions.

Even from a distance, Jonathan could see that the object was solid gold. Fish swirled about as he drew nearer, and his eagerness forced him impatiently along.

Before his feet, in the sand below, lay a Spanish cross, eight inches in length, six inches across, and three-quarters of an inch thick . . . solid gold. Its surface was embedded with rare jewels and polished pearls, and even though it was well over two-hundred

years old, it still glistened in the broken beams of sunlight. The cross's value was immeasurable, and it was, without a doubt, the greatest find he had ever made.

Slowly Jonathan swam to the surface of the water, never once taking his eyes off the find. He did not even think to look for the other divers to show them of his newly found prize—he simply ascended in a hypnotic trance to where the water met the sky.

The boat bobbed back and forth with a vacant deck. Jonathan pulled himself up the ladder clutching his golden cross. Quickly he removed his wetsuit and began meticulously cleaning the cross's surface. He paid no mind to the fact that the divers still remained beneath the sea, all he cared about, at that point in time, was the cross.

The jewels and the gold mingled in the sunlight and virtually blinded the eye with radiant brilliance. Jonathan continued to carefully clean and scrub the cross, and as he did so, he unmasked a small seal in its center . . . a solid silver seal. Of course, he immediately recognized the seal, for it was identical to the one that he had found before. Jonathan snapped out of his hypnotic state of mind and re-lived the warnings that were given to him.

His eyes panned the open sea, and then something strange happened. Jonathan raised the anchor, grabbed the spokes of the wheel and slowly turned the boat 180 degrees and aimed its wooden bow for the shores of home.

A crackled voice rang over the drone of the boat's motors, "Tis best to have an empty purse; because, old friend, the curse is worse . . ."

Jonathan throttled the boat to an even higher speed and focused only on the vast expanse of wealth he now held within his grasp, and never once did he look back. His crew perished in the icy seas above the *Anna Marie*.

Mr. Moore went on to receive the fame and fortune that he had long since lusted after. He explained to all who asked that his crew had been killed in a violent and sudden squall.

However, one night, while sitting alone by the fireplace in his mansion, something strange happened. On the mantel sat a beautiful conch shell that he had found when he was a young boy. Due to his boredom, Jonathan picked up and fondled the shell, remembering how he used to place it in his ear in hopes of hearing the ocean. The old wives' tale made a thin smile cross his lips, and he placed the conch to his ear, yet when he did so the simple smile ran away from his face, and beads of sweat arose upon his forehead. He heard the ocean all right, but he also heard the moans and wails of his crew, whom he had left behind to die. The conch dropped to the marble floor and shattered, but the dreadful sounds of dying men and ocean swells continued. Jonathan covered his ears, but the agonizing sounds only grew louder.

A raspy water-logged voice boomed within his brain, "Tis best to have an empty purse; because old friend, the curse is worse . . . because, old friend, the curse is worse . . ." and then the voice broke into a horrible laughter that flooded the corridors of his mansion.

Quickly, Jonathan drove to where his boat was docked and headed through the open water toward the *Anna Marie*. Jonathan Moore was never to be seen again.

Story Outline

I. Jonathan Moore is returning to find treasure lost at sea on the *Anna Marie* with a new crew of treasure hunters.

II. His partner on the first trip, Thomas Hues, had died during their earlier dives for the *Anna Marie's* treasure.

III. On the trip out to the site, Thomas Hues' ghost appears and warns his friend of the "Curse of the Silver Seal." "'Tis best to have an empty purse; because old friend, the curse is worse . . . "

IV. While the crew is diving on the site, Jonathan dives off the one side and finds a large gold cross which he brings to the surface.

V. He starts up the motor and leaves the crew behind, to perish in the ocean.

VI. He becomes wealthy from his treasure, but one day while listening to an old sea shell, he hears the moans of the drowned crew members.

VII. He takes his boat back out toward the *Anna Marie*, never to be seen again.

25

THE MONKEY'S PAW

by W. W. Jacobs

Without, the night was cold and wet, but in the small parlor of Laburnam Villa the blinds were drawn and the fire burned brightly. Father and son were at chess; the former, who possessed ideas about the game involving radical changes, putting his king into such sharp and unnecessary perils that it even provoked comment from the white-haired old lady knitting placidly by the fire.

"Hark at the wind," said Mr. White, who, having seen a fatal mistake after it was too late, was amiably desirous of preventing his son from seeing it.

"I'm listening," said the latter, grimly surveying the board as he stretched out his hand. "Check."

"I should hardly think that he'd come tonight," said his father, with his hand poised over the board.

"Mate," replied the son.

"That's the worst of living so far out," bawled Mr. White, with sudden and unlooked-for violence; "Of all the beastly, slushy, out-of-the-way places to live in, this is the worst. Path's a bog, and the road's a torrent. I don't know what people are thinking about. I suppose because only two houses in the road are let, they think it doesn't matter."

"Never mind, dear," said his wife soothingly; "perhaps you'll win the next one."

Mr. White looked up sharply, just in time to intercept a knowing glance between mother and son. The words died away on his lips, and he hid a guilty grin in his thin grey beard.

"There he is," said Herbert White, as the gate banged to loudly and heavy footsteps came toward the door.

The old man rose with hospitable haste, and opening the door, was heard condoling with the new arrival. The new arrival also condoled with himself, so that Mrs. White said, "Tut tut!" and coughed gently as her husband entered the room, followed by a tall, burly man, beady of eye and rubicund of visage.

"Sergeant-Major Morris," he said, introducing him.

The sergeant-major shook hands, and taking the proffered seat by the fire, watched contentedly while his host got out whisky and tumblers and stood a small copper kettle on the fire.

At the third glass his eyes got brighter, and he began to talk; the little family circle regarding with eager interest this visitor from distant parts as he squared his broad shoulders in the chair, and spoke of wild scenes and doughty deeds; of wars and plagues, and strange peoples.

"Twenty-one years of it," said Mr. White, nodding at his wife and son. "When he went away he was a slip of a youth in the warehouse. Now look at him."

"He don't look to have taken much harm," said Mrs. White politely.

"I'd like to go to India myself," said the old man, "Just to look round a bit, you know."

"Better where you are," said the sergeant-major, shaking his head. He put down the empty glass, and sighing softly, shook it again.

"I should like to see those old temples and fakirs and jugglers," said the old man. "What was that you started telling me the other day about a monkey's paw or something, Morris?"

"Nothing," said the soldier hastily. "Leastways nothing worth hearing"

"Monkey's paw?" said Mrs. White curiously.

"Well, it's just a bit of what you might call magic, perhaps," said the sergeant-major off-handedly. His three listeners leaned forward eagerly. The visitor absent-mindedly put his empty glass to his lips and then set it down again. His host filled it for him.

"To look at," said the sergeant-major, fumbling in his pocket, "it's just an ordinary little paw, dried to a mummy."

He took something out of his pocket and proffered it. Mrs. White drew back with a grimace, but her son, taking it, examined it curiously.

"And what is there special about it?" inquired Mr. White as he took it from his son, and having examined it, placed it upon the table.

"It had a spell put on it by an old fakir," said the sergeant-major, "A very holy man. He wanted to show that fate ruled people's lives, and that those who interfered with it did so to their sorrow. He put a spell on it so that three separate men could each have three wishes from it."

His manner was so impressive that his hearers were conscious that their light laughter jarred somewhat.

"Well, why don't you have three, sir?" said Herbert White cleverly.

The soldier regarded him in the way that middle age is wont to regard presumptuous youth. "I have," he said quietly, and his blotchy face whitened.

"And did you really have the three wishes granted?" asked Mrs. White.

"I did," said the sergeant-major, and his glass tapped against his strong teeth.

"And has anybody else wished?" persisted the old lady.

"The first man had his three wishes. Yes," was the reply; "I don't know what the first two were, but the third was for death. That's how I got the paw."

His tones were so grave that a hush fell upon the group.

"If you've had your three wishes, it's no good to you now then, Morris," said the old man at last. "What do you keep it for?"

The soldier shook his head. "Fancy, I suppose," he said slowly. "I did have some idea of selling it, but I don't think I will. It has caused enough mischief already. Besides, people won't buy. They think it's a fairy tale, some of them; and those who do think anything of it want to try it first and pay me afterward."

"If you could have another three wishes," said the old man, eyeing him keenly, "would you have them?"

"I don't know," said the other. "I don't know."

He took the paw, and dangling it between his forefinger and thumb, suddenly threw it upon the fire. White, with a slight cry, stooped down and snatched it off.

"Better let it burn," said the soldier solemnly.

"If you don't want it, Morris," said the other, "give it to me."

"I won't," said his friend doggedly. "I threw it on the fire. If you keep it, don't blame me for what happens. Pitch it on the fire again like a sensible man."

The other shook his head and examined his new possession closely. "How do you do it?" he inquired.

"Hold it up in your right hand and with a loud voice, declare your wish," said the sergeant-major. "But I warn you of the consequences."

"Sounds like the *Arabian Nights*," said Mrs. White, as she rose and began to set the supper. "Don't you think you might wish for four pairs of hands for me?"

Her husband drew the talisman from his pocket, and then all three burst into laughter as the sergeant-major, with a look of alarm on his face, caught him by the arm.

"If you must wish," he said gruffly, "wish for something sensible."

Mr. White dropped it back in his pocket, and placing chairs, motioned his friend to the table. In the business of supper the talisman was partly forgotten, and afterward the three sat listening in an enthralled fashion to a second installment of the soldier's adventures in India.

"If the tale about the monkey's paw is not more truthful than those he has been telling us," said Herbert, as the door closed behind their guest, just in time to catch the last train, "we shan't make much out of it."

"Did you give him anything for it, father?" inquired Mrs. White, regarding her husband closely.

"A trifle," said he, coloring slightly. "He didn't want it, but I made him take it. And he pressed me again to throw it away."

"Likely," said Herbert, with pretended horror. "Why, we're going to be rich, and famous, and happy. Wish to be an emperor, father, to begin with; then you can't be henpecked."

He darted round the table, pursued by the maligned Mrs. White armed with an antimacassar. Mr. White took the paw from his pocket and eyed it dubiously. "I don't know what to wish for, and that's a fact," he said slowly. "It seems to me I've got all I want."

"If you only cleared the house, you'd be quite happy, wouldn't you!" said Herbert, with his hand on his shoulder. "Well, wish for two hundred pounds, then; that'll just do it."

His father, smiling shamefacedly at his own credulity, held up the talisman as his son, with a solemn face, somewhat marred by a wink at his mother, sat down at the piano and struck a few impressive chords.

"I wish for two hundred pounds," said the old man distinctly.

A fine crash from the piano greeted the words, interrupted by a shuddering cry from the old man. His wife and son ran toward him.

"It moved," he cried, with a glance of disgust at the object as it lay on the floor. "As I wished, it twisted in my hand like a snake."

"Well, I don't see the money," said his son, as he picked it up and placed it on the table, "And I bet I never shall."

"It must have been your fancy, father," said his wife, regarding him anxiously.

He shook his head. "Never mind, though; there's no harm done, but it gave me a shock all the same."

They sat down by the fire again while the two men finished their pipes. Outside, the wind was higher than ever, and the old man started nervously at the sound of a door banging upstairs. A silence unusual and depressing settled upon all three, which lasted until the old couple rose to retire for the night.

"I expect you'll find the cash tied up in a big bag in the middle of your bed," said Herbert, as he bade them good night, "And something horrible squatting up on top of the wardrobe watching you as you pocket your ill-gotten gains."

He sat alone in the darkness, gazing at the dying fire, and seeing faces in it. The last face was so horrible and so simian that he gazed at it in amazement. It got so vivid that, with a little uneasy laugh, he felt on the table for a glass containing a little water to throw over it. His hand grasped the monkey's paw, and with a little shiver he wiped his hand on his coat and went up to bed.

In the brightness of the wintry sun next morning as it streamed over the breakfast table he laughed at his fears. There was an air of prosaic wholesomeness about the room, which it had lacked on the previous night, and the dirty, shriveled little paw was pitched on the sideboard with a carelessness that betokened no great belief in its virtues.

"I suppose all old soldiers are the same," said Mrs. White. "The idea of our listening to such nonsense! How could wishes be granted in these days? And if they could, how could two hundred pounds hurt you, father?"

"Might drop on his head from the sky," said the frivolous Herbert.

"Morris said the things happened so naturally," said his father, "that you might if you so wished attribute it to coincidence."

"Well, don't break into the money before I come back," said Herbert as he rose from the table. "I'm afraid it'll turn you into a mean, avaricious man, and we shall have to disown you."

His mother laughed, and following him to the door, watched him down the road; and returning to the breakfast table, was very happy at the expense of her husband's credulity. All of which did not prevent her from scurrying to the door at the postman's knock, nor prevent her from referring somewhat shortly to retired sergeant-majors of bibulous habits when she found that the post brought a tailor's bill. "Herbert will have some more of his funny remarks, I expect, when he comes home," she said, as they sat at dinner. "I dare say," said Mr. White, pouring himself out some beer; "but for all that, the thing moved in my hand; that I'll swear to." "You thought it did," said the old lady soothingly. "I say it

did," replied the other. "There was no thought about it; I had just
—What's the matter?"

His wife made no reply. She was watching the mysterious
movements of a man outside, who, peering in an undecided
fashion at the house, appeared to be trying to make up his mind
to enter. In mental connection with the two hundred pounds,
she noticed that the stranger was well-dressed, and wore a silk
hat of glossy newness. Three times he paused at the gate, and
then walked on again. The fourth time he stood with his hand
upon it, and then with sudden resolution flung it open and
walked up the path. Mrs. White at the same moment placed her
hands behind her, and hurriedly unfastening the strings of her
apron, put that useful article of apparel beneath the cushion of
her chair. She brought the stranger, who seemed ill at ease, into
the room. He gazed at her furtively, and listened in a preoc-
cupied fashion as the old lady apologized for the appearance of
the room, and her husband's coat, a garment which he usually
reserved for the garden. She then waited as patiently as her sex
would permit, for him to broach his business, but he was at first
strangely silent.

"I—was asked to call," he said at last, and stooped and
picked a piece of cotton from his trousers. "I come from Maw
and Meggins." The old lady started. "Is anything the matter?" she
asked breathlessly. "Has anything happened to Herbert? What is
it? What is it?" Her husband interposed. "There, there, mother,"
he said hastily. "Sit down, and don't jump to conclusions. You've
not brought bad news, I'm sure, sir;" and he eyed the other wist-
fully. "I'm sorry—" began the visitor.

"Is he hurt?" demanded the mother wildly.

The visitor bowed in assent. "Badly hurt," he said quietly,
"But he is not in any pain."

"Oh, thank God!" said the old woman, clasping her hands. "Thank God for that! Thank—"

She broke off suddenly as the sinister meaning of the assurance dawned upon her, and she saw the awful confirmation of her fears in the other's averted face. She caught her breath, and turning to her slower-witted husband, laid her trembling old hand upon his. There was a long silence. "He was caught in the machinery," said the visitor at length in a low voice.

"Caught in the machinery," repeated Mr. White, in a dazed fashion. "Yes."

He sat staring blankly out at the window, and taking his wife's hand between his own. pressed it as he had been wont to do in their old courting days nearly forty years before "He was the only one left to us," he said, turning gently to the visitor. "It is hard." The other coughed, and rising, walked slowly to the window.

"The firm wished me to convey their sincere sympathy to you in your great loss," he said, without looking 'round. "I beg that you will understand I am only their servant and merely obeying orders."

There was no reply; the old woman's face was white, her eyes staring, and her breath inaudible; on the husband's face was a look of such as his friend the sergeant might have carried into his first action.

"I was to say that Maw and Meggins disclaim all responsibility," continued the other. "They admit no liability at all, but in consideration of your son's services, they wish to present you with a certain sum as compensation."

Mr. White dropped his wife's hand, and rising to his feet, gazed with a look of horror at his visitor. His dry lips shaped the words, "How much?"

"Two hundred pounds," was the answer.

Unconscious of his wife's shriek, the old man smiled faintly, put out his hands like a sightless man, and dropped, a senseless heap, to the floor.

In the huge new cemetery, some two miles distant, the old people buried their dead, and came back to the house steeped in shadow and silence. It was all over so quickly that at first they could hardly realize it, and remained in a state of expectation as though of something else to happen—something else which was to lighten this load, too heavy for old hearts to bear.

But the days passed, and expectation gave place to resignation—the hopeless resignation of the old, sometimes miscalled apathy. Sometimes they hardly exchanged a word, for now they had nothing to talk about, and their days were long to weariness.

It was about a week after that the old man, waking suddenly in the night, stretched out his hand and found himself alone. The room was in darkness, and the sound of subdued weeping came from the window. He raised himself in bed and listened.

"Come back," he said tenderly. "You will be cold."

"It is colder for my son," said the old woman, and wept afresh.

The sound of her sobs died away on his ears. The bed was warm, and his eyes heavy with sleep. He dozed fitfully, and then slept until a sudden wild cry from his wife awoke him with a start.

"The paw!" she cried wildly. "The monkey's paw!" He started up in alarm. "Where? Where is it? What's the matter?"

She came stumbling across the room toward him. "I want it," she said quietly. "You've not destroyed it?"

"It's in the parlor, on the bracket," he replied, marveling. "Why?" She cried and laughed together, and bending over, kissed his cheek.

"I only just thought of it," she said hysterically. "Why didn't I think of it before? Why didn't you think of it?"

"Think of what?" he questioned.

"The other two wishes," she replied rapidly. "We've only had one."

"Was not that enough?" he demanded fiercely.

"No," she cried triumphantly; "We'll have one more. Go down and get it quickly, and wish our boy alive again."

The man sat up in bed and flung the bedclothes from his quaking limbs. "Good God, you are mad!" he cried, aghast.

"Get it," she panted "Get it quickly, and wish—Oh, my boy, my boy!"

Her husband struck a match and lit the candle. "Get back to bed," he said unsteadily. "You don't know what you are saying."

"We had the first wish granted," said the old woman feverishly; "Why not the second?" "A coincidence," stammered the old man.

"Go and get it and wish," cried his wife, quivering with excitement.

The old man turned and regarded her, and his voice shook. "He has been dead ten days, and besides he—I would not tell you else, but—I could only recognize him by his clothing. If he was too terrible for you to see then, how now?"

"Bring him back," cried the old woman, and dragged him toward the door. "Do you think I fear the child I have nursed?"

He went down in the darkness, and felt his way to the parlor, and then to the mantelpiece. The talisman was in its place, and a horrible fear that the unspoken wish might bring his mutilated son before him ere he could escape from the room seized upon him, and he caught his breath as he found that he had lost the direction of the door. His brow cold with sweat, he felt his way round the table, and groped along the wall until he found himself in the small passage with the unwholesome thing in his hand.

Even his wife's face seemed changed as he entered the room. It was white and expectant, and to his fears seemed to have an unnatural look upon it. He was afraid of her.

"Wish!" she cried in a strong voice.

"It is foolish and wicked," he faltered.

"Wish!" repeated his wife.

He raised his hand. "I wish my son alive again."

The talisman fell to the floor, and he regarded it fearfully. Then he sank trembling into a chair as the old woman, with burning eyes, walked to the window and raised the blind.

He sat until he was chilled with the cold, glancing occasionally at the figure of the old woman, peering through the window. The candle-end, which had burned below the rim of the china candlestick, was throwing pulsating shadows on the ceiling and walls, until, with a flicker larger than the rest, it expired. The old man, with an unspeakable sense of relief at the failure of the talisman, crept back to his bed, and a minute or two afterward the old woman came silently and apathetically beside him.

Neither spoke, but lay silently listening to the ticking of the clock. A stair creaked, and a squeaky mouse scurried noisily through the wall. The darkness was oppressive, and after lying for some time screwing up his courage, he took the box of matches, and striking one, went downstairs for a candle.

At the foot of the stairs the match went out, and he paused to strike another; and at the same moment a knock, so quiet and stealthy as to be scarcely audible, sounded on the front door.

The matches fell from his hand and spilled in the passage. He stood motionless, his breath suspended until the knock was repeated. Then he turned and fled swiftly back to his room, and closed the door behind him. A third knock sounded through the house.

"What's that?" cried the old woman, starting up.

"A rat," said the old man in shaking tones. "A rat. It passed me on the stairs."

His wife sat up in bed listening. A loud knock resounded through the house.

"It's Herbert!" she screamed. "It's Herbert!"

She ran to the door, but her husband was before her, and catching her by the arm, held her tightly.

"What are you going to do?" he whispered hoarsely.

"It's my boy; it's Herbert!" she cried, struggling mechanically. "I forgot it was two miles away. What are you holding me for? Let go. I must open the door."

"For God's sake don't let it in," cried the old man, trembling.

"You're afraid of your own son," she cried, struggling. "Let me go. I'm coming, Herbert; I'm coming."

There was another knock, and another. The old woman with a sudden wrench broke free and ran from the room.

Her husband followed to the landing, and called after her appealingly as she hurried downstairs. He heard the chain rattle back and the bottom bolt drawn slowly and stiffly from the socket. Then the old woman's voice strained and panting.

"The bolt," she cried loudly. "Come down. I can't reach it."

But her husband was on his hands and knees groping wildly on the floor in search of the paw. If he could only find it before the thing outside got in. A perfect fusillade of knocks reverberated through the house, and he heard the scraping of a chair as his wife put it down in the passage against the door. He heard the creaking of the bolt as it came slowly back, and at the same moment he found the monkey's paw, and frantically breathed his third and last wish.

The knocking ceased suddenly, although the echoes of it were still in the house. He heard the chair drawn back, and the door opened. A cold wind rushed up the staircase, and a long loud wail of disappointment and misery from his wife gave him courage to run down to her side, and then to the gate beyond. The street lamp flickering opposite shone on a quiet and deserted road.

Story Outline

I. The White family is at home one rainy evening when a former acquaintance, Sergeant Major Morris arrives.

II. He speaks of his travels and lets slip about a magical, dried monkey's paw that he has in his pocket.

III. A holy man in India had placed a spell on it to show that fate rules men's lives and those who interfered with it did so to their sorrow.

IV. The Sergeant-Major states that only three men can have three wishes. One man had taken his three—in fact his last wish was for death and that was when the Sergeant—Major got it.

V. The Sergeant-Major had taken his three, so there were no more remaining for him and, so saying, he tosses the paw into the fireplace.

VI. Mr. White recovers it from the fire, but the Sergeant-Major tells him he should let it burn.

VII. The Whites have everything they needed, but Mr. White, at his son's suggestion, wishes for two hundred pounds, which would pay off their house.

VIII. After their son goes to work the next day, they notice a stranger who comes to their door. He announces that their son has been killed and that the company which he worked for has sent them as compensation two-hundred pounds.

IX. The grief-stricken mother insists that her husband use his next wish to bring their son back from the dead.

X. After he does so there is silence for awhile (the cemetery is two miles away). Suddenly there is a rapping on the door.

XI. As his wife frantically tries to open the door, Mr. White finds the paw and makes his third and last wish.

XII. The pounding suddenly stops and as the wife opens the door, there is only an empty road.

26

THE VAMPIRE OF CROGLIN GRANGE

by Augustus Hare

Augustus Hare was an English writer who lived from 1834 to 1903. He wrote many travel books and stories of people he had known. One of them, Captain Fisher, related this strange tale of Croglin Grange, an actual place in Cumberland, England. When telling this story, be sure to dramatize the scratch, scratch, scratch, and the peck, peck, peck. Also, the running together of the sentences as used in the text, especially when the vampire comes into the room and grabs the girl, is a very effective technique. Claiming authenticity for this story, as it has been told as a true episode by Augustus Hare's friend Captain Fisher, also lends a creepy aspect to this tale.

"FISHER," said the Captain, "may sound a very plebian name, but this family is of a very ancient lineage, and for many hundreds of years they have possessed a very curious old place in Cumberland, which bears the weird name of Croglin Grange. The great characteristic of the house is that never at any period of its very long existence has it been more than one story high, but it has a terrace from which large grounds sweep away towards the church in the hollow, and a fine distant view.

"When, in lapse of years, the Fishers outgrew Croglin Grange in family and fortune, they were wise enough not to destroy the long-standing characteristic of the place by adding another story to the house, but they went away to the south, to reside at Thorncombe near Guildford, and then rented Croglin Grange.

"They were extremely fortunate in their tenants, two brothers and a sister. They heard their praises from all quarters. To their poorer neighbors they were all that is most kind and beneficent, and their neighbors of a higher class spoke of them as a most welcome addition to the little society of the neighborhood. On their part, the tenants were greatly delighted with their new residence. The arrangement of the house, which would have been a trial to many, was not so to them. In every respect Croglin Grange was exactly suited to them.

"The winter was spent most happily by the new inmates of Croglin Grange, who shared in all the little social pleasures of the district, and made themselves very popular. In the following summer there was one day which was dreadfully, annihilating hot. The brothers lay under the trees with their books, for it was too hot for any active occupation. The sister sat on the veranda and worked, or tried to work, for in the intense sultriness of that summer day, work was next to impossible. They dined early, and after dinner they still sat out on the veranda, enjoying the cool air which came with the evening, and they watched the sun set, and the moon rise over the belt of trees which separated the grounds from the churchyard, seeing it mount the heavens till the whole lawn was bathed in silver light, across which the long shadows from the shrubbery fell as if embossed, so vivid and distinct were they.

"When they separated for the night, all retiring to their rooms on the ground floor (for, as I said, there was no upstairs in that house), the sister felt that the heat was still so great that she could not sleep, and having fastened her window, she did not close the shutters—in that very quiet place it was not necessary—and, propped against the pillows, she still watched the wonderful, the marvelous beauty of that summer night. Gradually she became aware of two lights, two lights which flickered in and out in the belt of trees which separated the lawn from the churchyard, and, as her gaze became fixed upon them, she saw them emerge, fixed in a dark substance, a definite ghastly something, which seemed every moment to become nearer, increasing in size and substance as it approached. Every now and then it was lost for a moment in the long shadows which stretched across the lawn from the trees, and then it emerged larger than ever, and still coming on. As she watched it, the most uncontrollable horror seized her. She longed to get away, but the door was close to the window, and the door was locked on the inside, and while she was unlocking it she must be for an instant nearer to it. She longed to scream, but her voice seemed paralyzed, her tongue glued to the roof of her mouth.

"Suddenly—she could never explain why afterwards—the terrible object seemed to turn to one side, seemed to be going round the house, not to be coming to her at all, and immediately she jumped out of bed and rushed to the door, but as she was unlocking it she heard scratch, scratch, scratch upon the window. She felt a sort of mental comfort in the knowledge that the window was securely fastened on the inside. Suddenly the scratching sound ceased, and a kind of pecking sound took its place. Then, in her agony, she became aware that the creature was unpicking the lead! The noise continued, and a diamond pane of glass fell into the room. Then a long bony finger of the creature came in and turned the handle of the window, and the window opened, and the creature came in; and it came across the room, and her terror was so great that she could not scream, and it came up to the bed, and it twisted its long, bony fingers into her hair, and it dragged her head over the side of the bed, and—it bit her violently in the throat.

"As it bit her, her voice was released, and she screamed with all her might and main. Her brothers rushed out of their rooms, but the door was locked on the inside. A moment was lost while they got a poker and broke it open. The creature had already escaped through the window, and the sister, bleeding violently from a wound in the throat, was lying unconscious over the side of the bed. One brother pursued the creature, which fled before him through the moonlight with gigantic strides, and eventually seemed to disappear over the wall into the churchyard. Then he rejoined his brother by the sister's bedside. She was dreadfully hurt, and her wound was a very definite one, but she was of strong disposition, not even given to romance or superstition, and when she came to herself she said, 'What has happened is most extraordinary and I am very much hurt. It seems inexplicable, but of course there is an explanation, and we must wait for it. It will turn out that a lunatic has escaped from some asylum and found his way here.' The wound healed, and she appeared to get well, but the doctor who was sent for to her would not believe that she could bear so terrible a shock so easily, and insisted that she must have change, mental and physical; so her brother took her to Switzerland.

"Being a sensible girl, when she went abroad she threw herself at once into the interests of the country she was in. She dried plants, she made sketches, she went up mountains, and, as autumn came on, she was the person who urged that they should return to Croglin Grange. 'We have taken it,' she said, 'for seven years, and we have only been there one; and we shall always find it difficult to let a house which is only one story high, so we had better return there; lunatics do not escape every day.' As she urged it, her brothers wished nothing better, and the family returned to Cumberland. From there being no upstairs in the house it was impossible to make any great change in their arrangements. The sister occupied the same room, but it is unnecessary to say she always closed the shutters, which, however, as in many old houses, always left one top pane of the window uncovered. The brothers moved, and occupied a room together, exactly opposite that of their sister, and they always kept loaded pistols in their room.

"The winter passed most peacefully and happily. In the following March, the sister was suddenly awakened by a sound she remembered only too well—scratch, scratch, scratch upon the window, and, looking up, she saw climbed up to the topmost pane of the window, the same hideous brown shriveled face, with glaring eyes, looking in at her. This time she screamed as loud as she could. Her brothers rushed out of their room with pistols, and out of the front door. The creature was already scudding away across the lawn. One of the brothers fired and hit it in the leg, but still with the other leg it continued to make way, scrambled over the wall into the churchyard, and seemed to disappear into a vault which belonged to a family long extinct.

"The next day the brothers summoned all the tenants of Croglin Grange, and in their presence the vault was opened. A horrible scene revealed itself. The vault was full of coffins; they had been broken open, and their contents, horribly mangled and distorted, were scattered over the floor. One coffin alone remained intact. Of that the lid had been lifted, but still lay loose upon the coffin. They raised it, and there —brown, withered, shrivelled, mummified, but quite entire—was the same hideous figure which had looked in at the windows of Croglin Grange, with the marks of a recent pistol shot in the leg; and they did the only thing that can lay a vampire—they burnt it."

Story Outline

I. Two brothers and a sister moved into an ancient manor house called Croglin Grange. It was a one story building with grounds that stretched to the old churchyard cemetery.

II. One hot summer night, the sister noted someone—something coming from the churchyard cemetery towards the house. It came straight to her window and started scratching, (scratch, scratch, scratch) then pecking (peck, peck, peck)—removing the lead holding the glass panes.

III. She was so terrified she could not scream. The Creature unlatched the window with his bony finger. It came across the room right up to her, twisted her hair in its bony fingers, dragged her down on the bed and bit her on the side of the neck.

IV. Her screams brought her brothers, who broke into the room, scaring the creature away. She was badly wounded, but recovered and they left the area for a short time, traveling in Switzerland.

V. Upon their return the brothers moved to the room next to her, keeping their pistols loaded. Nothing happened until March, when she awoke in horror one night, again hearing the scratch, scratch, scratch upon her window.

VI. She screamed loudly; her brothers came and chased the creature away. One brother shot it in the leg.

VII. The next day they all opened the crypt from which the creature seemed to come. There they found many coffins which had been broken open, the bodies horribly mangled. In one coffin they found the same creature, with a bullet wound in its leg.

VIII. They did the only thing which they could with a vampire, they burned it.

27

A MUSICAL ENIGMA

as told by Rev. C. P. Cranch

This strange visit to an undertaker's establishment took his young employee by surprise. Frankly, I do not think that I have the courage that the undertaker in this story displayed. In this story by Rev. Cranch, we can share the surprise and fear of young William Spindles and his friends as they are paid a visit that they would never forget.

One chilly, windy evening in the month of December, three young men sat around a tall office-stove in Mr. Simon Shrowdwell's establishment, No. 307 Dyer Street, in the town of Boggsville.

Mr. Simon Shrowdwell was a model undertaker, about fifty years of age, and the most exemplary and polite of sextons in the old Dutch church just round the corner. He was a musical man, too, and led the choir, and sang in the choruses of oratorios that were sometimes given in the town-hall. He was a smooth-shaven, sleek man, dressed in decorous black, wore a white cravat, and looked not unlike a second-hand copy of the clergyman. He had the fixed, pleasant expression customary to a profession whose business it was to look sympathetic on grief, especially in rich men's houses. Still it was a kind expression; and the rest of his features indicated that he did not lack firmness in emergencies. He had done a thriving business, and had considerably enlarged his store and his supply of ready-made mortuary furnishings. His rooms were spacious and neat. Rows of handsome coffins, of various sizes, stood around the walls in shining array, some of them studded with silver-headed nails; and everything about the establishment looked as cheerful as the nature of his business permitted.

On this December evening Mr. Shrowdwell and his wife, whose quarters were on the floor above, happened to be out visiting some friends. His young man, William Spindles, and two of his friends who had come in to keep him company, sat by the ruddy stove, smoking their pipes, and chatting as cheerily as if these cases for the dead that surrounded them were simply ornamental panels. Gas, at that time, hadn't been introduced into the town of Boggsville; but a cheerful argand-lamp did its best to light up the shop.

Their talk was friendly and airy, about all sorts of small matters; and people who passed the street-window looked in and smiled to see the contrast between the social smoking and chatting of these youngsters, and the grim but neat proprieties of their environment.

One of the young men had smoked out his pipe, and rapped it three times on the stove, to knock out the ashes.

There was an answering knocking—somewhere near; but it didn't seem to come from the street-door. They were a little startled, and Spindles called out:—

"Come in!"

Again came the rapping, in another part of the room.

"Come in!" roared Spindles, getting up and laying his pipe down.

The street-door slowly opened, and in glided a tall, thin man. He was a stranger. He wore a tall, broad-brimmed hat, and a long, dark, old-fashioned cloak. His eyes were sunken, his face cadaverous, his hands long and bony.

He came forward, "I wish to see Mr. Shrowdwell."

"He is out," said Spindles. "Can I do anything for you?"

"I would rather see Mr. Shrowdwell," said the stranger.

"He will not be home till late this evening. If you have any message, I can deliver it; or you will find him here in the morning."

The stranger hesitated. "Perhaps you can do it as well as Shrowdwell. . . . I want a coffin."

"All right," said Spindles; "step this way, please. Is it for a grown person or a child? Perhaps you can find something here that will suit you. For some relative, I presume?"

"No, no, no! I have no relative," said the stranger. Then in a hoarse whisper, "*It's for myself!*"

Spindles started back, and looked at his friends. He had been used to customers ordering coffins; but this was something new. He looked hard at the pale stranger. A queer, uncomfortable chill crept over him. As he glanced around, the lamp seemed to be burning very dimly.

"You don't mean to say you are in earnest?" he stammered. And yet, he thought, this isn't a business to joke about. . . . He looked at the mysterious stranger again, and said to himself: "Perhaps he's deranged—poor man!"

Meanwhile the visitor was looking around at the rows of coffins shining gloomily in the lamplight. But he soon turned about, and said:—

"These won't do. They are not the right shape or size. . . . *You must measure me for one!*"

"You don't mean—" gasped Spindles. "Come, this is carrying a joke too far."

"I am not joking," said the stranger; "I never joke. I want you to take my measure. . . . And I want it made of a particular shape."

Spindles looked toward the stove. His companions had heard part of the conversation, and, gazing nervously at each other, they had put on their hats and overcoats, pocketed their pipes, and taken French leave.

Spindles found himself alone with the cadaverous stranger, and feeling very strange. He began to say that the gentleman had better come in the morning, when Mr. Shrowdwell was in—Shrowdwell understood this business. But the stranger fixed his cold black eyes on him, and whispered:

"I can't wait. *You* must do it—tonight. . . . Come, take my measure!"

Spindles was held by a sort of fascination, and mechanically set about taking his measure, as a tailor would have done for a coat and trousers.

"Have you finished?" said the stranger.

"Y—y—es, sir; that will do," said Spindles. "What name did you say, sir?"

"No matter about my name. I have no name. Yet I might have had one if the fates had permitted. Now for the style of the coffin I want."

And taking a pencil and card from his pocket, he made a rough draught of what he wanted. And the lines of the drawing appeared to burn in the dark like phosphorus.

"I must have a lid and hinges—so, you see—and a lock *on the inside*, and plenty of room for my arms."

"All r—r—ight," said Spindles; "we'll make it. But it's not exactly in our line—to m—m—ake co—co—coffins in this style." And the youth stared at the drawing. It was for all the world like a violoncello—case.

"When can I have it?" said the stranger, paying no attention to Spindles' remark.

"Day after tomorrow, I sup—p—ose. But I—will have to—ask Shrowdwell—about it."

"I want it three days from now. I'll call for it about this time Friday evening. But as you don't know me, I'll pay in advance. This will cover all expenses, I think," producing a bank-note.

"Certainly," stammered Spindles.

"I want you to be particular about the lid and the locks. I was buried once before, you see; and this time I want to have my own way. I have one coffin but it's too small for me. I keep it under my bed and use it for a trunk. Good evening. Friday night—remember!"

Spindles thought there would be little danger of his forgetting it. But he didn't relish the idea of seeing him again, especially at night. "However, Shrowdwell will be here then," he thought.

When the mysterious stranger had gone, Spindles put the bank-bill in his pocket-book, paced up and down, looked out of the window, and wished Shrowdwell would come home.

"After all," he said, "it's only a crazy man. And yet what made the lamp burn so dim? And what strange raps those were before he entered! And that drawing with a phosphoric pencil! And how like a dead man he looked! Pshaw! I'll smoke another pipe."

And he sat down by the stove, with his back to the coffins. At last the town-clock struck nine, and he shut up the shop, glad to get away and go home.

Next morning he told Shrowdwell the story, handed him the bank-bill as corroboration, and showed him the drawing, the lines of which were very faint by daylight. Shrowdwell took the money gleefully, and locked it in his safe.

"What do you think of this affair, Mr. Shrowdwell?" Spindles asked.

"This is some poor deranged gentleman, Spindles. I have made coffins for deranged men—but this is something unusual—ha! ha!—for a man to come and order his own coffin, and be measured for it! This is a new and interesting case, Spindles—one that I think has never come within my experience. But let me see that drawing again. How faint it is. I must put on my specs. Why, it is nothing but a big fiddle-case—a double-bass box. He's probably some poor distracted musician, and has taken this strange fancy into his head—perhaps imagines himself a big fiddle—eh, Spindles?" And he laughed softly at his own conceit. "Pon my soul, this is a strange case—and a fiddle-case, too—ha! ha! But we must set about fulfilling his order."

By Friday noon the coffin of the new pattern was finished. All the workmen were mystified about it, and nearly all cracked jokes at its queer shape. But Spindles was very grave. As the hour approached when the stranger was to call for it he became more and more agitated. He would have liked to be away, and yet his curiosity got the better of his nervousness. He asked his two friends to come in, and they agreed to do so, on Spindles' promise to go first to an oyster-saloon and order something hot to fortify their courage. They didn't say anything about this to Shrowdwell, for he was a temperance man and a sexton.

They sat around the blazing stove, all four of them, waiting for the insane man to appear. It wanted a few minutes of eight.

"What's the matter with that lamp?" said Shrowdwell. "How dim it burns! It wants oil."

"I filled it today," said Spindles.

"I feel a chill all down my back," said Barker.

"And there's that rapping again," said O'Brien.

There *was* a rapping, as if underneath the floor. Then it seemed to come from the coffins on the other side of the room;

then it was at the window-panes, and at last at the door. They all looked bewildered, and thought it very strange.

Presently the street-door opened slowly. They saw no one, but heard a deep sigh.

"Pshaw, it's only the wind," said Shrowdwell, and rose to shut the door—when right before them stood the cadaverous stranger. They were all so startled that not a word was spoken.

"I have come for my coffin," the stranger said, in a sepulchral whisper. "Is it done?"

"Yes, sir," said Shrowdwell. "It's all ready. Where shall we send it?"

"I'll take it with me," said the stranger in the same whisper. "Where is it?"

"But it's too heavy for you to carry," said the undertaker.

"That's my affair," he answered.

"Well, of course you are the best judge whether you can carry it or not. But perhaps you have a cart outside, or a porter?"

All this while the lamp had burned so dim that they couldn't see the features of the unknown. But suddenly, as he drew nearer, it flared up with a sudden blaze, as if possessed, and they saw that his face was like the face of a corpse. At the same instant an old cat which had been purring quietly by the stove—usually the most grave and decorous of tabbies—started up and glared, and then sprang to the farthest part of the room, her tail puffed out to twice its ordinary size.

They said nothing, but drew back and let him pass toward the strange-looking coffin. He glided toward it, and taking it under his arm, as if it were no heavier than a small basket, moved toward the door, which seemed to open of its own accord, and he vanished into the street.

"Let's follow him," said the undertaker, "and see where he's going. You know I don't believe in ghosts. I've seen too many dead bodies for that. This is some crazy gentleman, depend on it; and we ought to see that he doesn't do himself any harm. Come!"

The three young men didn't like the idea of following this stranger in the dark, whether he was living or dead. And yet they liked no better being left in the dimly-lighted room among the coffins. So they all sallied out, and caught a glimpse of the visitor just turning the corner.

They walked quickly in that direction.

"He's going to the church," said Spindles. "No, he's turning toward the graveyard. See, he has gone right through the iron gate! And yet it was locked! He has disappeared among the trees!"

"We'll wait here at this corner, and watch," said Shrowdwell.

They waited fifteen or twenty minutes, but saw no more of him. They then advanced and peered through the iron railings of the cemetery. The moon was hidden in clouds, which drifted in great masses across the sky, into which rose the tall, dim church-steeple. The wind blew drearily among the leafless trees of the burial-ground. They thought they saw a dark figure moving down toward the northwest corner. They then heard some of the vault-doors creak open and shut with a heavy thud.

"Those are the tombs of the musicians," whispered the under-taker. "I have seen several of our Music Society buried there—two of them, you will remember, last summer. I have a lot there myself, and expect to lay bones in it someday."

Presently strange sounds were heard, seeming to come from the corner of the graveyard spoken about. They were like the confused tuning of an orchestra before a concert—with discords and chromatic runs, up and down, from at least twenty instruments, but all muffled and pent in, as if underground.

Yet, thought the undertaker, this may be only the wind in the trees. "I wish the moon would come out, he said, "so we could see something. Anyhow, I think it's a Christian duty to go in there, and see after that poor man. He may have taken a notion, you know, to shut himself up in his big fiddle-case, and we ought to see that he don't do himself any injury. Come, will you go?"

"Not I, thank you." "Nor I," said they all. "We are going home—we've had enough of this."

"Very well," said the undertaker. "As you please; I'll go alone."

Mr. Shrowdwell believed in death firmly. The only resurrection he acknowledged was the resurrection of a tangible body at some far-off judgement-day. He had no fear of ghosts. But this was not so much a matter of reasoning with him, as temperament, and the constant contact with lifeless bodies.

"When a man's dead," said Shrowdwell, "He's dead, I take it. *I'll* never see a man or woman come to life again. Don't the Scriptures say, 'Dust to dust?' It's true that with the Lord nothing is impossible, and at the last day he will summon his elect to meet him in the clouds; but that's a mystery."

And yet he couldn't account for this mysterious visitor passing through the tall iron railings of the gate—if he really *did* pass—for after all it may have been an ocular illusion.

But he determined to go in and see what he could see. He had the key of the cemetery in his pocket. He opened the iron gate and passed in, while the other men stood at a distance. They knew the sexton was proof against spirits of all sorts, airy or liquid; and after waiting a little, they concluded to go home, for the night was cold and dreary—and ghost or no ghost, they couldn't do much good there.

As Shrowdwell approached the northwest corner of the graveyard, he heard those singular musical sounds again. They seemed to come from the vaults and graves, but they mingled so with the rush and moaning of the wind, that he still thought he might be mistaken.

In the farthest corner there stood a large old family vault. It had belonged to a family with an Italian name, the last member of which had been buried there many years ago—and since then had not been opened. The vines and shrubbery had grown around and over it, partly concealing it.

As he approached it, Shrowdwell observed with amazement that the door was open, and a dense phosphorescent light lit up the interior.

"Oh," he said, "the poor insane gentleman has contrived somehow to get a key to this vault, and has gone in there to commit suicide, and bury himself in his queer coffin—and save the expense of having an undertaker. I must save him, if possible, from such a fate."

As he stood deliberating, he heard the musical sounds again. They came not only from the vault, but from all around. There was the hoarse groaning of a double-bass, answered now and then by a low muffled wail of horns and a scream of flutes, mingled with the pathetic complainings of a violin. Shrowdwell began to think he was dreaming, and rubbed his eyes and his ears to see if he were awake. After considerable turning and running up and down the scales, the instruments fell into an accompaniment to the double-bass of a Beethoven mass.

The tone was as if the air were played on the harmonic intervals of the instrument, and yet was so weirdly and so wonderfully like a human voice, that Shrowdwell felt as if he had got into some enchanted circle. As the solo drew to its conclusion, the voice that seemed to be in it broke into sobs, and ended in a deep groan.

But the undertaker summoned up his courage, and determined to probe this mystery to the bottom. Coming nearer the vault and looking in, what should he see but the big musical coffin of the cadaverous stranger lying just inside the entrance of the tomb.

The undertaker was convinced that the strange gentleman was the performer of the solo. But where was the instrument? He mustered courage to speak, and was about to offer some comforting and encouraging words. But at the first sound of his voice the lid of the musical coffin, which had been open, slammed to, so suddenly, that the sexton jumped back three feet, and came near tumbling over a tombstone behind him. At the same time the dim phosphorescent light in the vault was extinguished, and there was another groan from the double-bass in the coffin. The sexton determined to open the case. He stooped over it and listened. He thought he heard inside a sound like putting a key into a padlock. "He mustn't lock himself in," he said, and instantly wrenched open the cover.

Immediately there was a noise like the snapping of strings and the cracking of light wood—then a strange sizzling sound—and then a loud explosion. And the undertaker lay senseless on the ground.

Mrs. Shrowdwell waited for her husband till a late hour, but he did not return. She grew very anxious, and at last determined to put on her bonnet and shawl and step over to Mr. Spindles' boarding-house to know where he could be. That young gentleman was just about retiring, in a very nervous state, after having taken a strong nipper of brandy and water to restore his equanimity. Mrs. Shrowdwell stated her anxieties, and Spindles told her something of the occurrences of the evening. She then urged him to go at once to a police-station and obtain two or three of the town watchmen to visit the graveyard with lanterns and pistols; which, after some delay and demurring on the part of the guardians of the night, and a promise of a reward on the part of Mrs. Shrowdwell, they consented to do.

After some searching the watchmen found the vault, and in front of it poor Shrowdwell lying on his back in a senseless state. They sent for a physician, who administered some stimulants, and gradually brought him to his senses, and upon his legs. He couldn't give any clear account of the adventure. The vault door was closed, and the moonlight lay calm upon the white stones, and no sounds were heard but the wind, now softly purring among the pines and cedars.

They got him home, and, to his wife's joy, found him uninjured. He made light of the affair—told her of the bank-note he had received for the musical coffin, and soon fell soundly asleep.

Next morning he went to his iron safe to reassure himself about the bank-note—for he had an uncanny dream about it. To his amazement and grief it was gone, and in its place was a piece of charred paper.

The undertaker lost himself in endless speculations about this strange adventure, and began to think there was diabolical witchcraft in the whole business, after all.

One day, however, looking over the parish record, he came upon some facts with regard to the Italian family who had owned the vault. On comparing these notes with the reminiscences of one or two of the older inhabitants of Boggsville, he made out something like the following history:—

Signor Domerico Pietri, an Italian exile of noble family, had lived in that town some fifty years since. He was of an unsocial, morose disposition, and very proud. His income was small, and his only son Ludovico, who had decided musical talent, determined to seek his fortune in the larger cities, as a performer on the double-bass. It was said his execution on the harmonic notes was something marvelous. But his father opposed his course, either from motives of family pride, or wishing him to engage in commerce; and one day, during an angry dispute with him, banished him from his house.

Very little was known of Ludovico Pietri. He lived a wandering life, and suffered from poverty. Finally all trace was lost of him, the old man died, and was buried, along with other relatives, in the Italian vault.

But there was a story told of a performer on the double bass, who played such wild, passionate music, and with such skill, that in his lonely garret, one night, the devil appeared, and offered him a great bag of gold for his big fiddle—proposing at the same time that he should sign a contract that he would not play any more *during his lifetime*—except at his (the fiend's) bidding. The musician, being very poor, accepted the offer and signed the contract, and the devil vanished with his big fiddle. But afterward the poor musician repented the step he had taken, and took it so to heart that he became insane and dead.

Now, whether this strange visitor to Mr. Shrowdwell's coffin establishment, who walked the earth in this unhappy frame of mind, was a live man, or the ghost of the poor maniac, was a question which could not be satisfactorily settled.

Some hopeless unbelievers said that the strange big fiddle-case was a box of nitroglycerine or fulminating powder, or an infernal machine; while others as firmly believed that there was something supernatural and uncanny about the affair, but ventured no philosophical theory in the case.

And as for the undertaker, he was such a hopeless skeptic all his life, that he at last came to the conclusion that he must have been dreaming when he had that adventure in the graveyard; and this notwithstanding William Spindles' repeated declarations, and those of the two other young men (none of whom accompanied Shrowdwell in this visit), that everything happened just as I have related it.

Story Outline

I. Young William Spindles sits amidst the coffins of Mr. Simon Shrowdwell's mortuary.

II. There is a strange knocking, the lights burn low, and a man desires to be measured for an unusually shaped coffin.

III. Spindles complies, but is scared.

IV. He pays his boss the next day and the coffin is made.

V. On Friday night the man returns with strange knocking, the light dims, but then reveals a death-like face. Even the cat is scared. He easily lifts the heavy coffin and leaves in the night.

VI. The three boys go with the brave undertaker to the cemetery, but upon hearing strange musical sounds, the boys go home rather than help investigate.

VII. The undertaker goes to the vault with the noise, the coffin slams shut. He hears the coffin being locked, but he tries to open it—an explosion takes place.

VIII. He is found outside the closed vault. The bank-note is found charred in the safe.

IX. We are told the legend of Signor Pietri's son Ludovico signing a pact with the devil not to play during his lifetime.

X. Mr. Shrowdwell, the undertaker, decides that he must have imagined the cemetery episode, but the three young men know this story to be true.

28

THE HAUNTING AT VINE STREET

by Ambrose Bierce

The original source for this story was Some Haunted Houses, *a collection of true hauntings by Ambrose Bierce. This has been altered for better ease in campfire story telling. The original title was "A Fruitless Assignment."*

This story is told as actually having happened to a newspaper reporter by the name of Henry Saylor. He was a reporter for the *Cincinnati Commercial*. In the year 1859 a vacant house in Cincinnati on Vine Street became the center of local excitement because of the strange sights and sounds said to be observed in it nightly. According to the testimony of many reputable residents of the vicinity, there was no explanation for these activities, unless the house was haunted!

Figures with something singularly unfamiliar about them were seen by crowds on the sidewalk to pass in and out. No one could say just where they appeared on the front lawn on their way to the front door, nor at exactly what point they vanished on the way out. It should be said that each witness knew where these things happened . . . it's just that no two people could agree.

Also, they all disagreed upon their description of the figures. Some of the bolder of the curious crowd ventured on several evenings to stand upon the door steps to intercept them, or to at least get a closer look at them. These courageous men, it was said, were unable to force the door by their united strength, and always were hurled from the steps by some invisible agency and even injured—the door immediately afterward opening, apparently of its own volition, to admit or let out some ghostly guest.

The dwelling was known as the Roscoe house. A family of that name lived there once, but one by one they disappeared, the last to leave being an old woman. Stories of foul play and successive murders had always been rife, but never were authenticated.

One day during the height of the excitement, Mr. Saylor was called to the editor's office of the *Commercial* for orders. He received a note from the city editor which read as follows: "Go and pass the night alone in the haunted house on Vine Street and if anything occurs worth while make two columns." Saylor obeyed his superior; he could not afford to lose his position on the paper.

Telling the police of his intention, he entered the house through a rear window before dark, walked through the deserted rooms, bare of furniture, dusty and desolate, and seating himself at last in the parlor on an old sofa which he had dragged in from another room, watched the deepening of the gloom as night came on.

Before it was altogether dark, the curious crowd had collected in the street, silent, as a rule, and expectant, with here and there an unbeliever uttering his incredulity and courage with scornful remarks or ribald cries. None knew of the anxious watcher inside. He feared to make a light. The uncurtained windows would have betrayed his presence, subjecting him to insult from the crowd, possibly injury. Moreover, he was too conscientious to do anything to alter any of the customary conditions under which the manifestations were said to occur.

It was now dark outside, but light from the street faintly illuminated the part of the room that he was in. He had opened every door in the whole interior, above and below, but all of the outer ones were locked and bolted.

Sudden exclamations from the crowd caused him to spring to the window and look out! He saw the figure of a man moving rapidly across the lawn towards the building—saw it ascend the steps; then a projection of the wall concealed it. There was a noise as of the opening and closing of the hall door; he heard quick, heavy footsteps along the passage—heard them ascend the stairs—heard them on the uncarpeted floor of the chamber immediately overhead!

Saylor promptly drew his pistol, and groping his way up the stairs entered the chamber, dimly lighted from the street. No one was there. He heard footsteps in an adjoining room and entered that. It was dark and silent. He struck his foot against some object on the floor, knelt by it, passed his hand over it.

It was a human head! The head of a woman! Lifting it by the hair this iron-nerved man returned to the half-lighted room below, carried it near the window and attentively examined it. While so engaged he was half conscious of the rapid opening and closing of the outer door, of foot-falls sounding all about him. He raised his eyes from the ghastly object of his attention and saw himself the center of a crowd of men and women dimly seen! The room was thronged with them. He thought the people had broken in.

"Ladies and gentlemen," he said coolly, "you see me under suspicious circumstances, but—" his voice was drowned in peals of laughter—such laughter as is heard in asylums for the insane.

The persons about him pointed at the object in his hand and their merriment increased as he dropped it and it went rolling among their feet. They danced about it with gestures grotesque and attitudes obscene and indescribable. They struck it with their feet, urging it about the room from wall to wall; pushed and overthrew one another in their struggles to kick it; cursed and screamed and sang snatches of ribald songs as the battered head

bounded about the room as if in terror and trying to escape. At last it shot out of the door into the hall, followed by all, with tumultuous haste. That moment the door closed with a sharp concussion. Saylor was alone, in dead silence.

Carefully putting away his pistol, which all the time he had held in his hand, he went to the window and looked out. The street was deserted and silent; the lamps were extinguished; the roofs and chimneys of the houses were sharply outlined against the dawn light in the east.

He left the house, the door yielding easily to his hand, and walked to the *Commercial* office. The city editor was still in his office—asleep.

Saylor waked him and said: "I have been at the haunted house."

The editor stared blankly, as if not wholly awake. "Good God!" he cried, "are you all right?"

"Yes, why not?"

The editor made no answer, but continued staring.

"I passed the night there—it seems," said Saylor.

"They say that things were uncommonly quiet out there," the editor said, trifling with a paper-weight upon which he had dropped his eyes. "Did anything occur?"

"Why, nothing whatever."

Story Outline

I. An empty house on Vine Street in Cincinnati is reported to be haunted, with ghosts entering and leaving.

II. Henry Saylor is given the assignment by the editor of the *Cincinnati Commercial* to spend the night alone in the house and to write a story about it, if anything happens.

III. Saylor tells the police, then enters the house through a back window. He does not use any lights, for he doesn't want the crowd gathering in front of the house to see him and he wants to avoid disturbing anything that might be happening within.

IV. He hears a noise from the crowd, looks out the window and sees a ghostly figure enter the front of the house. He hears its footsteps go upstairs, but when he goes up there, he can find nothing.

V. He hears footsteps in the adjoining room and enters it. His foot strikes something. When he touches it he realizes that it is a human head!

VI. He carries it to the half-lighted room below to examine it. When he gets there he realizes that he is surrounded by dimly seen figures. He tries to explain what he is doing there with a human head.

VII. The figures dance around him merrily, grotesquely—he drops the head and the figures kick it around the room.

VIII. The head bounces around the room as if in terror and trying to escape—it is finally kicked out the door and down the hall, followed by all. He is left alone, in dead silence.

IX. He returns to the newspaper office and tells the editor that he spent the night out there. When asked if anything happened he says, "Why, nothing whatever."

29

DELUSE'S GOLDEN CURSE

by Ambrose Bierce

The original source for this story was Some Haunted Houses, *a collection of true hauntings by Ambrose Bierce. This story has been altered for better ease in campfire story telling. The original title was "The Isle of Pines." Bierce was a famous writer of the late 1800's and also immortalized as the writer who disappeared into the Mexican Revolution in the movie:* Old–Gringo.
    The Isle of Pines was once a famous rendezvous for pirates—the Rev. Galbraith jokingly referred to Deluse's house as the Isle of Pines because of his supposed connection to pirates. —Doc

Those who have labored hard for their treasures, and who have done so at the cost of selling their souls, do not part with treasure easily. Such may be the cause of the tragic events which were recorded in a haunted house near the town of Gallipolis, Ohio, in 1867.

For many years there lived close to the town of Gallipolis an old man named Herman Deluse. Very little was known of his history, for he would never speak of it himself nor encourage others to do so. It was a common belief among his neighbors that he had once been a pirate—he would have been a young man in the early 1800's, a time in our history when pirates still frequented the coasts of the United States. He had a collection of old weapons—boarding pikes, cutlasses, and ancient flintlock pistols that, coupled with his secret ways, caused this rumor to persist.

He lived entirely alone in a small four room house which was falling rapidly into decay and never repaired further than was required by the weather. It stood on a slight elevation in the midst of a large, stony field overgrown with brambles, and cultivated in patches and only in the most primitive way. It was his only visible property, but could have hardly yielded him a living, even as simple and few as were his needs. He seemed to always have ready money. He paid cash for all his purchases at the village stores roundabout, seldom buying more than two or three times at the same place until after the lapse of a considerable time. He got no commendation for this equal distribution of his patronage; people were disposed to regard it as an effort to attempt to conceal his possession of such much money. That he had great hoards of ill-gotten gold buried somewhere about his tumbledown dwelling was not reasonably to be doubted by any honest soul in his neighborhood.

On 9 November 1867, the old man died. At least his dead body was discovered on the 10th, and physicians testified that death had occurred about twenty-four hours previously—precisely how, they were unable to say. The post-mortem examination showed every organ to be absolutely healthy, with no indication of disorder or violence. According to them, death must have taken place about noon, yet the body was found in bed. The verdict of the coroner's jury was that he "came to his death by a visitation of God." The body was buried and the public administrator took charge of the estate.

A rigorous search disclosed nothing more than was already known about the dead man, and much patient excavation here and there about the premises by thoughtful and thrifty neighbors went un-rewarded. The administrator locked up the house against the time when the property, real and personal, should be sold by law.

The night of 20 November was boisterous. A furious gale stormed across the country, scourging it with desolating drifts of sleet. Great trees were torn from the earth and hurled across the roads. So wild a night had never been known in all that region, but towards morning the storm had blown itself out of breath and day dawned bright and clear. At about eight o'clock that morning, the Rev. Henry Galbraith, a well-known and highly esteemed Lutheran minister, arrived on foot at his house, a mile and a half from the Deluse place. Mr. Galbraith had been away for a month in Cincinnati. He had come up the river in a steamboat, and landing at Gallipolis the previous evening had immediately obtained a horse and buggy and set out for home. The violence of the storm had delayed him over night, and in the morning the fallen trees had compelled him to abandon his horse and buggy and continue his journey on foot.

"But where did you spend the night?" inquired his wife, after he had briefly related his adventure.

"With old Deluse at the 'Isle of Pines,'" was the laughing reply; "and a glum enough time I had of it. He made no objection to my remaining, but not a word could I get out of him."

Fortunately for the interests of truth there was present at this conversation a visitor to the reverend's house, Mr. Robert Maren, a lawyer from Columbus, Ohio. The family was astonished at what the reverend had said, for they knew old Deluse had been dead almost over two weeks. Mr. Maren, with a gesture, stopped the others from saying anything and calmly inquired: "How came you to go in there?"

This is Mr. Maren's version of Rev. Galbraith's reply:

"I saw a light moving in the house, and being nearly blinded by the sleet, and half frozen besides, drove in at the gate and put my horse in the old rail stable, where it is now.

I then rapped at the door, and getting no invitation went in without one. The room was dark, but having matches I found a candle and lit it. I tried to enter the adjoining room, but the door was solidly shut, and although I heard the old man's heavy footsteps in there he made no response to my calls.

There was no fire in the hearth, so I made one and lying down before it with my overcoat under my head, prepared myself for sleep. Pretty soon the door that I had tried silently opened and the old man came in carrying a candle. I spoke to him pleasantly, apologizing for my intrusion, but he took no notice of me.

He seemed to be searching for something, though his eyes were unmoved in their sockets. I wondered if he ever walked in his sleep. He took a circuit a part of the way round the room, and went out the same way he had come in. Twice more before I slept he came back into the room, acting in precisely the same way, and departing as at first. In the intervals I heard him trampling all over the house, his footsteps distinctly audible in the pauses of the storm. When I woke in the morning, he had already gone out."

Mr. Maren attempted some further questioning, but he was unable to any longer restrain the family's tongues. The story of Deluse's death and burial came out, greatly to the good minister's astonishment.

"The explanation of your adventure is very simple," said Mr. Maren. "I don't believe old Deluse walks in his sleep—not in his present one; but you evidently dream in yours."

And to this view of the matter Rev. Galbraith was compelled reluctantly to agree.

Nevertheless, a late hour of that very night found these two gentlemen, accompanied by a son of the minister, in the road in front of the old Deluse house.

There was a light inside! It appeared now at one window, now at another. The three men advanced to the door.

Just as they reached it there came from the interior a confusion of the most appalling sounds—the clash of weapons, steel against steel, sharp explosions of firearms, shrieks of women, groans and curses of men in combat!

The investigators stood a moment, determined, but frightened. Then Rev. Galbraith tried the door. It was stuck fast. But the minister was a man of courage, a man, moreover, of tremendous strength. He retreated several steps and rushed against the door, striking it with his right shoulder and bursting it from the frame with a loud crash! In a moment the three were inside. Darkness and silence! The only sound was the beating of their hearts.

Mr. Maren had provided himself with matches and a candle. With some difficulty, due to his excitement, he made a light. They proceeded to explore the place, passing from room to room. Everything was in orderly arrangement, as it had been left by the sheriff. Nothing had been disturbed. A light coating of dust was everywhere. A back door was partly open, as if by neglect, and their first thought was that the people making the noise had escaped through it.

The door was opened and the light of the candle shone through upon the ground! [*Quicken your voice throughout this sentence for dramatic effect, then slowly utter the rest of the paragraph.*] The previous night's storm had left a light coating of snow. There were no foot prints—the white surface was unbroken.

They closed the door and entered the last room of the four that the house contained—that farthest from the road, in an angle of the building. Here the candle in Mr. Maren's hand was suddenly extinguished as if by a draught of air!

ALMOST IMMEDIATELY FOLLOWED THE SOUND OF A HEAVY FALL! When the candle had been hastily re-lighted, the preacher's son was seen lying flat on the floor, a little distance from the others! He was dead!

The boy's neck had been broken by a heavy bag of gold coins, coins that were later found to be Spanish pieces of eight. Directly over the body, a board had been torn from the ceiling—the place from where the bag had fallen!

The boy had paid the penalty for entering the haunted house. But with his death the old pirate's curse was ended, for the mysterious activities of the house were never heard of again.

Story Outline

I. An old man named Deluse lived alone in a four room house near Gallipolis, Ohio. Local people thought he night have been a pirate in the old days. He always had money and was very secretive.

II. He died on 9 November 1867. People searched for his gold, but none was found. The sheriff locked the house which was to be sold at public sale later.

III. On 20 November a tremendous storm hit the area, with sleet and winds that tore down trees. The Rev. Galbraith was trying to return home, but could not. He spent the night at the Deluse house, and travelled home on foot the next day.

IV. He told his family of the strange night he had spent with Deluse not talking to him. His family was amazed for

Deluse had been dead over two weeks. A friend of the family was visiting, Mr. Maren, a lawyer from Columbus, Ohio.

V. Rev. Galbraith, his son, and Mr. Maren visit the old Deluse house that night. On the front steps they hear a terrible clamor inside of fighting.

VI. Rev. Galbraith breaks the door down. They find themselves inside, but with the house empty and quiet. They can find no evidence of activity inside, or on the snowy ground when they look out the back door.

VII. They enter the fourth room. Suddenly the candle is blown out! They hear a thud! When they re-light the candle, the minister's son is dead, killed by a bag of gold that had fallen from the ceiling.

30

GOLD TOOTH

by Scott E. Power and Doc Forgey

One weekend Mr. Simpson and his thirteen year old son Jimmy were camping in the Jacksonville State Forest area. They had prepared this camp out with very little help from Mom. Well, except for some advice. She saw Dad packing a large can of sauerkraut and asked him what he planned to do with it. He responded that it was for supper on Saturday night.

Mom didn't think that was a very good idea. "I know what will happen," she said. "You'll go to bed right after supper because you'll both be afraid of the dark and Jimmy will have horrible nightmares after eating that sauerkraut."

"Nonsense," her husband remarked and he packed the sauerkraut anyway.

Friday night they went to bed early. Not because they were scared, but because they were tired. They had gotten up early, finished packing, and had driven half the day to reach the beautiful campsite which they were able to claim.

Saturday was a busy day. And even though they ate a good breakfast and lunch, the full day of hiking left them starving by supper time. That sauerkraut turned out to be a real treat that evening. It certainly complemented that grilled sausage! And for dessert, banana pudding washed down with hot chocolate.

After relaxing around the campfire a short while they turned on their AM/FM radio to hear the news.

Unexpectedly, an emergency flash news report came over the radio:

ATTENTION, ATTENTION, ALL CITIZENS:

JUST HOURS AGO A CONVICTED MURDERER ESCAPED FROM THE JACKSONVILLE CORREC-TIONAL CENTER. INITIAL ATTEMPTS TO CAPTURE HIM HAVE FAILED. HE IS AT LARGE AND IS CONSIDERED DANGEROUS. HE IS BELIEVED TO BE HEADING NORTH-NORTHWEST ON FOOT. HE STANDS ABOUT 6'4" AND WEIGHS APPROXIMATELY 280 POUNDS. HE HAS LONG BROWN HAIR WITH A BEARD AND MUSTACHE. HE ANSWERS TO THE NAME "GOLD TOOTH." IF YOU HAVE ANY KNOWLEDGE OF THE WHEREABOUTS OF THIS ESCAPED CRIMINAL PLEASE CALL YOUR LOCAL POLICE IMMEDIATELY.

FOR EVERYONE'S SAFETY, ANYONE CAMPING IN THE JACKSONVILLE STATE FOREST AREA SHOULD LEAVE IMMEDIATELY. THAT IS ALL.

Instantly, Jimmy turned to his dad in fear.

"Don't be afraid, Son. You have nothing to worry about. Jacksonville Correctional Center is twenty miles north over Jackson Ridge. Besides we're leaving in the morning and there is no way anyone could travel that distance on foot in twelve hours. Regardless, the news report said he's traveling north-northwest and we're due south."

"Dad, I don't care. I'm scared. I wanna go home," Jimmy replied.

"What if I gave you something to protect yourself with?"

"Like what, Dad? A Swiss Army knife?"

"No, of course not. I brought the rifle for a little target practice tomorrow morning before we leave. But if you'd like, I'll keep it in the tent tonight for protection."

"You will?"

"Yes, I will."

"Really? Do you promise?"

"Yes, I promise."

"OK, let's stay. But I'm getting tired. I want to go to sleep. And my stomach is acting up a little." Jimmy got up from sitting by the campfire and walked over to the tent and got in.

Mr. Simpson walked over to the duffle bags and began to look for the rifle, finding it in the red one.

Holding it in his hand, Mr. Simpson knew the gun was not loaded with bullets. And he did not plan to load any either. Mr. Simpson had no concern whatsoever that the escaped prisoner would threaten them in any way. He was merely providing a sense of security for his son. Mr. Simpson was more concerned about a possible bear attack than the prisoner at large.

Walking past the tent to put the fire out, Mr. Simpson could hear that Jimmy had already fallen to sleep. Smiling to himself, Jimmy's father picked up the pail of water and poured it over the fire. Immediately, the sizzle of steam rose into the air as the fire light disappeared into darkness.

Mr. Simpson turned on his flashlight to find his way back to the tent. As he walked over, he held the flash light in his right hand and the rifle in his left. Crawling into the tent he placed the rifle between the sleeping bags. Zipping the tent door behind him,

Mr. Simpson crawled into his sleeping bag, zipped it up and then turned the flash light off. As he laid in the darkness, he could hear Jimmy still snoring and the gentle noises from the crickets and the bullfrogs outside. For a moment, he thought about how happy he was to be there in such a beautiful peaceful place with his son who he loved so much. Everything was perfect. Peaceful. Serene.

Slowly, Mr. Simpson could feel himself falling to sleep and beginning to dream. Soon he was deep in sleep and snoring too.

In the middle of the night, probably around four in the morning, Jimmy awoke. He was squirming because his stomach was cramping and he was having nightmares.

As he laid on his back looking up at the top of the tent, he immediately thought about the escaped murderer.

He turned his head to look towards his father and then he saw the gun lying between them. Instantly, he was relieved. He felt safe again.

Then, in the distance he heard CRACK!!

It sounded like someone stepping on a fallen branch. Then, he heard CRUNCH!!

It sounded like someone stepping onto a pile of leaves. Then, he heard CRACK!!

Again. Another broken branch.

Jimmy tried to wake his Dad up, but he couldn't. He tried shaking him, but he was sleeping too deeply. Jimmy grabbed the rifle and pointed it at the door, not knowing it was loaded.

Then, outside the tent, Jimmy saw the shape of a man silhouetted by the light of the moon. Instantly, without thought he pulled the triggered of the unloaded gun.

POW!!!!

The gun fired and a bullet ripped through the tent striking the shadowy figure dead.

Mr. Simpson woke up in a panic and didn't understand what was happening. Everything seemed chaotic and confusing. His ears were ringing from the sound of the gun firing. He couldn't believe the gun was loaded. He thought for sure it was not. Good thing he was wrong.

Jimmy was sitting still holding the gun firm in his grip. His eyes were locked straight ahead in the direction he had fired. He was trembling with fear. Finally, he spoke.

"I saw him. It was him. The escaped prisoner. I know it was him. He was going to kill us. I had to do it. I had to do it. I had to do it." Jimmy repeated.

Hours later, the cops arrived on the scene. The man did not look like the escaped prisoner. He had short hair, no beard or mustache, and was wearing street clothes.

Jimmy felt sick that he had shot at someone without knowing who he was shooting. His dad felt terrible that he had made the awful mistake of thinking that a gun was unloaded without checking it by opening the breech.

Jimmy was arrested as a murderer and he was taken to Jacksonville Prison. There he was placed in the very cell that the escaped convict had been in.

"Kid, this cell is good enuff for you. You killed my brother-in-law, Henry. We'll just keep you here until I hope they hang you."

Later that night a man with long hair was brought in wearing handcuffs and leg chains. The guard laughed as he shoved him into Jimmy's cell.

"Hey, you two murderers should get along just fine in there, " he cackled as he slammed the door, locked it, and walked away down the hall leaving the two in there together.

"Aw. What e in fo her kid? You murda someone like me?" And as he laughed Jimmy saw the gold tooth shining though the

droopy long mustache covering his face. And Jimmy realized that he had finally met the killer face to face, locked in a cell together without anyone around to help. And all because he shot someone he didn't even know.

"Say kid," Gold Tooth exclaimed as he came closer and closer to Jimmy, "I hair you be har fer tryen to kill me?"

Jimmy backed up until he was finally trapped in a corner of the cell. Gold Tooth put his manacled hands out in front of him, reaching for Jimmy.

"I hate it when people try to kill me," Gold Tooth growled, snatching Jimmy around the waist as he tried to sneak past him.

Jimmy struggled with every ounce of his energy against the overwhelming strength of Gold Tooth, but he just couldn't break away. Gold Tooth had him and wasn't letting go!

Jimmy knew he was going to die. His breath was being squeezed out of him. His last chance for survival was to shout for help to the guard who had left them both in the cell.

"HELP!" Jimmy screamed at the top of his lungs.

"Jimmy, Jimmy! Wake up Jimmy!" a familiar voice was shouting and Jimmy suddenly realized he was not in the cell, but was in the tent being shaken by his father.

"Jimmy! You have been having a nightmare. Wake up."

What had been a great campout had turned into a nightmare. But they had both learned important lessons. Pay attention to the authorities when they make an announcement and follow their instructions. Never trust that a gun is not loaded and never shoot at a target without positive identification, even in a dream. And when your mother gives you some advice, even if it's just not to take sauerkraut on a camp out and eat it before going to bed—believe her!

Story Outline

I. Jimmy and his Dad were packing up for a weekend camping, when Mr. Simpson ignored his wife's advice not to pack a large can of sauerkraut as part of their food provisions.

II. Mr. Simpson and Jimmy were camping in the Jacksonville State Park when they heard a radio announcement that they should leave the area as a feared murderer "Gold Tooth" had escaped from the local prison.

III. Jimmy wanted to go home, but Mr. Simpson noted that the prisoner was heading a different direction from them and was 20 miles away.

IV. To calm Jimmy down, Mr. Simpson pulled an unloaded gun from their gear and placed it between them in the tent.

V. Jimmy woke up hearing noises outside the tent.

VI. He saw the shadow of a man on the tent and he shot at him, striking him dead.

VII. Jimmy was thrown into a jail cell by a relative of the man he killed.

VIII. The guard returns and throws another murderer in the cell with him who turns out to be the real "Gold Tooth."

IX. Gold Tooth knows that Jimmy tried to kill him, so he goes after him, squeezing the life out of him.

X. Jimmy wakes from his sauerkraut induced nightmare and realizes it had all been a dream!

XI. Jimmy and his Dad learned several lessons from this experience: Do not ignore the advice in official bulletins; never trust that a gun is empty; never shoot without identifying the target; and always pay attention to what Mom has to say!

31

WILLIE BROWN AND THE GRAVEYARD CORPSE

as told by Doc Forgey

This story is a modification of a traditional Irish folk story, changed to reflect a more American setting.

Once there was a scout named Willie Brown who lived with his family in a small cottage located far outside of town in southern New England. The shortest distance between his home and town was through the graveyard. One day his father was taking the short cut when he stopped to rest for awhile. It was only at dinner that evening when he remembered that he had left his black walnut walking stick at an open grave.

His wife noticed he was looking kind of troubled and asked him what was the matter.

"I stopped to rest today by a newly dug grave and I left my walking stick. It was the walking stick that your Dad gave me the night we were engaged. You know how much I love that cane. I am afraid someone might steal it during the night."

The children looked at one another and thought about those haunted tombs and they looked down at their plates.

Willie Brown alone stood up and said, "I'll get it father," and before anyone could stop him he was out of the house and into the darkness. He walked quite a ways until he came to the entrance to the graveyard. Then he followed the path along until he came to the new dug grave. He saw his father's walking stick laying there in the loose dirt. He reached his hand out for it . . . and a voice came from out of the grave!

"Leave that black walnut walking stick Willie Brown and help me out of this hole!"

Willie Brown was really frightened but a power took hold of him and drew him to the edge of that put and he looked down.

"Help me out of this hole!"

Willie Brown couldn't move. A nameless creature, a power from beyond death itself, crept out of that grave and climbed onto William's back. It put one hand around his neck and with the other silently pointed a finger for him to walk away from those graves. William was in kind of a daze. He walked for awhile. The weight of that frightful beast was getting so heavy on his back. Finally he stopped, he could go no further.

"Walk on, Willie Brown."

Willie Brown walked on. Eventually they came into the town where the houses sit side by side – kind of in rows up and down the street. It pointed for him to go into the first house. As they got close to the first door, the monster said, "Aahh!, we can't go in here, I smell the smell of holy water!"

So they went to the second house. As they got close to that door, again he said, "Aahh!, we can't go in here, I smell the smell of holy water!"

So he took him to the third. As they got close to that door he said, "Aahh, There is no holy water here." So they went inside. Willie Brown took that dead man from his back and he set it in a chair beside the TV set.

The the monster said in a raspy voice, "Now find me something to eat and drink."

Willie Brown went to the kitchen and after awhile he came back and brought a bowl of oatmeal.

"And where is something to drink?" it asked him.

"There is nothing to drink but dirty water," Willie Brown told him.

Aahh, he flew into a rage. "Bring a razor and a dish!"

Willie Brown did as he said. Once again the creature climbed onto his back. It pointed for him to go up the stairs to the second floor. When they got to the top of the landing, it motioned for him to go into the first room where there were 3 young brothers lying asleep. The monster took the razor and it cut the fingers of each of those boys and let the blood drop into the dish. With the first drop the flesh color left the boys' faces. With the second, their breathing stopped. With the third, they were as cold and white as the corpse himself.

"That is for leaving no clean water!" it said.

Once again the corpse creature climbed onto Willie's back and he was forced to take it down stairs.

"Now bring me two dishes and two spoons!"

After he had done that, the corpse mixed the blood and oatmeal together and divided it into two portions. It handed Willie Brown one part and said, "Now you eat this!" and he proceeded to gobble his own.

While the monster wasn't looking, Willie Brown took his scout neckerchief that was around his neck and rotated it from behind his head to the front. While he pretended to eat that concoction, he instead let it drop down into the neckerchief. Then he tied it so the blood mixture was hidden in a bundle.

Well, the corpse was so busy gobbling his own, he didn't even notice what Willie Brown was doing. After awhile he looked and said, "Are you finished?"

Willie Brown said that yes he was. "Then take me back to where you found me."

Willie Brown quaked at the thought of returning to the grave-yard. He was scared and exhausted, but he found the strength from somewhere, so he got up and began clearing the table.

He was afraid that the monster might smell the oatmeal around his neck, so while his back was turned, he untied the neckerchief, rolled it up, and put it up into the cupboard. Once again the ghostly being climbed onto his back and they walked out of the house.

It pointed for him to go back a different way, a short cut through the woods. When after they had been walking for awhile, Willie Brown asked, "Is there any cure for those 3 young boys?"

The monster laughed so hard that Willie Brown was shaken, then it said "There is none, for we have eaten it. But if any of that blood and oatmeal had been placed in their mouths, they would be alive and would never have known of their deaths. But there is no way now!"

And on they walked. After a while he pointed to a field over to the side that had 3 stone heaps in it. He said, "Under each of those stone heaps, there lies gold, but no one knows it except the dead."

Willie Brown shivered to hear that for he knew that he was not dead. At least he was not dead yet! And on they walked.

Suddenly the monster made him stop when he heard the crow of a rooster. "Augh," the monster wailed. "Was that the crow of a rooster?"

"No," Willie Brown said, thinking quickly, "It was only the bleating of a sheep for its mother."

Willie Brown slowed his pace as much as he could, hoping that the crow of the rooster might mean something bad for the monster. Finally they came to the back entrance of the grave yard. They followed the path but that weight was getting heavier and heavier. Again Willie Brown could hear the faint sound of a rooster crowing. He thought the monster might have heard it so Willie Brown said, "A barn owl must have eaten a rat."

The monster only cackled as if this was a delightful joke, but then shrieked in his ear "Hurry on!"

Willie Brown felt the grip around his neck tighten and tighten. It was if the closer they came to that open grave, the more the creature delighted at the thought of pulling him into the hole with him. Willie Brown went slower and slower, but the creature kept digging its bony knees into his back urging him on.

But finally, through the damp mist the yawning, open grave appeared before them. "Aahh, Willie Brown. It is into the grave with you."

The creature began pulling him down into that new dug grave. Willie Brown was so exhausted that he didn't have much strength left, but held back as hard as he could, trying to loosen the tight grip the rotten, decaying corpse had on him – he pulled and struggled and desperately felt himself being drug into that grave.

Just as he was afraid he might be pulled over the edge into the cold mist of the open grave, the rooster crowed for the third time. And the corpse fell lifeless into the coffin.

The creature said with its last breath, "Aahh, Willie Brown, if I had known the rooster would crow three times before I had you in the grave, I would have never told you of the gold."

And he was silent. Willie Brown took the lid to the coffin lying on the ground beside the grave and he put it on as tightly as he could, pounding the nails in with the end of his father's walking stick. Then, taking his father's black walnut walking stick, he headed for home.

The first light of dawn was just coming into the sky when he reached the cottage. Everything was very quiet. He walked in and placed the walking stick next to his father's favorite chair and then he fell into bed exhausted. About mid-morning he was awakened by his mother's rough shaking. "Willie Brown, get out of bed. Here you are still asleep and our neighbor's sons have died last night. Get up we must go to their wake."

He rolled over and he said, "Then go without me for I am sick with weariness."

His mother saw that he was just as pale as the sheets themselves, so she covered him back up again. His mother and the rest of the family left the house and went to the neighbor's. Around noon Willie Brown finally got out of bed still very tired and he fixed himself just a little bit to eat and then he headed for the neighbor's place. When he got there, there were a lot of people gathered around, all the friends and neighbors and family. He walked among them until he found the parents.

When Willie Brown saw them he said, "I am sorry that I am late, but I have felt very ill this morning. You see, I had a most horrible dream last night. I dreamed that your sons had all died. When Mom woke me this morning, I could hardly believe what she told me, that they had really died."

They looked at him and said, "Willie Brown, thanks for coming. You do look ill. We know how much you kids like to play together. Please, sit down over here."

But Willie Brown continued, "Yes, but there was much more to my dream. I also dreamed of a way to save them. A very simple way. I know that I can do it, but I have to be left alone with them,"

The parents, seeing that he was as upset as they, felt that this would do no harm and said that he could be alone with the boys just as he requested.

Before heading upstairs, Willie Brown went to the cupboard and he recovered his neckerchief with the blood and oatmeal. He got a spoon and went upstairs. Taking some of that mixture, he put a portion into the mouths of each of the boys. With the first bite, the warmth came back to their bodies, With the second, the color returned to their flesh. And with the third, they were breathing and deeply asleep.

Willie Brown called the parents who rushed into the boys' room. Then he turned to the parents and said, "Now call each son by his name."

When they did, each boy sat up in bed, amazed to find all of the people gathered around. William told them all that had happened the night before. Well, almost everything. But he mentioned nothing about that field with the gold. Well they turned that wake into a party of joy and celebration! It went on long into the night.

The amazed and grateful parents asked Willie Brown if there was anything they could do for him and he requested the field with the 3 stone heaps. Willie Brown got that field. After a while he dug up some of the gold and built a house where his family and friends could come visit. He lived a long and happy life. But he was always very careful to keep plenty of holy water by the door. And he never again fixed oatmeal.

Story Outline

I. Willie Brown's father left his black walnut walking stick by an open grave in the cemetery and Willie bravely returned to get it.

II. A corpse crawls from the open grave and climbs upon Willie Brown's back, forcing him to take him into the town.

III. They pass by two houses with holy water at the door, but then enter an unprotected house. When asked for something to eat, Willie Brown finds some oatmeal for the monster, but he cannot find water.

IV. The monster cuts the fingers of three sleeping brothers to catch their blood, causing them to lose their flesh color with the first drop, their breathing to stop with the second drop, and for them appear to die with the loss of the third drop.

V. The monster mixes the blood with the oatmeal and eats his share, but Willie Brown hides his in his neckerchief and places it in the cupboard.

VI. The monster climbs back on Willie Brown and makes him return to the graveyard. He tells Willie Brown that the boys could have been saved if there had been any of the oatmeal and blood left to place in their mouths.

VII. He shows him a field with three piles of stones and tells Willie that there is gold under the piles, but "only the dead know it."

VIII. A rooster crows, but Willie Brown cleverly tells the monster that it was a sheep bleating for its mother and tries to delay their return to the graveyard.

IX. Again a rooster crows, but Willie tells the monster that a barn owl must have eaten a rat.

X. When they reach the grave the monster tries to pull Willie Brown into it, but then a rooster crows for the third time and the monster falls into the grave dead.

XI. Willie Brown pounds the coffin lid shut and returns home with his father's black walnut walking stick.

XII. Willie Brown is exhausted the next day. His mother tells him of the boys dying, but lets him sleep longer. Willie Brown then goes to the neighbor's home and tells everyone he had a dream about the boys' death and how to bring them back to life.

XIII. He places the oatmeal and blood mixture in their mouths and the boys come back to life. The grateful parents give the field with the three stone piles to Willie Brown, who later digs up enough gold to live happily ever after.

If you feel like writing a new story, how about coming up with one titled: "Willie Brown and the Three Piles of Gold?" Inventing new stories for the campfire can be a great way to surprise the group with a new adventure!

LOST FACE

by Jack London

This little-known story is one of Jack London's best. The surprise ending, coupled with a scary woodland setting, make it an ideal campfire story. The initial paragraphs, relating to the hero's wanderings can be condensed in the telling, and place names can be eliminated or greatly simplified by the teller.

It was the end. Subienkow had traveled a long trail of bitterness and horror, homing like a dove for the capitals of Europe, and here, farther away then ever, in Russian America, the trail ceased. He sat in the snow, arms tied behind him, waiting the torture. He stared curiously before him at a huge Cossack, prone in the snow, moaning in his pain. The men had finished handling the giant and turned him over to the women. That they had exceeded the fiendishness of the men the man's cries attested.

Subienkow looked on and shuddered. He was not afraid to die. He had carried his life too long in his hands, on that weary trail from Warsaw to Nulato, to shudder at mere dying. But he objected to the torture. It offended his soul. And this offense, in turn, was not due to the mere pain he must endure, but to the sorry spectacle the pain would make of him. He knew that he would pray, and beg, and entreat, even as Big Ivan and the others that had gone before. This would not be nice. To pass out bravely and cleanly, with a smile and a jest—ah, that would have been the way. But to lose control, to have his soul upset by the pangs of the flesh, to screech and gibber like an ape, to become the veriest beast—ah, that was what was so terrible.

There had been no chance to escape. From the beginning, when he dreamed the fiery dream of Poland's independence, he had become a puppet in the hands of fate. From the beginning, at Warsaw, at St. Petersburg, in the Siberian mines, in Kamchatka, on the crazy boats of the fur thieves, fate had been driving him to this end.

Without doubt, in the foundations of the world was graved this end for him—for him, who was so fine and sensitive, whose nerves scarcely sheltered under his skin, who was a dreamer and a poet and an artist. Before he was dreamed of, it had been determined that the quivering bundle of sensitiveness that constituted him should be doomed to live in raw and howling savagery, and to die in this far land of night, in this dark place beyond the last boundaries of the world.

He sighed. So that thing before him was Big Ivan—Big Ivan the giant, the man without nerves, the man of iron, the Cossack turned freebooter of the seas, who was as phlegmatic as an ox, with a nervous system so low that what was pain to ordinary men was scarcely a tickle to him. Well, well, trust these Nulato Indians to find Big Ivan's nerves and trace them to the roots of his quivering soul. They were certainly doing it. It was inconceivable that a man could suffer so much and yet live. Big Ivan was paying for his low order of nerves. Already he had lasted twice as long as any of the others.

Subienkow felt that he could not stand the Cossack's sufferings much longer. Why didn't Ivan die? He would go mad if that screaming did not cease. But when it did cease, his turn would come. And there was Yakaga awaiting him, too, grinning at him even now in anticipation—Yakaga, whom only last week he had kicked out of the fort, and upon whose face he had laid the last of his dog whip. Yakaga would attend to him. Doubtlessly Yakaga was saving for him more refined tortures, more exquisite nerve racking. Ah! That must have been a good one, from the way Ivan screamed. The squaws bending over him stepped back with laughter and clapping of hands. Subienkow saw the monstrous thing that had been perpetrated, and began to laugh hysterically. The Indians looked at him in wonderment that he should laugh. But Subienkow could not stop.

This would never do. He controlled himself, the spasmodic twitchings slowly dying away. He strove to think of other things, and began reading back in his own life. He remembered his mother and his father, and the little spotted pony, and the French tutor who had taught him dancing and sneaked him an old worn copy of Voltaire. Once more he saw Paris, and dreary London, and gay Vienna, and Rome. And once more he saw that wild group of youths who had dreamed, even as he, the dream of an independent Poland, with a king of Poland on the throne at Warsaw. Ah, there it was that the long trail began. Well, he had lasted longest. One by one, beginning with the two executed at St. Petersburg, he took up the count of the passing of those brave spirits. Here one had been beaten to death by a jailer, and there, on that bloodstained highway of the exiles, where they had marched for endless months, beaten and maltreated by their Cossack guards, another had dropped by the way. Always it had been savagery—brutal, bestial savagery. They had died, of fever, in the mines, under the knout. The last two had died after the escape, in the battle with the Cossacks, and he alone had won to Kamchatka with the stolen papers and the money of a traveler he had left lying in the snow.

It had been nothing but savagery. All the years, with his heart in studios and theaters and courts, he had been hemmed in by savagery. He had purchased his life with blood. Everybody had been killed. He had killed that traveler for his passports. He had proved that he was a man of parts by dueling with two Russian officers on a single day. He had had to prove himself in order to win a place among the fur thieves. He had had to win that place. Behind him lay the thousand-years-long road across all Siberia and Russia. He could not escape that way. The only way was ahead, across the dark and icy sea of Bering to Alaska. The way had led from savagery to deeper savagery. On the scurvy-rotten ships of the fur thieves, out of food and out of water, buffeted by the interminable storms of that stormy sea, men had become animals. Thrice he had sailed east from Kamchatka. And thrice, after all manner of hardship and suffering, the survivors had come back to Kamchatka. There had been no outlet for escape, and he could not go back the way he had come, for the mines and the knout awaited him.

Again, the fourth and last time, he had sailed east. He had been with those who first found the fabled Seal Islands; but he had not returned with them to share the wealth of fur in the mad orgies of Kamchatka. He had sworn never to go back. He knew that to win to those dear capitals of Europe he must go on. So he had changed ships and remained in the dark new land. His comrades were Slavonian hunters and Russian adventurers, Mongols and Tatars, and Siberian aborigines; and through the savages of the New World they had cut a path of blood. They had massacred whole villages that refused to furnish the fur tribute; and they in turn had been massacred by ships' companies. He, with one Finn, had been the sole survivors of such a company. They had spent a winter of solitude and starvation on a lonely Aleutian isle, and their rescue in the spring by another fur ship had been one chance in a thousand.

But always the terrible savagery had hemmed him in. Passing from ship to ship, and ever refusing to return, he had come to the ship that explored the south. All down the Alaskan coast they had encountered nothing but hosts of savages. Every anchorage among the beetling islands or under the frowning cliffs of the mainland had meant a battle or a storm. Either the gales blew, threatening destruction, or the war canoes came off, manned by howling natives with the war paint on their faces, who came to learn the bloody virtues of the sea rovers' gunpowder. South, south they had coasted, clear to the myth land of California. Here, it was said, were Spanish adventurers who had fought their way up from Mexico. He had had hopes of those Spanish adventurers. Escaping to them, the rest would have been easy—a year or two, what did it matter more or less?—and he would win to Mexico, then a ship, and Europe would be his. But they had met no Spaniards. Only had they encountered the same impregnable wall of savagery. The denizens of the confines of the world, painted for war, had driven them back from the shores. At last, when one boat was cut off and every man killed, the commander had abandoned the quest and sailed back to the North.

The years had passed. He had served under Tebenkoff when Michaelovski Redoubt was built. He had spent two years in the Kuskokwim country. Two summers, in the month of June, he had managed to be at the head of Kotzebue Sound. Here, at this time, the tribes assembled for barter; here were to be found spotted deerskins from Siberia, ivory from the Diomedes, walrus skins from the shores of the Arctic, strange stone lamps, passing in trade from tribe to tribe, no one knew whence, and once, a hunting knife of English make; and here, Subienkow knew, was the school in which to learn geography. For he met Eskimos from Norton Sound, from King Island and St. Lawrence Island, from Cape Prince of Wales, and Point Barrow. Such places had other names, and their distances were measured in days.

It was a vast region these trading savages came from, and a vaster region from which, by repeated trade, their stone lamps and that steel knife had come. Subienkow bullied and cajoled and bribed. Every far journeyer or strange tribesman was brought before him. Perils unaccountable and unthinkable were mentioned, as well as wild beasts, hostile tribes, impenetrable forests, and mighty mountain ranges; but always from beyond came the rumor and the tale of white-skinned men, blue of eye and fair of hair, who fought like devils and who sought always for furs. They were to the east—far, far to the east. No one had seen them. It was the word that had been passed along.

It was a hard school. One could not learn geography very well through the medium of strange dialects, from dark minds that mingled fact and fable and that measured distances by "sleeps" that varied according to the difficulty of the going. But at last came the whisper that gave Subienkow courage. In the east lay a great river where were these blue-eyed men. The river was called the Yukon. South of Michaelovski Redoubt emptied another great river which the Russians knew as the Kwikpak. These two rivers were one, ran the whisper.

Subienkow returned to Michaelovski. For a year he urged an expedition up the Kwikpak. Then arose Malakoff, the Russian half-breed, to lead the wildest and most ferocious of the hell's broth of mongrel adventurers who had crossed from Kamchatka. Subienkow was his lieutenant. They threaded the mazes of the great delta of the Kwikpak, picked up the first low hills on the northern bank, and for half a thousand miles, in skin canoes loaded to the gunwales with trade goods and ammunition, fought their way against the five-knot current of a river that ran from two to ten miles wide in a channel many fathoms deep. Malakoff decided to build the fort at Nulato. Subienkow urged to go farther. But he quickly reconciled himself to Nulato. The long winter was coming on. It would be better to wait. Early the following summer, when the ice was gone, he would disappear up the Kwikpak and work his way to the Hudson's Bay Company's posts. Malakoff had never heard the whisper that the Kwikpak was the Yukon, and Subienkow did not tell him.

Came the building of the fort. It was enforced labor. The tiered walls of logs arose to the sighs and groans of the Nulato Indians. The lash was laid upon their backs, and it was the iron hand of the freebooters of the sea that laid on the lash. There were Indians who ran away, and when they were caught they were brought back and spread-eagled before the fort, where they and their tribe learned the efficacy of the knout. Two died under it; others were injured for life; and the rest took the lesson to heart and ran away no more. The snow was flying ere the fort was finished, and then it was the time for furs. A heavy tribute was laid upon the tribe. Blows and lashings continued, and that the tribute should be paid, the women and children were held as hostages and treated with the barbarity that only the fur thieves knew.

Well, it had been a sowing of blood, and now was come the harvest. The fort was gone. In the light of its burning, half the fur thieves had been cut down. The other half had passed under the torture. Only Subienkow remained, or Subienkow and Big Ivan, if that whimpering, moaning thing in the snow could be called Big Ivan. Subienkow caught Yakaga grinning at him. There was no gainsaying Yakaga. The mark of the lash was still on his face.

After all, Subienkow could not blame him, but he disliked the thought of what Yakaga would do to him. He thought of appealing to Makamuk, the head chief; but his judgment told him that such appeal was useless. Then, too, he thought of bursting his bonds and dying fighting. Such an end would be quick. But he could not break his bonds. Caribou thongs were stronger than he. Still devising, another thought came to him. He signed for Makamuk, and that an interpreter who knew the coast dialect should be brought.

"Oh, Makamuk," he said, "I am not minded to die, I am a great man, and it were foolishness for me to die. In truth, I shall not die. I am not like these other carrion."

He looked at the moaning thing that had once been Big Ivan, and stirred it contemptuously with his toe.

"I am too wise to die. Behold, I have a great medicine. I alone know this medicine. Since I am not going to die, I shall exchange this medicine with you."

"What is this medicine?" Makamuk demanded.

"It is a strange medicine."

Subienkow debated with himself for a moment, as if loath to part with the secret.

"I will tell you. A little bit of this medicine rubbed on the skin makes the skin hard like a rock, hard like iron, so that no cutting weapon can cut it. The strongest blow of a cutting weapon is a vain thing against it. A bone knife becomes like a piece of mud; and it will turn the edge of the iron knives we have brought among you. What will you give me for the secret of the medicine?"

"I will give you your life," Makamuk made answer through the interpreter.

Subienkow laughed scornfully.

"And you shall be a slave in my house until you die."

The Pole laughed more scornfully.

"Untie my hands and feet and let us talk," he said.

The chief made the sign; and when he was loosed Subienkow rolled a cigarette and lighted it.

"This is foolish talk," said Makamuk. "There is no such medicine. It cannot be. A cutting edge is stronger than any medicine."

The chief was incredulous, and yet he wavered. He had seen too many deviltries of fur thieves that worked. He could not wholly doubt.

"I will give you your life; but you shall not be a slave," he announced.

"More than that."

Subienkow played his game as coolly as if he were bartering for a fox skin.

"It is a very great medicine. It has saved my life many times. I want a sled and dogs, and six of your hunters to travel with me down the river and give me safety to one day's sleep from Michaelovski Redoubt."

"You must live here, and teach us all of your deviltries," was the reply.

Subienkow shrugged his shoulders and remained silent. He blew cigarette smoke out on the icy air, and curiously regarded what remained of the big Cossack.

"That scar!" Makamuk said suddenly, pointing to the Pole's neck, where a livid mark advertised the slash of a knife in a Kamchatkan brawl. "The medicine is not good. The cutting edge was stronger than the medicine."

"It was a strong man that drove the stroke." (Subienkow considered.)

"Stronger than you, stronger than your strongest hunter, stronger than he."

Again, with the toe of his moccasin, he touched the Cossack—a grisly spectacle, no longer conscious—yet in whose dismembered body the pain-racked life clung and was loath to go.

"Also the medicine was weak. For at that place there were no berries of a certain kind, of which I see you have plenty in this country. The medicine here will be strong."

"I will let you go downriver," said Makamuk, "and the sled and the dogs and the six hunters to give you safety shall be yours."

"You are slow," was the cool rejoinder. "You have committed an offense against my medicine in that you did not at once accept my terms. Behold, I now demand more. I want one hundred beaver skins." (Makamuk sneered.) "I want one hundred pounds of dried fish." (Makamuk nodded, for fish were plentiful and cheap.) "I want two sleds—one for me and one for my furs and fish. And my rifle must be returned to me. If you do not like the price, in a little while the price will grow."

Yakaga whispered to the chief.

"But how can I know your medicine is true medicine?" Makamuk asked.

"It is very easy. First, I shall go into the woods—"

Again Yakaga whispered to Makamuk, who made a suspicious dissent.

"You can send twenty hunters with me," Subienkow went on. "You see, I must get the berries and the roots with which to make the medicine. Then, when you have brought the two sleds and loaded on them the fish and the beaver skins and the rifle, and when you have told of the six hunters who will go with me—then, when all is ready, I will rub the medicine on my neck, so, and lay my neck there on that log. Then can your strongest hunter take the ax and strike three times on my neck. You yourself can strike the first three times."

Makamuk stood with gaping mouth, drinking in this latest and most wonderful magic of the fur thieves.

"But first," the Pole added hastily, "between each blow I must put on fresh medicine. The ax is heavy and sharp, and I want no mistakes."

"All that you have asked shall be yours," Makamuk cried in a rush of acceptance. "Proceed to make your medicine."

Subienkow concealed his elation. He was playing a desperate game, and there must be no slips. He spoke arrogantly.

"You have been slow. My medicine is offended. To make the offense clean you must give me your daughter."

He pointed to the girl, an unwholesome creature, with a cast in one eye and a bristling wolf tooth. Makamuk was angry, but the Pole remained imperturbable, rolling and lighting another cigarette.

"Make haste," he threatened. "If you are not quick, I shall demand yet more."

In the silence that followed, the dreary Northland scene faded from before him, and he saw once more his native land, and France, and once, as he glanced at the wolf-toothed girl, he remembered another girl, a singer and a dancer, whom he had known when first as a youth he came to Paris.

"What do you want with the girl?" Makamuk asked.

"To go down the river with me." Subienkow glanced her over critically. "She will make a good wife, and it is an honor worthy of my medicine to be married to your blood."

Again he remembered the singer and dancer and hummed aloud a song she had taught him. He lived the old life over, but in a detached, impersonal sort of way, looking at the memory pictures of his own life as if they were pictures in a book of anybody's life. The chief's voice, abruptly breaking the silence, startled him.

"It shall be done," said Makamuk. "The girl shall go down the river with you. But be it understood that I myself strike the three blows with the ax on your neck."

"But each time I shall put on the medicine," Subienkow answered, with a show of ill-concealed anxiety.

"You shall put the medicine on between each blow. Here are the hunters who shall see you do not escape. Go into the forest and gather your medicine."

Makamuk had been convinced of the worth of the medicine by the Pole's rapacity. Surely nothing less than the greatest of medicines could enable a man in the shadow of death to stand up and drive an old woman's bargain.

"Besides," whispered Yakaga, when the Pole, with this guard, had disappeared among the spruce trees, "when you have learned the medicine you can easily destroy him."

"There will be some part where he has not rubbed the medicine," was Yakaga's reply. "We will destroy him through that part. It may be his ears. Very well; we will thrust a spear in one ear and out the other. Or it may be his eyes. Surely the medicine will be much too strong to rub on his eyes."

The chief nodded. "You are wise, Yakaga. If he possesses no other devil things, we will then destroy him."

"But how can I destroy him?" Makamuk argued. "His medicine will not let me destroy him."

Subienkow did not waste time in gathering the ingredients for his medicine. He selected whatsoever came to hand such as spruce needles, the inner bark of the willow, a strip of birch bark, and a quantity of mossberries, which he made the hunters dig up for him from beneath the snow. A few frozen roots completed his supply, and he led the way back to camp.

Makamuk and Yakaga crouched beside him, noting the quantities and kinds of the ingredients he dropped into the pot of boiling water.

"You must be careful that the mossberries go in first," he explained. "And—oh yes, one other thing—the finger of a man. Here, Yakaga, let me cut off your finger."

But Yakaga put his hands behind him and scowled.

"Just a small finger," Subienkow pleaded.

"Yakaga, give him your finger," Makamuk commanded.

"There be plenty of fingers lying around," Yakaga grunted, indicating the human wreckage in the snow of the score of persons who had been tortured to death.

"It must be the finger of a live man," the Pole objected.

"Then shall you have the finger of a live man." Yakaga strode over to the Cossack and sliced off a finger.

"He is not yet dead," he announced, flinging the bloody trophy in the snow at the Pole's feet, "Also, it is a good finger, because it is large."

Subienkow dropped it into the fire under the pot and began to sing. It was a French love song that with great solemnity he sang into the brew.

"Without these words I utter into it the medicine is worthless," he explained. "The words are the chiefest strength of it. Behold, it is ready."

"Name the words slowly, that I may know them," Makamuk commanded.

"Not until after the test. When the ax flies back three times from my neck, then will I give you the secret of the words."

"But if the medicine is not good medicine?" Makamuk queried anxiously.

Subienkow turned upon him wrathfully. "My medicine is always good. However, if it is not good, then do by me as you have done to the others. Cut me up a bit at a time, even as you have cut him up." He pointed to Cossack. "The medicine is now cool. Thus I rub it on my neck, saying this further medicine."

With great gravity he slowly intoned a line of the "Marseillaise," at the same time rubbing the villainous brew thoroughly into his neck.

An outcry interrupted his play acting. The giant Cossack, with a last resurgence of his tremendous vitality, had arisen to his knees. Laughter and cries of surprise and applause arose from the Nulatos, as Big Ivan began flinging himself about in the snow with mighty spasms.

Subienkow was made sick by the sight, but he mastered his qualms and made believe to be angry.

"This will not do," he said. "Finish him, and then we will make the test. Here, you, Yakaga, see that his noise ceases."

While this was being done, Subienkow turned to Makamuk. "And remember, you are to strike hard. This is not baby work. Here, take the ax and strike the log, so I can see you strike like a man."

Makamuk obeyed, striking twice, precisely and with vigor, cutting out a large chip.

"It is well." Subienkow looked about him at the circle of savage faces that somehow seemed to symbolize the wall of savagery that had hemmed him about ever since the Czar's police had first arrested him in Warsaw. "Take your ax, Makamuk, and stand so. I shall lie down. When I raise my hand, strike, and strike with all your might. And be careful that no one stands behind you. The medicine is good, and the ax may bounce from off my neck and right out of your hands."

He looked at the two sleds, with the dogs in harness, loaded with furs and fish. His rifle lay on top of the beaver skins. The six hunters who were to act as his guard stood by the sleds.

"Where is the girl?" the Pole demanded. "Bring her up to the sleds before the test goes on."

When this had been carried out, Subienkow lay down in the snow, resting his head on the log like a tired child about to sleep. He had lived so many dreary years that he was indeed tired.

"I laugh at you and your strength, O Makamuk," he said. "Strike, and strike hard."

He lifted his hand. Makamuk swung the ax, a broadax for the squaring of logs. The bright steel flashed through the frosty air, poised for a perceptible instant above Makamuk's head, then descended upon Subienkow's bare neck. Clear through flesh and bone it cut its way, biting deeply into the log beneath. The amazed savages saw the head bounce a yard away from the blood-spouting trunk.

There was a great bewilderment and silence, while slowly it began to dawn in their minds that there had been no medicine. The fur thief had outwitted them. Alone, of all their prisoners, he had escaped the torture. That had been the stake for which he played. A great roar of laughter went up. Makamuk bowed his head in shame. The fur thief had fooled him. He had lost face before all his people. Still they continued to roar out their laughter. Makamuk turned, and with bowed head stalked away. He knew that thenceforth he would be no longer known as Makamuk. He would be Lost Face; the record of his shame would be with him until he died; and whenever the tribes gathered in the spring for the salmon, or in the summer for the trading, the story would pass back and forth across the campfires of

how the fur thief died peaceably, at a single stroke, by the hand of Lost Face.

"Who was Lost Face?" he could hear, in anticipation, some insolent young buck demand. "Oh, Lost Face," would be the answer, "he who once was Makamuk in the days before he cut off the fur thief's head."

Story Outline

I. Subienkow is a Polish adventurer who had escaped from Poland across Siberia after an attempt at independence had been crushed by the Russian Czar. He hopes to reach Europe by way of the rugged and unexplored North American wilderness, possibly by contacting the fur traders of Hudson's Bay Company.

II. To get to Alaska he fights his way across Siberia and joins fur thieves who are looting the Indians. Subienkow attempts to learn geography from the natives, hoping to eventually escape to a more civilized area.

III. A new leader arises, Malakoff, who leads the band of fur thieves deeper into the wilderness, eventually forcing the Indians into slave labor to build a fort. The Indians who try to escape are brutally punished.

IV. The women and children are held captive, forcing the Indians to hunt and trap fur for the thieves. But the Indians revolt, burning the fort and killing the surviving fur thieves by slowly torturing them to death.

V. Subienkow has to watch as they kill Big Ivan. He is being held to the last because he lashed the face of Yakaga. Subienkow does not mind dying, but he hates the thought that the Indians will reduce him to a whimpering pile of flesh.

VI. Subienkow tells Makamuk that he will not die because he has a powerful medicine that will prevent them from killing him. He asks the chief what he would give to learn the medicine's secret.

VII. Makamuk says he will give him his life and make him a slave the rest of his life. Subienkow is scornful. The chief then says he would not make him a slave, but Subienkow asked for more than that.

VIII. Subienkow demands that he receive a sled, dogs, and six warriors to provide him safety on his return to the base camp called Michaelovski Redoubt.

IX. Makamuk notices a scar on Subienkow's neck and says that the medicine is weak. Subienkow replies that it was a very strong person, stronger than Big Ivan, who drove that stroke, and that the medicine was weak because he lacked enough special berries at the place where the wound was made, but that there are plenty of these berries around their camp.

X. Makamuk agrees to provide the sled, dogs, and warriors, but Subienkow sneers that he was too slow in granting his demands, and that he now wants one hundred beaver, one hundred pounds of fish to feed the dogs, two sleds to carry the furs, and his rifle returned.

XI. Yakaga asks how they would know that the medicine is real. Subienkow explains that he will go into the woods (accompanied by twenty warriors) and pick the ingredients, then when ready he will smear it on his neck and the strongest of the Indians can take an ax and strike his neck three times.

XII. Makamuk agrees, but Subienkow says he answered too slowly, and now he demands more, he wants Makamuk's daughter. Makamuk agrees, but says that he personally will get to use the ax. Subienkow, with ill-concealed anxiety, makes the point that he must be allowed to apply more of the medicine to his neck between each of the blows.

XIII. Yakaga and the chief decide that they will kill Subienkow when they learn the secret of his medicine, as he will not cover his whole body, or if he does, they will be able to kill through an uncovered spot.

XIV. Subienkow quickly picks the ingredients. Makamuk and Yakaga watch as he mixes them together. He also needs the finger from a man and wants to cut off Yakaga's finger. (Just a small finger, he says, when Yakaga put his hands behind his back and scowled.)

XV. Makamuk commands Yakaga to give him a finger, but Yakaga points to all of the dead bodies lying around. Subienkow says that it must come from a live person, so

Yakaga cuts a finger from Big Ivan, who is still barely alive, and tosses it to Subienkow.

XVI. Subienkow rubs the medicine on his neck. When Big Ivan regains consciousness and starts flailing around in the snow, Subienkow demands that they kill Big Ivan to stop the noise. He makes Makamuk show that he can use the ax like a man, then places his head on the block.

XVII. Makamuk strikes a hard blow, cutting off Subienkow's head—and then realizes that he has been fooled. Subienkow had escaped their torture, and the chief was laughed at. He lost his position as chief and would forever be known as "Lost Face."

33

THE BLOODY HAND

Anonymous, adapted by Doc Forgey

This anonymous legend was gleaned from a book of short stories. Frequently short stories do not lend themselves well to campfire telling, but I found this one to be an exception.

In a certain village on the south coast, a widow and her two daughters were living in a house that stood rather apart from its neighbors on either side. It was situated on a wooded cliff, and about a quarter of a mile from its garden was a waterfall of some height. The two daughters were much attached to each other. One of them, Mary, was very attractive. Among her admirers were two men especially distinguished for their devotion to her. One of them, John Bodneys, seemed on the point of realizing the ambition of his life when a new competitor of a very different disposition appeared and completely conquered Mary's heart.

The day was fixed for the marriage, but though Mary wrote to the Bodneys family to announce her engagement and ask John to be present at her wedding, she had received no reply from him. On the evening before the wedding day, Ellen, the other sister, was gathering ferns in the woods when she heard a faint rustling behind her and, turning quickly around, thought she had a momentary glimpse of the figure of John Bodneys. Whomever it was vanished swiftly in the twilight. On her return to the house, Ellen told her sister what she thought she had seen, but neither of them thought much of it.

The wedding took place the next day. Just before the bride was due to leave with her husband, she took her sister to the room they had shared. It had a window that opened onto a balcony from which a flight of steps led down to the enclosed garden. After a few words, Mary said to her sister, "I would like to be alone for a few minutes. I will join you again presently."

Ellen left her and went downstairs, where she waited with the others. When half an hour had passed and Mary had not appeared, her sister went up to see if anything had happened to her. The bedroom door was locked. Ellen called but had no answer. Becoming alarmed, she ran downstairs and told her mother.

At last the door was forced open, but there was no trace of Mary in the room. They went into the garden, but except for a white rose lying on the path, they saw no sign of Mary. For the rest of that day and on the following days, they hunted high and low for Mary. The police were called in, the whole countryside was roused, but all to no purpose. Mary had utterly disappeared.

The years passed by. The mother and Mary's husband were dead, and of the wedding party only Ellen and an old servant were still alive. One winter's night the wind rose to a furious gale and did a great deal of damage to the trees near the waterfall. When workers came in the morning to clear away the fallen timber and fragments of rock, they found a skeleton hand, on the third finger of which was a wedding ring, guarded by another ring with a red stone in it. On searching further they found a complete skeleton, around whose bones some rags of clothes still adhered. The ring with the red stone in it was identified by Ellen as the one that her sister was wearing on her wedding day.

The skeleton was buried in the churchyard, but the shock of the discovery was so great that a few weeks later Ellen herself was on her deathbed. On the occasion of Mary's burial, she had insisted on keeping the skeleton hand with the rings, putting it in a glass box to secure it from accident. Now as she lay dying, she left the relic to the care of her old servant.

Shortly afterward the servant set up a hotel, where, as may be imagined, the skeleton hand and its story were a common topic of conversation among those who frequented its bar. One night a stranger, muffled up in a cloak, with a cap pulled over his face, made his way into the inn and asked for something to drink.

"It was a night like this when the great oak was blown down," the bartender observed to one of his customers.

"Yes," the other replied. "And it must have made the skeleton seem doubly ghastly, discovering it, as it were, in the midst of ruins."

"What skeleton?" asked the stranger, turning suddenly from the corner in which he had been standing.

"Oh, it's a long story," answered the publican. "You can see the hand in that glass case, and if you like, I will tell you how it came to be there."

He waited for the stranger's answer, but none came. The stranger was leaning against the wall in a state of collapse. He was staring at the hand, repeating again and again, "Blood, blood," and sure enough, blood was slowly dripping from his fingertips. A few minutes later, he had recovered sufficiently to admit that he was John Bodneys and to ask that he might be taken to the magistrate. He confessed to them that in a frenzy of jealousy, he had made his way into the private garden on Mary's wedding day. Seeing her alone in her room, he had entered and seized her, muffling her cries, and had taken her as far as the waterfall. There she had struggled so violently to escape from him that, unintentionally, he had pushed her off the rocks, and she had fallen into a cleft, where she was almost completely hidden. Afraid of being

discovered, he had not even waited to find out whether she was dead or alive. He had fled and lived abroad ever since, until an overpowering longing led him to revisit the scene of his crime.

After making his confession, Bodneys was committed to the county jail, where shortly afterward he died, before any trial could take place.

Story Outline

I. John Bodneys is very attracted to Mary, but she falls in love with someone else. She invites John to her wedding, but he does not reply.

II. Just before the bride is to leave with her husband, she goes upstairs to her room. But she never comes down! A search fails to find her.

III. Years pass, and everyone who had been at the wedding has died but her sister and an old servant. A storm destroys a large tree, whose roots pull up the remains of a woman in wedding clothes, with a wedding ring on her skeleton hand. The body is identified as Mary's.

IV. The body is buried in the churchyard, but her sister keeps the hand with its rings in a glass case. She soon dies and leaves the hand to the old servant.

V. The servant opens a tavern and hotel and displays the hand in a glass case.

VI. One day a stranger who overhears a conversation about the skeleton hand asks about it—the stranger stares at the hand and collapses.

VII. He admits to being John Bodneys and having killed Mary, leaving her in the crevasse by the old tree.

When telling this story, I do not have the hand dripping blood, as in the original version, but rather have John Bodneys recognize the rings and the hand as belonging to the murder victim and collapsing because of this grisly reminder from his past.

34

ONE SUMMER NIGHT

by Ambrose Bierce

This tale by the macabre Ambrose Bierce is about a topic that all medical students have to encounter—the dead body required for dissection in anatomy class. In medieval Europe a copy of the keys to the city cemetery was a legacy passed from one medical school class to the next. Voluntary donations have now replaced body snatching, but this tale returns to the time—not so long ago—when medical students had to fend for themselves in this grisly business.

The fact that Henry Armstrong was buried did not seem to him to prove that he was dead: He had always been a hard man to convince. That he really was buried, the testimony of his senses compelled him to admit. His posture—flat upon his back, with his hands crossed upon his stomach and tied with something that he easily broke without profitably altering the situation—the strict confinement of his entire person, the black darkness and profound silence, made a body of evidence impossible to controvert, and he accepted it without cavil.

But dead—no; he was only very, very ill. He had, withal, the invalid's apathy and did not greatly concern himself about the uncommon fate that had been allotted to him. No philosopher was he—just a plain, commonplace person gifted, for the time being, with a pathological indifference: The organ that he feared consequences with was torpid. So, with no particular apprehension for his immediate future, he fell asleep and all was at peace with Henry Armstrong.

But something was going on overhead. It was a dark summer night, shot through with infrequent shimmers of lightning silently firing a cloud lying low in the west and portending a storm. These brief, stammering illuminations brought out with ghastly distinctness the monuments and headstones of the cemetery and seemed to set them dancing. It was not a night in which any credible witness was likely to be straying about a cemetery, so the three men who were there, digging into the grave of Henry Armstrong, felt reasonably secure.

Two of them were young students from a medical college a few miles away; the third was a gigantic Negro known as Jess. For many years Jess had been employed about the cemetery as a man-of-all-work, and it was his favorite pleasantry that he knew "every soul in the place." From the nature of what he was now doing, it was inferable that the place was not so populous as its register may have shown it to be.

Outside the wall, at the part of the grounds farthest from the public road, were a horse and a light wagon, waiting.

The work of excavation was not difficult: The earth with which the grave had been loosely filled a few hours before offered little resistance and was soon thrown out. Removal of the casket from its box was less easy, but it was taken out, for it was a perquisite of Jess, who carefully unscrewed the cover and laid it aside, exposing the body in black trousers and white shirt. At that instant the air sprang to flame, a cracking shock of thunder shook the stunned world and Henry Armstrong tranquilly sat up. With inarticulate cries the men fled in terror, each in a different direction. For nothing on earth could two of them have been persuaded to return. But Jess was of another breed.

In the gray of the morning the two students, pallid and haggard from anxiety and with the terror of their adventure still beating tumultuously in their blood, met at the medical college.

"You saw it?" cried one.

"God! Yes—what are we to do?"

They went around to the rear of the building, where they saw a horse, attached to a light wagon, hitched to a gate post near the door of the dissecting room. Mechanically they entered the room. On a bench in the obscurity sat Jess. He rose, grinning, all eyes and teeth.

"I'm waiting for my pay," he said.

Stretched naked on a long table lay the body of Henry Armstrong, the head defiled with blood and clay from a blow with a spade.

Story Outline

I. Henry Armstrong had been very ill and was buried alive—he can tell that when he wakes up.

II. Up above him it is a dark night, complete with flashes of summer lightning. Three men are in the cemetery, digging up the grave of Henry Armstrong. Two are medical students, the other is a big fellow named Jess who is employed at the cemetery—a person who steals bodies often.

III. It is easy digging into the newly dug grave. Lifting the coffin out is less easy.

IV. When the lid is removed, a crack of thunder shakes the air—and Henry Armstrong sits up in the coffin.

V. The three men run in terror in different directions. The medical students meet at the college early in the morning, still scared and haggard from their horrible night.

VI. They go to the dissecting room, and there is Jess who says, "I'm waiting for my pay."

VII. And on the table is the body of Henry Armstrong, his head crushed from a blow with a spade.

35

THE STRANGER

by Ambrose Bierce

Some of Ambrose Bierce's tales of the supernatural make particularly good campfire stories—especially this one with its outdoors setting, around a campfire in remote wilderness, about someone—or something— that enters this group's lives.

A man stepped out of the darkness into the little illuminated circle about our failing campfire and seated himself upon a rock.

"You are not the first to explore this region," he said gravely.

Nobody controverted his statement; he was himself proof of its truth, for he was not of our party and must have been somewhere near when we camped. Moreover, he must have companions not far away; it was not a place where one would be living or traveling alone. For more than a week we had seen, besides ourselves and our animals, only such living things as rattlesnakes and horned toads. In an Arizona desert one does not long coexist with only such creatures as these; one must have pack animals, supplies, arms—"an outfit." And all these imply comrades. It was, perhaps, a doubt as to what manner of men this unceremonious stranger's comrades might be, together with something in his words inter-pretable as a challenge, that caused every man of our half a dozen "gentlemen adventurers" to rise to a sitting posture and lay his hand upon a weapon—an act signifying, in that time and place, a policy of expectation. The stranger gave the matter no atten-tion and began again to speak in the same deliberate, uninflected monotone in which he had delivered his first sentence: "Thirty years ago Ramon Gallegos, William Shaw, George W. Kent, and Berry Davis, all of Tucson, crossed the Santa Catalina Mountains and traveled due west, as nearly as the configuration of the country permitted. We were prospecting, and it was our intention, if we found nothing, to push through to the Gila River at some point near Big Bend, where we understood there was a settlement. We had a good outfit but no guide, just Ramon Gallegos, William Shaw, George W. Kent, and Berry Davis."

The man repeated the names slowly and distinctly, as if to fix them in the memories of his audience, every member of whom was now attentively observing him, but with a slackened apprehension regarding his possible companions somewhere in the darkness that seemed to enclose us like a black wall, for in the manner of this volunteer historian was no suggestion of an unfriendly purpose. His act was rather that of a harmless lunatic than an enemy. We were not so new to the country as not to know that the solitary life of many a plainsman had a tendency to develop eccentricities of conduct and character not always easily distinguishable from mental aberration. A man is like a tree: In a forest of his fellows he will grow as straight as his genetic and individual nature permits; alone, in the open, he yields to the deforming stresses and tortions that environ him.

Some such thoughts were in my mind as I watched the man from the shadow of my hat, pulled low to shut out the firelight. A witless fellow, no doubt, but what could he be doing there in the heart of a desert?

Nobody having broken the silence, the visitor went on to say: "This country was not then what it is now. There was not a ranch between the Gila and the Gulf. There was a little game here and there in the mountains, and near the infrequent water holes grass enough to keep our animals from starvation. If we should be so fortunate as to encounter no Indians, we might get through. But within a week the purpose of the expedition had altered from discovery of wealth to preservation of life. We had gone too far to go back, for what was ahead could be no worse than what was behind; so we pushed on, riding by night to avoid Indians and the intolerable heat, and concealing ourselves by day as best we could. Sometimes, having exhausted our supply of wild meat and emptied our casks, we were days without food and drink; then a water hole or a shallow pool in the bottom of an arroyo so restored our strength and sanity that we were able to shoot some of the wild animals that sought it also. Sometimes it was a bear, sometimes an antelope, a coyote, a cougar—that was as God pleased; all were food.

"One morning as we skirted a mountain range, seeking a practicable pass, we were attacked by a band of Apaches who had followed our trail up a gulch—it is not far from here. Knowing that they outnumbered us ten to one, they took none of their usual cowardly precautions, but dashed upon us at a gallop, firing and yelling. Fighting was out of the question. We urged our feeble animals up the gulch as far as there was footing for a hoof, then threw ourselves out of our saddles and took to the chaparral on one of the slopes, abandoning our entire outfit to the enemy. But we retained our rifles, every man—Ramon Gallegos, William Shaw, George W. Kent, and Berry Davis."

"Same old crowd," said the humorist of the party. A gesture of disapproval from our leader silenced him, and the stranger proceeded with his tale:

"The savages dismounted also, and some of them ran up the gulch beyond the point at which we had left it, cutting off further retreat in that direction and forcing us on up the side.

Unfortunately, the chaparral extended only a short distance up the slope, and as we came into the open ground above, we took the fire of a dozen rifles; but Apaches shoot badly when in a hurry, and God so willed it that none of us fell. Twenty yards up the slope, beyond the edge of the brush, were vertical cliffs, in which, directly in front of us, was a narrow opening. Into that we ran, finding ourselves in a cavern about as large as an ordinary room. Here for a time we were safe. A single man with a repeating rifle could defend the entrance against all the Apaches in the land. But against hunger and thirst we had no defense. Courage we still had, but hope was a memory.

"Not one of those Indians did we afterwards see, but by the smoke and glare of their fires in the gulch we knew that by day and by night they watched with ready rifles in the edge of the bush—knew that, if we made a sortie, not a man of us would live to take three steps into the open. For three days, watching in turn, we held out, before our suffering became insupportable. Then— it was the morning of the fourth day—Ramon Gallegos said,

"'Señore, I know not well of the good God and what please him. I have lived without religion, and I am not acquainted with that of yours. Pardon, señores, if I shock you, but for me the time is come to beat the game of the Apache.'

"He knelt upon the rock floor of the cave and pressed his pistol against his temple. 'Madre de Dios,' he said, 'comes now the soul of Ramon Gallegos.'

"And so he left us—William Shaw, George W. Kent, and Berry Davis.

"I was the leader. It was for me to speak.

"'He was a brave man,' I said. 'He knew when to die, and how. It is foolish to go mad from thirst and fall by Apache bullets, or be skinned alive—it is in bad taste. Let us join Ramon Gallegos.'

"'That is right,' said William Shaw.

"'That is right,' said George W. Kent.

"I straightened the limbs of Ramon Gallegos and put a hand-kerchief over his face. Then William Shaw said: 'I should like to look like that a little while.'

"And George W. Kent said that he felt that way too.

"'It shall be so,' I said. 'The devils will wait a week. William Shaw and George W. Kent, draw and kneel.'

"They did so and I stood before them.

"'Almighty God, our Father,' said I.

"'Almighty God, our Father,' said William Shaw.

"'Almighty God, our Father,' said George W. Kent.

"'Forgive us our sins,' said I.

"'Forgive us our sins,' said they.

"'And receive our souls.'

"'And receive our souls.'

"'Amen!'

"'Amen!'

"I laid them beside Ramon Gallegos and covered their faces."

There was a quick commotion on the opposite side of the campfire. One of our party had sprung to his feet, pistol in hand.

"And you!" he shouted. "You dared to escape? You dare to be alive? You cowardly hound, I'll send you to join them if I hang for it!"

But with the leap of a panther the captain was upon him, grasping his wrist. "Hold it in, Sam Yountsey, hold it in!"

We were now all upon our feet, except for the stranger, who sat motionless and apparently inattentive. Someone seized Yountsey's other arm.

"Captain," I said, "there is something wrong here. This fellow is either a lunatic or merely a liar—just a plain, everyday liar

that Yountsey has no call to kill. If this man was of that party it had five members, one of whom—probably himself—he has not named."

"Yes," said the captain, releasing the insurgent, who sat down, "there is something—unusual. Years ago four dead bodies of white men, scalped and shamefully mutilated, were found about the mouth of that cave. They are buried there; I have seen the graves—we shall all see them tomorrow."

The stranger rose, standing tall in the light of the expiring fire, which in our breathless attention to his story we had neglected to keep going.

"There were four," he said. "Ramon Gallegos, William Shaw, George W. Kent, and Berry Davis."

With this reiterated roll call of the dead, he walked into the darkness, and we saw him no more.

At that moment one of our party, who had been on guard, strode in among us, rifle in hand and somewhat excited.

"Captain," he said, "for the last half an hour three men have been standing out there on the mesa." He pointed in the direction taken by the stranger. "I could see them distinctly, for the moon is up, but as they had no guns and I had them covered with mine, I thought it was their move. They have made none, but damn it! They got on my nerves."

"Go back to your post, and stay till you see them again," said the captain. "The rest of you lie down again, or I'll kick you all into the fire."

The sentinel obediently withdrew, swearing, and did not return. As we were arranging our blankets, the fiery Yountsey said: "I beg your pardon, Captain, but who the devil do you take them to be?"

"Ramon Gallegos, William Shaw, and George W. Kent."

"But how about Berry Davis? I ought to have shot him."

"Quite needless; you couldn't have made him any deader. Go to sleep."

The original story glosses over the fact that Berry Davis sat with the dead bodies of his friends a full week before he killed himself, so that his friends could rest unmutilated by Indians "for a little while" as requested by William Shaw and George W. Kent. I generally make more a point of this when telling the story—actually drawing out his staying in the hot cave with his dead friends, holding off the Indians' attacks, and starving until he could stand it no longer—then killing himself.

Story Outline

I. A group of cowboys is seated around a campfire in Arizona when a stranger steps into the light of their fire and tells them a story.

II. He relates how Ramon Gallegos, William Shaw, George W. Kent, and Berry Davis had been prospecting in that area many years before.

III. They nearly starved and died from thirst as they struggled through the unexplored desert, shooting what game they could find at water holes.

IV. They traveled by night to avoid the heat and Indians, but their luck ran out one morning when a band of Apaches caught up with them and trapped them in a gully.

V. The men found refuge from Indian bullets in a cave, but were trapped without food or water.

VI. After three days they could stand it no longer, and Ramon Gallegos said he did not want to be tortured by thirst and hunger and shot himself.

VII. His body was laid out with a handkerchief over his face. William Shaw and George W. Kent said that they would like to look like that without being mutilated by the Indians, if only for a little while. Their leader said, "It shall be so. The devils will wait a week."

VIII. The two men were laid out alongside Ramon Gallegos, their faces covered.

IX. Some of the cowboys think that this man escaped the massacre and abandoned his friends, or that he is a fifth member of this group.

X. The cowboy foreman says that four mutilated bodies were found at a cave entrance near where they are camping many years ago, and that their graves are close by.

XI. The stranger repeats that there were only four in the party—and again gives their names. He then leaves the camp.

XII. The guard comes in and says he noted three men just standing outside of their camp. He is told to return to his guard duty, and the rest of the men are ordered to bed.

XIII. The foreman is asked who the three men are, and he answers, "Ramon Gallegos, William Shaw, and George W. Kent." When a cowboy says he should have shot the cowardly Berry Davis, the foreman answers, "Quite needless; you couldn't have made him any deader. Go to sleep."

If you have trouble remembering the slain men's names, try substituting the names of relatives or coworkers.

THE MANOR

by Sir Walter Scott

This story is an adaptation of an old Sir Walter Scott story by the same name. It has been placed in a modern setting to provide more relevance for the campfire audience. Some old stories are best left in their ancient settings, while others seem to work better with modernization.

The road and the scenery whizzed by, but the country's beauty was lost to the driver. His thoughts weren't on the local charms or even on the destination for which the car was headed; his mind was on a war, a war in a faraway land.

But the war was over for Lt. Col. Brad Rallings, at least the combat was over. A Viet Cong land mine had seen to that. It was strange the way things had turned out. He was one of the few who had become exactly what he had always wanted to be, a combat officer. Now he would finish his career behind a desk at a training command, a career that had taken him through four tours of Viet Nam, earned him a chest full of medals and now a leg that would never function as it should again. Yeah, it was strange the way things turned out sometimes.

A sudden curve in the road brought him back to reality, and the colonel took notice of the picturesque countryside that was all around him. His thoughts turned to his destination and a friend he had not seen since he first entered the service. It would be great seeing his childhood buddy again. He and Ken had been chums since they were old enough to walk. They did everything together. They were even roommates in college. Ken went into business, and Brad entered the military. But they had always kept in contact with each other, no matter where their careers took them.

Ken had inherited an old country manor a few years back. Actually it was more of an estate. Ken had converted it into a resort, the opening of which occurred just a few weeks earlier. Now that the colonel had several weeks of medical leave, he couldn't think of a better place to recuperate than at a quiet manor out in the country. Three weeks of total peace and quiet would hopefully give him a new frame of mind with regard to his new command behind a desk.

The road wound through the countryside like a shiny ribbon, enshrouded on either side by thick green woods, which, from time to time, gave way at different points to offer the eye a fleeting glimpse of the truly magnificent scenery. It was through one of these woodland portholes that the colonel first caught sight of the manor. The colonel stopped his car and gazed across the valley at the manor resting sedately on the side of the adjacent hill. The sight was enough to bring a sense of calm to the haggard soldier's mind. His heart warmed at the thought of his lifelong friend in possession of such a delightful place. He couldn't picture a better place to rest up before returning to his duties as a soldier. He quickly pulled away, now anxious to see his friend and get settled in for a much needed rest.

On his arrival the colonel was greeted by a porter, who when learning his identity, quickly sent word of his arrival to the owner. As he waited, the colonel looked about in awe. The manor was even more splendid than he had imagined. It was then that the colonel first saw Ken, and although the years had been many, he instantly recognized him. But for a moment his childhood friend seemed to hesitate and looked at him like a stranger. Col. Rallings had the face of a soldier, upon which war with its fatigues and wounds had made a great alteration. But the uncertainty lasted only until the colonel spoke. The hearty greeting that followed was one that could only be shared between those who had spent countless days of childhood and early youth together.

"If I had but one wish," said the soldier's friend, "it would be that you had been here to share the opening of my manor!"

The colonel made a suitable reply and congratulated his friend on the fine manor he had acquired.

"You ain't seen nothing yet ole buddy!" his friend replied and proceeded to give the colonel a personally guided tour of the manor.

"Don't think that your exploits haven't been watched," Ken told him at one point. "I've kept close track of your career, and a glorious one it's been. Twice decorated for valor, a Distinguished Service Cross, and so many more honors that I can't count them all."

The tour ended when they came to an isolated area of the manor. The colonel's friend led him down a hallway that ended in front of a large oak door that strangely did not match the rest of the decor. "This is part of the original manor," his friend explained, "It's much like it was when the house was first built, and I've reserved it especially for you. Now why don't you freshen up. I'll see you for dinner at about eight in the dining room." With that the owner of the manor took his leave.

The colonel found the room to be something right out of the 1800s, with heavy ornate wood trim and plastered walls. The furnishings were antique and centered around a very large four-poster bed. All in all the room was quite nice and seemed the perfect place to relax.

After unpacking, the colonel took a stroll on the large balcony that ran the length of the manor and adjoined his room. He had access to it by way of two large patio doors. He felt relaxed and comfortable. The colonel looked forward to dinner with his friend.

A celebration took place that evening in the dining hall. Ken had prepared a special banquet in the colonel's honor, and it was attended by many of the owner's friends and guests. The soldier was introduced as a man of great honor and bravery. His exploits and awards were revealed to those attending, and the colonel was coaxed by his host to speak of his adventures. All who were present looked on the soldier as a brave officer, one who was sensible, cool under fire, and who had gained the respect of his fellow officers and the men who fought under him.

After dinner the evening turned to entertainment and dancing. The atmosphere was that of a relaxed party. The festivities ended at a respectable hour, and the guests returned to their rooms. The host accompanied the colonel to his room, and when they reached the door, he inquired if his friend found his accommodations to his liking. The colonel answered that it was most comfortable, and because it was the property of such a dear friend, he would rather be here than anywhere else. The two childhood friends bid each other good night with a warm handshake. "I'll see you at breakfast promptly at eight," his host said as he retreated down the hall.

The colonel entered his room, looked around, and thought to himself how different it was here, how comfortable compared with the hardships and pain he had suffered the past few weeks. With this he prepared himself for bed and a luxurious night's sleep.

The next morning found the host and a few friends assembled for breakfast at eight without the colonel. Because he was the desired guest, his absence was justly noticed. More than once Ken expressed his surprise at the soldier's lack of promptness and finally sent a porter to check on the colonel. The porter came back to inform him that the colonel was not in his room and had been seen walking about the terrace and grounds since very early that morning, which seemed strange because the weather had turned cold and misty.

"Just like a soldier," said the host to those around the table. "Many of them have the habit of not sleeping past light because their duty calls for them to be alert at early hours." But his explanation didn't really sit well with Ken, and he soon excused himself to find his boyhood friend. Ken found the colonel as the porter had said, roaming aimlessly about the grounds. The colonel looked extremely fatigued and feverish. His clothes were wrinkled and hung on him with a careless negligence that was surprising for a military man. His hair was mussed and damp with dew, his face haggard and ghastly in some strange way.

"You look absolutely horrible this morning, Brad," commented Ken with some concern. "Are you feeling all right? Why were you wandering around so early this morning? You okay?"

"I'm fine," the colonel replied quickly, but with the air of embarrassment that made it obvious that he was not telling the truth.

"Why don't you come in and get a cup of coffee and eat some breakfast. You'll feel better," Ken said.

"No thanks, Ken," answered the colonel with a quiver in his voice. With a hesitation that didn't go unnoticed, the colonel said that he had asked the porter to collect his bags and bring his car around.

"Why?" asked Ken with surprise. "You said you'd spend at least a couple of weeks. Why the sudden change of heart?"

"I'm sorry, Ken. I know it's sudden, but I must get to my next command," announced the much-decorated soldier with obvious embarrassment.

"That's a bunch of bull, and you know it!" his friend said firmly. "Now level with me, what happened last night that has you so rattled?"

After a long hesitation the colonel turned and looked into the eyes of the man with whom he had shared his childhood and who was undoubtedly his best friend. It was then that Ken noticed something he had never before seen in the eyes of this modern-day warrior. He saw fear!

"Brad, as my oldest and dearest friend and on the honor of a soldier, I want you to answer me honestly: How did you sleep last night?" asked the owner of the manor.

There was once again a long hesitation. Then with a sigh of resignation, the brave colonel answered, "I've never in my life spent such a horrible night. It was so miserable that I couldn't run the risk of spending another night, not for anything, not even for you."

"This is unbelievable," said the host as if speaking to himself. Ken turned back to the colonel and said, "For God's sake, Brad, be candid and tell me everything that happened last night. Tell me what could possibly have done this to you."

The colonel seemed very distressed by his friend's request and paused at length before he replied. "Ken, what happened last night was so bizarre and frightening that I wouldn't want to recount it to anybody, not even you. But I feel somehow honor bound to tell you what happened. If I told anyone else they would think I had completely flipped out, but you know me, and you should know that I would never make up something as unthinkable as what I'm about to tell you."

With this the colonel paused and looked directly into the eyes of his friend.

"Believe me Brad, I know there's something really bothering you. I know that you'll be telling the truth no matter how strange it sounds!" replied Ken. "Now tell me what happened."

"All right," said the veteran soldier, "I'll tell you as best I can, relying on your discretion; and yet I'd rather face a company of Viet Cong than recall what happened last night!"

The brave colonel paused again; Ken's silence confirmed his attention and willingness to hear him out. So with great reluctance and a sense of uneasiness, the colonel related the events of the worst night in his life.

"After you left me last night, I got ready for bed. The fire in the hearth burned brightly, and I lay thinking of our childhood and growing up, how our lives had changed over the years. All of these were fond memories. I was glad to be here, spending this time with my best friend." Again the colonel paused, then almost forcing himself, he continued. "I was just about to doze off, when I was aroused by the sound of footsteps, like that a woman would make in high heels as she walked across the floor. I could also hear the rustling of material, like a woman's gown would make. As I sat up in bed and focused my eyes, I saw the figure of a woman pass in front of the fireplace. Her back was to me, but by the way she held herself, her neck, her shoulders, I could tell that it was an old woman whose dress was an old-fashioned gown, like those you see in a movie about the Civil War."

The colonel closed his eyes for a moment, then cleared his throat to continue. "I really didn't think much of the intrusion. I figured it to be no more than an elderly (perhaps senile) guest who was confused as to the room in which she belonged. So I shifted myself to accommodate my injured leg and coughed to let her know I was there. That's when she slowly turned toward me. I swear, Ken, nothing in my life prepared me for what I saw."

The soldier's eye looked skyward, and Ken could see the fear that was in them as his friend forced himself to continue. "There wasn't any doubt as to what she was, or even any chance that she was still among the living. Her face had the fixed features of a corpse, yet somehow manifested the vile, hideous passions she possessed while alive. Her form was like some demonic soul that the Devil sent back from the grave! Some fiendish creature whose guilt was too great to lie quietly in eternity. In my horror I pushed myself backward to the head of the bed, supporting myself on my palms. Too scared to move, I watched as this hideous specter, in what seemed a single move, climbed right onto the bed. No more than a foot away from me, she squatted over the top of me. Her eyes were wide and wild, as if she was completely insane. Her grin was that of demonic maniac, mocking and full of malice."

Here the colonel stopped and wiped away the cold beads of sweat that had formed during the recalling of that horrible night. His breathing was labored, and he tried to calm himself before he went on.

"My Lord, Ken," the colonel continued in a trembling voice. "I'm no coward. I've proven that a hundred times on the battlefield, and I've never dishonored myself or my men. But having this thing hovering over me with those horrible demonic eyes and being so close that . . . that horrid evil incarnation . . ." He paused to recapture his labored breath. "I . . . I couldn't control my fear. My blood seemed to turn to ice. The hair stood up on the back of my neck, and I shook with panic . . . that's when I must have passed out."

The soldier's head seemed to fall in shame. When he again spoke, his voice was weak and shaky, "How long I was out I couldn't tell you."

The haggard soldier, the person that Ken was sure possessed no fear, slowly walked a few steps and gazed out over the terrace, gathering himself before going on with his terrible story.

"When I finally came to, I lay with my eyes closed for some time for fear of seeing that horrible hag hovering above me once again. When I finally gathered enough courage to look, she was no longer there. It's to my own shame that I'll tell you, I was so afraid of crossing paths with that terrible creature again that I laid huddled in that bed, too afraid to get out. I can't even begin to tell you of the hideous things that ran through my mind as I lay there waiting for dawn. But those were all in my mind, I knew the difference. At first light of day I quickly threw on my clothes and got out of that haunted room. I wandered the grounds trying to soothe my nerves. Now you know why I can't spend another night under the same roof with that demon hag."

As strange as the colonel's tale was, Ken had no doubt as to the conviction in his friend's recollection of the previous night. He never questioned the possibility that it all could have been a bad dream. Quite the contrary, Ken didn't seem to doubt a single word of the soldier's tale. A look of sorrow and regret had taken over his normally jovial face.

"I'm truly sorry for the pain and anguish you have suffered," Ken began slowly, "for I'm afraid I'm to blame for what happened last night! That room I gave you last night has been closed up for many, many years because it was said to be haunted. When I inherited the manor, I reopened the room, not believing at all that it was haunted. Everybody around here knows of the room, and I figured that they would be biased toward it and rekindle the rumors if they were to spend the night there. So when you called and said you were coming, I thought it the perfect opportunity to dispel the rumors and make the room useful again. Your courage is indisputable, and with no prior knowledge of the room, you were perfect for my little experiment."

"Thanks a lot, Ken," said the colonel, somewhat hastily. "I'll be forever in your debt, as I'm likely to remember for some time the consequences of your so-called little experiment. Next time, find some other guinea pig!"

"Now you're being unfair, Brad," Ken said. "I would never have put you through that if for a moment I believed it would cause you so much grief. You know that. If I had told you ahead of time, you would have jumped at the chance to stay in that room. Perhaps I was wrong in my method, but what happened last night was not my fault. You must remember that until this morning, I honestly didn't believe that the room was haunted."

"You're right, Ken," said the colonel, the anger no longer in his voice. "I know I have no right to be mad at you. Until last night I didn't believe in ghosts either and most likely would have taken that room if you had told me. Look, I see that my car's here, and I don't want to keep you from your guests any longer, so I'll be going now."

"Brad, wait. I know there's no way I can talk you into remaining now, but can't you stay for a while? There are some things that I want to show you," pleaded the colonel's friend.

The shaken colonel accepted the invitation, although somewhat reluctantly. Brad Rallings would not breathe easy until he was far away from this manor, but he owed it to his lifelong friend to at least grant his request.

The colonel followed his host through several rooms and into a long gallery hung with portraits, which Ken pointed out were his ancestors and former owners of the manor. As they moved down the gallery, Ken would point out certain paintings, telling their names and giving some account of who they were. The colonel had little interest but followed along quietly. They were about halfway down the gallery when Ken noticed that the colonel suddenly stiffened and jumped back in the utmost surprise and not without some fear, if the way his eyes were riveted to a portrait of an old lady in a sacque, the fashionable dress of the end of the seventeenth century, were any indication.

"There she is!" he exclaimed. "That's her, the woman from the room! Not as hideous as last night, but it's her nonetheless!"

"If that's the case," said the colonel's friend, "there's no doubt as to the horrible reality of your ghost. That is a picture of a wretched ancestress of mine. Her crimes are too numerous to count, too horrible to name. Let's just say that the crimes committed in that room were unnatural acts of violence and death. I will reseal the room, leaving it to the isolation to which the better judgment of those before me consigned it; and never again, as long as I can help it, will anyone go through the anguish that you have."

Thus the two friends who had met with such happiness, parted in very different moods: Ken to dismantle the haunted room and have it sealed; and the colonel to finish out his career, hoping to forget that horrifying night he passed while at the manor.

Story Outline

I. A wounded Vietnam war hero, Lt. Col. Brad Rallings, is home on sick leave and plans to visit a high school friend whom he has not seen for years.

II. His friend, Ken, inherited an old country manor and has turned it into a resort, inviting Brad to spend several weeks there to aid in his recuperation.

III. The colonel is the guest of honor at dinner. Everyone admires the war hero and gives him great respect because of his demonstrated heroism.

IV. Ken takes the colonel to the special guest room that has been prepared for him, a room strangely isolated in an unused portion of the old manor house.

V. The next morning the colonel fails to appear for breakfast. When Ken finds him wandering outside, the colonel appears fatigued and rumpled.

VI. Ken asks him how he slept and finally learns that the brave colonel has just spent the most terrifying night of his life.

VII. The colonel relates that just as he was falling asleep, he heard the footsteps of a woman.

VIII. He could see an old woman pass between him and the fireplace. Thinking that she was a guest who had wandered accidentally into his room, he coughed to let her know he was there.

IX. But an evil, dead creature turned toward him and leaped upon his bed, causing him to feel such concentrated horror that he became paralyzed with fear and passed out.

X. When he awoke, he was afraid to open his eyes, fearing that the hideous face would still be hovering over him.

XI. He stayed frozen in fright until dawn appeared, when he immediately threw on his clothes and left the mansion to soothe his nerves.

XII. His friend apologizes for placing him in the haunted room but points out that he needed someone with great courage, who had not heard of the ghost, to test the room and find the truth.

XIII. Ken then tells the colonel that he had to show him something. Taking him on a tour of the manor, he shows him a series of family portraits. Suddenly the colonel recognizes one as being that of the woman whose ghost he had seen he night before.

XIV. Ken tells the colonel that she had been an evil wretch, and that she had committed horrible crimes in that room. He swears that he will seal the room forever so that no one will ever again have to experience the fear that his friend did.

37

THE MINNESOTA MAGGOT OF DEATH

by Doc Forgey

This old folk tale is simple, yet it readily conjures up thoughts of an evil and hideous ghoulie—one that becomes particularly dreadful around a campfire, deep in the woods on some dark night. Try to personalize the introduction, much as I have.

During a recent visit with my old canoe buddy, Cliff Jacobson, I was shown an overgrown church cemetery near his hometown of Hastings, Minnesota. Perhaps the most loathsome and terrifying apparition ever seen there was a maggoty creature that was said to have haunted this little Minnesota churchyard years ago.

The first man to see it was Mr. Thomas, the baker. He was passing the graveyard on his way home on a bright moonlit night when his attention was caught by a large blob of luminous ooze, issuing from the fresh grave of a recently dead villager named Jenkins. The giant, ugly glowworm wriggled and grew bigger as it slithered from the ground. Repulsed and horrified, Thomas was nevertheless fascinated by the creature. It looked exactly like a giant glowing maggot. He never liked cutting through the cemetery by himself, so it took all of the courage that he could muster to even watch the monster. When he saw its eyes, he was forced to look away from it, for the evil creature stared in a strangely human fashion. Its hideous face seemed to recognize him, yet it was decidedly not human—it was a creature from beyond the grave that exuded pure evil.

Thomas followed the ghastly monster as it slithered along the ground, leaving a gleaming trail of disgusting slime in its wake. The maggot wriggled along the paths between the tombstones and soon reached the edge of the graveyard. Thomas followed the slimy trail until it ended at the door of the village postmaster's house nearby.

The next day Thomas told his wife and his best friend about the incredible experience. That night the three of them went to the cemetery to see if they could discover anything more about the hideous monster. Suddenly the ground above Jenkins's grave quivered and the dreadful creature oozed forth. The three friends followed at a distance until it disappeared once again at the postmaster's house. The next day the Thomases and their friend were shocked to learn that the postmaster and his entire family had taken ill. Worse, by the time the sun set that night, all members of the family were dead. The perplexed doctor taking care of them decided that they had all died of carbon monoxide poisoning.

Resolved now more than ever to learn about the glowing maggot's origin, Thomas, his wife, and their friend returned to the grave that very night. Again the ground above Jenkins's grave trembled and the glowing maggot poked its slimy head above the surface. The creature slithered up from the grave, glanced in their direction, and then crawled between the tombstones. Following the familiar trail of glowing slime, the three friends followed the trail until it vanished at the house of the village school principal. There was no need for the creature to visit the principal a second time, nor did Thomas have a chance to warn him. The principal became ill in the morning and died before sunset, like the postmaster and his family, of carbon monoxide poisoning.

Now completely frightened and more bewildered than ever, Thomas and his companions decided to return to the graveyard

that very night. Almost to their astonishment, nothing happened. They were afraid to tell anyone of their sightings for fear they would be made to look hysterical or even implicated in the deaths. They decided to maintain their nightly vigil at the grave for at least two weeks.

On the tenth night of watching, the creature again emerged from Jenkins's grave, this time slithering purposefully straight toward the Thomas home. The Thomases were horror stricken. Rushing into their house, they grabbed their five-year-old son and rushed him outside. That night they all stayed at their friend's house. In the morning they found their pet dog, Jack, dead—the vet said of carbon monoxide poisoning.

That very night, their hearts filled with anger and fear, Thomas and his wife, accompanied by their friend, went back to the grave site. This time they meant to strike back at the monster. Equipped with a kerosene lantern and shovels, they dug up the grave of the late Mr. Jenkins.

When they struck the coffin, Mrs. Thomas held the lantern, while her husband and his friend pried the lid off. Mrs. Thomas shrieked when she saw the corpse, dropping her lantern. Mr. Thomas and his friend sprang back from the coffin, allowing the lid to slam shut. But before it closed, they could both see that a hideous green glow emanated from it.

The two men then placed a rope around the coffin and dragged it from the graveyard to a nearby field. Taking the now-broken lantern, they poured the remaining kerosene over the coffin and lit it on fire, burning it to cinders. After returning to the cemetery, they filled the grave and covered all traces of their having been there.

The monstrous maggot of death was never seen again. Mr. Thomas later learned that the dead man had been on bad terms with both the postmaster and the school principal. He had never had any trouble with Jenkins, but he remembered with a shudder how the evil glowing maggot had stared at him as it crawled away from the cemetery on its way to perform its hideous deeds.

Story Outline

I. Mr. Thomas passes through the cemetery one night when he sees a hideous blob of luminous ooze wriggle up from a fresh grave.

II. A glowing, monstrous maggot slithers out of the grave-yard, leaving a trail of gleaming slime until it disappears into the postmaster's house.

III. Thomas, his wife, and best friend return to the cemetery the next night, and again the glowing maggot slithers from the grave to the postmaster's house.

IV. The next day the postmaster and his entire family take ill and are dead by sunset—the doctor feels from carbon monoxide poisoning.

V. The three companions return to the churchyard the following night and again watch as the glowing maggot leaves the grave and makes its way to the school principal's house.

VI. The school principal becomes ill in the morning and dies before the three friends can warn him. Carbon monoxide poisoning is said to be the cause of the principal's death.

VII. Thoroughly alarmed, yet afraid to look foolish to the authorities, Thomas and his companions watch the cemetery nightly, but nothing happened for ten days.

VIII. When it reappears, the glowing maggot heads directly for the Thomas house. Terrified, they take their son and spend the night at their friend's home.

IX. On returning home they find that their pet dog, which had been left behind in their haste, is dead—the vet says from carbon monoxide poisoning.

X. That night the three friends return to the graveyard and dig up the corpse from Jenkin's grave.

XI. They remove the coffin to a nearby field and burned it to cinders.

XII. They learn that the dead man had hated the postmaster and school principal. He had never had any trouble with Jenkins, but Thomas remembers with a shudder how the evil glowing maggot had stared at him as it crawled away from the cemetery on its way to perform its hideous deeds.

38

RUNNING WOLF

by Algernon Blackwood

Algernon Blackwood has produced many stories of the occult. Because of his interest in the outdoors, and his experiences canoeing and camping in Canada and Europe, many of these stories deal with the mysterious aspects of deep wilderness. Two of his longer stories that are must reads for outdoorsmen are "The Wendigo" and "The Willows." Both of these stories are rather long, however, and are difficult to tell around a campfire in their entirety. "Running Wolf," however, is an ideal campfire story by the master of the wilderness macabre.

The man who enjoys an adventure outside the general experience of the race, and imparts it to others, must not be surprised if he is taken for either a liar or a fool, as Malcolm Hyde, hotel clerk on a holiday, discovered of course. Nor is *enjoy* the right word to use in describing his emotions; the word he chose was probably *survive*.

When he first set eyes on Medicine Lake, he was struck by its still, sparkling beauty, lying there in the vast Canadian backwoods; next, by its extreme loneliness; and, lastly—a good deal later, this—by its combination of beauty, loneliness, and singular atmosphere, due to the fact that it was the scene of his adventure.

"It's fairly stiff with big fish," said Morton of the Montreal Sporting Club. "Spend your holidays there—up Mattawa way, some fifteen miles west of Stony Creek. You'll have it all to yourself except for an old Indian who's got a shack there. Camp on

the east side—if you'll take a tip from me." He then talked for
half an hour about the wonderful sport; yet he was not otherwise
very communicative, and did not suffer questions gladly, Hyde
noticed. Nor had he stayed there very long himself. If it was such
a paradise as Morton, its discoverer and the most experienced rod
in the province, claimed, why had he himself spent only three
days there?

"Ran short of grub," was the only explanation offered; but to
another friend he had mentioned briefly, "flies," and to a third,
so Hyde learned later, he gave the excuse that his half-breed "took
sick," necessitating a quick return to civilization.

Hyde, however, cared little for the explanations; his interest in
these came later. "Stiff with fish" was the phrase he liked. He took
the Canadian Pacific train to Mattawa, laid in his outfit at Stony
Creek, and set off thence for the fifteen-mile canoe trip without
a care in the world.

Traveling light, the portages did not trouble him; the water
was swift and east, the rapids negotiable; everything came his way,
as the saying is. Occasionally he saw a big fish making for the
deeper pools, and was sorely tempted to stop; but he resisted. He
pushed on between the immense world of forests that stretched
for hundreds of miles, known to deer, bear, moose, and wolf, but
strange to any echo of human tread, a deserted and primeval wilderness. The autumn day was calm, the water sang and sparkled,
the blue sky hung cloudless over all, ablaze with light. Toward
evening he passed an old beaver dam, rounded a little point, and
had his first sight of Medicine Lake. He lifted his dripping paddle; the canoe shot with silent glide into calm water. He gave an
exclamation of delight, for the loveliness took his breath away.

Though primarily a sportsman, he was not insensible to
beauty. The lake formed a crescent, perhaps four miles long, its

width between a mile and half a mile. The slanting fold of sunset flooded it. No wind stirred its crystal surface. Here it had lain since the redskins' god first made it; here it would lie until he dried it up again. Towering spruce and hemlock trooped to its very edge, majestic cedars leaned down as if to drink, crimson sumacs shone in fiery patches, and maples gleamed orange and red beyond belief. The air was like wine, with the silence of a dream.

It was here the red men formerly "made medicine," with all the wild ritual and tribal ceremony of the ancient day. But it was of Morton, rather than of Indians, that Hyde thought. If this lonely, hidden paradise was really stiff with big fish, he owed a lot to Morton for the information. Peace invaded him, but the excitement of the hunter lay below.

He looked about him with quick, practiced eyes for a camping place before the sun sank below the forests and the half-lights came. The Indian's shack, lying in full sunshine on the eastern shore, he found at once; but the trees lay too thick about it for comfort, nor did he wish to be so close to its inhabitant. Upon the opposite side, however, an ideal clearing offered. This lay already in shadow, the huge forest darkening it toward evening; but the open space attracted. He paddled over quickly and examined it. The ground was hard and dry, he found, and a little brook ran tinkling down one side of it onto the lake. This out fall, too, would be a good fishing spot. Also, it was sheltered. A few low willows marked the mouth.

An experienced camper soon makes up his mind. It was a perfect site, and some charred logs, with traces of former fires, proved that he was not the first to think so. Hyde was delighted. Then, suddenly, disappointment came to tinge his pleasure. His kit was landed, and preparations for putting up the tent were begun, when he recalled a detail that excitement had so far kept in the background of his mind—Morton's advice. But not Morton's only, for the storekeeper at Stony Creek had reinforced it. The big fellow with a straggling moustache and stooping shoulders, dressed in shirt and trousers, had handed him out a final sentence with the bacon, flour, condensed milk, and sugar. He had repeated Morton's half-forgotten words:

"Put your tent on the east shore, I should," he had said at parting.

He remembered Morton, too, apparently. "A shortish fellow, brown as an Indian and fairly smelling of the woods. Traveling with Jake, the half-breed." That assuredly was Morton. "Didn't stay long, now, did he," he added to himself in a reflective tone.

"Going Windy Lake way, are yer? Or Ten Mile Water, maybe?" he had first inquired of Hyde.

"Medicine Lake."

"Is that so?" the man said, as though he doubted it for some obscure reason. He pulled at his ragged moustache a moment. "Is that so, now?" he repeated. And the final words followed him downstream after a considerable pause—the advice about the best shore on which to put his tent.

All this now suddenly flashed back upon Hyde's mind with a tinge of disappointment and annoyance, for when two experienced men agreed, their opinion was not to be lightly disregarded. He wished he had asked the storekeeper for many details. He looked about him, he reflected, he hesitated. His ideal camping ground lay certainly on the forbidden shore. What in the world, he wondered, could be the objection to it?

But light was fading; he must decide quickly one way or the other. After staring at his unpacked dunnage, and the tent, already half erected, he made up his mind with a muttered expression that consigned both Morton and the storekeeper to less pleasant places. "They must have some reason," he growled to himself. "Fellows like that usually know what they're talking about. I guess I'd better shift over to the other side—for tonight, at any rate."

He glanced across the water before actually reloading. No smoke rose from the Indian's shack. He had seen no sign of a canoe. The man, he decided, was away. Reluctantly, then, he left the good camping ground and paddled across the lake, and half an hour later his tent was up, firewood collected, and two small trout were already caught for supper. But the bigger fish, he knew lay waiting for him on the other side by the little out fall, and he fell asleep at length on his bed balsam boughs, annoyed and disappointed, yet wondering how a mere sentence could have persuaded him so easily against his own better judgment. He slept like the dead, the sun was well up before he stirred.

But his morning mood was a very different one. The brilliant light, the peace, the intoxicating air, all this was too exhilarating for his mind to harbor foolish fancies, and he marveled that he could have been so weak the night before. No hesitation lay in him anywhere. He struck camp immediately after breakfast, paddled back across the strip of shining water, and quickly settled in upon the forbidden shore, as he now called it, with a contemptuous grin. And the more he saw of the spot, the better he liked it. There was plenty of wood, running water to drink, an open space about the tent, and there were no flies. The fishing, moreover, was magnificent. Morton's description was fully justified, and "stiff with big fish" for once was not exaggeration.

The useless hours of the early afternoon he passed dozing in the sun, or wandering through the underbrush beyond the camp. He found no sign of anything unusual. He bathed in a cool, deep pool; he reveled in the lonely little paradise. Lonely it certainly was, but loneliness was part of its charm; the stillness, the peace, the isolation of this beautiful backwoods lake delighted him. The silence was divine. He was entirely satisfied.

After a brew of tea, he strolled toward evening along the shore, looking for the first sign of a rising fish. A faint ripple on the water, with the lengthening shadows, made good conditions. *Plop* followed *plop*, as the big fellows rose, snatched at their food, and vanished into the depths. He hurried back. Ten minutes later he had taken his rods and was gliding cautiously in the canoe through the quiet water.

So good was the sport, indeed, and so quickly did the big trout pile up in the bottom of the canoe, that despite the growing lateness, he found it hard to tear himself away. "One more," he said, "and then I really will go." He landed that "one more," and the evening was curiously disturbed. He became abruptly aware that someone watched him. A pair of eyes, it seemed, was fixed upon him from some point in the surrounding shadows.

Thus, at least, he interpreted the odd disturbance in his happy mood; for thus he felt it. The feeling stole over him without the slightest warning. He was not alone. The slippery big trout dropped from his fingers. He sat motionless and stared about him.

Nothing stirred; the ripple on the lake had died away; there was no wind; the forest lay a single purple mass of shadow; the yellow sky, fast fading, threw reflections that troubled the eye and made distances uncertain. But there was no sound, no movement; he saw no figure anywhere. Yet he knew that someone watched him, and a wave of quiet unreasoning terror gripped him. The nose of the canoe was against the bank. In a moment, and instinctively, he shoved it off and paddled into deeper water. The watcher, it came to him also instinctively, was quite close to him on the bank. But where? And who? Was it the Indian?

Here, in deeper water, and some twenty yards from the shore, he paused and strained both sight and hearing to find some possible clue. He felt half ashamed, now that the first strange feeling passed a little. But the certainty remained. Absurd as it was, he felt positive that someone watched him with concentrated and intent regard. Every fiber in his being told him so; and though he could discover no figure, no new outline on the shore, he could even have sworn in which clump of willow bushes the hidden person crouched and stared. His attention seemed drawn to that particular clump.

The water dripped slowly from his paddle, now lying across the thwarts. There was no other sound. The canvas of his tent gleamed dimly. A star or two were out. He waited. Nothing happened.

Then, as suddenly as it had come, the feeling passed, and he knew that the person who had been watching him intently had gone. It was as if a current had been turned off; the normal world flowed back; the landscape emptied as if someone had left a room. The disagreeable feeling left him at the same time, so that he instantly turned the canoe in the shore again, landed, and paddle in hand, went over to examine the clump of willows he had singled out as the place of concealment. There was no one there, of course, nor any trace of recent human occupancy. No leaves, no branches stirred, nor was a single twig displaced; his keen and practiced sight detected no sign of tracks upon the ground. Yet, for all that, he felt positive that a little time ago someone had crouched among these very leaves and watched him. He remained absolutely convinced of it. The watcher, whether Indian hunter, stray lumberman, or wandering half-breed, had now withdrawn, a search was useless, and dusk was falling. He returned to his little camp, more disturbed perhaps than he cared to acknowledge. He cooked his supper, hung up his catch on a string, so that no prowling animal could get at it during the night, and prepared to make himself comfortable until bedtime. Unconsciously, he built a bigger fire than usual, and found himself peering over his pipe into the deep shadows beyond the firelight, straining his ears to catch the slightest sound. He remained generally on the alert in a way that was new to him.

A man under such conditions and in such a place need not know discomfort until the sense of loneliness strikes him as too vivid a reality. Loneliness in a backwoods camp brings charm, pleasure, and a happy sense of calm until, and unless, it comes too near. It should remain an ingredient only among other conditions; it should not be directly, vividly noticed. Once it has crept within short range, however, it may easily cross the narrow line between comfort and discomfort, and darkness is an undesirable time for the transition. A curious dread may easily follow—the dread lest the loneliness suddenly be disturbed, and the solitary human feel himself open to attack.

For Hyde, now, this transition had been already accomplished; the too intimate sense of his loneliness had shifted abruptly into the worst condition of no longer being quite alone. It was an awkward moment, and the hotel clerk realized his position exactly. He did not quite like it. He sat there, with his back to the blazing logs, a very visible object in the light, while all about him the darkness of the forest lay like an impenetrable wall. He could not see a yard beyond the small circle of his campfire; the silence about him was like the silence of the dead. No leaf rustled, no wave lapped; he himself sat motionless as a log.

Then again he became suddenly aware that the person who watched him had returned, and the same intent and concentrated gaze as before was fixed upon him where he lay. There was no warning; he heard no stealthy tread or snapping of dry twigs, yet the owner of those steady eyes was very close to him, probably not a dozen feet away. This sense of proximity was overwhelming.

It was unquestionable that a shiver ran down his spine. This time, moreover, he felt positive that the man crouched just beyond the firelight, the distance he himself could see being nicely calculated, was straight in front of him. For some minutes he sat without stirring a single muscle, yet with each muscle ready and alert, straining his eyes in vain to pierce the darkness, he only succeeded in dazzling his sight with the reflected light. Then, as he shifted his position slowly, his heart gave two big thumps against his ribs and the hair seemed to rise on his scalp with the sense of cold that gave him goose flesh. In the darkness facing him he saw two small and greenish circles that were certainly a pair of eyes, yet not the eyes of an Indian hunter, or of any human being. It was a pair of animal eyes that stared so fixedly at him out of the night. And his certainty had an immediate and natural effect upon him.

For, at the menace of those eyes, the fears of millions of long dead hunters since the dawn of time woke in him. Hotel clerk though he was, heredity surged through him in an automatic wave of instinct. His hand groped for a weapon. His fingers fell on the iron head of his small camp ax, and at once he was himself again. Confidence returned; the vague, superstitious dread was gone. This was a bear or wolf that smelled his catch and had come to steal it. With beings of this sort he knew instinctively how to deal, yet admitting, by this very instinct, that his original dread had been of quite another kind.

"I'll damned quick find out what it is," he exclaimed aloud, and snatching a burning brand from the fire, he hurled it with good aim straight at the eyes of the beast before him.

The bit of pitch-pine fell in a shower of sparks that lit the dry grass this side of the animal, flared up in a moment, then died quickly down again. But in the instant of bright illumination he saw clearly what his unwelcome visitor was. A big timber wolf sat on its hindquarters, staring steadily at him through the firelight. He saw its legs and shoulders, he saw also the big hemlock trunks lit up behind it and the willow scrub on each side. It formed a vivid, clear-cut picture shown in clear detail by the momentary blaze. To his amazement, however, the wolf did not turn and bolt away from the burning log, but withdrew a few yards only, and sat there again on its haunches, staring, staring as before. Heavens, how it stared! He "shooed" it, but without effect; it did not budge. He did not waste another good log on it, for his fear was dissipated now; a timber wolf was a timber wolf, and it might sit there as long as it pleased, provided it did not try to steal his catch. No alarm was in him anymore. He knew that wolves were harmless in the summer and autumn and even when "packed" in the winter, they would attack a man only when suffering desperate hunger. So he lay and watched the beast, threw bits of stick in its direction, even talked to it, wondering only why it never moved. "You can stay there forever, if you like," he remarked to it aloud, "for you cannot get at my fish, and the rest of the grub I shall take in my tent with me!"

The creature blinked its bright green eyes, but made no move.

Why, then, if his fear was gone, did he think of certain things as he rolled himself in the Hudson Bay blankets before going to sleep? The immobility of the animal was strange, its refusal to turn and bolt was still stranger. Never before had he known a wild creature that was not afraid of fire. Why did it sit and watch him, as with purpose in its gleaming eyes? How had he felt its presence earlier and instantly? A timber wolf, especially a solitary wolf, was a timid thing, yet this one feared neither man nor fire. Now, as he lay there wrapped in his blankets inside the cozy tent, it sat outside beneath the stars, beside the fading embers, the wind chilly in its fur, the ground cooling beneath its planted paws, watching him, steadily watching him, perhaps until the dawn.

It was unusual, it was strange. Having neither imagination nor tradition, he called upon no store of racial visions. Matter of fact, a hotel clerk on a fishing holiday, he lay there in his blankets, merely wondering and puzzled. A timber wolf was a timber wolf and nothing more. Yet this timber wolf—the idea haunted him—was different. In a word, the deeper part of his original uneasiness remained. He tossed about, he shivered sometimes in his broken sleep; he did not go out to see, but he woke early and unrefreshed.

Again with the sunshine and the morning wind, however, the incident of the night before was forgotten, almost unreal. His hunting zeal was uppermost. The tea and fish were delicious, his pipe had never tasted so good, the glory of this lonely lake amid primeval forests went to his head a little; he was a hunter before the Lord, and nothing else. He tried the edge of the lake, and in the excitement of playing a big fish, knew suddenly that it, the wolf, was there. He paused with the rod, exactly as if struck. He looked about him, he looked in a definite direction. The brilliant sunshine made every smallest detail clear and sharp—boulders of granite, burned stems, crimson sumac, pebbles along the shore in neat, separate detail—without revealing where the watcher hid. Then, his sight wandering farther inshore among the tangled undergrowth, he suddenly picked up the familiar, half-expected outline. The wolf was lying behind a granite boulder, so that only the head, the muzzle, and the eyes were visible. It merged in its background. Had he not known it was a wolf, he could never separate it from the landscape. The eyes shone in the sunlight.

There it lay. He looked straight at it. Their eyes, in fact, actually met full and square. "Great Scott!" he exclaimed aloud. "Why, it's like looking at a human being!"

From that moment, unwittingly, he established a singular personal relation with the beast. And what followed confirmed this undesirable impression, for the animal rose instantly and came down in leisurely fashion to the shore, where it stood looking back at him. It stood and stared into his eyes like some great wild dog so that he was aware of a new and almost incredible sensation—that it courted recognition.

"Well! Well!" he exclaimed again, relieving his feelings by addressing it aloud. "If this doesn't beat everything I ever saw! What d'you want anyway?"

He examined it now more carefully. He had never seen a wolf so big before; it was a tremendous beast, a nasty customer to tackle, he reflected, if it ever came to that. It stood there absolutely fearless and full of confidence. In the clear sunlight he took in every detail of it—a huge, shaggy, lean-flanked timber wolf, its wicked eyes staring straight into his own, almost with a kind of purpose in them. He saw its great jaws, its teeth, and its tongue hung out, dropping saliva a little. And yet the idea of its savagery, its fierceness, was very little in him.

He was amazed and puzzled beyond belief. He wished the Indian would come back. He did not understand this strange behavior in an animal. Its eyes, the odd expression in them, gave him a queer, unusual, difficult feeling. *Had his nerves gone wrong?* he almost wondered.

The beast stood on the shore and looked at him. He wished for the first time that he had brought a rifle. With a resounding smack he brought his paddle down flat upon the water, using all his strength, till the echoes rang as from a pistol shot that was audible from one end of the lake to the other. The wolf never stirred. He shouted, but the beast remained unmoved. He blinked his eyes, speaking as to a dog, a domestic animal, a creature accustomed to human ways. It blinked its eyes in return.

At length, increasing his distance from the shore, he continued fishing, and the excitement of the marvelous sport held his attention—his surface attention, at any rate. At times he almost forgot the attendant beast; yet whenever he looked up, he saw it there. And worse: When he slowly paddled home again, he observed it trotting along the shore as though to keep him company. Crossing a little bay, he spurted, hoping to reach the other point before his undesired and undesirable attendant. Instantly the brute broke into that rapid, tireless lope that, except on ice, can run down anything on four legs in the woods. When he reached the distant point, the wolf was waiting for him. He raised his paddle from the water, pausing a moment for reflection; for his very close attention—there were dusk and night yet to come—he certainly did not relish. His camp was near; he had to land; he felt uncomfortable even in the sunshine of broad day, when, to his keen relief, about a half mile from the tent, he saw the creature suddenly stop and sit down in the open. He waited a moment, then paddled on. It did not follow. There was no attempt to move; it merely sat and watched him. After a few hundred yards, he looked back. It was still sitting where he left it. And the absurd, yet significant, feeling came to him that the beast divined his thought, his anxiety, his dread, and was now showing him, as well as it could, that it entertained no hostile feeling and did not meditate attack.

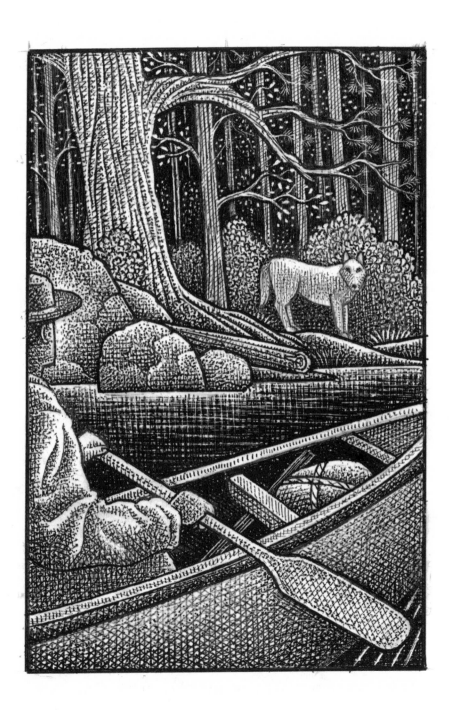

He turned the canoe toward the shore; he landed; he cooked his supper in the dusk; the animal made no sign. Not far away it certainly lay watched, but did not advance, and to Hyde, observant now in a new way, came one sharp, vivid reminder of the strange atmosphere into which his commonplace personality had strayed: He suddenly recalled that his relations with the beast, already established, had progressed distinctly a stage further. This startled him, yet without the accompanying alarm he must certainly have felt twenty-four hours before. He had an understanding with the wolf. He was aware of friendly thoughts toward it. He even went so far as to set out a few big fish on the spot where he had first seen it sitting the previous night. "If he comes," he thought, "he is welcome to them. I've got plenty, anyway." He thought of it now as "he."

Yet the wolf made no appearance until he was in the act of entering his tent a good deal later. It was close to ten o'clock, whereas nine was his hour, and late at that, for turning in. He had, therefore, unconsciously been waiting for him. Then, as he was closing the flap, he saw the eyes close to where he had placed the fish. He waited, hiding himself, and expected to hear sounds of munching jaws; but all was silent. Only the eyes glowed steadily out of the background of pitch darkness. He closed the flap. He had no slightest fear. In ten minutes he was sound asleep.

He could not have slept very long, for when he woke up he could see the shine of a faint red light through the canvas, and the fire had not died down completely. He rose and cautiously peeped out. The air was very cold, he saw his breath. But he also saw the wolf, for it had come in, and was sitting by the dying embers, not two yards away from where he crouched behind the flap. And this time, at these very close quarters, there was something in the attitude of the big wild thing that caught his attention with a vivid thrill of startled surprise and a sudden shock of cold that held him spellbound. He stared, unable to believe his eyes, for the wolf's attitude conveyed to him something familiar that at first he was unable to explain. Its pose reached him in the terms of another thing with which he was entirely at home. What was it? Did his senses betray him? Was he still asleep and dreaming?

Then, suddenly, with a start of uncanny recognition, he knew. Its attitude was that of a dog. Having found the clue, his mind then made an awful leap. For it was, after all, no dog its appearance aped, but something nearer to himself, and more familiar still. Good heavens! It sat there with a pose, the attitude, the gesture in repose of something almost human. And then, with a second shock of biting wonder, it came to him like a revelation. The wolf sat beside that campfire as a man might sit.

Before he could weigh his extraordinary discovery, before he could examine it in detail or with care, the animal, sitting in this ghastly fashion, seemed to feel his eyes fixed on it. It slowly turned and looked him in the face, and for the first time Hyde felt full-blooded superstitious fear flood through his entire being. He seemed transfixed with that nameless terror that is said to attack human beings who suddenly face the dead, finding themselves bereft of speech and movement. This moment of paralysis certainly occurred. Its passing, however, was singular as its advent. For almost at once he was aware of something beyond and above this mockery of human attitude and pose, something that ran along unaccustomed nerves and reached his feeling, even perhaps his heart. The revulsion was extraordinary, its result still more extraordinary and unexpected. Yet the fact remains. He was aware of another thing that had the effect of stilling his terror as soon as it was born. He was aware of appeal, silent, half expressed, yet vastly pathetic. He saw in the savage eyes a beseeching, even a yearning, expression that changed his mood as by magic from dread to natural sympathy. The great gray brute, symbol of cruel ferocity, sat there beside his dying fire and appealed for help.

The gulf betwixt animal and human seemed in that instant bridged. It was, of course, incredible. Hyde, sleep still possibly clinging to his inner being with the shades and half shapes of dreams yet about his soul, acknowledged, how he knew not, the amazing fact. He found himself nodding to the brute in half consent, and instantly, without more ado, the lean gray shape rose like a wraith and trotted off swiftly, but with stealthy tread, into the background of the night.

When Hyde woke in the morning, his first impression was that he must have dreamed the entire incident. His practical nature asserted itself. There was a bite in the fresh autumn air; the bright sun allowed no half lights anywhere; he felt brisk in mind and body. Reviewing what had happened, he came to the conclusion that it was utterly vain to speculate; no possible explanation of the animal's behavior occurred to him. He was dealing with something entirely outside his experience. His fear, however, had completely left him. The odd sense of friendlessness remained. The beast had a definite purpose, and he himself was included in that purpose. His sympathy held good.

But with the sympathy there was also an intense curiosity. "If it shows itself again," he told himself, "I'll go up close and find out what it wants." The fish laid out the night before had not been touched.

It must have been a full hour after breakfast when he next saw the brute; it was standing on the edge of the clearing, looking at him in the way that had now become familiar. Hyde immediately picked up his ax and advanced toward it boldly, keeping his eyes fixed straight upon its own. There was a nervousness in him, but kept well under, nothing betrayed it; step by step he drew nearer until some ten yards separated them. The wolf had not stirred a single muscle as yet. Its jaw hung open, its eyes observed him intently; it allowed him to approach without a sign of what its mood might be. Then, with these ten yards between them, it turned abruptly and moved slowly off, looking back first over one shoulder and then over the other, exactly as a dog might do, to see if he was following.

A singular journey it was they made together, animal and man. The trees surrounded them at once, for they left the lake behind them, entering the tangled bush beyond. The beast, Hyde noticed, obviously picked the easiest track for him to follow; for obstacles that meant nothing to the four-legged expert, yet were difficult for a man, were carefully avoided with an almost uncanny skill, while yet the general direction was accurately kept. Occasionally there were windfalls to be surmounted; but though the wolf bounded over these with ease, it was always waiting for the man on the other side after he had laboriously climbed over. Deeper and deeper into the heart of the lonely forest they penetrated in this singular fashion, cutting across the arc of the lake's crescent, it seemed to Hyde; for after two miles or so, he recognized the big rocky bluff he had seen from his camp, one side of it falling sheer into the water; it was probably the spot, he imagined, where the Indians held there medicine-making ceremonies, for it stood out in the isolated fashion, and its top formed a private plateau not easy of access. And it was here, close to a big spruce at the foot of the bluff upon the forest side, that the wolf stopped suddenly and for the first time since its appearance gave audible expression to its feelings. It sat down on its haunches, lifted its muzzle with open jaws, and gave vent to a subdued and long-drawn howl that was more like the wail of a dog than the fierce barking cry associated with a wolf.

By this time Hyde had lost not only fear, but caution too; nor, oddly enough, did this warning howl revive a sign of unwelcome emotion in him. In that curious sound he detected the same message that the eyes conveyed—an appeal for help. He paused, nevertheless, a little startled, and while the wolf sat waiting for him, he looked about him quickly. There was young timber here; it had once been a small clearing, evidently. Ax and fire had done their work, but there was evidence to an experienced eye that it was Indians and not white men who had once been busy here. Some part of the medicine ritual, doubtless, took place in the little clearing, thought the man, as he advanced again toward his patient leader. The end of their queer journey, he felt, was close at hand.

He had not taken two steps before the animal got up and moved very slowly in the direction of some low bushes that formed a clump just beyond. It entered these, first looking back to make sure that its companion watched. The bushes hid it; a moment later it emerged again. Twice it performed this pantomime, each time, as it reappeared, standing still and staring at the man with as distinct an expression of appeal in the eyes as an animal may compass, probably. Its excitement, meanwhile, certainly increased, and this excitement was, with equal certainty, communicated to the man. Hyde made up his mind quickly. Gripping his ax tightly, and ready to use it at the first hint of malice, he moved slowly nearer to the bushes, wondering with something of a tremor what would happen.

If he expected to be startled, his expectation was at once fulfilled; but it was the behavior of the beast that made him jump. It positively frisked about him like a happy puppy dog. It frisked for joy. Its excitement was intense, yet from its open mouth no sound was audible. With a sudden leap, then, it bounded past him into the clump of bushes, against whose very edge he stood, and began scraping vigorously at the ground. Hyde stood and stared, amazement and interest now banishing all his nervousness, even when the beast, in its violent scraping, actually touched his body with its own. He had, perhaps, the feeling that he was in a dream, one of those fantastic dreams in which things may happen without involving an adequate surprise; for otherwise the manner of scraping and scratching at the ground must have seemed an impossible phenomenon. No wolf, no dog certainly, used its paws in the way those paws were working. Hyde had the odd, distressing sensation that it was hands, not paws, he watched. And yet, somehow, the natural, adequate surprise he should have felt was absent. The strange action seemed not entirely unnatural. In his heart some deep hidden spring of sympathy and pity stirred instead. He was aware of pathos.

The wolf stopped in its task and looked up into his face. Hyde acted without hesitation then. Afterwards he was wholly at a loss to explain his conduct. It seemed he knew what to do, divined what was asked, expected of him. Between his mind and the dumb desire yearning through the savage animal, there was intelligent and intelligible communication. He cut a stake and sharpened it, for the stones would blunt his ax edge. He entered the clump of bushes to complete the digging his four-legged companion had begun. And while he worked, though he did not forget the close proximity of the wolf, he paid no attention to it; often his back was turned as he stooped over the laborious clearing away of the hard earth; no uneasiness or sense of danger was in him anymore. The wolf sat outside the clump and watched the operations. Its concentrated attention, its patience, its intense eagerness, the gentleness and docility of the gray, fierce, and probably hungry brute, its obvious pleasure and satisfaction, too, at having won the human to its mysterious purpose—these were colors in the strange picture that Hyde thought of later when dealing with the human herd in his hotel again. At that moment he was chiefly aware of pathos and affection. The whole business was, of course, not to be believed, but that discovery came later, too, when telling it to others.

The digging continued for fully half an hour before his labor was rewarded by the discovery of a small whitish object. He picked it up and examined it—the finger bone of a man. Other discoveries then followed quickly and in quantity. The cache was laid bare. He collected nearly the complete skeleton. The skull, however, he found last, and might not have found at all but for the guidance of this strangely alert companion. It lay some few yards away from the central hole now dug, and the wolf stood nuzzling the ground with his nose before Hyde understood that he was meant to dig exactly in that spot for it. Between the beast's very paws his stake struck hard upon it. He scraped the earth from the bone and examined it carefully. It was perfect, save for the fact that some wild animal had gnawed it, the teeth marks being still plainly visible. Close beside it lay the rusty iron head of a tomahawk. This and the smallness of the bones confirmed him in his judgment that it was the skeleton not of a white man, but of an Indian.

During the excitement of the discovery of the bones one by one, and finally the skull, but more especially, during the period of intense interest while Hyde was examining them, he had paid little if any attention to the wolf. He was aware that it sat and watched him, never moving its keen eyes for a single moment from the actual operations, but sign or movement it made none at all. He knew that it was pleased and satisfied, he knew also that he had now fulfilled its purpose in a great measure. The further intuition that now came to him, derived, he felt positive, from his companion's dumb desire, was perhaps the cream of the entire experience to him. Gathering the bones together in his coat, he carried them, together with the tomahawk, to the foot of the big spruce where the animal had first stopped. His leg actually touched the creature's muzzle as he passed. It turned its head to watch, but did not follow, nor did it move a muscle while he prepared the platform of boughs upon which he then laid the poor worn bones of the Indian who had been killed, doubtless, in sudden attack or ambush, and to whose remains had been denied the last grace of proper tribal burial. He wrapped the bones in the bark; he laid the tomahawk beside the skull; he lit the circular fire round the pyre; and the smoke rose upward into the clear bright sunshine of the Canadian autumn morning till it was lost among the mighty trees overhead.

In the moment before actually lighting the little fire he had turned to note what his companion did. It sat five yards away, he saw, gazing intently, and one of its front paws was raised a little from the ground. It made no sign of any kind. He finished the work, becoming so absorbed in it that he had eyes for nothing but the tending and guarding of his careful ceremonial fire. It was only when the platform of boughs collapsed, laying their charred burden gently on the fragrant earth among the soft wood ashes, that he turned again, as though to show the wolf what he had done, and seek, perhaps, some look of satisfaction in its curiously expressive eyes. But the place he searched was empty. The wolf had gone.

He did not see it again; it gave no sign of its presence anywhere, he was not watched. He fished as before, wandered through bush about his camp, sat smoking round his fire after dark, and slept peacefully in his cozy little tent. He was not disturbed. No howl was ever audible in the distant forest, no twig snapped beneath a stealthy tread, he saw no eyes. The wolf that behaved like a man had gone forever.

It was the day before he left that Hyde, noticing smoke rising from the shack across the lake, paddled over to exchange a word or two with the Indian, who evidently now returned. The Indian came down to meet him as he landed, but it was soon plain that he spoke very little English. He emitted the familiar grunts at first; then bit by bit Hyde stirred his limited vocabulary into action. The net result, however, was slight enough, though it was certainly direct:

"You camp there?" the man asked, pointing to the other side.

"Yes."

"Wolf come?"

"Yes."

"You see wolf?"

"Yes."

The Indian stared at him fixedly a moment, a keen, wondering look upon his coppery, creased face.

"You 'fraid wolf?" he asked after a moment's pause.

"No," replied Hyde, truthfully. He knew it was useless to ask questions of his own; though he was eager for information, the other would have told him nothing. It was sheer luck that the man had touched on the subject at all, and Hyde realized that his own best role was merely to answer, but to ask no questions. Then, suddenly, the Indian became voluble. There was awe in his voice and manner.

"Him no wolf. Him big medicine wolf. Him spirit wolf."

Whereupon he drank the tea the other had brewed for him, closed his lips tightly, and said no more. His outline was discernible on the shore, rigid and motionless, an hour later, when Hyde's canoe turned the corner of the lake three miles away and landed to make the portages up the first rapid of his homeward stream.

It was Morton who, after persuasion, supplied further details of what he called the legend. Some hundred years before, the tribe that lived in the territory beyond the lake began their annual medicine-making ceremonies on the big rocky bluff at the northern end; but no medicine could be made. The spirits, declared the chief medicine man, would not answer. They were offended. An investigation followed. It was discovered that a young brave had recently killed a wolf, a thing strictly forbidden, since the wolf was the totem animal of the tribe. To make matters worse, the name of the guilty man was Running Wolf. The offense was unpardonable, the man was cursed and driven from the tribe:

"Go out. Wander alone among the woods, and if we see you we slay you. Your bones shall be scattered in the forest, and your spirit shall not enter the Happy Hunting Grounds till one of another race shall find and bury them."

"Which meant," explained Morton laconically, his only comment on the story, "probably forever."

Story Outline

I. Morton of the Montreal Sporting Club tells Malcom Hyde of a great fishing place—Medicine Lake—a place that he has never returned to even though he spoke of the fishing enthusiastically. Hyde is told in passing to camp near an Indian's cabin on the east side of the lake.

II. On the way to the lake, Hyde stops by a general store and is again told to put his tent on the east shore. The store owner acts surprised that he would even be going to Medicine Lake.

III. After canoeing to the lake, he is delighted with its beauty. He sees a perfect place to camp on the west shore, but because of what everyone else has said, he camps on the east side near the Indian's cabin.

IV. Early the next morning, he canoes over to the perfect camping place on the west shore, sets up camp, and starts serious fishing.

V. He fishes until dusk, when suddenly his happiness is disrupted by the feeling that someone is watching him. Fear suddenly comes over him without warning. He canoes quickly away from the clump of bushes he is close to against the shore, but sees nothing. The feeling leaves.

VI. He returns to the shore and checks the clump of bushes, but sees no evidence of any animal or human.

VII. If possible, remember Blackwood's comments on loneliness in a backwoods camp.

VIII. He feels the presence again of something watching him in the dark. Throwing a burning log into the woods, he sees a large timber wolf staring at him. The wolf stays, but he is not afraid of a timber wolf.

IX. The next day while fishing, he senses the strange wolf on the shore. Their eyes meet, and the wolf comes down to the bank. The wolf follows him toward his camp that night, trotting along the lake's edge as he paddles back.

X. That night the wolf again comes to his camp, but this time sits next to the fire—just as a human being would sit.

XI. Hyde decides to find out what the wolf wants. The next day he approaches the wolf, then follows it on a journey through the woods.

XII. At the foot of the large bluff, an area sacred to the ancient Indians, the wolf indicates to him to dig in a certain spot.

XIII. He uncovers a human skeleton, probably the skeleton of an Indian. The wolf also shows him where to find the skull a few yards away.

XIV. He feels compelled to build a funeral pyre. After burning the remains of the skeleton, he turns and finds that the wolf has gone.

XV. He does not see the wolf during the rest of his trip at the lake. The Indian on the other side of the lake sees him during his last day there and tells him that it was no wolf, but a spirit wolf.

XVI. Morton later tells him the legend of the brave called Running Wolf, who had killed a wolf, the totem animal of his tribe. He was condemned to death and to have his spirit wander until one of another race would find his bones and properly bury them.

39

THE PREDATOR OF SOULS

Written by Scott E. Power,
Edited by Doc Forgey

Many years ago in 1598, when the North American wilderness belonged to its rightful owners, there was a Cree Indian Shaman named Eagle Eyes who was very wise and very old. He was called Eagle Eyes because he could see into the future things that were to happen.

Eagle Eyes was a holy man in his tribe. Tribe members honored him and followed his sage advice. He had been the spiritual leader of his tribe since the age of 10 when the tribe became convinced of his supernatural aptitude.

When Eagle Eyes was the age of 10, a holy number within Cree culture, he walked up to a wild timber wolf and touched its head by caressing the wolf's fur. The wolf stood still, immediately sitting at rest in a submissive manner showing all the witnesses that this little boy had supernatural power; the power to command wild animals into submission.

Later that day, the little boy predicted a "ground storm" that would destroy the plains by "swallowing the grass." Two days later, an earthquake hit north of the tribe's camp and twenty-five acres of the earth's surface sank into itself. It was on this day the tribe named the little boy Eagle Eyes, and appointed him the spiritual leader and shaman of the tribe.

One day many years later, a woman in the tribe was in labor to give birth. She was having extreme difficulty, so Eagle Eyes

assisted in the birth. It was a very scary time. The woman was in great pain and near death. However, the shaman was able prevent a tragedy by delivering the baby without harm to the mother. It was a boy. However, something unusual happened when the baby was born. It did not cry. Sensing something was wrong, Eagle Eyes spanked the baby to provoke it, but it did not work. Eagle Eyes looked into the baby's eyes and saw that it was alive and well. Immediately, the mother named the baby boy Wacha, Cree for Strong Spirit.

As Wacha grew older, Eagle Eyes sensed there was something very special about the boy. As he talked with the boy he realized that Wacha was an old soul, probably in his fourth incarnation. He was wise beyond his years and very interested in things unseen, spiritual matters and shamanic powers. Eagle Eyes began to teach Wacha The Ways of the Shaman, making him an apprentice.

As Wacha grew older he became very confident in his abilities and spiritual knowledge. Eagle Eyes had taught him well. However, something began to stir within Wacha, something powerful. Wacha started to become aware of himself. He became conscious of his spiritual power. He desired more. And he wanted more knowledge. His curiosity swelled within him. So, at night while the rest of the tribe was sleeping Wacha would meditate, searching his soul for answers he did not have.

One day, Wacha asked Eagle Eyes about his thirst for the unknown. Immediately, the wise shaman exclaimed the danger of searching for such answers:

"There is only confusion in knowledge. Trust only in The Great Spirit. Trust not what you think. Trust in the mind over The Spirit is certain death. Trust in The Spirit and there is life forever. The Spirit never dies. Mind and its knowledge die and are gone forever. Trust not the tricks of the mind on the body.

Meditate on what The Great Spirit has shown us, not on The Unknown. To do otherwise is certain death."

This upset Wacha greatly. He left Eagle Eyes' teepee feeling very angry and disappointed with what his mentor had said. Wacha didn't understand. He didn't think it was fair. He wanted more than what he had. More knowledge, more spiritual power. No! For Wacha this would not do. He would take it upon himself to probe even harder for The Unknown, for the answers he sought. He would continue his nightly meditations, despite what Eagle Eyes had told him.

As time passed and Wacha continued to search The Unknown, something in him began to change. His demeanor and his posture changed. He became very sour faced and slouched over. He began to take on the appearance of an older person up in the seasons. Wacha's attitude changed too. He became more withdrawn. He stopped speaking to others. He stopped smiling. And he started to hate Eagle Eyes.

Wacha became bitter about what his mentor had taught him. He felt cheated. He felt Eagle Eyes had cheated him out of vital knowledge about The Unknown. Wacha hated Eagle Eyes passionately. So, he devised a plan. He would cast a spell to steal Eagle Eyes's spirit from his body and be rid of him for good!

So, using his spiritual powers Wacha cast a spell. He called for a wolf to wander into camp and brush against Eagle Eyes's leg and steal his spirit upon contact.

Wacha couldn't wait for his spell to be realized. He began to fantasize about how great life would be without Eagle Eyes. Now, Wacha would become the tribe's new shaman!

Later that day, Eagle Eyes was found dead lying in his teepee. There was no sign of physical harm done, but his body was found lifeless on the floor. Upon further investigation, the tribesman who found the body said he saw a timber wolf leaving Eagle Eyes' teepee, which is what caused him to peer inside the teepee.

Wacha listened carefully, as if to appear concerned. All the while, laughing on the inside as a very evil spirit began to grow inside Wacha. Others from the tribe, not knowing what was really going on, began to approach Wacha about adopting all Shamanic responsibilities immediately. He accepted.

It was a very dangerous time in the life of the tribe.

Early the next morning another wolf was spotted leaving Wacha's teepee. Soon after, Wacha's body was found dead on the floor of the teepee. As people gathered in and around Wacha's tent to examine his body and mourn this double tragedy, Eagle Eyes walked through the crowd. People began to faint, falling onto the ground. They thought they were seeing a dead man walking. Quite the contrary. Eagle Eyes was alive!

Once the tribe knew that it was truly him and not some ghostly illusion, Eagle Eyes explained that Wacha had cast a spell for a wolf to steal his spirit. Which indeed worked and was why his body laid dead. But, what Wacha didn't realize is that Eagle Eyes's power of the animals would be intact and that he could control the wolf's actions.

So, during the early morning Eagle Eyes went into Wacha's teepee and pulled his spirit out of his body and into the wolf. Then, went back to his own tent and rubbed up against his day-old corpse and swapped his spirit back. He then condemned Wacha to a life trapped inside an animal's body never to be reversed.

Story Outline

I. A Cree Indian boy became the tribe shaman by showing his control over a wolf and predicting a "ground storm" (earthquake).

II. Many years later a boy was born who didn't cry at birth.

III. This boy was called Wacha (Strong Spirit).

IV. Wacha was not content learning the ways of the Great Spirit—he wanted to control it.

V. He was rebuked by Eagle Eyes, so he plotted revenge.

VI. He caused a wolf to steal Eagle Eyes's soul one night, thus assuming the role of the tribe shaman.

VII. But Eagle Eyes's soul in the wolf caused it to steal and trap Wacha's soul instead and to release his.

VIII. The tribe was rid of the evil spirit and Eagle Eyes resumed his role as the tribe shaman.

40

THE WINDIGO AND THE FORK

by Doc Forgey

My old friend Calvin Rutstrum once said to me, "How do you tell your partner you hate his guts by the way he holds his fork?" Anyone who has ever gone on long trips in the wilderness with others knows how this strange and almost inexplicable situation can easily come about. But that conversation got me to think about developing this story.

Scott and Dave were lucky. Or at least they started out feeling very lucky. They were deeper into the North Woods than they had ever been in their lives. A remote cabin, 120 miles from the town of Churchill, Manitoba, a small town located halfway up the east coast of Hudson's Bay. Scott was the Junior Assistant Scoutmaster of Troop 16 and Dave was the Senior Patrol Leader. Scott's Dad had arranged for the boys to fly in to a small lake, about three miles from the cabin and to spend 10 days there over Christmas vacation when Boris, a trapper who lived in Churchill, was to arrive by snow mobile to bring them out.

The cabin was located at the very edge of the tree line. For thousands of miles north of them there was nothing but Arctic muskeg, "the barrens" as it is often called. While to the south a thousand miles of forest stretched to the plains of southern Canada and the US border. This cabin would have also been in the barrens except that it was in a valley that had protected the local trees from the severe blasts of Arctic cold that prevented their growth on the plateau above.

The incredible cold of this Canadian Arctic land made the remoteness even more impressive. In fact survival would not be possible if it was not for the down parkas and pants, heavy wool clothing and "polypro" underwear that Scott and Dave were wearing. But the cabin made the country not only safer to stay in, but allowed their adventure to be enjoyable. And what a cabin! Cut from local black spruce logs, the twelve foot square building had a sleeping loft, a wood burning stove, and a storage room that made the place appear like a palace in the north woods. To prevent cold leaks the cabin only had one small window on the ground floor, but two Plexiglas windows had been installed in the sleeping loft to catch the early morning and afternoon light.

Catching light was important, for there is little of it at that time of year in Northern Manitoba. The sun would peak above the horizon at 8:30 in the morning, then stay low on the southern horizon until it set by 2:30 in the afternoon. The rest of the time kerosene lights, and the flickering of light from the wood stove, was their only source of light. Unless they were outside after dark when the snow would reflect moonlight and frequently incredible displays of northern lights that could fill the entire sky with curtains of mysterious, flickering fire.

What an adventure! The plane flight in from Churchill allowed them a glimpse of the 100 miles of frozen barrens where they would soon be traveling over in a snow mobile. And then the edge of the forest with the tiny cabin tucked into the Manito River valley finally appeared through the frosty window of the plane.

The pilot buzzed the cabin, but they could not tell from the snow-covered mound whether it was ok or not. He swooped twice more over the river checking out the landing conditions before setting the plane down, actually bumping to a stop only a few hundred feet from the gap in the trees where the path probably led to the cabin.

The excitement of first stepping out of the plane was matched only by the hushed expectation of the boys as they snow shoed their way to the long abandoned cabin's door—hoping that the building was intact and habitable—or else their great adventure would have to be called off. The pilot went with them. The quiet of the frozen north seemed impressive after the engine noise during the hour and a half flight from Churchill. The only sound was the crunch of the snow shoes against the frozen snow and the excited puffing of their breath as they bound up the bank to the cabin site. The cabin was located only a short distance from the stream, but hidden by the trees well enough that it couldn't be easily seen.

As they approached the cabin they could see that the stovepipe was intact and the shutters were still fastened over the lower window. The Plexiglas windows in the sleeping loft above looked ok. They removed the large crow bar used to barricade the door—for in the tradition of the North Country this cabin had no lock, only a barricade to prevent animals from easily shoving the door open.

As they peered into the dark, empty cabin they could easily see that nothing was disturbed. There was no mess from animal destruction, the walls still had their chinking, the wood stove and its flue of stovepipe looked functional, and a variety of lamps, parts, and various tools were all in their proper place.

The pilot returned with the boys to the plane and helped them unload everything. They had kerosene, winter sleeping bags, extra clothes, a .30-.30 Winchester rifle and a 12-gauge shotgun

—enough food to last the 10 days until Boris arrived and for the 3 day sled trip back to town—even food for the dogs for that return trip. The pilot was anxious to be off before his engine froze and possibly adding him to the guest list. And the boys were also eager for him to depart so that they could be on their own, away from all traces of civilization.

There was much to do at first. The shutters had to be taken down, the frozen pile of firewood uncovered, a water hole cut through 3 feet of river ice, and the stove started to heat the cabin. It was impossible to work with bare hands for the temperature hovered at 20 degrees below zero! With all of the hustle and bustle of their first day in the bush, it wasn't long before 2:30 came and the sunset. The boys enjoyed their first meal in the bush—a beef stew they had allowed to cook nearly all day on the hot wood stove.

That evening they stood beside the river's edge. The Windigo River seemed much wider in the night. They could barely see the dark splotch of the water hole against the pristine snow. And since they had been too busy to explore around that day, there were no other tracks that they could see in the fresh snow. While they stood beside the river, a dim yellow light began to glow above the stunted tree growth, slowly creeping higher in the sky. Their excitement grew as they witnessed a phenomenon strange and eerie. Growing stronger and more intense, the wavering light soared overhead, dancing wildly like a long silk scarf in a breeze. Swirls and whirlpools of light were oozing from its depths, while the shimmering enchantment danced across the sky in a fluorescent glow.

They stood in awe, in almost disbelief. Troops of bright yellow spears began marching vertically toward the west. After a time, the light began to fade, hanging in the heavens motionless, dissolving. The boys had witnessed their first grand display of the northern lights. It was more than the remoteness, the cold, and the unusual natural phenomena that gave the boys a strange thrill as they stood there that night. The cabin they were being allowed to use was almost never occupied. And for a reason. No Indian or white man would trap or live there, for it stood in a mysterious area. The very name of the river "Windigo River" was a warning of the awe which this area had for the persons who had named it. The windigo creature is known in nearly every northern Indian legend, sometimes translated as "he who walks on water and eats human bones." The myths about the windigo were known as far south as the Illinois Indians who had lived in the state that now bears their name.

"Tomorrow we will get breakfast before daylight so we can start to explore this area," Dave remarked, as much to himself as to his companion. Scott voiced his agreement. The short hours of daylight were too precious to be wasting inside cooking. There was much to do outside—and exploring this countryside, especially looking for tracks to examine the signs of animal life that surrounded them was high on the priority list. They felt certain that many unseen eyes were watching them. It would be nice to learn more about those eyes by examining their tracks in the snow tomorrow.

As the boys banked the stove and then snuggled into their sleeping bags in the loft, they were only vaguely aware of a muffled sound coming from the river.

Scott's wristwatch alarm went off the next morning at 7 A.M., otherwise they would have surely overslept. It was hard getting up. The cabin temperature had dropped since the stove fire had died many hours before. Shining a light at the thermometer attached by a bracket outside the loft window, Scott could see that it was

38 degrees below zero! The muffled sounds had continued from the river all night. Dave had remarked that he was sure that it was the heaving of the frozen ice, as it cracked beneath the snow due to the intense cold. Scott felt that the thermometer proved that the cold was certainly intense.

The same fire that heated their cabin back to a comfortable temperature also cooked their breakfast of Red River cereal, a traditional north country breakfast which they had purchased in Winnipeg. The boys also prepared extra coffee for a mug-up on the trail and packed away hunks of fruit cake, beef sausage sticks, and pilot biscuits for a trail lunch.

Leaving the cabin just as the sun was glowing over the southeast horizon, the temperature had not warmed at all. Even getting into the snowshoes was an adventure, requiring quick work and many pauses to warm their fingers. But soon they were plowing their way through the snow, crossing the river with plumes of frozen breath hanging behind them in the still air.

They found just what they hoped they would see across the river. An incredible record of the otherwise invisible wildlife was written in the snow. Not a creature was stirring in the bitter cold, but the tracks of their recent activity gave away their presence. It was apparent that there had been martin, mink, and considerable movement of spruce grouse in the woods. The boys also discovered a fox trail. But they were not just looking at trails. They had also brought their sleds and a bow saw and axes, for they needed to cut more firewood to replace what they were using from the cabin woodpile.

Each day they repeated the adventure and the work required to live in the deep winter of the far north. Each night they huddled in the frozen cabin listening to the strange muffled sounds of the deep wilderness. They were becoming more and more acclimatized to the bitter cold, a process that was to be important if they were to successfully tolerate the long dog sled trip to the town of Churchill on Hudson's Bay.

As their trips took them further afield, they were not only seeing evidence of more and more species of wildlife, but also reading the dramas of life and death as they found several sites of recent kills marked by bloody, disheveled snow. These sights gave greater fascination to the wild sounds that they could not quite grow accustomed to hearing each night, sounds drifting into their cabin from that frozen wilderness. They could not but feel the wildness of the area. Perhaps it was the incredible remoteness, or the evidence of death and the struggle for survival that was evident all around them, but without any doubt there was an uneasiness that they were both feeling.

Call it what you will ... the Windigo, the Manito ... the remote wilderness had a spiritual component that was capable of drawing you into it deeper and deeper. It was not entirely unpleasant, but the constant evidence of death, the survival of the fittest, also cast a questionably evil sense to the experience.

That was the scary part. The mystery of this remote area had always had a fascination for both boys. They never quite understood why they would be drawn so strongly to being in the outdoors. This wasn't simply being outdoors, however. They were deep in the heart of the outdoors and were near the point of origin of the powerful pull that wild places had always exerted upon them both.

After spending a week in this frozen wilderness, the boys could almost feel that civilization was a dream and that what they were struggling with was the only reality of life. Dave particularly became fixated on the mysterious pull that this wildness seemed to generate. Especially at night, while listening to the muted sounds of the groaning ice. Or was it ice? Dave's excuse at first was that he wanted to check out these night noises and confirm that they were coming from the river. His solo sojourns into the night started one night with a simple ten-minute hike onto the river. The next night, however, he felt the need to go again, this time for half an hour. He knew it wasn't just to feel the ice rumble, but to be closer to the wildness all around him. To feel even more a part of it.

Scott, however, was looking forward to the dog sled trip more and more. It would be an adventure in itself, it would break the drudgery of daily life in the cabin, but more importantly, deep inside of him he was beginning to long for a link with humans again. To long for a break from the wildness of the frozen forest.

The third night Dave was gone for almost an hour and a half. Scott was concerned for his safety—who wants to be left alone in the North? But also genuinely worried about what was going on with Dave. And Dave gave very little explanation for the length of his absence upon his return. He seemed almost mesmerized by the beckoning call of this wild place. And that's when they had their big argument.

Now Dave and Scott were very good friends before this trip, and in fact had made many trips together. But Scott's annoyance with Dave's wandering started to expand into other areas. Perhaps he felt he was being abandoned, that Dave was taking risks by traveling alone that would threaten both their safety. Regardless, he started noticing other aggravating traits that Dave had. For example, the way he brushed his teeth and then spit the water out between his front teeth. At first this was nothing, but as the tension mounted, it became somehow annoying. Then there was the matter of how Dave so thoroughly cleaned his plate. Now everyone is hungry during a wilderness trip. There never seems to be enough food. But Dave would literally scrape his plate clean with his fork. Scrape, scrape, scrape. Finally Scott had just about had it watching this happen with every meal.

How do you tell your partner you hate his guts by the way he holds his fork? Tension like this is without doubt contagious. So Dave's strong attachment to the call of the wild seemed to accelerate, partially to serve a selfish purpose, to enjoy the wilderness, partially to get away from the tension in the cabin.

And Scott's opinion of all of this? "Good, I'm glad the Manito is calling him. Maybe it will teach him how to eat properly!"

The fourth night Dave did not return at all. When Scott awoke at 4 A.M. and found himself alone, he felt a sudden cold chill strike through him that even the bitter temperature could not account for. He had another 5 hours before daylight, so he started a fire to warm the icy cabin, hoping the light and warmth would ease the fear in his heart. But, of course it did not.

Alone on the edge of the barrens. The more he thought about it the more he realized how much Dave had been changing. He had seemed more than just interested in the wilderness. He had become captured by it. It was as if the Manito itself was achieving a presence within Dave. And that damn fork!

But even with that thought, Scott became more concerned about Dave. He could hardly wait for the sun to come up to go out to look for him. The wind had been gradually building until the snow started blowing off the Arctic plateau above them, dumping larger and larger amounts of snow into the valley. The five hours was like five years. But finally the glow brightened and a gray stormy day dawned. Scott rapidly saw it would be impossible to attempt to find Dave. The continuing storm made travel impossible. The wild seemed to have swallowed Dave whole.

And thus the day was spent alone. While the wilderness seemed to call to Dave, it was doing the very opposite at this time to Scott. He was feeling crushed by it. He wanted to stay in the cabin and was reluctant to go outside at all.

A cabin can be a place of refuge in the wilderness, but it also easily becomes a prison. And while a prison would be a horrible experience, it pales compared to the position that Scott was in. His best friend, and the only other human in this vast wilderness, Dave, had disappeared leaving him alone in it. He feared for Dave and he feared for himself. He did not know which of these emotions was the strongest. There is the cut to the quick fear that one has for his own survival; possibly nothing is stronger than that. But if there is, it is one thing; it is the fear that something has happened to your best friend, no matter how he holds his fork. And when that best friend is also your only link to civilization, it magnifies the combination of personal danger and grief that one could feel. And imagine doing all of this alone.

Eventually the long night came to a close—daybreak arrived. It was the day that Boris was to arrive. The day that was to represent the start of another adventure, but now was expressing something much more basic. Raw survival. Just to get out of this place had become Scott's strongest feeling. But just behind it was the loneliness of not knowing where or what happened to Dave.

Finally Scott heard the distant noise of a snow machine, a powerful snowmobile that Boris was riding. The sounds rose and fell, seeming at one moment close and the next far away, until finally there was the consistent racket of the powerful machine grinding it's way up the river near the cabin.

It stopped outside the cabin. The loud racket was replaced first by silence, and then the soft crunching of a person's making his way around the side of the cabin to the front door. Scott waited with baited breath until suddenly the door burst open and Boris stood there with a great grin on his face.

"How ya doing here, eh? Bet you're getting a bit lonely!" he exclaimed with a grin. But seeing Scott sitting, more or less cowering, dumbfounded, in the corner by the table, he immediately added "Well, I brought a present for you!"

Scott could hardly make sense of what he heard. He was safe! But his partner was gone. "I found him about 6 miles out, near the junction with the Churchill River, all cuddled up in a snow cave. Bet you thought the Manito got 'em, eh?"

And with that Dave crunched his way through the door. "Hi Scott! I never thought I'd be so glad to see a person this much in my life! I'm sorry I got carried away with the pull of the wilderness. It really taught me a lesson. I'm sorry that I pulled that stunt and left you here alone."

And Scott felt he had been given a great present, indeed. He was so thankful that Dave was alive and that he was no longer alone. But he never wanted to have to watch David eat with a fork again.

Story Outline

I. Dave and Scott fly to a remote cabin on the Windigo River in Northern Manitoba to spend ten days, before being joined by Boris with a snowmobile for a return trip to Churchill.

II. The mysterious wilderness exerts a pull on Dave, causing him to travel alone to enjoy it better.

III. Scott feels the stress of the lonesome wilderness and soon starts to notice minor problems with Dave's mannerisms.

IV. Finally Scott concentrates on Dave's use of his fork and it starts to drive him nuts. ("How do you tell your partner that you hate his guts because of the way he holds his fork?")

V. Dave disappears into a storm one night and Scott is left alone. Scott feels sorry that his relationship with Dave has deteriorated over such minor things, and also feels the fear of being alone and anger at Dave for having put him into this situation.

VI. Boris arrives with the snowmobile. He has found Dave who was in a snow cave seeking refuge from the storm.

VII. Scott is thankful that his best friend is safe. But, he never wants to watch him eat with a fork again!

EPILOGUE

"AND WHAT IS DEATH? . . .

Do you know it?" "Ey! I know it," answered the old Negro woman. ". . . Hit's er shadder en er darkness. . . . En dat shadder en darkness hit comes drappin; down on yer, creepin' up on yer; hit gits hol 'er yo' feet. Den hits slips up ter yer knees, den hit slips up, up twel hit gits ter yo' breas'. Dat reap-hook hit gi's er wrench ter de breaf er you' breas'. Dat reap-hook hit gi's er wrench ter de breaf er you' mouf, en dar! Yer gone, caze yer breaf, hit's yer soul!"

—Eli Shepard

ABOUT THE AUTHOR

William W. Forgey, M.D., FAWM, CCHP-P, CTM® is a National Committee member of the Boy Scouts of America. He is a volunteer Clinical Professor of Family Medicine, Indiana University School of Medicine and member of the Board of Directors of the International Association of Medical Assistance to Travelers. He is a Fellow of the Academy of Wilderness Medicine, a Fellow of the Explorers Club, and holds the Certificate of Travel Medicine from the International Society of Travel Medicine. He has been associated with Scouting and outdoor education for over 40 years.

ABOUT THE ILLUSTRATOR

Paul Hoffman's work graces books of many genres—children's titles, textbooks, short story collections, natural history volumes, and numerous cookbooks. His illustrations can also be found in Globe Pequot Press's *Spooky* series. He lives in Massachusetts.

ABOUT THE CONTRIBUTORS

David R. Scott and his friend **Scott E. Power** spent a year in the wilderness of Northern Canada in 1991-1992 on an expedition sponsored by Dr. Forgey (see www.forgey-cabin.com). On this adventure they were given several assignments, which included rigorous trips into the sub-Arctic, writing stories, and staying alive. Dave is now an advertising specialist working in Chicago and Scott a brand imagining specialist living in Los Angeles. Dave married Nicole, a travel agent, and spends his spare time on tropical beaches. Scott married Channing Dungey, the President of ABC, and spends his spare time taking care of their children. Dave and Scott go on occasional great adventures to this day.